from SMART MOUTH . . .

The young teacher heard the boy's hoarse whisper behind her. "The water's almost to the top of the second stair."

She was glad Dylan had the sense to keep this information between them. The rest of the team chattered excitedly amongst themselves, pointing out the windows like they were on the Pirates of the Caribbean ride at Disneyland.

She tried not to look but the temptation was too much. Glancing over, she was paralyzed by the flood water pouring into the bus, a heavy, musty steam reaching for her. The white vapor floated above water filled with swirling dead leaves, multicolored plastic confetti, and indeterminable brown chunks. *If I spot a condom, I'm going to freak. 'Cause that's my breaking point. Garbage in the water.*

SMART MOUTH
a novel

Holly L. Lörincz

SMART MOUTH

This is a work of fiction.
Names, characters, places and incidents are either the products of the
author's imagination or are used fictitiously. Any resemblance to actual
persons (living or dead), events, or locations is entirely coincidental.

Copyright © 2013 by Holly Lorincz
Represented by Chip MacGregor
MacGregor Literary Agency
PO Box 1316
Manzanita, OR 97130
chip@macgregorliterary.com

ISBN:-13: 978-1495336362
ISBN:-10: 1495336360

cover design: Sarah Aageson Creative
www.sarahaagesen.com
cover photo: Laura Grauwen
www.grauwenphotography.com

For Auggie Mar

CHAPTER 1
ADDY

Am I wearing underwear?

Her thoughts congealed. The twenty-three year old flashed on well-worn panties: pilled white cotton, weak elastic around the legs sliding over her morning gooseflesh.

Thank God.

Five seconds ago Addison Taylor's only concern had been controlling the nervous vomit crawling up her throat. Lips compressed, she'd stepped behind her battered desk, dismissed the rickety nature of the office chair, and dropped into the seat.

And fell over backward.

Now the overturned chair cradled her like a calf in a chute. On her back, legs in the air, long tweed skirt flipped over her face, Addy decided this was an omen. She was not meant to be here. Fluorescent light filtered through the loose weave.

Why me? Did I trip the Pope in a past life?

The top buttons on her blouse popped open as she twisted herself free. Honey-stained hair burst into statically charged frizz. The chair's wheels continued to roll in the air next to her head.

Out of sight, the classroom door snicked open. Brisk steps quickened her heartbeat, stopped her wind-milling legs. She turned her head, cringed. A gap between the floor and the desk revealed a well-oiled pair of men's black dress shoes.

"Ms. Taylor?" A deep voice rolled through the room. Troy Ford, the vice-principal.

If she answered, he'd see her Goodwill panties. If she stayed quiet, a herd of fourteen year olds were going to show up and capture this on their cell phones.

Her silence didn't matter. A cleft chin filled the air above her, followed by gladiator cheekbones and water-blue eyes. Ford, cartoon handsome, placed his fists on the desktop and leaned over, quirking an eyebrow. "Ms. Taylor."

She closed her eyes, willed herself to die.

The administrator stepped around the desk. "Let me help." He managed to sound condescending and polite while crouching his long body close to hers, grasping her arms and heaving her to her feet like a first aid dummy. His superior facial features twitched but did not break.

"I see you've encountered The Chair."

"Gah." Addy couldn't clear the last, small bit of dignity from her throat.

He cocked his head at her. "Are you all right?"

She nodded as he hefted the chair upright, the abrupt halt of the wheels disconcerting. He glanced at her, lifted an eyebrow. A beautiful eyebrow, set in a tan, expectant face.

Talk.

"Suh-sorry. Fine." She shook like a wet Labrador, smoothed her skirt down, let her brain focus. "Uh, thanks." She surreptitiously rebuttoned her gaping blouse.

"Well, if I can be of no further assistance . . ." he shrugged. He may or may not have been amused, Addy couldn't read his stiff face. She teetered on her high heels, still unsteady, and wondered if she had the strength to sprint down the hall, jump in her car and disappear from this place.

Why am I such an idiot? I should have filled my gas tank. The thought reminded her, though, of why she was here. Money.

Money to buy gas to put in her gas tank. And to prove she could survive in the adult world. So far, so . . . *damn*.

"Welcome to Oceanside." The vice-principal stepped back to the other side of the desk, expressionless, her attractive young boss apparently unfazed by a woman flashing her threadbare panties. She almost sat back down.

Skittering away from the chair, she tripped over the edge of a clear plastic floor mat, her open toed pumps betraying her after years of service. She caught herself on the desk, sweeping attendance sheets into the garbage can.

"Careful there," Ford said, retrieving the papers from the bin.

Embarrassment and a growing lump on the back of her head vied for attention. Her head on fire, she leaned one hip against the desk, aiming for professional cool but settled for awkwardness. Her apple cheeks flushed as she blinked away stray bangs.

He picked up a stack of documents he must have dropped on her desk earlier, uncovering the framed photo of her boyfriend, Rick. Ford glanced at the picture, her, then his papers, a lock of auburn hair falling across his forehead.

"I'm here to give you a list of committees with open seats. The English teacher you replaced was on the Community Council, The Tsunami Safety Committee, the Respectful Pirate Committee and the Sunshine Committee."

Respectful Pirates. Seriously.

"We also need coaches. This has the list of extra positions. Most are not paid." Suddenly he loomed over her, a toothy great white circling a baby seal. "Legally, administration can't force you to accept extra duties. But everyone pulls their weight in a family, right?" Ford shifted the documents from one hand to another. "I'm lucky enough to be the athletic director *and* the vice principal."

Was that sarcasm? Addy bit her lip, not sure what to say. She looked him in the eye, feeling brave, but she didn't speak.

"I've marked a few activities you'll find interesting." He handed her the type-covered pages, tilted his head, stared her down. She was afraid to breathe or do anything that might suggest agreement. She couldn't yet call herself a teacher, much less be responsible for big decisions.

He blinked first. "You don't talk much, do you?"

She opened her mouth to respond but he turned, strode to the door, and twisted the knob with authority. Her lips re-sealed. Her daddy would have approved, often remarking how her best quality was her silence—she didn't say anything stupid when she was silent.

Troy Ford exited her new classroom, throwing one final spear over his shoulder. His eyes had softened but his words remained hard.

"The debate team will be a good fit. I'd seriously consider it if I were you. It's been defunct for ten years. The Parent Group is grumbling." The door shut.

The Debate Team. Yelling. Conflict.

I can't do it.

But Addy realized this for what it was: an ultimatum. Ford was her superior, reviewing state test scores, sitting in her classroom, evaluating her performance. If he thought she wasn't cutting it as a teacher, or staff member, he would end her. In short, he was the dark lord and she was a hapless clone.

Trying to see past the corpse of her ego, she muted her jangling nerves by reading the list while adjusting her underwear.

The door was flung back open, bounced off the wall. Addy froze, hand under her skirt. A tiny girl with a black mohawk and lip rings smirked and pushed past. Addy jerked her hand free.

A wall of youth followed mohawk girl. The chemical smell of new clothes and Axe body spray overwhelmed the room, teenage bodies pinging off each other, finding seats on the first day of school, stiff notebooks slapping well-worn wood, the pencil sharpener grinding, grinding, grinding . . . *What the hell was I thinking?* Addy's armpits dripped as she faced the enemy. A sour bouquet of terror rolled off her. She might as well be thirteen again, a brace-faced book-nerd hoping for invisibility. The seething mass of teenagers before her was about to catch the ungodly whiff of fear and attack like a pack of wild dogs. Time to move.

The class bell rang. *I can't do this.*

She squared her spongy shoulders and pretended to straighten stapled handouts stacked on the podium, buying time, hiding behind a sheath of swinging hair, crazed with attempts to interpret the mutters of discontent as a sweet babbling brook. She shuffled more papers, moved books. Moved them back, shuffled papers. Cleared her throat, shuffled papers. She had yet to speak. Not good. Thirty-two kids: hickory shirts, sport jerseys and bedazzled tshirts melded together, morphing into one cold-eyed monster.

Addy reminded herself she'd come into Room Seven that morning fully prepared to be despised by the end of the day. How could they *not* hate her, a high school English teacher with a pert nose and freckles screaming uppity-twelve-year-old. She was about to make them read archaic poetry, write essays for nonexistent readers, and give speeches in front of posturing, poop-throwing orangutans. But in order to despise her, she had to first talk.

Addy prayed none of the desk-bound fourteen year olds staring at her were gifted at making, or using, pencil shivs. Freshmen were notoriously adept at creating torture devices out of a paper clip, a pencil eraser nub, and a sliver of rubber from the sole of their shoe.

Time to stop screwing around. Her eyes swept over the freshmen. Her freshmen. *Just pick a teacher from one of those movies. Michelle Pfeiffer. Act like her.*

"Miss Taylor, will you go to the prom with me?"

Addy's heart stopped. *Ok, Angelina Jolie. Act like her. Kick some ass here.*

Addy tucked her hair behind her ears, injected faux steel into her bowing spine. The unexpected male advance gave her something to focus on. Someone to focus on. The carrot-headed hormone in the window row smirked as she stepped away from the podium, his lax posture an irritant. Every face, acned and clear, looked up from their conversations. Suddenly focused and intent, the class melded back into the single beast, cocking its head, waiting.

Picture the words, say the words. Angelina Jolie wouldn't panic. She'd throw a knife at his head. Addy was pretty sure her career counselor would not approve of this imagery but it helped all the same.

"First, my name is Ms. Taylor. That's Miz, not Miss. Second, we definitely run in different circles, kid." She curled her lips in the shape of a grin to soften the blow, glanced around the room. "But I'm glad to see you guys don't seem overwhelmed by the thought of your first high school class." The tick-tick of raindrops hitting the window filled the silent room.

"Obviously it's time we went over the class rules." She grabbed a stack of papers off the podium and walked with a faked confidence down the window aisle. "Here you go, Romeo," she said lightly, stopping at the joker's desk. "A reminder of acceptable human behavior."

Someone whistled. The boy smiled and leaned back. Fingers laced behind his head, he winked. Addy's eyes bulged. *Where's that knife?*

She continued down the aisle, shoulders slumped. She'd opened her mouth, finally, but it didn't accomplish much. Regardless, she kept moving, negotiating through strewn backpacks and scuffed tennis shoes.

The tension in the air eased as she handed out papers. The great mass was not necessarily behind her but, for the moment, they didn't seem to be against her. Then she noticed three kids texting, one using a pencil as a carving tool, and another handing out what appeared to be cigarettes. They had transitioned from middle school to high school just fine.

I am so getting fired.

At 3:35 the last bell rang. Addy watched the surge of bodies nearly break down the door. Shell-shocked, she slunk behind the gun-metal grey desk. She picked up the small stack of papers Ford had left behind and started flipping through them. Anything to avoid processing the string of failures from her first day as an adult in a real job.

In her hands was a list of extra, mostly unpaid duties. *Ah, on to thinking about future failures.* Ford's pen denoted her "choices," boxes marked with a bold red checkmark. First was Literacy Council, a one year seat with a group of grammar Nazis. The next red mark tagged Freshman Class Advisor, a stint spent planning fundraisers, dances, and finding out who held fake i.d.'s.

Then her breath stopped. Ford wasn't kidding around. Clearly, he did not know her. Speech and Debate Team Coach, two heavy red checks. This particular coaching position remained vacant for a damn good reason: the outline described a competitive season which began in September and ended in June. Black dots dangled in her vision. Months of talking.

She gingerly eased the desk chair out from under the desk.

It fell over.

Addy heaved a sigh, sitting on the edge of the desk. The teacher stupid enough to coach spent most evenings working with teenagers instead of curling up on the couch with a cold beer and a warm boyfriend. The pressure of training lawyers, business giants, ambassadors and the next president of the United States might be rewarding but it would be relentless. Never-ending relentless pressure from pushy parents and nerdy kids. Pressure and time. Relentless. Fucking relentless. That is, if said stupid teacher could dig up enough kids for a team and then convince them public speaking was a regular hoot, way better than attending football games or running black-ops on a video game.

She glared at the chair lying at her feet. Ford wanted her, Addison Taylor, to gestate and birth a debate program. Her first day as a high school English teacher. She hadn't even gestated an adult backbone yet. This was too much. Her nostrils flared, her eyes twitched in her head, her hair streamed in the air around her, a wild horse rearing to bust out of the corral.

Breathe. Breathe. Addy reeled in the panic, put the brakes on her spinning eyeballs. She crossed the room, pried open a window. The rain stopped, giving way to a September sun wrapped in grey—wet mist rolled in from the Pacific, blurring her view of the surf across the highway but giving body to the salty, musky aroma. She breathed.

She could always quit.

Addy wasn't here for the kids. Hell no. She was here in the hallowed halls of education and derision, of conflict and drama, because she nodded a real job to pay her bills, like her horrifying college loans. The hand of God wasn't going to reach down and do it for her. She closed her eyes and sighed, dropped her chin to her chest. There was a deeper reason. This was her Everest. To stop now was to die. If she didn't get on top of this stultifying shyness currently dictating her days, she was going to end up an old lady dressed in cat hair sweaters with only a chin wart for company.

As a teen, she'd been a potato. A silent, ugly potato who read books to avoid eye contact with a derisive "children should be seen, not heard" father and her "wha's up, Potato Face?" classmates. She skulked out of her high school graduation, staring at the ground—only to be hit by Tim

Smith's Camry as he rushed out of the parking lot to get to a kegger she had not been invited to. Having her teeth knocked out saved her life. She entered college with a beautiful new set of teeth, a new nose, new haircut, and a new desire to look up.

So, no she couldn't quit. She had to prove she could do this, that she could be a functioning cog in the wheel of adulthood, that she could stand in front of others and open her mouth, make others listen. She'd thought standing in front of high school kids would be easier than talking to adults, but was seriously questioning that theory now. Bad idea or no, here she was.

And let's be honest. I'm an English major. What else am I going to do?

She dragged her lesson plans and a few textbooks onto a student desk by the bank of windows, sinking into the small but stable seat. Her tired brain pondered tomorrow's lessons. She quickly sketched out notes for classroom lectures and created corresponding worksheets.

Time to go home.

I'll make copies in the library on my way out. She gathered up her coat and tattered messenger bag, shut off the light, standing in a dim room.

Addison Taylor was no General. She was never going to marshal troops with a simple stern look, an authoritative point of the index finger. No, she was shaky Private Taylor, gruffly asked for identification at every checkpoint. The stink of new ink wafted around the battleground, the smell a reminder of her freshly minted Oregon Teaching Certificate. The framed pristine document stood alone, a single sentry on the otherwise empty walls of the classroom. Her classroom.

Her shoulders relaxed for the first time in twelve hours as she locked the door of Room Seven and started down the hallway, eyes half-lidded with exhaustion, hoping to get her copies and be off.

Day one, down. I'll give it a week. I can do that.
The library door was locked.

CHAPTER 2
ED

"**W**ait for me, ass hat!"

"Watchyer mouth, kid," Ed growled. "It's the first day of school, for Chrissakes." He grabbed the cursing, gawky senior loping down the hall after his friends. The fifty-year old social studies teacher squeezed the back of the boy's neck once, a pulse of tough love, then gently thrust him away. The teen, surprised by the assault, almost knocked down two sophomores huddled by their lockers, texting each other. The victim straightened, turned as if to say something, then laid eyes on Ed's vein-laced cheeks, bulbous stomach, whistle necklace, and short-shorts. He shut his mouth and backpedaled.

Ed smirked.

"Sorry, Coach Nielson."

"I guess you are."

The kid dashed away, tripping over his size thirteen Nikes until he hit his stride. Ed shook his head, leaned against the wall outside his classroom, and yelled, "No running in the halls!"

Ass hat. I'll have to remember that one. I know a few ass hats. His arched back and nylon-clad hips crumpled a poster on the wall behind him. A poorly painted pirate yelled into the teacher's well-endowed buttocks: OHS NEEDS YOU! GO PIRATES!

Ed scratched the fringe of grey hair clinging to his scalp, staring at the young bodies as they shot past on their way to their first classes of the new school year. They evaded eye contact. *Yeah, you fuckers better be afraid of me. I own you.*

His ears perked up as he heard a loud thump reverberate from Addison Taylor's room across the hall. Probably related to The Chair. *Ouwwwwch*, he thought, squinting his eyes in empathy. *Not a great way to start the day.* Every year one new teacher was saddled with that stupid trick chair, at least until he or she smartened up and snuck it into the next unsuspecting sucker's room. Ed mustered the waistband of his pants, preparing to saunter to the rescue of the little lady with whom he had yet to make formal acquaintance. Then he noticed that suave bastard Ford striding down the hall toward him.

The Athletic Director, a peacock in an expensive suit, brushed past Ed, leaving the stink of aftershave in his wake. Ed watched as Ford jerked open the door to Room Seven, barely deigning to acknowledge the social studies teacher's existence, offering only a slight tilt of his ridiculous square jaw.

Ed bridled at the slam to his manhood. Ford was the reason he, Ed, was rejected for the head football coach position every time it opened. Ed had taught social studies at OHS for the past twenty some years. He was sick of being the assistant coach, forced to sit at the goddamn little kid's table.

Jesus. I hope that guy sticks his gelled-up head into an open flame. A Ford candle would be a great birthday present. He smirked to himself until it hit him, his birthday was next week. *If I'm not careful, these new teachers might just think I'm too old to share some beers.* He pushed himself off the wall with a kick, ripping the cheerleaders' already wrinkled poster, the material of his shorts flapping, revealing yellowing tighty-whities. *No one is going to look down their nose at ol' Ed Nielson. I still got what it takes, baby. Fifty is the new thirty.*

Brrrrinnnnngggg. Ed assumed it was the bell warning staff and students to finish their lattes and get their asses to class, but then it rang again. The phone in his classroom. *Gah.* Only two people ever called his room. One was the brainless, catty secretary. The other was his ex-wife, probably calling to tell him once again his son refused to stay with him. *It's not like it matters,* he thought bitterly, approaching his desk. *He never looks up from his stupid video games anyway, unless it's to roll his eyes.*

He ignored the wave of sadness trying to engulf him.

Ed picked up the phone. "Yeah?"

"Hey, this is Pike." The head football coach spoke with a fake drawl. Ed heard his pointy red beard scrape against the phone receiver. "I need you to pick up a copy of the football budget from the office before practice today. Ford needs us to go over our accounts, get our books balanced. That douche bag says there's some big discrepancy in the athletic department funding. He won't stop bitching at me about it." Pike's high-pitched rant paused. "I don't know what's going on. You better fix this, Ed."

"Me? I don't have anything to do with the budget."

"Your job is to assist me, isn't it? So assist, goddamn it! Do your job!"

You little fuck. I've done your job and mine since those morons hired you.

Ed took a deep breath, mentally balanced his need of a paycheck against opening fire. "I've got some grading to do right after school. I'll bring the budget down when I'm done."

"The first day of school hasn't even started yet. How do you have papers to grade already?"

"Well, Pike, I plan to actually teach in my classes." Ed dropped the receiver, hoping Pike's ginger head exploded.

Seven hours later, Ed pushed the last stinking freshman out the door and settled at his desk. He aimed to spend no more than ten minutes wielding a heavy red pen on the eleventh graders' Battle of the Little Bighorn worksheets. Then he'd stop by the office to get the stupid budget. His main goal was to get into the weight room with the football players, pump a little iron in front of the mirror, show the boys how a man did it.

Ed harrumphed out loud when he noticed one kid's answers. The dumbass believed the battle involved food—specifically, custard and cayenne. He flipped through the other worksheets. *Holy shit! Did I give this lecture as an internal fucking monologue?* Over half the class wrote in the wrong historical dates; the year 1502 must have originated from one of the more popular kids, spreading like syphilis to the majority of idiots. *Can't even cheat with common sense,* he thought, knuckles pressed into the wrinkled flesh on his forehead. *I hope to God these kids aren't ever in charge of nuclear weapons. Or my social security benefits.*

He'd put the papers from the dumber kids on the bottom of the stack, staving off the pain as long as possible. He'd had these same students last year, as sophomores, and they had not gotten any smarter over the summer. *Johnny Bergman. Here we go.* The kid could handle a ball all right, but his communication skills were minimal, generally relying on shoving or snorting to make his point.

Johnny had written, "I dont know what started that war but I think war is freking stupid. Soldurs get hurt and dont know why. my dad came back from Irac with no foot and now my mom cant get him to leave the gurage. He screams alott"

Well, shit. Ed put down his pen and ran a tired hand over his face, telling himself the stinging in his eyes came from sweat.

The question was worth five points; Ed gave him twenty. Then he fired off an email to the counselor. "Bill, I know you're busy yakking with the anorexic kids, but talk to Johnny Bergman, make sure he's not getting ready to stick his hand in a garbage disposal."

What else could he do?

He was going to be here for a while. He had to plan for tomorrow, figure out a different method of teaching these idiots. No gym tonight. Damn. Coach Pike was going to have to run scrimmages and fix the budget without him. Ed settled his hefty weight into the office chair, loosened the drawstring on his nylon shorts, opened a squeaky drawer, removed a grimy pair of eyeglasses and a package of HoHos. He shoved the sticking drawer, hard, cursing at the clang. *Nothing works around here.*

He ripped open the HoHo with his teeth. A loud guttural sigh of appreciation escaped with the first savage bite into the waxy chocolate.

A timid knock at the door unnerved him, more so when the door popped open and the beautiful new English teacher stood before him, flushed and flustered. He gulped, a wad of HoHo catching in his throat.

"Yeah?" *Oh fuck. Did she hear me groan?* He put his hands on the desktop, leaned back, let her view his zipper, fully in place. *Nothin' to see here.*

"Hi. Sorry to bug you, sir. My name's Addy." Her voice was throaty, almost a whisper.

He swiped his hand on his synthetic shorts, offering to shake from his chair. "Don't call me sir. Name's Ed. Ed Nielson." He pumped her hand once, limply, then crossed his arms. "Did ya' need somethin'? I've gotta' get down to the weight room." He tightened his shoulder muscles.

"Oh, no, sorry, it's just that the library door is locked." She tucked long blonde curls behind an ear, eyes cast down shyly. "I need to make copies for tomorrow. Can I use the copier in the main office? Are staff allowed to do that?"

Ed snorted. "Yeah, you can use the office copier. But the question is, do you want to? You never know who might be lurking around in there. Besides, your classroom key should unlock the library. Did you try it?"

"Dang it. No, I didn't even think of that." She smacked her lovely forehead, freckled cheekbones pinking like a doll's. "I'll go try that now."

"That it?"

She quickened her step to the door, nervous. "I'm good, thanks . . ." her voice petered out. "Well, it was nice to meet you. Guess I'll see you around."

"Yeah. All right then," he said gruffly, tugging open another squealing drawer, withdrawing a red pen. He didn't really want her to go. "Let me know if you need anything else. I've been around awhile. I know every asshole in this place."

She didn't say anything, only furrowed her brow.

He chuckled. "I'm not talkin' about the kids. Not today, anyway."

Addy's sweet, unaffected laughter coiled around his heart. "Oh, then I think I encountered one already."

"Hey, I'm right here. If you gotta' call me names, at least do it behind my back."

"No, no, not you—" she stammered.

"Come on, kid, stop bein' so fragile. I was kidding."

She grimaced, shamefaced. "I'm not normally dim. I'm tired, I guess."

"No shit. You just survived your first battle. Go home, pour some whiskey on your wounds. I'll see you tomorrow."

The young teacher withdrew silently, Ed staring after her. *Whiskey sounds damn good.*

16

CHAPTER 3
ADDY

Addy walked the long hallway to the staff parking lot, irritated by the tick-tick-tick of her heels on tile. She had nothing left to give this day.

Her old Volvo chugged out of the parking lot. Across the highway, the Pacific beat a constant tempo, wave upon wave sliding up the beach, toward the road. The cadence slowed her own heartbeat.

She sighed. Her Carmello-eating, wine-drinking, movie-watching girlfriends were back in the city, far away from this burg she now called home. Rick, her boyfriend of three years and now her roommate, did not count. Sure, he was a good guy. Sometimes controlling, generally oblivious, but a good guy. He wasn't *trying* to be mean or belittling when he would change the channel to football, strip to his boxers and drink all the wine. He wasn't *trying* to be a jerk while barely faking interest if she had worked up enough courage to share angst or feelings. He would politely respond with a poetic litany of "uh huh, uh huh" and "do we have more chips?" and "the wine's gone, any beer?" She loved him, she even liked him sometimes, but he was not who she turned to when she needed emotional support. Squeezing out a tear when the quarterback was knocked out for the season did not equate being in touch with the feminine side.

And, yet, she'd talked him into moving to Oceanside with her. He liked that she was excessively quiet, she liked that he helped pay rent. Partnership made in heaven.

Her mind on Rick, she barely noticed the wild blooming rhododendrons, the Manzanita trees or the glimpses of the ocean as her car chugged along the small town roads. Addy frowned, hoped her man would learn to be happy here, away from the city and his friends. His attachment to her had always been tight, even when he had others onto which to spread his intensity. A lonely Rick was a smothering Rick.

He or Addy had yet to meet any of their Oceanside neighbors. They weren't busy unpacking the boxes stacked haphazardly throughout their tiny rental house on Main Street, nor were they busy investigating the five streets in the town. No, they'd spent the past few nights eating frozen dinners while laying prostrate on separate couches, reminiscing about Portland's breweries, coffee houses, galleries, gyms and Powell's Book Store, barely acknowledging the pastoral landscape outside their window. Oceanside's one stop light would change to a blinking yellow light every night at eight, a light free to strobe Addy's living room walls, unimpeded by the drapes lying on the floor, highlighting the change in their lives. Inertia dominated their days so far.

The only items Addy had bothered to unearth were her Goodwill tweeds and a potpourri burner. She planned to take time tonight to find some dishes and, hopefully, her toothbrush. Her finger wasn't cutting it. Then, maybe, she could begin looking for friends.

The Volvo coughed to a stop on the street ten feet from the front stoop of her rental bungalow. She could see clearly through the fish bowl window. *Note to self: no walking around naked tonight.* Rick stood in the living room with a PBR in one hand and a tablet in the other, a purposefully tight tshirt accentuating his wrestler's body, exuding smart sexiness in dark horn-rimmed glasses. He must've finished work early; she'd thought he was working the late shift.

Addy could complain for days about his annoying manly habits but never would she fault his work ethic. She'd met him in college, while he was cooking at the local pizzeria to supplement his wrestling scholarship. Framed in their window, her boyfriend still looked like that guy, the first boy to find Addy attractive, to actually want to be with her. She owed him loyalty, if nothing else.

She hefted open her car door, watching Rick as he maneuvered around their shared living space. They moved to Oceanside a week ago and already he'd finagled a desk at the county's one computer repair shop. He wasn't thrilled to be working on private computers, doing upgrades and hitting the reset button for old people in what he called "our village." He wanted to be an IT guy at a big corporation in Portland but the jobs weren't there right now. They both agreed it was time to leap into the unknown, the small town life, when Oceanside High School offered her a teaching position. Portland wasn't a huge city, but it was a city. Oceanside had one grocery store. The local post office was inside the grocery store. Oceanside was no city. This was barely an outpost.

Yet, here they were. She tottered up the narrow cement walkway to her tiny house. Rick waved to her through the tiny window. He opened the door, waving her inside with a pompous flourish; the queen of tiny-ville had arrived.

"Hey babe," said Rick, brown eyes lit with amusement, "Trying out a new look for the grapefruits today?"

She looked down. Damn. Why couldn't her shirts stay buttoned? She dropped her messenger bag, papers spilling everywhere, and ran into Rick's arms.

"Ok, ok." After a minute he tried to break the clinch. He managed to move her back enough to look into her face, his smile becoming concerned. "Was it really that bad?" When she didn't answer, just clasped him back into a bear hug, he said, "Really? Come on. Those kids loved you. How could they not? You must be the cutest teacher in the history of schools." He reached inside her gaping shirt, cupping her breasts, "If I had an English teacher that looked like you, I might've actually learned to read."

She shoved his hands away, laughing. "Please." She unwound herself from his tower of comfort. Her body crumpled onto the worn couch instead. Feet propped up on a box of outdated stereo equipment, Addy leaned back and practiced yoga breathing. "Rick, you have no idea how good it feels to be out of the crosshairs."

He shoved her over and dropped next to her. "Okay, tell me. Do you still have a job? Have you been fired?"

She covered her face but tears spurted out between her fingers. A dying crow tried to get out of her throat.

"Jesus! What'd you do? Punch a kid?" Now he was alarmed.

"Nuh . . . nuh . . . no!" She stuttered through her sobs, "I have to read seventy-six essays by tomorrow." She sobbed harder for a second, stunning Rick into silent patting. When she stopped breathing like an obese man with sleep apnea, her ability to speak returned. "And, yes, they did hate me. Well, maybe not all of them. Most were irritated. Four percent outright despised me. I'm pretty sure one of them spit in my coffee."

"Oh. Well. Don't leave your coffee sitting around." He patted her back when her breath hitched. "Honey. It can't be that bad," he tried to corral her wild blonde waves, pushing clumps of hair behind her ears. Addy sensed him give up, surreptitiously try to grab his beer from the side table without disturbing her blubbering.

Her hysteria subsided to snot runnels and hiccups, the occasional tear. Rick slowly brought the beer to his lips, gulping silently, behind Addy's head. *My hero*, she thought.

Addy wiped her eyes, blew out her breath hard enough to stir the hair out of her face. "Sorry."

"Tomorrow will be better. You'll find your groove." Rick gave her the one armed hug. "You knew it was going to be hard. My God. You're practically their age. Sucks being so brilliant, so young, huh?"

They sat quietly for a minute, sharing warmth. She loosened up, cat-stretched, and curled around her boyfriend. "Okay, I'm okay. I just needed to vent. And I'm not that young. *Someone* thought I was old enough to be responsible for children."

Rick opened his mouth. Addy bent forward and playfully bit his lower lip. "Don't say it or you'll lose skin, I swear," she growled, crinkling her nose.

Then she sat back, eased faux-leather pumps from her swollen feet. In a soft, tired voice, picking absently at her red toenail polish, she said, "So, speaking of responsibilities . . . remember the Athletic Director I was telling you about? Troy Ford? After school he came in to tell me about my *extra* responsibilities."

"Extra responsibilities? What does that mean? Like all those papers you have to grade tonight?"

"No," she said, "that's just part of teaching English. No, there's a bunch of committees . . . and stuff." Pause. "Actually the main thing I'm supposed to help with . . ."

He looked at her over the rim of his beer can.

His hand no longer played with her hair.

Uh oh. Here we go. She began again, words bursting like starlings exploding from a nest. She wanted to catch Rick before his mood went to that cold place, a place where he was the king, a dictator demanding loyal, ever-present servitude, a moody ruler with abandonment issues and manic-depressive outbursts. She'd maneuvered through this land for a long time. The trip no longer amused her. She planned on changing the path they were on, somehow, just not tonight.

She pretended nonchalance. "Honey, it's no big deal." Why did it always come to this? Her placating him even when she was the one who was upset? "Look, it's just . . . Ford is making me start up a speech and debate team. He says the parent council is requiring it." She shrugged and snuggled into his shoulder. "But I seriously doubt I'll have any kids join. Anyway, I don't have a choice."

He leaned away. "How much time is this stupid team going to take?"

She held her tongue. A plethora of retorts bucked and bit against her teeth, never to be freed. "Uh, we'll probably have practice a couple of times a week, just a few hours."

"What in the hell are you practicing? Talking to each other? That sounds *real* exciting."

She pictured a miniature red box residing in the pit of her stomach. Her miniature stomach-self balled up her frustration and shoved it into the box. Miniature stomach-self had to sit on the lid in order to close it—it was pretty full. She promised her miniature stomach-self a lemon drop martini. Stomach-self gave an enthusiastic thumbs up.

She breached the distance, reaching out to rub Rick's arm. "Hey, it's been a rough day. Wanna' walk down to the pub, get a burger? We should try those sweet potato fries."

After a beat, Rick nodded. "Yeah." He grabbed her hand, tugged her closer. "Though you might want to change your shirt. Then again, maybe the grapefruits can get us some free beers."

She tried to ease the stiffness in her body, not wanting him to feel her true response to his crazy mood swings. His brooding soul had been sexy years ago, as she sat in the Philosophy 101 lecture hall, mooning over the darkly handsome boy. However, the increasingly erratic responses from a twenty-four year old man was no longer sexy. Far from sexy. As a matter of fact, it led to less sex.

She tucked her hair behind her ears and stood up. She wasn't about to get in a confrontation with Rick. Arguing, especially with Rick, made her stomach cramp and her brain fuzz.

She frowned. Tonight's plan: quietly watch him eat fried food and drink Pabst Blue Ribbon. *You're gonna' need Rick to pay rent when you get fired. Just chill out.*

The pub's burgers were made from local beef—beef possibly garroted, exsanguinated, and butchered behind the restaurant. Blood ran down Rick's chin, dripping from his hands. "Delicious," he said, his mouth a gaping maw. She shut her eyes and wondered once again if she really did need his rent money . . . but then pictured her clothes and books and shoes used as bedding in her Volvo and decided she could make this work. She ordered the lemon drop martini.

Addy sat next to him at the bar, keeping her eyes averted and her mouth shut. She endured her boyfriend with caresses and smiles, staying fixated on his emotional recounting of the Seahawk's last win, relaxing as he talked. She grasped his biceps and giggled as they walked back through the warped door of their bungalow. She wasn't acting, not exactly, but she heaved a sigh of relief when he announced his intention to hole up in front of the tv, watch the game. She'd been sure he was going to want his ego soothed with a round of unsatisfying, three minute sex. At least she'd be able to skip the faked orgasm and the shower and get right to work.

As he hopped and gesticulated like a tree monkey, screaming at the quarterback on their living room big screen, she snuck back in to the office. Easing the door shut, she flinched at the click of the handle. No response from the other room. She placed a cup of chamomile tea (a balm against the martinis boiling in her belly) onto the worn old captain's desk and ruefully appraised the notebook pages spread across the surface.

Earlier that day, a lifetime ago, she had thought it would be a good idea to get to know her students by having them write short response papers, asking them to describe their issues with reading and writing.

I hate reading. It makes me feel stupid its too hard. Why cant we read easy stuff?

I don't like to read made up bullshit. Who cares about some Afghanistan kid and his kite. We need to learn about the liberal regime and how it is ruining this great democracy.

Me no can rite reel good.

My dad said writing stories is for faggots.

I've had to read Call of the Wild three years in a row. Please don't make me read it again.

English class suckz. You suck.

I love English. It's my favorite class. I read all day long, at least until I get in trouble. Can you talk to the math teacher for me, ask him if we can read when we get stuck?

Can we eat in here?

Mom says you are going to feel the wrath of God if you try to make me read "dirty" books. Don't worry, I usually hide my English books from her. Especially The Odyssey. She really hates that Homer guy.

We waste so much paper in this class. I have an issue with the fact that we use bleached paper and don't recycle.

Oh, they had issues, all right.

Addy threw the stack of papers up in the air, shoving herself away from the desk and out of the way as they wafted slowly down—too slowly, considering the weight of the words. She accidentally tread on three or four before reaching the door, stepping into the hall, stretching back to flip out the light without looking.

Her soul hung around her ankles. *Time to get some sleep. Maybe I can wake up tomorrow a superhero. Or maybe someone who has her shit together. Or, at least, find the perfect movie character to emulate.*

CHAPTER 4
ADDY

The ending bell rang, cutting the moist air. The first period freshmen pushed out the door, whacking each other with textbooks and swinging backpacks. *Are their asses on fire? What's the rush?*

Addy, bemused, double-checked the buttons on her blouse and skirt, straightening her light cardigan. The class had gone well. Even the smart-mouthed hormone, Travis Diamond, stayed on task, keeping his comments to himself. When she handed out flyers announcing a lunch meeting for anyone interested in the speech and debate team, the bulk of the brightly colored flyers were jettisoned into the blue recycling bin while at least three kids rolled their eyes muttering "that's so gay." She cringed but remained quiet, choosing to focus on their savvy environmental habits while pretending to be momentarily deaf.

I have to be brave—or at least look confident. Robert DiNero. She stood straighter, puffed out her chest, squinted her eyes, thought about lecturing in a Bronx accent while throwing chairs around the room. On to second period, senior English.

The seventeen and eighteen year olds funneled in the narrow, peeling portal as she tried to organize last period's paperwork: completed assignments in one basket, extra handouts in another pile, late homework in yet another, still another stack of assignments for the absent kids who cared enough to collect and make up missing work. She wrote with papers balanced on her knee.

The volume slowly climbed in the room. *I've got to get these guys settled down, set the tone from the first minute.* Her breath hitched. *This is where DeNiro would begin his slow rant. Do it.*

A willowy girl glided in and stood before Addy, intimidating with her sophisticated up-do, a vintage Betty Paige skirt, expensive ballet slippers, and a fringed scarf strewn around her neck in complicated folds. She handed Addy a yellow slip of paper, then carefully readjusted a thick band of fine metal bracelets. "I'm Nina DuBois, a new student. Sorry I wasn't in class yesterday, my paperwork just came through. The office personnel asked me to give you this." A slight upper class Boston accent hummed in her words—much smoother than Addy's newly acquired Bronx sound.

Addy bit back the jealously of Nina's style and poise. *Better perfect the 'gunna' go huntin', fishin' and muddin'' talk right quick.* The local kids weren't illiterate hillbillies but sometimes it was hard to tell. The lazy northwest rural diction prevailed among the current in-crowd, while the Queen's English was to be mocked and, if possible, hung from the flagpole by its underwear.

Addy read the admittance slip. *Hmmm, red flagged by the counselor. What's that even mean?*

"Well, hi Nina. Good to have you." Addy decided to try out Robin William's fake teacher persona, throwing back her shoulders, formalizing her voice. "I see you're a senior. Where'd you move from? You sound like you're from the east coast."

"I came from a private prep school in Massachusetts. I lived there with my father." The teenager coolly surveyed the carved, mismatched desks, the three beat up dictionaries on the shelf. "This school seems a lot different."

Addy laughed. "I'm sure. But you'll do fine. Don't worry, you'll make friends in no time." Then epiphany hit. "Hey! You should consider joining Oceanside's Speech Team, that'd be a good way for you to meet people."

Nina eyeballed her. "Umm. I don't have a speech impediment, Ms. Taylor. I'm sure the kids in the club are nice . . ."

"No, no," Addy cringed, realizing she had this particular conversation to look forward to many times. "The speech team competes in debates, even some acting events. It's not a club for students with disabilities." She dithered. "Though a kid in a wheelchair or with a lisp certainly can compete. Anyone can compete. Anyone. Anyone at all."

Do I sound desperate? Stop talking, Addy.

Nina eyed the clock, gracefully edging away from her. Addy needed to work on her sales pitch. The regular crew of seniors pushed past, looking at Nina suspiciously, eying her east coast fashion and the black sketchbook in her hands. The tight-knit local kids would not make this transition easy for her. *Tread lightly, girly,* thought Addy, wanting to protect a teen she barely knew, while at the same time wishing her own wardrobe was half as nice.

"Your seat is right there," Addy pointed to a pocked desk in the second row.

A cheerleader with a beautiful cascade of crimson red hair falling over her black and white uniform patted the desktop. She chirped, upbeat. "Here, next to me!"

"Ugh." A pretty girl dressed in a tight tshirt and low-slung jeans dropped into a desk and rolled her eyes. "Billie, you're not the school greeter."

Billie turned to the snotty girl nonchalantly, smiled sweetly at the haughty remark. "And you don't always have to give in to your inner emo."

"All right, everyone please be seated." Addy spoke forcefully to the class, hoping to put the kibosh on any conversations that might spin out of control. "You need to be ready to begin when the bell rings so as not to be marked tardy. Now, go ahead and take out a clean sheet of paper and a pen or pencil. Your heading will need to—"

"Ms. Taylor?" A dark haired boy, looking to be barely in his teens, much less a senior, sat lounging at his desk, hood tight around his eyebrows, hoisting a finger as if to hail a cab.

"Yes?"

"Do you have any paper? And a pen?"

"Uh." *Really? Didn't he think a language arts class might require writing materials?* "Sure. Does anyone else need paper?" Hands shot up. "There's a stack of notebook paper on the back shelf. And some extra pencils. Go ahead and grab what you need now, but please put the pencils back at the end of the period." The stampede to the back of the room shocked her. When the room quieted down, paper on everyone's desk, she asked, slightly irritated, "How come you guys don't have paper or pencils? You must need this stuff for other classes."

Then she realized her error. It struck her when some of the students looked down, shame apparent on their faces. The shoes. The shoes were the real give away. Many of the students wore dingy, ill-fitting tennis shoes, and clothes that had gone through the washing machine and the hand-me-down network many times—even though it was only the second day of the school year. This was not a wealthy crew. Their families probably struggled to buy a can of chili and gas for the log truck. Scanning the young faces, she wondered how many of them had eaten breakfast. *Man, I'm a total jerk.* Tomorrow she would silently restock the pencil jar and keep a couple of extra peanut butter and jelly sandwiches on hand.

Billie waved her hand, drawing her black and red uniform tight, magnetizing the boys around her. "We don't need paper in other classes—we get packets of worksheets," she smiled sweetly. "That is, if we aren't watching a movie or getting free-time. We're seniors, ya' know? "

"I remember being a senior. I'm pretty sure you still have some learning to do," said Addy, relieved to have dodged a bullet, yet despairing at the bubbly girl's description of other classes; hopefully she exaggerated the lack of learning.

"You're gonna' need to come in here prepared and ready to work, every day. If you don't know how to read or write coherently by the end of the year, be prepared to bag groceries forever."

The class erupted into catcalls and loud conversations. Addy put her hands up, patting the air. "Alright, alright, quiet. I get it. You just want to bide your time, play the game—get out of this prison. But I'm the Warden.

"Please head your paper on the left, like this." She pointed to the example of the proper heading she'd written on the whiteboard earlier. Looking out, she saw a handful of kids writing on the wrong side of the paper. She sighed.

"Next, I'd like you to write a paragraph in response to this question." She gestured to the whiteboard again, tapping her handwritten question.

Old stories always have a hero. Compare a mythological hero to a real-life hero in today's world. What are some common characteristics? Differences?

She liked this question. Apparently, so did the class. They settled into their desks, the only sound pencils scratching across paper. She caught the new girl's eye; Nina smiled then began to write with the others. Addy stood with her hands clasped in front of her, amazed at the bent heads. They were doing what she asked. *My God.* They were treating her as an authority figure. *Silly kids.*

"Ms. Taylor?" The dark haired boy again. She looked at the seating chart. Dylan Setton. She acknowledged his query with a nod and an inquisitive eyebrow.

"Uh, could you give me an example of a hero? I get Odysseus or Beowulf. They were warriors, smart, like Superman . . . but today? Nobody really has super powers."

A few others piped up, "Yeah—we don't have any heroes—this is a stupid question—I'm comparing my mom to Medusa—can I have the hall pass?"

Addy smiled and interrupted the flow of chatter. "I'm going to give you a couple more minutes to ponder modern heroes. But consider this: heroes aren't only the smartest or strongest warriors. Their most important characteristic is courage. Some heroes, then and now, were weak, average people who stepped up, displaying bravery in the face of evil or danger when it threatened others. Anyone you know of who is like that today?"

One by one, the heads bent back over their papers, some still a bit hesitant.

Who would I list as my hero? Addy wondered. She thought about fire fighters and soldiers, or activists, or doctors who worked pro-bono in ghettos. They were heroes. She just didn't know any of them personally. It would be nice to have a hero in her life.

"Ms. Taylor?" Dylan again. At least he wasn't shy.

She smiled. "Yes?"

"Can I list my mom as my hero? She was a single mom and kept our family together even when she was dying of cancer. She found us a place to live. If it wasn't for her, my sister and I would be in foster care. She was brave." Dylan leaned forward, his face tight, earnest. "She's a hero, right?"

Addy sucked in her breath sharply, bit the back of her tongue until she tasted iron. Dylan asked the question without crying, the least she could do was control her own tears. This kid. How fucking, unbearably sad. She wanted to cradle him in her arms, pet his head, tell him it would be okay. But who was she to say it was okay? Obviously, his mom had loved him and then she died. That was not okay. The rest of the class was quiet, waiting for her to answer.

"Yes, yes, absolutely Dylan. Your mother is the perfect example of a modern day hero." Addy knew her eyes were shiny. That couldn't be helped. She tried to diffuse the emotion in the room. "Does anyone else want to share their examples of today's heroes?"

Billie flung her hand in the air again, much to the delight of the males. "I do! I do! I'm writing about Anderson Cooper."

"The news reporter?"

"Yeah, he went to Iraq and reported on our troops, telling Americans the truth about the war."

Addy smothered her surprised response. *Teenage hottie watching CNN. Who knew?* "Good, yes. Anyone else?"

A quiet, pretty girl sitting in the back, surrounded by friends, tentatively raised her hand.

"Yes," Addy said, nodding at the girl, her internal rolodex refusing to barf up the name.

"Umm," the girl twisted a delicately beaded strand at her neck, blushing to match her light pink sweater. "I think I know a hero."

"Okay. Great." Addy shuffled through papers, looking for the seating chart. Not wanting to interrupt the flow of the discussion, she gave up. "I'm sorry, what's your name?"

"Oh, that's ok." Her eyes were down, voice quiet, but the class was listening. She was obviously well liked. "I'm Jamy Lock." She pushed her brown pixie cut of her eyes and shyly made eye contact with the young teacher.

Addy dipped her head, a bobble head doll exuding encouragement.

"So, last year, during that big flood, my dad and my uncle were using their logging equipment to help our neighbors shore up slides. They got trapped at the bottom of a valley by a huge mud slide."

Jamy told her story, speaking faster and faster, as if someone was going to interrupt her before she finished. Her voice shook. Addy felt a strong beat of empathy.

"It was pouring, and super windy, but the Coast Guard guys got their helicopter, lowered that bucket thing in the crazy wind gusts. They saved them. The whole freaking mountain was about to come down but those guys didn't care. They even rescued our dog." She took a breath, eyed the other kids around her. "You guys remember that." A number of kids nodded, somber. *That must have been one hell of a storm,* Addy thought.

"Anyway, those guys, the Coast Guard guys, I think they were heroes. They weren't fighting monsters, or anything, but they could have died trying to help my dad. They didn't even know us!" She stopped, breathing heavy from her racing speech. Her creamy cheeks stained with embarrassment.

"Jamy! That's a great story! And, yes, the Coast Guard are heroes. That's a perfect example for this essay." The senior seemed so young, so naïve, compared to the rest of the class, tentative but not jaded or cynical.

Jamy's mouth relaxed, the furrowed lines on her forehead easing.

Addy readdressed the class. "Okay, I bet you've thought of your own modern hero now. If you still have questions, raise your hand, I'll come around. " Pencils immediately started scratching, papers shifted. Those staring into corners or at the ceiling were at least doing it quietly.

Is this teaching? Am I teaching?

CHAPTER 5
NINA

What am I doing here?

New student Nina DuBois pressed a hand to her nose. *It smells like the fifth circle of hell.*

Oceanside High School loomed behind the teenager—a grey, squat building threatening to release a torrent of hardened criminals or homicidal maniacs from dark, hidden depths, the educational façade barely intact. Nina shuddered, shutting her eyes to the aesthetics.

She sat on the cold concrete bench in front of OHS, scarf fluttering in the sea breeze, the scent of decaying clamshells stinging her nostrils. The parking lot held a handful of cars, hunkered down, no people in sight. Standing abruptly, unsteady on the cracked sidewalk, she began pacing, scowling at the Pacific Ocean loudly surging onto the beach across the highway.

Nina needed this moment to breathe before her mother arrived. It had been a long day. Long week. And now buried urges were clawing their way into the light. Like an alcoholic seeking the last drop of Nyquil, her unruly fingers slipped inside the thick ring of bracelets, caressing the welts and scarring on the inside of her forearms. *Careful.* A fingernail snagged a ridge of flesh, making her catch her breath.

Where's my mother? Glaring down Highway 101, she realized she needed a Plan B.

Her mother. Her genius, work-crazy mother. How could her father send Nina back here? He knew her mother wasn't nurturing, or 'mothering' in any sense of the word. He knew *so* well that he left ten years ago, packing Nina and her stuffed animals into the back of the Lincoln Continental while Margo was at the hospital, in her big office, ruling her domain.

Now, Nina once again waited for her mother to choose her over the hospital. "Plan B" moved from figuring out how to get to Margo's house to plotting how to get back to where she belonged, with her dad.

She missed her father. He didn't understand Nina, or even know how to talk to her, but he cared for her. And now he had become afraid for her. "Honey, you say you're done cutting . . . but you said that last time. Your mom, she'll know medically when something is wrong." He had paused, face laden with fear and frustration. If she had touched him, they would both have started crying. He had choked up anyway, looking down at his lap as he said, "I just want you to be safe. Safe and happy. I'd rip out my heart and give it to you, kid, if I could make you happy."

Sitting in that exit room at Greenhaven's, she understood. Her cutting, and subsequent stay at the loony bin, changed the trajectory of her life. No surprise her father couldn't cope with her "issues." After all, *she* wasn't able to cope with her issues, much less define them. Nor did she see her mother, a career-obsessed woman, as part of the solution. An anxious, overworked adult living with a depressed, overwrought teen didn't seem smart.

Waiting. Alone. Thousands of miles away from daddy. Their phone calls were sporadic and short. Her mother didn't do much to fill the void. She was rarely home. Nina communicated by sticky note when the kitchen cupboards were empty or she needed a ride somewhere. In Boston, she used public transit, or simply ordered takeout. Here? No transit, no takeout, and no Margo—her non-existent chauffeur. She needed her mother, considering the five-mile jaunt to a store or restaurant, in a rural area with no public bus system. The highway didn't even have decent walking easements.

The woman forgot she had a daughter at least once a day. *Thank God I know how to make my own pesto penne.* Margo lived at the hospital, barely visiting her own bed, attending carefully to the needs of hospital staff and patients. When home, the director entered their kitchen to make coffee and find a lighter for her cigarettes, never to cook or sit down for a chat.

Shivering, Nina checked her watch for the umpteenth time. Her mother said she would pick her up ten minutes after school was out. It had been forty minutes since the mad cattle exodus from the school. She threw herself back on the hard seat in a huff, muttering to herself. "Why am I even here? She's supposed to be taking care of me."

"Is this conversation private or can I sit here?"

A short, dark haired boy stealthily emerged from behind the gym, much like Puck from the woods. She recognized him from one of her classes. He had a sweet, devilish face though his clothes were pure kid, thread-bare jeans bagging to his knees, revealing red and white striped boxers. While trying to look gangster he inadvertently oozed Christmas elf. He sat down, pulling his hood up and over his eyebrows, scanning the parking lot with furtive glances.

"Uh, sorry. Yes," Nina replied, hitching her tote close to her body. She could see this boy was no threat but he was awfully jumpy. He made her nervous. She startled when he turned to her, quickly.

"Hey, I know you. From English. Whatcher' name? Are you new?" He threw the questions at her, tossing them like grenades. He noticed her flinch and visibly dialed himself back a notch, offering a small smile. "Sorry, I'm amped up. Don't mean to be nosy. We don't get many new kids here. Most kids move away."

"Yes, I just moved here. I'm Nina." She didn't want to seem rude so she asked, "How about you? What's your name?"

"Dylan." He snatched his hand out of his hoody pocket, proffering it to Nina. She shook it, quickly putting her hand back in her own pockets, chilled by the ever-increasing wind. She tried not to shiver while Dylan talked.

"Hey, tell me if you see the football coach, will ya'? I'm supposed to be at practice."

She looked at him skeptically. "Don't take this the wrong way, but . . . really? Aren't you a little short for the football team?"

He snorted. "I'm not short, I'm just not a hulking moron like most of those guys. I bet I'm taller than you." He eyed her up and down and then broke into a grin. "Whatever. I don't care. I fucking hate football. Unfortunately, I promised my parole officer I'd get into an after school program. It was that or picking up litter along the highway in those orange jumpsuits." He noticed her edging away and grinned again.

"I didn't knife anyone, you don't have to worry. I got caught shoplifting. I was hungry. Damn girl, not every criminal is violent."

"I wouldn't know. You're my first criminal." She couldn't believe it, finally having a real conversation with someone her own age here and he had a parole officer. Life was certainly more interesting in Oceanside. Even the crazies in her Boston neighborhood had been upscale.

An older Volvo came lumbering around the side of the building, from the staff parking lot. Dylan tugged the drawstring on his hood until only his nose stuck out. Nina held back a laugh, not wanting to hurt his ego further. As the car approached she saw the English teacher, Ms. Taylor, who waved. Nina waved back, an unexpected warm feeling of affinity for the woman making her smile. She turned to Dylan, lightly touching his arm. "Hey. You can uncover your face. It was just our English teacher."

His face slowly broke free from the hood, revealing a chagrined countenance. "Ms. Taylor?" Then a naughty grin spread across his face. "She's hot."

Nina grimaced. "Uh yeah. So, what happens if you aren't at practice?"

"I told Coach Pike I hurt my ankle. I'm supposed to be soaking it in the locker room. That dick's not gonna' notice I'm missing, not unless he happens to sit in the cold spot on the bench I been keepin' warm. No skin off my nuts, dude, I can't play for shit." He shrugged. "I just hope my ride gets here before I get caught skippin'. If I'm busted then I have to meet with Mr. Bob. My parole guy." He shivered, hunkered down into his hoody. "Damn it's cold. Aren't you cold?"

"Is it always this windy? My mom was supposed to be here an hour ago. I don't think I can wait much longer." She looked down at her blue fingers, tapped her frozen toes on the pavement.

"What side of town do you live on? Maybe we can give you a ride," Dylan asked, eyeballing the locker room doors across the parking lot.

Nina considered this, rubbing the Goosebumps on her calves, pinning her floating skirt down with her elbows. It was highly likely her mother had forgotten about her, was right now showing an intern how to insert a tube into an old man's urethra or arguing with a hospital board member over the cost of Viagra. Dylan seemed harmless. She smoothed the flying tendrils out of her eyes and looked at the diminutive senior boy. The next gust decided her. "Is your mom picking you up?"

"Nah. My mom's dead. It's my buddy Ben."

"Oh God, that's right. You said that in class. I am so sorry . . ."

"Whatever. It was a long time ago. Cancer." He sounded gruff, then cleared his throat, asking, "So where do you live?"

Nina wanted to touch him again, caress this soft, lost soul. She'd developed an affinity for a second person today. *Great, my teacher wants me to join the dork team and I'm making friends with a degenerate. I'll be Ms. Popular.* She touched the scars on her arms again. *I could stand to be unseen for a while, I guess. Just until I figure out how to get back home, to dad.*

"I live on the north end."

Miraculously, her mother's Jaguar careened into the lot, halting in front of Nina's bench. The passenger window slid down. Margo, hair akimbo, dressed in a power suit, bent her head and yelled across the seats, "Hop in, kid, I gotta' head back for a meeting!" The window rolled back up, no apologies.

"Well. I guess my mom is here." Nina stood up, looking down at Dylan. "Can we give you a ride?"

She was kind of relieved when he ducked his head, all of a sudden shy.

"Ah, no, no thanks. I live on the south end." He grinned. "Don't worry about me. I know how to keep out of sight. Ben'll be here any second." He gave a salute, drawing his knees up to his chest, emphasizing his elfish nature.

"Okay. See you tomorrow." Nina waved and slid into the front seat, relieved to be stepping out of the wind. Margo did not wait for her to put on her seatbelt, peeling out just as Nina tugged the door shut. *And hello to you, too, mother.*

CHAPTER 6
ADDY

Rick roused Addy at the crack of eight a.m., long after the weekend edition of the Oceanside Daily News slammed into the front door, long after the watery dawn crept into her bedroom, but long before her body released its hold on Dreamland. Shifting her head without lifting it off the pillow, she saw rain drops clinging to the window, gray streaky shadows darkening the walls. *No sun today. Me no get out of bed.* She nestled into the dingy-white down comforter, pulling it over her head, ignoring the feather stems poking her cheek.

Her boyfriend came close to losing his life when he grabbed the blankets and tugged, tossing them on the floor at the foot of the bed. Addy popped up, her face red, her goose bumps white.

"Seriously?" She army crawled down the naked bed and dropped heavily into the blankets. Curling into the fetal position on the floor, she re-cocooned, the down quilt firmly wrapped around her body, her nose peeking out.

"Honey, I don't think you've taken a good look at that rug," Rick whispered by her ear, smoothly stepping back when her hand shot out, searching for skin to slap. He threw a pair of jeans and a Cleanline sweatshirt in a heap next to her. "I can't find your underwear." Her hand waved him away then withdrew to the nest.

"Come on, get up. I haven't seen you all week. You're going to have breakfast with me before I go to the office."

"Urgle bagurble."

"I can't understand you through your blankie." He ripped the quilt off her, threw it back onto the bed. "Stop being a baby."

Addy slit an eye. *It's going to be one of those days.* "Why are you being so mean to me?" She stretched alluringly, her tattered nightgown showing a toned leg. "Can't you bring me breakfast in bed?" She purred like a kitten. "I promise to keep my underwear off."

He slid into khakis, sifted through ties, frowning at the interior of the miniscule closet. She sighed. The appeasement-sex strategy only worked if he thought he was instigating it, otherwise it was an affront to his manhood to have a woman take the lead. *Are all men this insecure? Is that cat urine I smell?* The nubby brown carpet felt like astroturf and definitely emitted a stink. She wrinkled her nose and sat up, knowing she couldn't push the sleepy act much longer or he would become pissy. She had yet to learn how to let his bad moods roll off her. Addy, always the people-pleaser, moved into the familiar basketball stance, on the lookout for fleeting glances or words that might lead to hours of sulking or arguing. Time to get up, move around the court, play a little offense.

Re-wetting the gel in her wavy blonde hair, she drug the thick tendrils back into a messy ponytail. Wearing the red surf-shop hoody, she stopped in the bathroom to wash mascara rings from below her green eyes. After a hard scrub, the mascara was gone, leaving a swath of splotchy skin. As she ran a tube of pale cover-up over her flesh, Rick stepped up behind her.

"You don't need that." His brown eyes smirked. He pinched her behind. "You're not ugly anymore." He walked out. "Let's go."

Wow. Sometimes I hate you. She poked her image in the mirror, jamming a long finger into her eye, pretending it was Rick. Then she squinted, in a spaghetti western showdown with the retorts bubbling around her brain. She shoved the caustic comments she wanted to shout at Rick into the depths of her boiling stomach, waylaying an argument that would do no good anyway.

Rick and Addy, true Oregonians, bore the light rain without an umbrella, making their way down the hill to Oceanside's one café. Rosie's Roost boasted a great view of the Pacific, organic foods, coffee beans roasted on-site, and menu prices based on the tourist clientele. "We can't afford to eat here," Addy whispered, peeling off a damp jacket. Rick sat, tilting back in a wooden chair, the newspaper already fluffed and folded to reveal the sport's section.

"We're fine. Just don't order the lobster."

She looked at the choices. "No lobster. Can I order the crab?"

He continued to read, ignoring her. *Turnabout is fair play.* Out of her messenger bag she withdrew a thick binder, stuffed with a hundred pages off the internet describing the rules and regulations of high school Speech and Debate. *Light reading for the morning.* Thumbing through pages of dense text, Addy's brain seized. The words appeared to be in a foreign language. Addy imagined herself dropped from a plane into the middle of an African village. Licking a fingertip tasting of hair gel, she turned the pages to find a list of the twelve speaking events and four types of debates. *Just the simple stuff, I'll start there.* A glossary of definitions made her go pale, sweat beading her forehead. The text was anything but simple. *Rhetoric? I barely understood Plato, not to mention his weird fascination with chairs in his man cave.*

The cracked dam holding back her insecurities split in a few key places, allowing voices from her past to taunt her. Her father's voice boomed the loudest, old standbys regarding her lack of intelligence and common sense, her inability to put together a coherent sentence . . . a review of his litany from her teen years. She shut her eyes and rubbed her make-up slick temples, tamping down the internal noise.

Rick was still behind the newspaper; she flipped the pages of her binder, trying to make it into a funny flipbook cartoon. It didn't work. The text did not come alive. *They're going to think I'm a moron. Oh, hell. I am a moron.*

"What are you doing?" Rick peered at her over the paper, his brown eyes serious behind his horn-rimmed glasses.

"I'm reading about speech teams." She frowned. "I don't know why Ford thought I could do this job. I majored in literature. Books. I avoided speech classes like the plague."

"You don't need to figure it out today. We're supposed to be spending time together."

"Oh, I should watch you read the paper instead?" She regretted her retort instantly.

He frowned. "I'm just scanning the stats."

"Hmm. Well, what didya' want to talk about?" She kept her voice light while huffily sliding her binder out of the way, trying to reel back in her irritation, wanting to stop the conflict. She needed an easy morning.

"Jesus, Addy." He scrunched up the paper and threw it to the side. His voice got louder, his face hurt. "I don't give a fuck what we talk about. Is it so unpleasant to hang out with me?" He pushed away from the table, sloshed coffee spreading in rings on the white tablecloth. "I don't need this. I just wanted to spend time with you."

"Hey, you're overreacting." Her voice turned high pitched, cajoling. She tried reaching across the table to touch his hand, but he jerked away from her. Watching herself from afar, she hated this weak girl.

"Oh, I'm overreacting now? Thanks a lot." Low, slow mutter. He stood up, shoving his arms into his rain-slicker.

She gripped the table, knuckles whitening, wood giving under her fingernails. *Really? Now?* He could fire up his temper tantrums with a flick of a switch. If only she knew

42

the location of said switch. "Rick, please sit down," she whispered. "You know I love you."

He bent over her, an angry whisper spraying her cheeks. "Not much." He walked out, the bell over the door reverberating a long, hard peal of complaint.

Wow. Okay. I didn't see that coming. She watched him through the window, walking up the hill, shoulders hunched. Addy was used to Rick's manic-depressive moods but he usually reserved the show for her eyes only, behind closed doors. Regardless, he'd cold-cocked her. She was here, doing what he wanted. It wasn't enough for him. Still, she felt a deep pity for him, recognizing his Sisyphean effort to fill some un-fillable void in his psyche, a void she couldn't touch, no matter what she tried to do to show him that she loved him, cared about him.

"Are you going to order?" The Asian waitress, sporting bleached dreadlocks to her tiny waist, looked pointedly at the empty chair. "Is he coming back?"

"I don't know." She opened the menu. "What's the most expensive thing on the menu?"

Dreads smiled. "Honey, you might want to re-think that." She tapped the laminated page with an ornately manicured orange fingernail. "Filet mignon, sun dried tomatoes and goat cheese frittata. That bitch'll break the bank."

"Oh. My God. Yeah."

"Try today's special. Organic, whole wheat pancakes. Pretty good. Way cheaper."

Addy snorted. "I need a treat. I'll get the pancakes plus an egg, over easy."

"Live it up, sister."

Rick did not return, giving Addy plenty of time to drink gallons of coffee and build her anxiety level to heart attack status. She sloshed her way down to the beach. The rain had settled into a mist, steaming as it touched Addy's hot face. The monotonous surge of the waves slapping the wet sand was hypnotic, soothing. Her lungs filled with fresh, salty air and her face cooled; calmer, she traversed the six blocks home.

She spent the day taking notes, highlighting debate terms and doing internet searches. By the time she heard Rick's car pull into the driveway, the air was tinged with the wet, purple smells of the coming night. Her brain was full. She pushed away from the computer, more informed but even less sure of her ability to coach in the massive world of words.

She trudged down the hall, through the living room, to the front door, waiting for Rick to enter. She timidly smoothed her hair. She had no idea what to say to him.

CHAPTER 7
ADDY

Addy sat on a tall stool at her podium, head in hands, unable to bear the weight of the insecurity swirling through her brain. The tiny classroom seemed immense, an Alice in Wonderland room stretching for miles, vacant desks as far as the eye could see. The peace should have been pleasant. Instead, the quiet shouted obscenities at her.

It was lunch. The OHS Speech & Debate Team meeting was scheduled to be happening right now. In this room. This empty, empty room.

Well. She forced a cheery thought. *The team should be easy to coach. And I will have plenty of time to grade papers.* She looked down at her sandwich, narrowing her hazel eyes, biting a pen. The odorless peanut butter and butter on dried-out sourdough was holding down a stack of hero response papers.

The door opened. Nina glided in, quiet, swathed in soft, floating materials, a light scent of soap and lavender in her wake.

"Oh Nina! I'm so glad you're here!"

"Uh, I just forgot my scarf."

Addy's face melted.

"Ms. Taylor?"

"No, no, I'm fine," Addy muttered. Then a sound crawled out of her painfully stretched lips that sounded suspiciously like maniacal laughter. She watched the girl hasten her step and quickly grab her scarf from under a desk.

"Hey, Nina." Nina froze, a look of soft panic crossing

her porcelain features. "Did you know the meeting for the speech team was today?"

Nina looked away.

"No one showed up!" Addy took a deep breath, reeled her emotions back in. She took a second to breathe, to gather her wits. In the bigger world, the weak October sun strained to light up the beach. *Who in the hell cares about a speech team. No one out there, in the real world, even knows what it is.*

"I'm just a little, uh . . . flustered. I thought at least two or three kids would be here. Not all the flyers were thrown away. At least not in here." *I'm so glad I fought with Rick over nothing. And read the legal dictionary.*

"Ms. Taylor, I think you've forgotten who your audience is. You need to sell to your audience, right?"

"Ohhkay."

"Yeah. How about food? The target is teens, teens who love food, especially free food. Offer donuts. Better yet, pizza. If they sign up for the team."

Addy looked at Nina appreciatively. She watched Nina move confidently back into the wide world of high school with a smile and wave. *Damn. She's smart. I should've thought of that.*

Two hours later, Addy left her sixth period class reading quietly and walked to the front office, the senior girl's advice directing her steps. A secretary with teased brunette hair looked at Addy over a high counter, peering down her long thin nose. The nameplate stated "Candi Tencil."

Her voice was nasal, the opposite of a well-modulated phone voice. "May I help you?"

Daunted, Addy said, "Hi, I'm Addison Taylor. I'm the new English teacher? Your name is Candi? Well, Candi, I was wondering if I could make an announcement over the intercom?"

"You can't interrupt classes." Candi did not give the impression of warmth or caring.

"Oh. Can I make an announcement right before the end

of school?"

"The time is okay. But has Mr. Ford approved it?"

"Didn't you just say it was okay to announce at the end of the day?"

"No, I mean, Mr. Ford has to approve the wording of your announcement. You can't say anything over the intercom without Mr. Ford okaying it."

"Mr. Ford wants me to start a Speech Team. That's what the announcement is about."

The big-haired secretary just looked at her, not saying a word, her face blank.

"Okaaay. Is Mr. Ford in his office?"

The secretary looked at her as if she had a blistering pimple on her nose. "Do you have an appointment?"

Addy tamped down her irritation, hoped it didn't show on her face. Her education professors claimed the two most important people to befriend in a school building were the custodian and the secretary. Candi would certainly be a delight on a Friday night, hanging out, swapping girlie stories.

She answered with a forced calm, "I didn't know I was going to need an appointment. I did not know until this very second an announcement had to be vetted by an administrator." She tried to smile winningly, leaning in personably. "But now, thankfully, I have you to help me. Whew! It's a good thing you filled me in. Do you think I could talk to Mr. Ford for a quick second? Ask him about this short little announcement?"

In order to have this inane conversation with a pissy secretary she'd illegally left her sixth period class of thirty-two freshmen unsupervised. God knew what they were doing in her room, alone. *By the time this is resolved, two of my students will have conceived a baby and multiple drug deals will have gone down. Damn. Why did everything have to be so complicated?*

By the time she finally made it back to her classroom, she was afraid to open the door. She peeked through the door window, careful to avoid the smeary lip impressions. She'd been gone at least ten minutes, telling the class she would be gone for two, having them read the introduction to *The Iliad* while she was away. She breathed a sigh of relief to see them in their seats, though how many of them were reading versus sleeping or talking to their neighbor was a tough count. She didn't care so long as none of them had snuck out for a meth break. She strode in to her room.

"Hey, Ms. Taylor! I thought you said you were going to make an announcement. I didn't hear anything," said a joker from the back of the room.

"The secretary is going to announce it for me just before the last bell. Which is in . . . three minutes. Wow. We didn't get much done today. Sorry guys."

"That's okay." Susan, a punky girl with raven black spikes, said, " We're happy sitting here . . . reading." On the desk in front of her was someone else's math homework. No book.

"Hey, you guys, I'm going to have free pizza at lunch tomorrow for anyone who signs up to join the new speech team. Are any of you interested in joining? Come on, free ride to college! Overnight stays at a hotel –"

"What? Really? When is this meeting?"

"Tomorrow at lunch."

"And did you say you were giving out pizza?"

"Yep."

DING. The intercom came on.

"Are you interested in joining a new club? Go to Room Seven tomorrow at lunch. There will be free pizza. Sorry for the interruption. Have a good day."

Wow. The secretary had gone off script. Now Addy was going to be giving pizza to kids ranging from young republicans to teen lumberjacks, all hoping to start a new club. Where was she supposed to get this pizza? And how exactly was she going to pay for it? She didn't get her first paycheck until the end of the month. She sighed. At least the ball was rolling. Mr. Ford would see she was trying to fulfill her duties.

The next day at lunch her room smelled delicious; the heady scent of pepperoni, tomato and garlic wafted into the hallway. A small fan whirred on the desk next to the pizzas, aiming the fumes out at the foot traffic hurling past. There were stacks and stacks of pizza boxes, thanks to a local pizza place willing to bill her until the end of the month, including the generous delivery fee and tip. Addy had arrived to work an hour early so she could make more fliers and post them everywhere: the halls, the library, the metal shop, the locker rooms, the bathrooms, the infamous make-out spot under the bleachers, and on the trees leading up to the smokers' hill behind the school. And then she made another announcement, reading the invitation herself.

Between the pizza-fan ploy and the loud speaker, Addy managed to capture the attention of a few kids. And a few teachers, most of whom apologetically grabbed a slice and skipped out with a thanks. One teacher, rather short, sporting a pointy red goatee, jeans and cowboy boots, sauntered in, punched a few of the guys in letterman jackets on the shoulder and walked back out carrying a box almost half full of pizza. He had not so much as glanced in Addy's direction. She was trying to decide what to do about it when social studies teacher from next door slouched in and hovered by her desk, a slice in each hand, dripping grease.

"Hey, thanks for the grub. Smart way to get kids sucked in to your little club." He snatched two more pieces, walked away, tossing Addy a weird look over his shoulder. His mien suggested flirtiness. *Gahh*. She hoped not. She had enough to deal with, she didn't want to worry about hurting some old guy's feelings.

With her attention focused on the odd behavior of her male colleagues, a few more students slithered in, sliding into desks, slices shoved into their mouths. Addy recognized a few.

"I'm here, as promised. I hope the pizza is as delicious as it smells," said Nina, more teenager than ballerina in the face of food. She succumbed to her own suggestion.

The elfish, black-haired Dylan lurked behind her. He smiled shyly at Addy and then turned to Nina. "Hey, Nina, I like pizza too."

The girl lifted an eyebrow theatrically. "How bizarre. So few humans actually like cheesy goodness."

He grinned, unabashed. "Sit next to me. You can help me sign my name correctly."

Addy could faintly hear their conversation as they wandered off. She grimaced when they sat, eating at the bacteria-laden desks. Then the teacher grinned to herself, happy to see the new girl find friends.

"Are you really signing up for the team?" she heard Nina ask.

The boy, Dylan, answered with his mouth full. "Better this than football. My parole officer is starting to get suspicious about so many injuries keeping me from practice. And I don't think the debaters will enjoy picking me up and hanging me off hooks as much the apes on the football team."

Pretending to sort handouts, Addy raised an eyebrow. *Parole?! Nice. Better lock down the utility knives.*

"Really? They were that mean to you?" Nina seemed curious.

Dylan played it cool while his brown eyes hinted at a quashed soul, making Addy wince with empathy. "Nah, not all of them. I've known most of the guys since pre-school, playing tag on the soccer field and stuff like that. Only a couple of them like to pick on the little guy, really let their inner asshole shine. I'm adept at avoiding them, though. I've learned a lot about evasion over the past few years. I'm thinking of joining the CIA when I graduate, show 'em my mad skills in hide and seek."

Seats around Nina and Dylan were filling up, the level of noise rising with the body count. It became impossible to hear the boy any longer. Her gaze lingered him on a moment longer. *What is the smallest senior in Oregon on parole for?*

Addy sighed, counted twenty-seven kids; time to start the meeting. *This is crazy. Are all these kids really interested in speech and debate? God, I hope not. What would I do with them? I can't watch twenty kids give speeches at the same time.* A logistic that had not occurred to her until now. How did one person do this job?

She spent the next twenty minutes passing out contracts, handbooks, rules, event descriptions, insurance papers, and emergency contact information; at least sixteen trees died in the effort to start a new team at Oceanside. She took a deep breath, centering herself before she spoke. *It's actually getting easier. At least when I talk to kids.* She began, explaining the acting events, persuasion events and informational events, attempting to lure them with promises of a soapbox from which to rant about any topic their teenage hearts' desired.

"Anything?" Tori, the Student Body President, asked. Her straight blonde ponytail brushed her face as she leaned forward intently.

"Sure, anything."

"Even —" The cracking voice ejected from the big, awkward body of freshman Travis Diamond, wearing a football jersey, orange hair sticking up in all the wrong places.

"Nope, not that." Addy cut him off. The group laughed.

"But you don't even know what I was going to say!"

"Oh, yes, I do, Travis. Look, you guys get to make the choice, but you might as well make a choice the adult judges are gonna' want to hear about. Like the life cycle of the venus flytrap. Or how eyeshadow causes cancer."

"You want me to talk about a plant?" Travis kept going,

loving the stage.

"No. Come up with something better."

"Can I act out a scene from *Dumb and Dumber*?"

An older boy sitting next to Travis pulled a meaty hand out of his Carhart jacket and slapped the freshman on the back of the head. "Cuz, .why don't you try something new?"

The room filled with laughter again as Travis grinned and rubbed his head. Addy coughed into her hand to cover her own giggle. "Hey, okay, no need to get violent here. But, to answer your question, my guess is no, judges are not going to consider that quality literature."

And finally, debate. Arguing and conflict. *Ugh*.

"There are three or four types of debate but we're going to focus on a style called Lincoln-Douglas debate, at least for now. It's one person against another person. The topic changes every two months so you don't have time to get bored. You'll have to debate both the affirmative and negative side of each topic, whether you like it or not. Hate abortion? Despise coal mining? Keep your real opinion to yourself. The only thing that matters is selling a side to the audience."

Some of the kids were actually listening. Nina raised her hand, bracelets jingling. "Isn't that kind of unethical? Trying to make people believe in something you don't even believe in yourself?"

Addy shrugged. "Yep. This is an exercise in analysis and audience manipulation." Addy paused, sweeping the room with her eyes. "One way to think of this is that you will be learning how to think and speak like a politician or a lawyer. Is that good or bad?"

Dylan leaned over his desk, speaking slowly, "Well, I guess it's good, if you consider we'll be learning to understand The Man. We'll be able to figure out what they're *really* saying, how much of it's bullshit and how much of it's real." His face pinched. "Uh, sorry for cussing. Please don't give me a referral, I won't do it again."

Addy sent him a fake glare. "Keep it clean, kid." *Some criminal.* She stepped closer, tapping his shoulder. "And you're right. But the most important aspect of debating in high school is that you're learning how to look at both sides of an argument before making a decision. You guys should walk out of here as employable smart mouths. That, my friends, is good."

"Ms. Taylor?" Travis interrupted. "What if I don't want to debate? I thought you said in class we could do funny stuff, like stand up comedians?"

"Travis, you don't have to debate. You're talking about After Dinner Speaking. You write your own comedy routine." She looked him in the eye. "Of course, you have to keep it rated pg. For you, maybe g. This is still a school thing."

"Of course, of course." He leaned back in his desk, hands behind his head. "I'm always appropriate. Addison."

"Ms. Taylor, Travis."

"And what about football? I have practice after school. Coach'll rip off my arm and beat me with it if I miss practice. Am I gonna' be able to do both?"

"Speech practice is going to be after school in the library on Tuesdays and Thursdays. I'm willing to stay after football and volleyball practice lets out, work for an extra hour or so with you kids. If you really mean it, you wanna' to do both."

Travis started to say something but was cut off by Billie, the bubbly cheerleader with amazing crimson hair. "What about cheerleaders? Will you stay late for cheerleaders?"

Addy tried not to insult the girl by showing, once again, she had not expected a cheerleader to want to be part of an academic program. *God, I never knew I was such a stereotyping asshole.* "Of course. I'm sorry, your name's Billie, right? You're in senior English?"

"Oh that's okay, yeah, I'm Billie. I am in that class, but I'm only a junior. I want to start taking college classes next year, while I'm a senior."

"Good for you, Billie." Once again, stereotyping gone awry.

A few minutes later, the meeting wrapped up and the kids filed out, at least fifteen of them putting their names on the blue sign up sheet. *The phone numbers they listed may or may not be real, their names may or may not be real, unless Harry Butt was a popular family name around here, but Troy Ford and the Parent Group should be pleased.*

"Why the smile?" Speaking of the tall patrician, Troy's grey suit filled the door frame.

"Oh, Mr. Ford, hello." Why was she instantly flustered when he was around? *Maybe because he's seen my underwear.* "The meeting went better than expected." She picked up the sign up sheet. "At least ten of these names are from kids who're really interested. We're going to have our first practice tomorrow, after school."

"Good to hear." His smile was warm, his lips so . . . "You need to sign an extra duty contract to make this legal. Can you stop by my office later? I'll have Candi draw it up, have it ready for you to sign."

That sounded very adult. "By the way, how much does this coaching position pay?"

He looked amused, cocking his head as he said, "Pay? I thought it was clear, this is an unpaid position."

"Um. What?"

"In fact, you'll have to get the School Board to approve this group before they will begin paying for transportation or event fees."

"So, we can practice but we can't go to competitions? I'm pretty sure kids are expecting to compete."

"I didn't say you can't compete. You'll have to fundraise." He shrugged apologetically. "That's why I'm here. I signed up the speech team to run the football concessions this Friday. See, you're on your way all ready." He pushed himself out of the doorframe, where he'd been leaning. "Candi will email you the details.

"Oh, one last thing. Coaches are required to balance the cash box to the penny, always have three people present when the box is in use, and return the box to my office immediately after the event." Addy quailed as the tall vice-principal's face darkened. "Someone has been stealing club funds. But not for long."

With that, he was gone.

She sank onto the stool by the podium. *Great. My math skills rival that of a kindergartner.* Addy could not believe an adult was stealing from his or her own team. It was unbelievably unethical. And stupid. How could the money be worth the risk? Oceanside was a poor school in the middle of nowhere, it's not like there was some secret, deep pocket of cash to access.

She unscrunched the paper in her hand, looked at the list of names. *Unpaid? Are you kidding me?! You kids better be worth it.*

OCEANSIDE SCHOOL DISTRICT
Site Council / Public Meeting
September 8   6:30 am

Student Concerns: None—no student representative attended the meeting

Old Business:
Staff Development & Accountability: Committee has yet to meet

Student Life and Expectations: There was a delay in receiving the student's school planners (numerous misspellings). The company sent temporary planners (school rules are missing).

New Business:
Site Council Secretary: Approved Penny Knicker as the Site Council Secretary.

New High School Activity: Addison Taylor has requested funds from the Site Council to buy supplies and provide bussing for the newly instituted Oceanside Speech Club. Athletic Director Ford is going to look into using monies from the Small Schools Grant the high school received last month. Jennifer requested a budget report from the Grant funds. Mr. Ford had to leave for another meeting at this point.

Open House: There was a lengthy discussion regarding the name change for the summer Open House. Due to the fact that not all Oceanside Public School staff members are in attendance for the August Open House (many have second jobs), it can be misleading to parents under the assumption they will be meeting their child(ren)'s teacher and touring classrooms. Further discussion regarding this subject will be held in October, led by Mr. Seuss.

School Board Meeting Sign Up Sheet: Mr. Ford left a roster of dates and times that Site Council members will volunteer as reporter at the monthly School Board meetings.

Important Side Notes:

- Athletic Director Ford apologized for forgetting the donuts; he asked Mr. Nielson to bring the donuts from now on.
- Mr. Suess and Mr. Blank expressed interest in the high school providing interns to work in the community; both offered their place of business as a training ground; *item shelved*
- Tisha asked (repeatedly) for the group to consider a later meeting time; *item shelved.*
- Mr. Nielson suggested paying a student to fulfill the Federally-required student position on Site Council. Jennifer reminded the council all seats are unpaid.

CHAPTER 8
ADDY

"**T**hank you for giving me time to speak to you," she squeaked, refusing to look up from her notes. "I know it's short notice." Addy cleared her throat but couldn't get rid of the lump of terror climbing up her throat, stealing her voice.

"I didn't realize I was the OHS Speech Coach until just this week." *A mouse has inhabited my larynx. Yep, perfect fit for the speech coach, right here.*

She stopped, sipped her water, quaking hand sloshing the liquid. She peeked through her eyelashes at the audience before her. She'd suckered herself into believing that, since she was apparently able to direct a group of high school students, she'd be able to speak in front of her peers without fainting. The spots in front of her eyes begged to differ. The fact she was sitting saved her.

Eight adults with eight coffee mugs were seated before Addy at a round table in the high school library. Not one of them was looking at her. *Well, that's not true. Ed is looking at my breasts. At least part of him is paying attention.* The same could not be said for Bill Blank, the owner of the local gas station serving on the Site Council. His eyes were open but the soft puffs of air escaping from his wet lips were snores. Worse yet, Troy Ford was a witness to this fiasco, though so far he had only nodded hello and spent the rest of the time writing notes on a document in front of him. She hoped to god it wasn't about her as he would occasionally mutter and make angry red slashes on the paper.

Talk. She chose Angelina Jolie this time, hoping to project strength and sexiness. That hope ended when she bumped the table and sloshed everyone's coffee.

"Oh, sorry! So sorry." Irritated grumbles. "Anyway, I was informed yesterday we need money in order to travel and compete. I'm scrambling to find funds." She wiped her palms on her skirt, leaving a wet streak on her hips. "Apparently the Speech Team has been out of the line-up for quite a few years. No one knows where their allotted club money is . . . right now." The yawning, scratching council members continued to avert their eyes and pick their fingernails. Penny Knicker, her blue denim jumper and white tights clearly labeling her an elementary school teacher scrabbled notes between loud slurps of coffee from her oversized "#1 Teacher!" mug.

This was the monthly meeting of the Site Council, a public committee required by the federal law known as No Child Left Behind, dubbed by insiders as No Teacher Left Standing. Addy knew the Oceanside district schools set the meeting at 6:30 in the morning to make it "easier" for teachers from all the schools to attend. A seat on the Site Council was voluntary, hence the negligible response when it came time to fill a community, parent or student seat. Teachers didn't have a choice; staff members were "volunteered" on a rotating, yearly basis. Addy hoped to God her turn was years in the future, after she, too, mastered sleeping with her eyes open.

"One of the secretaries told me—" A sharp voice cut her off.

"Candi? If Candi told you something, it was probably wrong. Or she lied. She's an idiot." A diminutive, rat-faced woman practically yelled. Addy couldn't know that Tisha Ives, the abruptly irate parent council member, had applied for the same high school secretary position as Candi twelve years ago. Now Tisha worked at Denny's and was married to a man missing a front tooth. No, Addy could not have known any of that, but she was smart enough to sense danger.

"Uh, well, apparently there is a budget for the Speech Team in the club funds," Addy, shaky-voiced, spoke quickly as Tisha opened her mouth again. "I saw the account on the list of clubs. But since there hasn't been an actual team for so many years, the money is, uh, missing."

At this, Troy Ford looked up from a sheaf of documents he'd been manhandling brusquely for the past minutes. "Surely the secretary did not tell you the funds are missing. That is a misinterpretation of the funding process. The money has been re-allocated properly. But for now, we need to find you a new source of money in order to get the team started. As I said yesterday, fundraising is going to be key."

Addy wanted to die.

Ed startled her when he suddenly sat up, his belly pushing him back from the table. The assistant football coach looked fiercely at Ford, who blatantly ignored the searing stare.

"Hey, Ford," Ed said slowly, knowingly, "I think you're forgetting about the Small Schools Grant."

Ford frowned. "Ah yes. The grant. Now why hadn't I thought of that? Good thinking, Nielson." His glare suggested something other than praise for Ed's suggestion. Addy put her head down, uncomfortable with the aggressive mood in the air. Ford's voice rolled over her. "We'll have to look further into that, but it's not something that can happen immediately, Ms. Taylor. You'll still have to fundraise to get started, and to pay for supplies. I will get back to you on the grant monies."

She didn't look up, simply nodded.

Jennifer Haden, site council treasurer and middle school math teacher, propped her head up on her hands and said, "What's this about a grant? How come I don't know about it?"

Ed put in, "Oh, it was announced by our principal that the Site Council would be in charge of these new funds. It is weird we haven't heard more about it."

"We just received the money this past month," said Ford. "Principal Nakamura hasn't been available to do deal with this yet."

"I'd like to see a budget report. And then we should establish request parameters," said Jennifer, peering sternly over thick glasses. "Let's not wait for the principal to spare a minute from his constant stream of 'meetings'."

"Yes, well. I'll have to bring the report to the next meeting." Ford stood up, shoving papers into his expensive leather satchel. "We'll discuss this next month, I have another meeting right now." The comment hung in the air as Ford disappeared. Only his cologne remained in the room.

What just happened? Addy heard the library door click shut. *I guess Ford's not really Mr. Helpful. But he is a magician.* She tucked her hair behind her ears, blowing out her breath, glad she was out of the spotlight. For the moment.

Ed awkwardly shoved his bulk further back from the table. "Look, I need to go, too. I have to figure out what to do with my classes today."

The math teacher turned to him, her mouth twisted in judgment. "Really? You aren't prepared? How shocking."

Michael Mason, a dad bludgeoned by his wife into attending, put down his coffee cup and stood up, "Hey, I totally understand. I gotta' go myself."

Tisha, the other parent, snorted. "Michael, sit down. You know we aren't done. Those Victoria Secret catalogs aren't going anywhere."

"Wha' the—what's *wrong* with you?" the poor man sputtered, dropping back in to the plastic chair.

Tisha ignored him. Ed drummed his fingers, hard, on the peeling veneer of the dark table. "Okay, then, let's get this over with. Come on, Penny. What's next on this stupid agenda?"

Addy did not feel particularly blessed when, after the meeting, Ed escorted her back to her classroom. Students passing them in the hall sent side-long glances to each other, smirking. Addy noticed. She also noticed Ed inch closer to her every time she tried to gain some personal space. She tried "accidently" sloshing coffee onto his pants, to see if he would back off. He absentmindedly swiped at the dripping liquid on his yellow nylon tracksuit, taking a step closer.

"You look kinda' nervous in there." He clapped her on the back, knocking her slightly off balance. "Don't waste sweat on that crowd. If anyone in this building was to throw a stone, their house would shatter."

"Yeah. I just have . . . uh, a little problem. With talking to new people."

He gave her a sidelong glance, twitching his eyebrows. "You did fine, kid. Anyway, I've got a list of fundraisers I can give you. I recommend car washes." His eyes squinted as he talked. She was sure he was envisioning white tshirts and water hoses spraying out of control.

"That would be helpful. Thank you." She thought of something. "Hey, how much does it actually cost to get a bus to take the team into Portland?"

He looked disgruntled. "I don't know. The head coach takes care of that. I just show up, ride the bus. Have fun with that, by the way. Nothing better than going around corners with early morning puke sliding over the floors."

She didn't want to think about that aspect yet; she was trying to figure out how to pay for the bus.

"I've got to go make copies before first period. Can I get the fundraising list from you later?" Addy asked, easing herself out of step with Ed, hoping he wouldn't follow her to the office copier. He was a little much to take this early in the morning.

He strode forward, a strutting, molting peacock. "Catch ya' later," he crowed over his shoulder. Addy saw the students part before him but none tried to talk to him. Ed bumbled along, alone in a hallway packed with bodies. Addy felt sorry for him. Not sorry enough to want to hang out with him but, still, sorry.

She managed to slide into the office unnoticed. She hunched over the warm, whirring copier, avoiding eye contact with the secretary. Candi's hair-sprayed tower was like a train wreck, gruesome but magnetic. The secretary ignored Addy until her foot was hovering above the doorjamb, close to escape.

"Oh, Addy, good, I caught you." Her smile showed every yellow tooth. "Mr. Ford asked me to give you this." She held up an envelope with her name on it. "These are instructions for setting up tomorrow's football concession stand. Also, there's a checklist for clean up. Make sure everything is checked off or your club'll be docked money."

"Uh, ok. Hey, listen not to sound petty, but the speech team is a team, not a club. We travel and compete. And since we are a team, following the same state rules as a sport team, shouldn't we have the same kind of budget?"

"Hmmm, interesting point." Her lowered unibrow and pursed lips said something different. "I will mention that to Mr. Ford." She forcefully dropped the envelope onto the stack of papers cradled in Addy's arms. "Also, there's a contract in there for the speech coach position. Sign it, give it back to me, and then Principal Nakamura and the school board will have to approve it."

"Principal Nakamura? I thought Ford was in charge of this stuff?"

Candi snorted, looked around and leaned forward. "Ford's in charge of everything, whether he wants to be or not. I haven't seen Principal Nakamura since the staff meeting the first day of school. And I'm kinda' thinking that was a hollow grant."

Confused, Addy asked, "Do you mean hologram?"

"Psh. Whatever." She clawed her nails through the air and turned to her computer screen.

"Thank you." Addy fought the spring on the office door, trying to get out. *Maybe the school board won't approve me. That would make life a whole lot easier.* She walked quickly back to her room, hoping to give herself enough time to write some notes on the board and get the room set up for group discussions. She had a lot to do today before school was let out. Somehow she needed to find time to get stuff ready for the speech and debate team, like hunting for play scripts and interesting persuasive topics, something other than legalizing marijuana.

Tomorrow's the first speech practice. Will they accept me as the authority figure in the room? I wouldn't. She caught her reflection in the trophy case glass. Floating in front of metal Lilluptian champions was the soft face of youth.

CHAPTER 9
ADDY

The first OHS Speech and Debate Team practice was going so well Addy was sure someone slipped her ecstasy. She surreptitiously sniffed her coffee. *Does ecstasy have an odor?*

"Hey, guys, why don't you sit back down for a minute? Let's have a quick talk before it's time to go," she called across the large, open room, her slender body weaving between round tables covered in handouts listing the events, stacks of poetry books, teetering Time Magazines, and government textbooks. The last two hours transformed the quiet, stale air of the high school library into a whirlwind of excited chatter, books and magazines ripped off the shelves, giggled oral readings, shouted ethical debates. A trickle of students, in ones and twos, had hedged their way through the double doors after the last class bell but all hesitancy was gone now. The room throbbed with energy. A head count revealed ten wildly different young adults, ranging from fourteen to eighteen years old, some emo, some prep, some glam, some jock, some shy, some adHd, some intense. Ten kids. A team.

Addy glowed like a proud mamma as the tables before her filled with warm bodies. She'd surprised herself with the ease with which she was able to talk to this group, after only a few halting starts. Her new babies. Seniors Nina and Dylan, quiet Jamy Lock, Billie in her cheerleader outfit, and carrot-topped freshman Travis were students she knew from her classes.

She didn't teach sophomores or juniors, which meant meeting some of the team for the first time: a funny junior girl with glasses and a mass of black curls named Erin; a sophomore boy in a suit who insisted his name was Ace; a lanky Hispanic junior named Gavin with spiky blonde hair and a skinny tie; the pretty, purse-lipped School Body President, Tori, a junior; and husky Wyatt, a sophomore dressed from head to toe in Carharts, verbally able to diagram the family tree of the Greek gods whether or not it was requested of him.

"Before I forget, tomorrow night is our first fundraiser. At least five of you have to show up to help run the football concession stand. We'll use the money to pay for our entrance fees to the first tournament. Unless one of you has two hundred bucks you wanna' cough up for the good of the team."

Billie popped up. "I can work concessions in between cheers. Remember guys, there's no heat out there. Dress warm! And pray it doesn't rain because the concession shack leaks like a sieve." She sat back down with a flounce.

"What in thee hell is a sieve?" Travis asked. The only freshman in the room was trying to make a name for himself but then lost his thunder when he tipped too far back in his chair and fell over backwards. The group laughed at him, not with him. Except Addy. She felt his pain.

Tori, her long, straight blonde hair pulled firmly back into a ponytail, ignored Travis and held up a piece of paper. "I'll pass around a sign up sheet, Ms. Taylor. I think it's important we all take turns, make this fair. I can create a schedule. I do it for the student government events."

"Why, thank you, Tori, great idea. Thanks for organizing that. Did you guys hear Tori? Make sure to talk to her before you leave today."

Dylan raised his hand, his narrow face taken over by a toothy grin. "Hey, if we're working do we get free food? Like hot dogs and stuff?"

"Sure." *I have no idea if that's true.* Addy picked up a stack of papers, waving it at the team. "I know I've already handed these out but I wanna' remind you to go over the rules with your parents, have them sign it. Bring it back to me tomorrow. Also, make sure they fill out the proof of insurance forms and the travel release. If I don't get these three pieces of paper back, I can't let you come to practice. School rules."

"My dad isn't going to sign any of that," said Wyatt loudly, shaking his big shaggy head. He grimaced. "He doesn't like to be on the grid."

"Uh," Addy searched for the right response. "Tell him he doesn't have to give his social security number and no one will see this but the school office. He can call me if he still has issues."

"Oh, he'll call, don't worry." Wyatt, however, did look worried. *Great,* Addy thought, *looking forward to that phone call. Better brush up on my Crazy-ese.*

"What if we don't have insurance?" Erin had been joking around all practice, cracking up the kids and Addy with her string of one-liners, but this question was asked seriously. Her long black curly hair bobbed as she looked around, pushing her wire rim glasses back with a thick forefinger. "I don't think I'm the only one here on the free lunch program." Addy was surprised at her openness, making the girl even more likable.

"Hmm, that's a good question. I'll ask at the office and call you tonight."

"You can't call, we don't have a phone."

"Is your cell broken?"

"No, we can't afford a phone." Erin laughed at Addy's look. "Don't worry, we can use the neighbor's phone if there's an emergency. Really, it's not as big a deal as everyone thinks." She held up a textbook. "I have more time for homework."

"Okay, you're right. Stop by my room tomorrow morning, I'll tell you what the office wants us to do about the insurance. Bring in the rest of the forms, signed. We'll figure out the rest."

"Are we almost done, Ms. Taylor?" asked Tori, politely standing up, eying the big wall clock. "The activity bus is going to be here in five minutes. The driver will leave if we aren't out there."

"I didn't know there was a bus running this late."

"Some rich family pays for it so the poor kids without transportation can be here after school," said Tori, the one with all the answers. Addy knew she was going to be handy to have around.

Gavin, channeling a young Kevin Bacon, his Converse breaking into a nervous foot shuffle, said, "Really, it's to make sure there are enough kids here to field a football team. But we all take advantage of it." He stacked his textbooks, gathered pencils. "And being one of those po' folk, I'm stoked we have a bus. My mom hasta' work and I don't have a car," said Gavin. He caught Addy's eye then glanced away, shrugging. "Whatever. It's worth the shoving and the farting. I just don't sit in the back. It's a way home."

Addy said nothing, heart sinking with the weight of high school kids' realities. *There's just so much. Bullying, poverty, self-loathing . . . how can I deal with this? I couldn't deal with it when I was in school.*

She gathered them in with her gaze. "One last thing then. I'm proud of you for being here. I know it can be kinda' scary, trying something new. I have a lot to learn, too, but I'm thrilled to make this happen for you guys. As long as you're willing to be here and try your hardest, so will I, I promise," Addy smiled. "First I need to memorize your names. Then the events. That'll make it a lot easier to pretend I know what I'm doing."

The practice broke up with half-hearted pity laughs as the kids scrambled to fill their backpacks and hustle out the doors, throwing waves and goodbyes over their shoulders.

Dylan and Nina hung back.

"Don't you guys have to catch the bus?"

The girl smoothed a hand over her knotted hair, her bracelets softly jangling. "No, my mom is coming to pick me up. We have to get some groceries. If I don't go with her, she'll forget everything we need and come home with cigarettes and yogurt," She peered out the window. "She should be out front in a minute." She frowned. "Here's to hoping."

Dylan, zipping and unzipping his sweatshirt, said, "Yeah, I gotta' go. But I just wanted to ask. Ah," he zipped and unzipped faster. "This is something that I can do, right?" Addy nodded confused, but he continued, "And if I get good at it, maybe I can go to college? Or at least get a job?" He stopped moving. "I can get out of here?"

"Yes—"

"That's all I needed to know. Thanks." He ran out the door, ripped up backpack banging against the back of his thighs.

"Uh, ok." Bemused, the young coach started picking up discarded paper and candy wrappers, irritated to be cleaning up after kids old enough to know better. Nina trailed behind.

"I get it," Nina said. "I'm in the same boat as Dylan; I'm hoping this team is going to help me get into a good school. I think most of us are looking at it as a tool to escape this town."

"Wow, you've been here a whole five days and you want out already."

Nina looked her directly in the eye. "Yes," she said simply.

Addy nodded, flashing back to her own desperate need to escape her hometown, her old self. "Alright, point taken. So. What did you think of our first practice?"

"There were quite a few students here." Nina's posh Boston accent became stronger as she spoke, making the graceful girl seem elegant. "And I had no idea there were so many events."

"I know, it's kinda' like being in track, so many different things to do. Are you considering debating? Or are you more interested in acting?" Collecting trash, she put her hand in something and tried not to gag. *I'm going to act like throwing away this piece of chewed gum doesn't bother me.*

Nina gave Addy a wry smile as the coach frantically rubbed her palms together, cleaning with friction. "I apologize on behalf of my teammates. Kids are pigs. Anyway, I'd like to try debate someday. I'm thinking of doing poetry interpretation first, or maybe reading aloud a short story."

Addy gave her hands one last swipe and then raised an eyebrow at the girl. "I'm surprised you're not going for the straight-up acting stuff."

"I know. I'm considering Dramatic Interpretation, too," said Nina. "I was bummed when I found out Oceanside doesn't have a drama program but I think this might be better. I'll get to choose my own scripts."

"How about Duo? You and a partner can act out a scene."

The girl twisted her bracelets around and around. "I don't think I'm ready to work with someone else just yet."

"Dylan seems like he's ready."

"Ha ha, very funny, Ms. Taylor." She waved her hand in the air, adamantly. "We're just friends."

"Sorry, no more teasing." Addy looked around the room, at the abandoned books and magazines, and sighed. "I have to clean up or the librarian is going to kill me. I hope the kids didn't sneak any books out. We can't afford to have the librarian pissed at us."

Nina helped shelve materials for a few minutes before she left to meet her mother. Addy continued circling the room, putting away books and magazines, recycling extra handouts. She thought she'd be tired, having stood in front of a classroom, managing teens all day, then spending two more hours running from kid to kid, helping them understand the events and begin the search for speaking material. She'd rolled into the foggy parking lot at 6:45 this morning; looking at the clock now, she saw it was once again 6:45.

She wasn't tired, though. She was floating on clouds of glee. *These kids want to be here.* The team actually liked reading political essays and poems. Addy didn't have to ask them to be quiet three times when she wanted to say something. *I'm going to have to thank Ford; this may end up being the best part of my week.*

The realization that these same kids were now relying on her to provide a path out of this place put a stop to her dancing feet. Suddenly, the responsibility became too much. Now she had to worry about failing them, not just herself. Damn. She refused to let her brain fixate on that any longer.

Instead, she looked at the clock again. *I need to figure out how to get out of here earlier.* Rick was going to be grumpy. Hopefully he'd eaten. Rick could cook, he simply chose not to. Usually this was perfectly fine with Addy, since Rick choose not to clean, either, leaving a swath of dirty pans and burnt dishtowels in the wake of ill-prepared chicken. However, tonight she was hoping there was at least a tray of tater tots waiting for her. She was starving.

She hefted her overstuffed messenger bag onto her shoulder and shut out the lights. *Wow, it's pretty dark in here.*

This place could use more windows. As she pulled open the library doors she heard another door slam further down the hall. She paused. *Huh. Thought everyone was gone. That's not creepy at all. A dingy, old building filled with empty rooms.*

Addy had no desire to see what this place was like after the sun set. The long, jittery shadows lining the high-ceilinged corridor were bad enough. *I think they shot one of the Freddy Krueger movies here.*

She quickly slid into the hallway and strode out to the parking lot, telling herself she was not afraid. She jogged into the fading sunlight, a sprightly ocean breeze splashing her face. Drawing a deep breath, she laughed at herself. Why would she run from this school?

CHAPTER 10
ADDY

Relief flooded through Addy as she opened the door to a cold, empty house. Ahhh, a break. No arguments, no guilt-laden looks as she worked. No tater tots, no dishes, no fast-paced, repetitive music throbbing the walls as Rick watched ESPN highlights. No buzz kill. She was free to escape, to dine on a well-cooked meal in a cheery atmosphere, free to drip Rosie's secret sauce onto student essays to her heart's content. Rick's note said he wouldn't be home until late, that he was playing basketball over at the city park. She wrote a response on the flip side, telling him he could join her at the restaurant if he returned in time, otherwise she'd bring him home a cheeseburger.

Rosie's Roost glowed like a lighthouse, guiding in the lonely, hungry souls as they passed by on this chilly autumn night. The bell over the door tinkled sweetly as she emerged into the warm room, a small fire bobbing lazily in the corner fireplace. She could swear she smelled nutmeg and pumpkin pie.

Someone sat at her favorite table. She couldn't decide if she was more disappointed the table was occupied or that the person sitting at the table looked up from his paper. She tried to look away, pretend she didn't see him, but he caught her eye and waved her over. *Ugh. I thought I was done talking for the day.*

"Hi, Ed. You don't mind if I sit here with you?" She ducked her head shyly but caught herself and straightened up.

"Hell no, I haven't talked to another adult for a week." The older man moved his bulk back from the table, shoved an empty plate off to the side. In his red athletic jacket, he looked like a balding Santa, past his jolly prime.

"I'm totally beginning to see how that can happen." She sighed as she sat down. "I'm pretty sure I wouldn't recognize my boyfriend if I saw him right now, I've been so busy editing papers and writing lessons." She pulled a folder out of her messenger bag and held it up. "As a matter of fact, I have some quizzes I need to grade before tomorrow. Do you mind?"

"It don't bother me. But you shouldn't be bringing this shit home. You're gonna' burn out. Figure out how to keep your work at work."

She didn't say anything, just looked at him skeptically. *You sound like Rick.*

"Yeah, I know, I know." Ed threw up his hands in a "don't shoot me" gesture. "You English teachers are all the same, complaining about the goddamn reading of the essays. Here's a no-brainer: stop assigning 'em."

"You can't be serious."

"Okay, maybe you could assign them but not read them. That's what I do."

"You're such a liar!" She barked a laugh and then stopped awkwardly, looking at Ed quickly to make sure he didn't take her spasmodic response the wrong way. "I saw you making comments on that stack of papers earlier this week."

"Nah. I was just reminding that kid to return his extra football helmet."

Addy shook her head. "I don't believe you." She grabbed a menu. Flipping through, she cringed, reminded of the expensive prices. "I get what you're saying. I see the other teachers, the shell-shocked faces, the hollow eyes . . . it terrifies me. I want to believe things will get easier." She shook her head again, more adamantly this time. "But I can't think about that. I'm not expecting much of a life this year, not until I get this coaching thing down. Our first practice was great but it's taking a hell of a lot more time than I ever imagined."

"Oh, I know. Kids. They're a time suck. Wait until you have kids, then you'll really wanna' different profession. And a dark cave to hide in."

"So you have kids, Ed?"

He took a long, hard gulp from a bottle of Terminator Stout. "That is a good question." He took another quick drink and then held up the bottle, inspecting it. "Damn, this is good. Lizzie!" His chubby cheeks quivered as he yelled across the crowded room. The petite, dreadlocked waitress held up a finger in his direction, not looking at him, continuing unfazed with her mantra of the specials for the table of tourists before her.

"Did she just flip me off?"

"If she did, you deserved it. But no."

"Anyway. Kids. Yeah. I got one, a boy, a middle schooler. He spends most of the time with his mother, in the next town over. I don't get to see him much. There's always some lame excuse about sports or art camps or music lessons." Ed's face sagged. "It's a load of crap."

Addy sipped her ice water, no idea what to say, a surge of pity puckering her forehead.

The social studies teacher noticed. "Whatever. Life on the Oregon coast. It's the same everywhere, kids ignoring their parents and pissing off their teachers." He took the final swallow of the stout and suppressed a belch.

The hip, twenty-something waitress approached, waving a bill in her hand. "Here, you loud-mouthed hooligan." She slapped the bill on the table in front of Ed, making Addy cringe.

"I wanted another beer."

"No. You told me to cut you off. I'm cutting you off."

"I meant if I got drunk!"

"You got annoying. Same thing."

"Damn it, Lizzie –"

"Watch it, Ed. I'm seeing my mom tonight. She might not be so fond of you if she hears about this little incident." She put her fist on her hip, waited with a raised eyebrow.

"Pshh. What incident—me trying to get you to do your job?" He waved his empty bottle.

"No, you referring to me as a Jap."

Addy choked on her spit. Ed groaned, rolled his eyes, and said, "She knows I'd never say that. How'd you get such a mouth, anyway?"

"Don't test me, old man." Then Lizzie turned to Addy, grinning. "This pasty old man is sweet on my mother. It's fun."

"So, this is word play. Gottcha'." Addy relaxed, thankful the conflict wasn't real.

Ed growled a response. "Look, Lizzie. First time is funny, second time is annoying, third time's a spankin'. I believe we are on our third round of you using your momma against me. Bend over."

"Ugh." She stomped away, her dreads swinging with indignation.

"He he. Sorry you had to witness that, Addy. But I have to admit, it's not often I get the better of that vixen." He continued to chuckle, pulling a thick, worn leather wallet from his back pocket. He stood, zipping his athletic jacket over his bulging belly. "Don't worry, I'm leavin' a good tip to smooth down the edges." He threw a lump of cash on the table. "Last bit of advice: build a wall around yourself. Trust me, lettin' 'em in will suck your soul dry. See you tomorrow," he said and huffed his way out the door.

Lizzie reemerged from the kitchen, carrying a bottle of stout. "What, he really left? He wasn't mad, was he?" She proffered the beer to Addy, who happily took it. *Now I need to worry about my soul?*

"You're Addy, right? The new English teacher? I'm Lizzie."

"How did you know?"

"Honey, this is a small town. Even if I don't know you, I know you."

Addy dipped her head, frowning. Homesickness for the city and her comfortable, anonymous world welled up, filled her body, pulled her shoulders down further.

Lizzie patted her back. "Living in a small town has its perks, too. Take Ed there. I wouldn't have spent four seconds of my time on him when I lived in Portland. He would have put a serious hurt on my Hawthorn District vibe. But here . . . well, here I've been forced to talk to everybody, whether I want to or not. I've learned to appreciate Ed's . . . tics."

Maybe that's it, maybe he has Tourette's Syndrome. Or maybe teaching ruined him. Addy drank, picturing herself twenty years in the future, wearing mom jeans and a permanent grimace, lugging around a bag of poorly written essays.

Addy clopped up the sidewalk, heading home slowly, early dregs of moonlight clinging to the whitecaps on the Pacific. She consciously stuck her negative thoughts in a lock-box, focusing instead on earlier that afternoon, her success on the first day of practice. *I need to find balance. I don't want to end up like Ed. But I also don't want to give up. Not just yet.* The lights were on at the house; Rick was home. She smiled a small smile until she realized she'd forgotten to bring him a hamburger. *Why can't life be easy?*

CHAPTER 11
ADDY

Could it be any mother-lovin' colder? Addy huddled inside a thick cardigan. Yesterday's sun was but a memory. She stood in the concessions shack, peering out a hole cut in the plywood, barely able to spy the fuzzy outlines of kids on the football field through a smeary shield of Oregon rain. She pressed her cold white hands to the popcorn maker and eyed the machine's frayed cord leading to the molding wall. She gingerly stepped out of the water puddle she was standing in. *I don't wanna' die young. Especially while making green-tinged hotdogs and government cheese nachos.*

Almost half time. The boys were out there, in the deluge. *They're probably the only ones having fun, slipping and sliding in the mud.* The parents huddled under the small covered stands, a wobbly wooden structure that had been rained on weekly, if not daily, since 1922. Damp, depressed fans watched the big farm boys from the neighboring town hammer their sons under the Friday night lights.

"Ms. Taylor? We're out of hot dog buns. Do you know where to find more?" Tori was anxious, eyeing the non-existent line at the window. *This kid needs to take up yoga,* Addy thought. *How's she gonna' survive death rays from an audience?*

"I'm not really sure. I'll go see if I can find Mr. Ford. Think you guys will be ok?"

"Come on, Ms. T.," said Dylan, nacho cheese on his hands, shirt and pants, deliberately laying his mucky arm across Tori's stiff shoulders; she shook him off with a hiss of disgust. "Most of us have basic math skills. Except maybe

Gavin." From a dingy corner Gavin made a face, holding up the calculus book he'd been hunched over for the last half hour. Dylan turned to the ancient cash register, banging on the keys. "If only I could figure out what this here thing is for."

"Alright, point taken. Now stop pummeling the equipment unless you wanna' pay for it."

Addy stepped through the door, covering her head with a black garbage bag as she sprinted the 100 yards to the bleachers. *Should have worn a sports bra. My boobs are hitting me in the chin.* She hoped Ford was somewhere close. She did not look forward to body surfing the press of wet wool and whiskers. In answer to her prayer, a voice boomed from the old fashioned speakers, suggesting fans buy raffle tickets to support the team, maybe win a quilt or a rifle. The voice belonged to Ford. *Okay, now where is the Great Oz?* She scanned the structure, finally noticing a tiny ladder nailed to the wall, leading to a hole in the ceiling. *Well, of course. Of course, I'm wearing a skirt and I get to climb a ladder, a ladder hovering directly above the heads of students and parents. Nice. At least I have new underwear on this time.*

"Pardon me, excuse me, sorry," Addy apologized as she squeezed through the grouchy people bunched together below the opening. She stepped onto the bench hesitantly. The last time she climbed a ladder was when she was twelve, playing in her cousins' tree house. There had been no audience or skirt involved. *Time to gird my overies.* Addy twisted her skirt through her legs, hauling herself up while trying to keep her knees pressed together. She squeezed her eyes shut, having no desire to see the bearded grandfathers leering at her legs. *Goddamn. Why didn't I wear tights? Pants? Leg warmers? Now I understand Grandma's love of the skort.*

The ten second climb ended ten hours later. She pulled herself through the jagged square, half laying on the rough floor planks as she tried to scramble up—a worm wriggling in the dirt, unable to gain purchase. A strong pair of hands grasped her shoulders, yanking her to her feet. She stumbled, catching herself on the wall. Her savior was, of course, Troy Ford.

He smelled like man-heaven, sending a zing up her spine. His warm fingers clenched her arms for a second, then swung away. His eyes had widened briefly, she'd swear to it. Then he stepped back, a cold draft between them.

"Yes?" His blue eyes appraised her with curiosity.

"Hey, yeah, hi." *Yes, yes, I am an imbecile.* "We need more hot dog buns. I think they're in the storage room by the kitchen, but I don't have the key."

"I guess you should have thought of that before." He ran a hand through his hair, sounding irritated. "I can't just hand out keys to anyone, Ms. Taylor."

Stung, she barely had the strength to fight on. "I can bring them right back—"

"No."

Addy looked at Ford. Was he kidding? He stared down into the field, hands clasped behind his back, the dictator.

"Uh, okay. I guess I can find a janitor." What was happening here? *I thought he was starting to be nicer. I even thought . . .*

"There you go. That's a better idea." He sat down on a rusty folding chair in front of a tabletop microphone. Looking out, he spoke again. "Don't forget to leave the money box in my office before you go tonight. Be sure there's a tally sheet, denoting how much you made and how much the football team made."

"What do you mean?"

"What do you mean what do I mean? You have to be accountable, Ms. Taylor." He wouldn't look at her.

"No, I mean, about the football team. They get some of the money we make?"

"Yes, Ms. Taylor." The tone of his voice would have made a room full of children cry. "You are sharing the proceeds with the football team, fifty-fifty. They are the reason you're able to sell concessions in the first place."

"But—"

Ford flipped a switch on the side of the microphone. "Good evening, Oceanside! A few reminders: you may not smoke on school property . . ." Ford purred loudly into the black mesh topping the phallic silver microphone, his back to Addy. The conversation was done.

Addy cursed him internally, stomping down the ladder, skirt swinging free, her face flushed with anger instead of embarrassment this time around. She hardly noticed the crowd as she maneuvered her way through the stadium. Luckily, she spotted someone she thought she recognized as a janitor heading toward the main building. *I refuse to sprint again. Yeah, that's right, I have some pride,* Addy lied to herself. The rain was a cold drizzle as she jogged across the parking lot. She caught up to the custodian as he keyed open the front door.

"Oh good," she gasped, skittering to a halt next to him. "I need hot dog buns."

"Yeah? I need a new job," the man muttered, turning. Ed peered out at her, his face florid underneath an Oceanside Pirate baseball cap. "Oh, hi Addy."

"Sorry, I thought you were the janitor," Addy said lamely, not expecting to see the social studies teacher.

"The janitor gets more respect than I do." Ed shoved the door open. It exploded inward, bounced off the wall, sprang back with such force it smacked his belly and knocked the brim of his hat askew.

"Goddamn it." He pushed through the opening and strode across the foyer, not bothering to hold the door for Addy. She caught it and hurried inside.

"Hey! Ed!" She called after him, trying to catch up without breaking into a run. *Seriously, do I need to wear exercise clothes to work?* Ed's red running pants swished loudly as he continued to move across the room.

"Ed! I need to get into the storage room!" She was frustrated. Why did everyone ignore her? "Mr. Ford won't let me use his key, can you let me in?"

She followed him around a corner and then almost bumped into his stationary figure wrangling a key into the storage room door. He didn't say anything but he did let her in. They stumbled around the dark room for a minute before they found the light string. She prayed that was Ed's arm grazing against her.

"Ford's a tight ass. Wha'd, he think you were goin' to make a copy of his key? Maybe steal some toilet paper?"

Addy agreed but didn't want to commit verbal treason, not just yet. "I'm sure there's some policy against giving out the special keys." She looked around the shelves as she spoke, collecting plastic-packaged buns and other items they might need, shoving cocoa envelopes and ketchup packets into her cardigan pockets. "I better get back out there, I left the kids in charge. I can't be sure they won't light a fire to stay warm. Not that I would blame them."

Ed hugged a large orange Gatorade tub to his torso. "If I don't get back out there, Coach Pike might havta' do something for himself. You done?"

They weaved their way back through the school, the parking lot and the entrance to the football field. The assistant coach spent the time ranting. "Just because Ford hates it here at this rinky-dink school doesn't mean he should take it out on us," Ed huffed. "Not my fault the swanky private school didn't want to keep him."

"He was fired?"

"That's my guess. He certainly ain't acting like he's happy here." He grunted, looking around the parking lot with broken streetlights and beat up trucks. "But who can blame him." He started scanning the ground. "I gotta' go, I need ta' find a hose."

He reached the field and pushed through the crowd.

"Thanks, Ed," Addy yelled after him, "Good luck with the game."

The young teacher made her way back to the shack, glad to know there was someone on her side, even if that someone was a curmudgeon. Her warm feelings were short lived, however, as she drew closer to her destination. The pizza-stealing, pointy-bearded short guy was bellowing through the shack's window at her cowering students.

"Waddya' mean you don't have any more Diet Pepsi?! The rule is, you save me a Diet Pepsi!" His beard twitched as he slammed his fists on the wooden counter. The kids seemed unable to answer, struck mute in terror.

Addy rushed in. "What's going on here? Can I help you, sir?"

"Sir?! Ha. That's right. Listen, girly, you gave away my pop. Unacceptable."

Addy had just today discovered that this evil leprechaun was the head football coach; he'd stood up at the early morning staff meeting and announced "his boys" needed more time to make up their homework from game days. The majority of the staff muttered to each other behind coffee cups but nobody said anything directly to the coach as he strode back to his seat.

Now, Addy offered her most charming smile, touching his hand. "Look, we didn't know. Can't I get you something else?"

"Didn't know? What, that sign isn't big enough?"

His finger, a skeleton bone, pointed at a faded note pinned to the wall next to the refrigerator: *Coach Pike will kill you if you don't save him a Diet Pepsi.*

Still trying to smooth things over, she said, "Gosh, sorry about that, guess we were sidetracked. Let me buy you something else. It's on the speech team."

"Of course it'll be on you. Wait a minute. Holy Bejuzus! Are you tellin' me you're really bringin' that dead, stinking dog back?! I thought that was a joke!"

Addy looked at him, confused.

"The speech team." He raked his glaring gaze over the stunned students. "Like you kids needed help being nerdy." His eyes targeted Dylan, who was trying to turn into a section of the wall. "I should've known. Setton. This is a good place for you, you scrawny little prick."

"You can't talk to students like that," Addy whispered, stuttering, indignant, her blood dropping from her brain to her stomach, making her ill. She wanted so badly to open her mouth and let him have it. Her mouth rebelled, the cowardly tongue hiding behind a fortress of teeth. *You clearly have a small penis, you ugly gnome. But then, so do I.*

"Kid, you've been teaching all of one week. Talk to me when you have a goddamn clue. Now find me a soda. I'll be with my team." He scraped her with his eyes. "A real team." He surged away, a malignant man dressed in khakis and high-heeled cowboy boots.

Addy and the teens were quiet for a minute, damp statues.

Shaking, enraged at herself for letting him bully the kids and then walk away, Addy felt like a whipped child. *But what could I do?* "Dylan, are you okay?"

Dylan stood up straight, all five foot four inches of him, and swaggered to the nacho machine. He began filling paper trays with chips, his back to the small group. "Whatever. That guy's a dick."

Gavin exchanged concerned looks with Nina and Erin, who'd been bent over poetry books by the door before the maelstrom. Jamy, Tori and Wyatt were staring at Dylan like he might explode. They started to speak, words tumbling, uncontrolled, into the air, Gavin saying the loudest, "Dylan, why is Coach Pike picking on you?"

"Because he's a douche! His team is losing and I'm the dog he needs to kick."

"He was pretty harsh, dude. That wasn't cool," Gavin, running his hands through his blond spikes nervously, seemed more upset than Dylan.

Dylan looked surprised, not expecting to see a circle of caring faces surrounding him, on his side, wanting to assuage his pain. "Hey, don't worry about it. I'm fine. He was rude to all of us, not just me. I mean, what was that shit about the speech team? "

Tori poked him, saying gently, "Watch your mouth." She looked at Addy, "Why is he so upset there's a new speech team? What does he care?"

Addy pondered that question. She had no clue. Speech was academic, football was a sport; what was the problem for Coach Pike? *It can't be financial,* thought Addy. *We aren't being given any budget money, and half our earnings tonight will go to them. They should love us.* She frowned. *Damn. I hate conflict.*

"Hey guys, what's up?" Billie, adorable in her black cheerleader outfit, and Travis, hulking in his too-clean football uniform, stood at the counter.

"I can help now that it's halftime. Do you need me?" Billie chirped, flipping her hair in Travis's face. The freshman didn't seem to mind.

Tori answered before Addy had a chance. "Sure, come on back. Travis, shouldn't you be with the team?"

"Yeah. Coach Pike sent me for his Diet Pepsi. I'm a bench warmer right now, since this is a varsity game and I play jv." He gestured to his pristine red, black and white livery. "They needed my meat suit to have enough guys to play. Coach will never let me on the field." He shrugged. "Did you find a pop for him? Please say you did."

Nina dug in the back of the refrigerator. She dramatically slammed the door, her multiple thick bracelets jingling, and hoisted a silver can as if it was the grail being held to the sun. "Ta-da!" She tossed the can to Travis, almost nailing Billie in the head as she came through the door.

"Sorry!" The new girl was horrified.

Nice. The speech team is going to need the ambulance before a kid from the football team does, thought Addy.

"Wow, I thought you guys wanted me in here." Billie smiled at the senior. "No worries. You're Nina, right? Love your scarf. Gavin! You're doing homework! Jamy! Stop reading that book!" She twirled around, pleats flying. "And where's Ace? Come on guys! Let's get this show on the road. Look at all these hungry people." Three teens waiting at the counter waived back at Billie, who exuded the energy of an infomercial salesman.

"I've been saying the same thing," grumbled Tori, clearly displeased at this display of charismatic leadership. "Ace is working at his parent's grocery store. He told me yesterday he couldn't be here, when *I* took the sign-up sheet around."

Addy inwardly chuckled, happy to see the politics of teenagers usurping the Coach Pike incident. Travis left with Coach's drug of choice while the speech team pulled together to feed the masses for marginal profit, maximum camaraderie. *Maybe that's what we needed, a common enemy to bond us. If only I knew why we were enemies. I'd ask Napoleon, if I didn't think I'd pee my pants in terror.*

CHAPTER 12
ED

Fucking Oregon. Gonna' haveta' up my meds if this rain is gonna' last through winter. Again. Ed fumbled with Coach Pike's key ring, trying to get the front doors to the school open. He was on the verge of kicking the sheet metal, giving into the rage, built up over the day. *All week. Fuck. All year.*

"Oh good," a woman purred behind him. "I need hot dog buns."

I'll give ya' a bun, Ed thought, rage fizzling to annoyance, turning with anticipation. "Yeah, well, I need a new job," he muttered, seeking the source of the sultry voice.

Peering up at him was a wet, vulnerable young thing. "Oh, hi Addy." *She is so cute. Too bad she looks like a kid.*

"Sorry, I thought you were the janitor."

Jesus. What a bitch.

He did not forgive Addy right away, not until he honed in on the anxiety rolling off the pretty young teacher while she dashed around the supply room, going on about Ford; she was just as unhappy as he was.

The bright orange of the Gatorade container caught his eye, reminding him he needed to bust a move before Pike busted his ass. He also wanted to go over tactical changes with the offense, get those boys rolling, but first he had to play waterboy.

He regretted parting ways with Addy, her scent delighting his nostrils. He had to stay focused, find water for the Gatorade powder, get the boys back in the game. He hefted the barrel. *This fucker isn't gonna' fit in a sink. Where did I see that hose?* He pictured Ford bent over, screaming, the missing hose made useful as a torture device. *Hmph. If only.* It took him five minutes of wandering around with his uncomfortable burden before he found the dirty green hose behind the bleachers. *Why do we only own one hose? And what in the hell needs watering back here? The Dorito bags and cigarette butts?* He swiped the mud, grass and grit off the nozzle, jammed it into the tub's mouth and pondered the futility of his days.

Finally making it to the locker room, Ed waddled under the weight of the high-priced Kool-Aid until an orange-headed doofus stepped forward, grabbed the tub, set it on the bench in front of the showers. Boys crowded around, Dixie cups eagerly outstretched.

Ed stopped in front of Coach Pike, towering over the health teacher, a cockroach who couldn't teach or coach worth a shit. The wee man was tense, the team's losing streak a heavy weight in the air.

"Jesus, Ed. Where ya' been?" Coach Pike hucked a loogie through his wiry beard, splattering the locker room floor. "These kids need some fluids. Be nice if you gave a crap about something other than your gut."

Ed grunted. Within that grunt were some obscenities.

Pike did not hear Ed. He had not heard Ed for two years. "Did you find any Diet Pepsi? The stupid hooch in the concession stand doesn't know her head from her well shaped ass." He stroked his VanDyke beard, and then pointed a bony finger at Travis, who shivered visibly. "Boy, go find me that pop. God knows, you ain't doin' shit here." He turned to Ed. "So what's our plan for the second half, Nielson?"

Pike often relied on Ed to call the shots. *It works out perfectly, he gets the glory, I get the shaft,* Ed thought. The hydrated team circled around them. Within five minutes, the white board was covered in arrows and x's, the boys were howling and hooting; it was time to retake the field.

Ed was happy. It took him a minute to diagnose the weird feeling. Twenty-five pairs of eyes had been watching him, silently absorbing his words of wisdom. *Damn. That doesn't happen often. Or ever. If the little fuckers listened to me more, we might actually win a game.* The boys sent up a prayer, asking God to watch over the local boys but squash the shit out of the neighbors. They ended with a blood curdling scream and made for the door.

"Did you know that new English teacher got the debate club started up again?" Pike asked. "Chh. Stupid. What a fucking waste of time." Ed followed him out of the locker room, the short man aggressively taking the lead.

"Yeah. So?"

"Well, Jesus, when were ya' going to tell me?"

Ed scratched his balding head. Pike's bad mood was starting to piss him off. The dwarf moved from irritating to irrational. "Why in the hell would you care?"

Pike jutted out his long, hairy chin and thundered, "You there! Ignoramus! Get out of the way!" A hapless cheerleader stood bumbling with the center of the sagging break-through banner, directly in the path of charging, helmeted footballers. She burst into tears, dropped the poster, but didn't move. One of the older boys shoved her out of the way, knocking her into a gaggle of cursing cheerleaders. With that, the team exploded onto a quiet field, not even the cheerleaders rooting them on.

Ed groaned. He let himself fall behind, a lone man, the neon red tracksuit glowing under the field lights.

CHAPTER 13
ADDY

"Look, Addison. These three kids aren't going to be on your little speech team, much less any real teams. They do not have insurance," said the snide secretary, safe in her desk bunker.

Addy entered the office Tuesday morning unprepared for this healthy dose of bullshit as she sought to make sure everyone on the burgeoning speech team was eligible to compete. Candi continued her tirade, speaking through her nose. "The district absolutely will not let them stay on campus after school hours without health insurance." Pause. Smirk. "Though I can't see how anyone could get hurt while talking."

Addy slowly breathed out. "Well, Candi, what would you suggest? Are there any loopholes? Kids in poverty play other sports, don't they? What do *they* do for insurance?"

"Their coaches pay for their insurance."

"What? Seriously?" *And why didn't you offer that suggestion in the beginning? By the way, your bangs look like a peacock's ass.* "How do I do that? Do you have the paperwork?" Addy wasn't exactly rolling in dough, especially after she'd paid for twenty pizzas last week, but breaking out her Visa appeared to be the only way to get the problem resolved by the end of the day. *Oh, Rick is going to love this. I wonder if the mailman will deliver my bank statements to the high school instead of to our house?*

She walked out of the office $150 lighter, the three unpaid kids caught up for the year. She purchased the cheapest plans, which barely covered anything and made her feel like an asshole. But now Erin, Wyatt and Dylan could stay. *Don't get pneumonia, kids, you can't afford the hospital.*

She brought peanut butter sandwiches to practice that afternoon, the first food she had time to eat since breakfast, possibly the first food some of her kids had eaten since morning. Though over half the school was on free or reduced lunch, word in the staff room was that the majority of those students were too proud to use the glowing pink tickets. Scanning the kids in the library after school, she still wasn't sure how many of her team lived below the poverty level. Regardless of their home lives and issues, they were here, back at practice, committing to this team.

Ace, the hero of the day, trumped her sandwiches when he showed up with a paper bag full of outdated Hostess donuts, claiming he stole them out of the pig farmer bins behind his parent's grocery store. "Sorry I had to work Friday night. Thought you might not be so mad at me if I brought sugar offerings." Passing around Old Fashioned Glazed, the sophomore boy reminded Addy of Alfalfa, dark cow licks breaking free from the accountant slicked down hair, wearing a tie and suit pants too short in the crotch, two inches of white athletic sock screaming from the cheap shiny loafers. He carried a cracked vinyl briefcase.

"What's with the briefcase, Ace?" Erin asked, pushing up her glasses. "How did you *not* get dunked in the toilet, carrying that thing around?"

He carefully put it on the table in front of him, opened it, and pulled out a stack of yellow notepads. "I am ready to debate. Don't I look like a debater, Ms. Taylor?" He looked at her, calf eyes begging for validation to make it worth the bullying he had to have endured that day.

She lightly touched his shoulder. "Yes, Ace, you look like a debater. But you don't need to dress up for practice. Keep your professional clothes for tournaments." Addy remembered something. "How many of you have dress clothes?"

"Well, what kind of dress clothes? I have a dress for the Homecoming Dance," said Billie. "It's red. The top is kinda' low, but the sequins hide a lot."

Addy pictured her team filing off the bus at the first tournament, wearing slutty evening dresses and ties with flannel shirts. *Oh shit. I should have thought of this sooner.* "Competitors are expected to wear professional clothes, which is different from evening wear."

"I have no idea what you're saying," Travis said, exchanging an uncomfortable look with Wyatt. "But I have a feeling this means I'm gonna' to have to buy a tie. I don't even know how to tie a tie."

"I don't either. We can look it up on YouTube."

"That's what clip-ons are for," Gavin said, enthusiastically pulling on his skinny tie.

Ace tugged his own lumpy red power tie, saying, "I'm an expert."

"Right. So, boys, you will need a button-down shirt, a tie and a pair of dress pants. Or at least khakis. No jeans for any of you, ever, not at a competition."

"Don't forget dress shoes, Ms. Taylor." Ace stood on one leg, holding up a foot like an awkward crane.

"Ah, thank you, Ace, yes, you will need nice shoes. And black socks." She hoped Ace heard that without feeling deflated. She didn't look at him. "Girls, you don't have to wear a dress, but no jeans for you, either, only dress pants. Shirts must be, umm, not revealing. And skirts have to reach your knees."

"Pshh, Ms. Taylor." Dylan sat low in his chair, blew a raspberry. "I thought you were cool. You sound like a freakin' nun."

"These aren't my rules, these are requirements you can find posted online when you look up state rules." She took a step closer to the group, making sure her freckled face was as serious as possible. "Remember what I said at our first meeting? Giving a speech is about manipulating the audience, get them to buy what you're selling. The very first thing you're selling is yourself. If you know the audience expects you to be taking the event seriously, you can't slap them in the face while dressed like a hooker and then expect them to give you a first place trophy. That's not how the world works." She frowned. "At least the speech world."

Nina pursed her lips, disdainful. "I thought this was about giving young people a voice, treating our opinions with respect?"

"Sure, in theory," Addy nodded, "But at the same time, you're dealing with judges that are much older and think you have the right to be a teenager, talk like an adult, and dress like a professional. As soon as they see your tongue ring and peeling black fingernail polish, they forget all about your rights, reverting to their gut instinct—which is to secretly despise youth."

They looked perplexed. She said, "Come on, guys. It isn't so bad. You have to learn to play the game sometime. If you must, find a way to stick it to the adults, but do it subtly. Not with your first impression."

Tori looked around, her straight blonde ponytail an inverse exclamation point. "Jeez. People. Pull on your big girl panties. Would you go into a job interview wearing a ripped *Team Edward* tshirt? No. Not if you really wanted that job. What Ms. Taylor's saying is common sense. If we want to win, we need to dress the part."

"Easy for you to say." Erin grimaced, poking Tori's American Eagle tshirt, making the student government president squirm. "My dress clothes couldn't get me a job at the local dollar store."

Jamy had been quiet, her pink cardigan and pearls suddenly standing out. She cleared her throat. Quietly, quickly, she said, "I dress nice and my dad's a logger. My mom tends bar. I go to Goodwill and garage sales. I can help you guys find stuff." Her voice sped up. Addy could barely tell what she was saying. Everyone else seemed to be having the same problem, leaning toward Jamy with their heads cocked to one side. "Seriously, I would love to shop for the team. Of course, you'd have to give me the money, or come with me."

Wyatt put his hand gently on Jamy's forearm. "Jamy, were you in *Pretty in Pink*?"

Travis laughed. "Is that a porn movie?" He sang "Bow chicka chicka wou wou" in a creepy voice until Billie loudly hit him on the head with a book of Maya Angelou poems.

"You're so disgusting, Travis."

Addy held up her hands, pleading for quiet. "Jamy, great idea. But first, everyone go home and raid your family's closets, look for old suits and stuff. I'll ask around the staff lounge, see if any teachers have clothes they want to donate."

"Gross. I'm not wearing anything Nielson's butt rubbed against."

"He only wears clothes made from plastic. Use Lysol."

Addy again silenced them. "Anyhoo. We have a lot more to talk about than clothes. We can deal with that later. For now, let's focus on finding pieces."

Ten voices at once said, "Pieces of what?"

She felt vindicated, having endured a weekend of bitching and then the silent treatment from Rick while gleaning nuggets of wisdom from websites for hours on end. Suddenly, she was an authority figure. *At least to this ignorant group.* "A 'piece' is a piece of text you use during a speech, like from a script, or book excerpt, or essay you've written."

"Yo, got my piece wit' me, how 'bout you, dog?" Dylan pulled a finger cocked like a gun from his saggy pant pocket. Wyatt shot back at him, proficiently cocking a fake shotgun.

"You're an idiot. And you're an idiot." Billie handed the book of poems to Jamy. "Here. You said you were looking for some poems. How many do you need for a poetry ... piece? Three or more? I love Phenomenal Woman, maybe you can use that for part of the collection."

"Ewwww, phenomenal woman. That's you, alright."

"I know where you live, Travis. Don't go to sleep tonight."

The lighthearted bickering continued for the next hour but so did the research and exchange of ideas. Ace found the current debate topic and squealed like a toddler. "Yes! Resolved: Economic sanctions ought not be used to achieve foreign policy objectives!"

Addy faded away before he could ask her any questions. She was going to need half an hour of alone time to process the concept and to secretly look up the term 'sanction.' Luckily, Ace jabbered away with Gavin at high speed, already lining out arguments.

Jamy, Billie, Erin and Nina were sequestered in the corner, poetry and short story books surrounding them. Tori stood humped over the copy machine with a pile of magazines, making copies of articles. Addy glanced through Tori's stack, finding articles on the Doomsday Clock, gays in the Boy scouts, the acceptable level of feces in canned vegetables, and how to read palms.

She patted the junior girl's shoulder. "This is good stuff, Tori! I could listen to any of these things for eight minutes." Tori nodded but didn't look up, trying to reassemble pages into the correct order. Walking around a book stack, Addy came across Wyatt and Travis reading aloud to Dylan from what looked to be a book of plays. Their voices were stilted, droning on.

And on.

"Well, then who's playing first?" Wyatt asked, sounding like a cartoon robot.

"Yes." Travis responded, equally as robotic.

"I mean the fellow's name on first base."

"Who?"

Oh my God. She tried not to cringe. Travis and Wyatt must have raided the library at an old folk's home to find the Abbot and Costello script; *Who's On First* was barely funny in the 1940's. Any judge under seventy was in for ten minutes of pure, mind-numbing, hell.

Thankfully, Nina called her away, asking Addy to come over to the small group of girls.

"Jamy found an interesting poem. We were wondering if it would work for the poetry event."

"Ok, let's hear it."

Jamy, shy, read quickly. She finished the poem, the lines of Langston Hughes' *Mother to Son* simple but powerful.

> "Don't you fall now—
> For I'se still goin', honey,
> I'se still climbin',
> And life for me ain't been no crystal stair."

Addy tilted her head, listening intently. *I'm not a huge fan of poetry but I can see how this would work in front of an audience.*

"You know what that reminds me of?" Nina, thoughtful, peered at the ceiling as she verbally processed her thoughts. "Our discussion on heroes in class the other day. The mom is trying to save her son." She gazed around the group and shrugged her shoulder, her Boston accent adding credence to her lecture. "I know it's a stretch, but you could say she's a hero."

"Hmm. Maybe. Then you need to find two more hero poems to have enough for the poetry event," Addy's voice petered out as her mind began picturing the table of contents from Norton Anthologies, trying to recall poems.

"You're the English teacher, don't you know any?"

Ducking her head in shame, the twenty-three year old said, "Not really, not off the top of my head. I've only read poetry in my college classes. I have to admit, though, I'm seeing this speaking event in a different light. I liked your poem, Jamy. Good job, girls."

The girls didn't appear to be phased by her confession of ignorance. "Ms. Taylor, where can we look for poems that match a theme? How do you do that kind of search?"

They're asking me like I'll know. Addy picked up an anthology, flipped to the back and started talking. Eventually, she shifted the topic to plays, and discussed script options with Nina.

"Nina, I'll come back and help you in a minute. I need to make a couple of overheads for my morning classes before I forget." The young teacher took a couple of books to the copy machine, shooing Tori and the boys out of her way.

It was a heady few moments, Addy feeling in charge. The universe allowed her that one brief beat of control.

And then the copy machine lit on fire.

CHAPTER 14
NINA

She doesn't know any poems off the top of her head? I'm not impressed, Nina thought, trying to keep her face from showing disappointment in her new coach. *On the other hand, she openly admitted to not knowing something while joining the search for an answer.* Ms. Taylor was definitely not like her private prep school teachers.

Nina's mental chart of pros and cons regarding Oceanside High School was lopsided; the positive entries were limited, while the fat negative column was in serious need of an exercise regime. She found herself alone in a world of childish cliques and adult workaholics, frozen in the face of multiple rejections. The speech team kids talked to her on a limited level, except Dylan, who had diarrhea of the mouth. He made her nervous. The rest of the high school kids erected a shield of silence as if Nina was a powerful foe. She tried to remain impassive, telling herself their reaction was due to her stranger status, that her newness would wear off and everything would be fine.

She could probably handle the alienation at school if she had human interaction at home. Instead, she was the quintessential latchkey kid, her isolation lasting far into the night and sometimes into the morning. The only people who knew the thoughts and feelings ricocheting inside her skull were her favorite authors. Unfortunately, Gabriel Garcia Marquez and Isabelle Allende, the magical realists, not only remained silent, they were unwilling to throw any magic her way. *I'm spending too much time in the land of books.* She looked around the library table, at Erin and the other girls talking easily, about nothing. The appealing land of humans. She opened her mouth. Then closed it. *Baby steps.*

Nina let the girls' babble flow over her as she pondered the art hanging behind Billie's head on the library wall, a curling poster of *Starry Night*, done in browns, accented by the yellowing masking tape in the corners. The lack of aesthetics in the one room that should have been a haven for culture hurt her heart. Literally. When she caught sight of a censored poster halfway behind a bookcase, her heart palpitated; a grainy picture of Michelangelo's David with the penis blacked out, sloppily, with a sharpie. *Maybe I should skip my senior year, go straight to college. Is that possible?* She crossed her arms on the table in front of her, almost put her head down. *I can't believe Ms. Taylor is describing how to use an index and the girls are acting like it's news to them.*

"Nina?" Ms. Taylor was looking at her. *I hope she can't read my mind. Probably not. She can't read poetry.*

"Have you found a piece you might like to perform?"

"I've been flipping through this scene book. I found a section from *Agnes of God.*" Pause. "Have you read it?" Nina's voice was snide, even to her. She tried to negate her words by tilting her head and smiling into Ms. Taylor's eyes. If nothing else, Nina was a master of manipulating grown ups. No reason to hurt the feelings of the one adult who seemed to be interested in her, even if that adult turned out to be dense.

Ms. Taylor didn't seem to notice Nina's snootiness. She grabbed the script book from Nina's hand. "Oh yes! The nun that has sex with an angel and kills her baby. I love this play." She flipped through the pages. "You know what, we might be able to link two scenes together, add more drama for a ten minute performance." She continued to thumb through the book. "The lines I'm thinking of aren't in this book, I think I have the whole play in a box at home. Oh." Ms. Taylor slapped her forehead hard enough to start her long blonde waves swinging. "Duh. I have two boxes of playbooks at my house. Why didn't I think of that sooner?"

Billie leaned forward, crumpling her cheerleader costume against the desk. "Were you in plays in college?"

"God, no. I'm a horrible actress." Ms. Taylor giggled, dissolving the last shred of her dignity. "But I love to read plays, and watch them. That might be helpful with our acting events, huh? Erin, I think I know the perfect scene for you to try. It's funny. Have ya' heard of a guy named David Ives?"

Ms. Taylor might not be a shallow imbecile reaching beyond her abilities—we'll see.

"Nina, I'll come back and help you in a minute. I need to make a couple of overheads for my morning classes before I forget." Nina watched the young teacher bulldoze her way to the copy machine. She knew her condescending attitude was unfairly harsh toward adults; the resentment of her father abandoning her and her mother ignoring her was hard to shake. But she wanted an adult to trust in her life, she wanted to give Ms. Taylor a chance. *She genuinely cares about us. And there might be a brain in there.*

"Fire! Shit! Fire!"

Ms. Taylor threw her hands up in the air and danced in a circle like a Rajneeshi. Tori and the boys yelped like puppies, recoiling away from Ms. Taylor and the machine to reveal a tiny yellow tongue spurting from one corner, a minute stream of smoke creating a tail. Mid-spin, the young coach caught site of the wall fire extinguisher, pried it free, and sprayed down the half-inch flame with an entire container of foam. Nina's teammates stood frozen in various poses, unsure of what had just happened.

Then the fire alarm went off. Nina, half expecting the sprinklers to go off, too, cranked her head back, scanned the ceiling tiles. There were no sprinklers.

"Alright! It's time to go home anyway! Grab your stuff! Everyone out!" Ms. Taylor pushed them out, a crazed look in her eye. The speech kids filed out under the pulsing lights and bleating sirens, awkward in their bewilderment. Ms. Taylor barged through them and sprinted down the hallway, shouting for a janitor. As the team made their way outdoors, a handful of teachers emerged from their classrooms, blinking, staring after the frantic new teacher.

Nina decided to take the activity bus home. The buses were already lined up, the drivers standing in a huddle, holding Styrofoam coffee cups. The coaches showed up and started yelling at kids to get on the buses, head on home. The football, volleyball, cross country and soccer kids climbed aboard, irritated at missing their showers, and the buses maneuvered out and around the incoming fire trucks and outgoing teen jalopies. Nina jostled her way onboard, shaking her head at the mess.

No one sat with her. She'd have to walk about half a mile in the misty twilight from the bus stop to her mom's house but at least she wouldn't be sitting in the misty twilight on the school bench, waiting in the wind for her elusive mother. She wanted to get home, start working on memorizing lines from her scene. Nina decided she wasn't going to wait around for help that may or may not be forthcoming from Ms. Taylor, who clearly was overwhelmed. *The first competition is in two weeks, I want to be ready. I don't want to look stupid.*

"Hey."

Nina heard the Neanderthal grunting behind her but didn't turn around, unsure if he was directing his monosyllabic utterance at her.

"Hey. New girl. Are ya' deaf?"

She turned to the football player in the seat behind her. He had wet hair as if he had just showered but the powerful scent of body odor rolled over Nina. Sniffing unobtrusively, she had to admit his smell wasn't offensive, kind of like a musky gingerbread cookie. His stubbly face was attractive in a bad boy sort of way. He looked at her expectantly.

"What?"

"What? That's not very nice. How 'bout hello?"

His body language was impossible to read. His face was pleasant, his posture wasn't threatening, but his conversation so far left much to be desired. She decided to face him head on, nip any crap in the bud. She hoped he couldn't see her heart thumping against her shirt. "I'm not trying to be impolite; I'm trying to decide if you're an asshole or just a poor conversationalist."

He hooted. "Sassy, ain't cha'? Hey, were you in the library? Was there really a fire in there?"

"It was just the copy machine. There wasn't much of a fire." She shrugged, began to turn back around.

"What's yer name?" His fingernails, resting on the back of her seat, were square and clean. She didn't know what to think of him. Her eyes narrowed, she said quietly, "Nina."

"Ya' don't have to look at me like that. I'm Jake." He pulled on the drawstring of his black hoody. "I'm harmless."

Another boy, clad in a football jersey, stood up behind Jake, slapping the back of his head. "Jake? Harmless?! Better not let Coach Pike hear ya' say that!"

"Trent! I'm gonna' kick your ass." Jake went back into the other kid's seat, playfully punching and wrestling. Nina looked at the bus driver. The old man, wearing a Rastafarian hat, caught her eye in the mirror, shook his head in disgust, and went back to driving.

Nina sighed audibly. When the bus rumbled into her stop five minutes later, the boys were still grappling like children. Jake did not attempt to speak with her again. Part of her hoped he would say something as she departed. It did not happen, not even a glance as she moved down the metal stairs and out the yellow folding door. *Boys here are as stupid as they are in Boston, just more open with the evidence.*

The gravel road leading out of town wound through a damp forest dotted with small homes. Her mother's house was at the end of the road. The three-story house stood out in the neighborhood, twice as large with a new, bright yellow paint job and professionally manicured lawns. Firs, cedars and manzanitas were a backdrop to blooming rhododendrons; the deep greens and pinks momentarily stunned Nina into bliss. She tilted her head back, eyes closed, soft smile on her lips, mist caressing her porcelain cheeks, moisture beading in her dark brown hair. Then her cell phone rang.

Digging it out of her backpack, she saw it was her mother.

"Hello."

"Hey there, baby. I wanted to let you know I won't be home until late tonight. Big budget meeting." Margo's voice was stuttery, distracted.

"Ok." *Why are you calling? You've been late every night.*

"You don't have to get pissy."

"I'm not—"

"I heard your tone." Nina heard papers rustling, talking in the background.

"I'm sorry mom. I'm just—"

"I have to go. Order pizza if you don't want to cook."

"Mom."

"I'm sorry. Really." Click.

Her world was grey once again. Stomping through the door, she let it slam behind her. The solid thunk was satisfying. Yanking open a kitchen drawer, she dug around for the Pizza Pantry menu, grumbling. She ordered a thin crust vegetarian, large, prophesying the need for leftovers tomorrow night. It wasn't until she began the address spiel that she was informed the Pizza Pantry did not deliver.

That's handy for a girl without a driver's license. Top Ramen it is. Numbly, she grabbed a silver pot, slipped off her bracelets, and pushed up her sleeves to fill the basin with fizzy tap water.

The pink scars on the inside of her pale forearm called to her. Sang. Throbbed with life. *Touch me. Stroke me. Open me up.*

She pulled her sleeves down, firmly, and stepped away from the silverware drawers.

CHAPTER 15
ADDY

Beep beep beep beep
Oh no! The fire alarm!
"Addy."
Beep beep beep beep
Fire. Fire!
"Addy! Turn that damn thing off!"
She sat up, heartbeat accelerated, unable to breath.
No fire. Alarm clock.
"Seriously Addy? It's 4 o'clock in the morning. Fuck."
Panicking all over again, she finally found the screeching clock under a limp tshirt.
"I'm sorry." *Ha ha, sucker. It's 3:45.*
Rick growled and rolled over, facing the wall, nestling into his pillow.
She tiptoed into the bathroom, trying to calm her heart. Peering into the mirror with shuttered, crusty eyes, she saw Ford standing before her, shaking his head, holding up a black molten lump that had once been a piece of lamination. She groaned at the memory, still fresh after two weeks. How could she forget? Everyday, every goddamn day, at least one teacher had handed her a box of laminating overheads and said, "This is the only kind that can go through the copy machine. Just thought you should know."
She rubbed her eyes. *Okay, it's over. Let it go. The librarian will forgive you. Someday.* The cold finally seeped into her consciousness, giving her the shivers and something else to focus on.

Her carefully chosen clothes were hanging on the back of the door; she dressed in the chill for her first speech tournament. On the mirror was a yellow Post It note: "Coach: Good luck at the tournie. I'll miss you. Call me, let me know how it's going. Love, your lonely boyfriend. P.S. Please don't wake me up."

Oops. She folded the note, tucked it into her bra.

Quiet, quiet. She didn't mind swabbing down with a cold wet washcloth rather than run a loud shower, she didn't mind shaving her legs with Lubriderm, she didn't mind brushing her teeth with a single drop of water rather than run the faucet, she didn't even mind digging through her makeup bag carefully so as not to clink and clang powder tubes. But the ban on the hairdryer killed her. The mirror reflected serious bed-head. She needed major repair, which required a good wetting, blowing the flat spots out and curbing the sprongs. Instead she slicked her long blonde waves back into a ponytail. *We'll be walking into a den of tigers and I might as well be sucking my thumb, clutching a teddy bear.* Addy straightened her pencil skirt, buttoned her black blazer, checked her nylons. *Sitting on a bus seat for two hours in pantyhose? My thighs will be branded by the time we get to Hillyard.* She dabbed purple nail polish on the beginnings of a run in the crotch. She crept out of the bathroom, high heels in hand, *quiet, quiet*, out of the house, shoes on, into her car. She turned the key, whispering "shhhh."

Gah. I'm not a role model. These kids have to live out loud, especially today. She rolled away from the curb and gunned it.

"Sorry, baby." No one heard her.

Her Volvo trundled into Oceanside High's parking lot by 4:20, head foggy from lack of sleep. A few kids milled about under the one working street lamp, no bus in sight. *We've got ten minutes before we're supposed to leave, we should be okay.* Someone tapped on her window. She jumped three inches off the velour seat, her teeth clicking together.

"Sorry, Ms. Taylor." Erin's nose pressed against the window. She waggled her eyebrows, moving her glasses up and down. Then she yelled, over-mouthing the words, "I need into the school. I left my speech in my locker last night."

Addy waved her back so she could open the car door. A sandy ocean breeze stung her face as she emerged. "I take it you didn't practice last night, then."

"Oh no, I did, I have it memorized. But the rules say I have to have the script with me."

"Well alright! I'm proud of you. Except for the forgetting your manuscript part."

"Do you have a key to let me in?"

Addy retrieved her key ring from the steering column. As she approached the school's steel double doors, a red light strobed through the window, blinking brighter as she approached.

Wha's tha—

Oh shit.

Weeks ago, new teachers had been given a short training on how to disarm the building's alarm. The training consisted of Ford handing her a business card with alarm instructions, saying "Don't set off the alarm." Luckily she found the crumpled card mashed into the bottom of her messenger bag. She read it three times. *These instructions were written by a chimpanzee. Or one of my freshmen.*

There was no way she'd set off the alarm twice in two weeks. The law of averages was in her favor. *I'm going to use common sense, see if that works.*

It didn't work.

Five minutes later, the bus still had not arrived but half the police department screeched into the lot, Troy Ford close behind. Oddly, the vice-principal was in a beat up green Toyota, a surfboard strapped to the top. Addy and ten high school kids sat along the curb, hands over their ears. The siren worked not only as a deterrent but also as a marker, since anyone trapped in the building with the searing scream would immediately start bleeding from the ears.

Ford jumped out of his truck, making a beeline for Addy. He did not look like an administrator. His auburn hair was tousled, sticking up on one side. Wearing a green U of O sweatshirt with scraggly cargo shorts and flip flops, he was awfully tan. And adorable. For a second. Then he spoke.

"Of course." He shook his head at her, just like in her vision. "You're an English teacher. You can't follow instructions?"

"I'm –"

"Don't bother."

Ford released the police, once he got them to believe he was in charge. He reset the alarm, contacted the alarm company, and escorted a chagrined Erin to her locker while Addy tried to decide if it was okay to breathe or not. She wondered if Rosie's Roost was hiring.

"Why are you still here? Shouldn't you be on your way?" He towered over her scrunched up form on the curbside.

"The bus is late." She squinted at her watch. "Fifteen minutes late."

Ford rolled his eyes, sighed deeply and brought a cell phone to his well-formed lips.

"Hello, this is Troy Ford at the high school. There's a team here, waiting for transportation. No, The Speech Team. What? Who cancelled it? I see. No, it'll be too late by then, thank you." He turned to Addy. "Did you catch that? Someone cancelled your bus. I take it that wasn't you." He looked around the parking lot. "How many parents are still here? They'll have to drive."

"Drive to Hillyard?! Isn't that two hours away?"

"Do you have a better suggestion? What time does your competition start?"

He was right. The speech team kids were standing in a half circle around her, waiting for direction. Tori stepped forward, sleek in her power suit, not a hair out of place. All business. "Ms. Taylor, my mom says she can drive. We can fit four in our car."

Addy began organizing drivers and passengers. Most parents, still in pajamas or sweats, avoided eye contact and drove away without a word. Luckily, ten kids fit into three vehicles. Not comfortably, maybe not even legally, but they fit. Tori's mom's CRV had seen some hard miles but it was in much better shape than Gavin's mother's dilapidated Le Mar Tacos' van, which was missing seats and parts of the floor, a steamer oven taking up a good chunk of the interior. *We just need to make it there. We'll worry about looks later.*

Wyatt watched his dad pull out of the driveway, heading down Highway 101 without a backward glance. The big farm kid shrugged. "Believe me, we didn't want him there anyway. He would've interrupted speeches, telling kids they're wrong. And then he'd have tried ta' sell them weed." He climbed into the backseat of Addy's Volvo.

Addy almost gave herself whiplash making sure Ford was out of earshot.

He was right behind her, glowering, but not saying a word. She ushered kids into cars like a nervous hen clucking after her chicks. "Ok then. Thank you, Mr. Ford, and again, I apologize profusely—"

"We'll talk on Monday." He loped across the parking lot to his truck. The green Toyota chugged away, the surfboard a white flag racing parallel to the Pacific Ocean. Addy shook herself. Time to get moving.

Driving the winding county highway into Portland at 70 miles per hour gave Addy time to relax, refocus on the tournament. Listening to Dylan repeat, mechanically, forty-five times in a row his extremely boring oratory speech detailing violence in video games made Addy realize a few things. First, violence can be boring. Second, Dylan's speech was written at a seventh grade level. Finally, Addy was hearing this new script for the first time, having only time to listen to his other event at practice last week, and now she was driving him to the beast that was going to eat him. He represented the best Addy could do.

That's gonna' change. I don't care if I have to divide myself in two, I've gotta' step it up.

By the time the Oceanside High School Speech and Debate Team caravan arrived at Hillyard High School, the students had changed into their dress clothes and practiced their speeches. Endlessly. Her brain was numb.

Dylan, Travis and Wyatt staggered out of Addy's car, pale with puckered lips.

"I hope I don't barf."

"I need some water."

"You drive like a maniac, Ms. Taylor."

"Where's Ace? I need him to tie this stupid thing."

She'd avoided looking into the back seat for the last twenty miles as they exchanged flannel shirts and hoodies for dress shirts and ties. She assessed Travis in the early morning gloom. The white shirt sleeves hit his wrists on the short side, his tie bore singing chipmunks, and he was wearing white athletic socks with his black dress shoes. Dylan and Wyatt looked similar, though Wyatt was wearing Carhart pants. *At least they're a dark color. I'm going to pretend I can't see the rat nest on his head.*

Gavin strolled over, rocking a red sweater vest and faded khakis, followed by Ace in a woolen brown suit reeking of moth balls. Nina and Jamy wore cardigans and skirts, Erin tugged on a flowered dress that once served as a tablecloth, and Billie wore tight pants and a sequined tank top. *Good lord, girl, please don't drop your speech, you can't bend over.* The team gathered around, a group of awkwardly dressed kids scared out of their minds; as one, they turned to face the front of the building.

Addy filled her lungs. "Ok. Let's go in."

I have no freaking idea what I'm doing here. Remember, role-model. She squared her shoulders and strode confidently up the sidewalk. "Come on, Pirates."

CHAPTER 16
ADDY

The kids followed close behind Addy, herding together, shoulder to shoulder, hip to hip, puppies huddling together for safety. She could feel the weight of their exuberant terror on her back, propelling her forward. Emerging into a commons area, they stumbled to a stop, surrounded by tempered chaos.

Well-dressed teenagers were jammed together like Romans at the bloody Pantheon, sitting at tables, or on the floor, laying under tables, running and pushing through the crowds, frantically flipping through yellow legal pads. On the east side of the cavernous room, a line of young professionals prostituted their craft, yelling and gesticulating at a blank white wall. The speakers were alone in their world of words, practicing their speeches as though a rapt audience was before them, pretending other passionate orators were not smacking their elbows. The cacophony made Addy's head hurt, her pulsing brain trying to fit the shouted random phrases into a cohesive thought.

"The dingoes ate my baby!"

"The economy will never recover under this administration."

"Your mother was a hamster and your father smelt of elderberries."

Dylan spread his thin arms, his baggy dress shirt becoming a white sail. "These are my people. I'm home." *He really is adorable,* Addy thought. *Let's hope Elf Boy doesn't turn into a demon by the end of the day.* She had not had discipline problems with any of her team yet. Yet. The day was young.

Erin used her pinky to push up her glasses and then used the same pinky to point at a tiny girl shrieking about the dingo. "She's fourteen. Think she really has a baby?" Erin's voice was high-pitched, nervous. Jamy, dressed like a young librarian, patted her shoulder.

Nina touched Erin's other shoulder. "Don't worry, she's only practicing. You'll look just as crazy by the end of the day. It's a lot like a drama workshop." Nina's chestnut hair was coiffed, her skirt was calf length and her shoes were tasteful ballet flats while Erin looked uncomfortable, her dress bursting at the buttons and her black curls straining out of a sparkly headband.

Billie, her red hair teased Texas style, her sparkly blouse taped into place, and her stilettos bordering on four inches, sashayed through the group and wrapped an arm around Erin's middle. "I'm just as nervous as you are, we'll be okay."

Erin eyed her suspiciously. "You don't look nervous. You look like you're trying to find a mate."

Addy stepped in before blood could be drawn. "Be careful, we tend to hurt the ones we love when we're upset or scared."

Erin, sheepish, said, "I'm sorry Billie, you look nice." Billie hugged her again.

"Why don't you guys find a spot to camp out while I look for the registration table?" The new coach spun slowly in a circle, distracted from her task by the press of people so early on a Saturday morning. *Someone in this room will graduate to the Forbes Top One Hundred list, someone else is going to walk on stage to accept an Oscar.* She glanced at her ill-prepared team, hoping they made it through the day without major meltdowns or burnouts—or the disheartening realization that they were the tiny David school with no chance against the gigantic Goliath schools. She wanted them to believe in themselves, try their best. The day would be more enjoyable for them if they could relish the process while remaining ignorant of the insurmountable mountain in their way.

"Ms. Taylor?" Tori, a Future Business Leader of America, was the only member of the speech team who seemed at ease in her power suit, in her element. "I saw a sign for registration right inside the door. Do you want me to come with you? I can help register."

"No, thank you Tori. I had to register on the website a few days ago. I just need to check us in and get your speaking schedules for the day." She left Wyatt and Travis to bulldoze a path, gently, through the seething multitudes to an empty table on the far side of the commons; their eight teammates followed them gratefully, Ace and Gavin closing up the rear, bobbing along to their ipods. They seemed okay for the time being.

Stutter-stepping back down a cave-like corridor, Addy found her way to the school's library, where a number of coaches were filtering in the doors. Addy joined the queue. When she finally reached a desk with an official looking woman, she withdrew a copy of her registration.

"What school are you with?" the grey haired woman asked curtly. Her chest bore a nametag with no name, just a title: President. The corners of the woman's mouth were turned down, queenly, disparaging.

"Oceanside High School. I was wondering—"

"Your school code is 'M'. Individual competitors have codes inside this folder. Write down any drops on the sheet over on that table. Your judges must check in here. Ocean Side High School owes $386. How're you going to pay?"

Oh, sweet mother, what is happening? Addy was flustered more than usual. "Please, I have a few questions—"

"Are you paying with check or money order?"

Addy tried to stabilize her shaking voice, hating any conflict, especially with an authority figure, no matter how tiny the figure. "I thought we'd be billed, I don't have a check."

The queen of mean harrumphed. "I'm not running a charity here."

"Uhhh," Addy's eyes rolled in panic.

"For God's sake. Write down your address, I'll send a bill." Fire darted from her red eyes. She muttered something under her breath.

"Thank you. I'm sorry for the inconvenience." *You look like a grandma but you, sir, are no grandma. At least I hope not.*

"Step out of the way now. You're holding up the line." The woman's cat sweater quivered with the force of her jutting arm, a knarled index finger pointing off into the distance, a place Addy longed to be already.

"Oh, okay, but can someone help me—"

The President cut her off again, visibly shaking with anger. "Juanita! Get this lady out of the way!"

Addy could feel tears trembling on her eyelashes. Embarrassment equaled a red, wet face. *I want to go home.* The other coaches around her shuffled nervously, avoided eye contact. No one stuck up for Addy, including Addy.

After a lifetime, possibly five seconds, another grandmotherly woman, one with a much softer face, came out from behind a neighboring table and gently grabbed Addy's arm, pulling her to the side. "Hi, I'm Juanita, don't worry, I can explain some things. Grab your school's folder."

The President shoved the thick manila folder into Addy's hands, glared at her for a second and then barked, "Next! Come on people! The first round starts in fifteen minutes."

Addy meekly allowed herself to be pulled aside, surreptitiously wiped her eyes. "I'm sorry, I don't know what I'm doing." She tried to suppress the hitch in her voice, leading to a case of the hiccups.

Juanita tsked, her look consoling as she leaned in and whispered conspiratorially, "Leila gets a little worked up. She runs a solid tournament but has a hard time venting her stress without burning a few people in the process." She settled her polyster-clad bottom on a plastic orange chair. "Now, how can I help?"

"Well, for one, I have no idea what Leila was talking about." Her voice rose, reaching glass-breaking heights. "Drops? Judges? Rounds?"

"You'll pick up the lingo soon enough, don't worry. Let me see your folder, I'll show you what you need." Juanita spent five minutes patiently answering Addy's questions.

Once she deciphered the coding system, she hurried back down the beige hallways, seeking her team. *I have to remember, this isn't about me. I'm here for the kids. Time to gird my loins. Better yet, gird my ovaries.* Addy's miniature stomach-self smirked at the brave words, knowing Addy would dwell on the unpleasant encounter for hours, beating herself up.

Tori and Billie had broken the team into two groups. They were practicing their speeches in front of each other. Wyatt and Travis were struggling to remember the words of their duo piece but were having fun, hamming up the delivery. Even though the team had seen their performance at least twenty times, the group broke out in encouraging laughter, urging the boys on. By the time they were done, they were flushed with pride and other teams sitting nearby joined in the final clapping. Ace had his phone out, videotaping the performance and the crowd so he could give the footage to the Oceanside AV Club. The team would be famous on the local cable channel.

Addy couldn't believe it. Her team was practicing and even the other competitors were being supportive. *That seems too good to be true.* As she called the kids to her, she spied the delightful President Leila taping a raft of papers across a wall on the outskirts of the common room. Kids rushed to the documents en masse. Addy pointed to the wall. "Check there to find where you're speaking in the next few minutes. They post your code, not your name. You'll have to look at the postings each time you perform today, you'll be in a different room with a different judge each time."

"We know, Ms. Taylor." Dylan said. "Tori made us listen to a spiel on the inner workings of a tournament yesterday at lunch."

The team had lunch together? When they didn't have to? That is so freaking sweet. She put her hand on Tori's shoulder, smiled at the group. Then Addy pointedly looked at the wall clock, which showed only five minutes before the first round of speeches were to begin. "Don't be late. You need to go to the postings, find your code and room. A judge is probably waiting there for you already."

She'd forgotten something. "Wait!" They turned back to her, speeches in hand, displaying nerves by licking their lips, scowling, or straight up popping beads of sweat on their foreheads.

"I'm so proud of you guys. Seriously." Her throat tightened, garbling the words.

"Don't freak me out, Ms. Taylor!" groaned Dylan, tucking in the volumes of excess shirt material. "See ya' later."

With that, the group dispersed, blending into the surging, suited crowd.

Addy watched them go. She was surprised. She'd been expecting some breakdowns, possibly vomiting. She'd prepared herself to be the tough mommy, picturing herself wiping their faces, steering them gently back into the fray, putting her hands on her hips and smiling as they stepped up in front of an audience, thanking her for her support. In reality, they didn't seem to need her, not really.

Then she overheard two boys in matching three piece black suits, red ties, and Wall Street haircuts, noisily gathering yellow notepads and buckets of egotism. "Did you see that Oceanside kid's shirt? Looks like the hillbillies found a ride to town."

"Don't make fun of the dude's clothes . . . make fun of his team. I heard 'em practicing. A bunch of illiterate junkies."

They strode off, prep-school ties swinging, two young classicists out to right the world.

She felt a slow simmer. *Whether they know it or not, my kids do need me. I'm not going to let snide smart asses like that beat us, not if I can help it.*

CHAPTER 17
NINA

Slightly embarrassed, Nina entered the front double doors of Hillyard High School with her team, a rag-tag group of kids. They were acting like krill being sucked into the maw of the big, bad whale, crowded around Ms. Taylor as if she was a savior. *Peons*, she thought, rolling her eyes. The big-city teen felt comforted by the smash of bodies and pulse of brainpower in the large school's commons. A huge rush of homesickness for Boston swayed down her spine.

Waiting to perform, however, was an exercise in consciously controlling her bodily functions, such as slowing her hummingbird heartbeat and ordering her bowels to return home. In the commons area with six hundred heavily-scented teenage speech competitors, Nina stood straight, shoulders back, hands tucked into the sleeves of her soft blue cardigan, grey eyes fastened on Travis and Wyatt; the two hicks were decimating a famous piece of slap stick comedy in front of a growing audience. She admired the boys for their gusto but was secretly superior, and glad she'd done some acting before this competition. These two football players were going to be tasteless hors d'oeuvres for the more experienced competitors.

While she pretended to watch them, she was mentally running lines from her own speech, a dramatic scene which, within ten minutes, referenced sex with an angel, a nun's bloody vagina, and a dead baby in a trash bin. She wondered how she was going to go from discreet high school girl to screaming murderer in the next half hour. The only thing that stopped her from stealing the Red Bull out of Gavin's hands was the fact that Gavin was about to perform a piece in which he had to play both a female prostitute and the Elephant Man. She let him keep his energy drink. She'd have to tap her inner crazy, hope that worked.

"Okay, here're your codes and school maps." Ms. Taylor returned slightly disheveled, bearing a manila folder. She withdrew a stack of yellow maps and passed them around, making sure each student wrote their speaking code on their map. They were one map short, Nina receiving the last copy. Dylan tried to snatch it. She twisted gracefully, pirouetting, leaving him to grasp air, empty-handed.

He cocked an eyebrow. "Don't worry, I'm street smart. I can find my way around this place with a blindfold on." He wrote his code on his hand with a flourish.

"Psht. I doubt you can find the restroom." Nina smiled at him, softening the blow. Hillyard High School was three stories and the square footage of a small mall. Oceanside High School had six hallways and a tiny cafeteria.

"Don't get uppity." Dylan stuck his nose in the air, mocked her Boston accent. "I suppose your old school was gargantuan." He dropped the dialect, looking around. "This place reminds me of a college, or a hospital."

That's right, Nina thought. *My old high school was as big as a hospital. And, for a couple months, it was a hospital. Boston's finest sanatorium for the mentally ill high school population.*

She shook the thought free.

A tiny senior citizen with a bad perm and a hideous cat sweater was taping a raft of papers across a wall on the outskirts of the common room. Kids rushed to the documents en masse, the old lady yelling at them to back off until she could pad out of the way. Ms. Taylor pointed to the wall. "Check there to find where you're speaking in the next few minutes. They post your code, not your name. You'll have to look at the postings each time you perform today, you'll be in a different room with a different judge each time."

"We know, Ms. Taylor." Dylan said. "Tori made us listen to a spiel on the inner workings of a tournament yesterday at lunch." What Dylan wasn't saying was how Tori somehow managed to deliver them official messages from the office yesterday morning, directing the speech team students to meet in the conference room for lunch. Tori showed up with an agenda, a copy of the state rules, and the air of God. She had gone on and on about how Oceanside needed to represent itself respectfully. The boys hooted like apes, the girls texted. In the end, Tori stomped out, leaving behind an F bomb so powerful Nina was sure she felt a breeze. The new senior sat quietly through the whole show, not sure of her place in the pecking order, or why the kids were being so rude to Tori. They needed the information, so why give her such a bad time? Public school offered new mysteries every minute of every day.

Ms. Taylor pointedly looked at the wall clock, which showed only five minutes before the first round of speeches were to begin. "Don't be late. You need to go to the postings, find your code and assigned room number, and then high tail it to those classrooms. A judge will be waiting there for you."

Jamy thrust her map in Nina's face. Her petite face was drawn, obscured beneath her brown pixie cut. "Where are we?"

Or at least that's what Nina thought Jamy said, considering Jamy had been speaking in nervous high-speed squirrel tongue ever since the school alarm went off that morning. Erin and Billie had made a game of trying to decipher the meaning behind Jamy's verbal explosions but Nina could see Jamy was about to explode for real. She showed the girl how to orient herself from the commons area and the front door, places Jamy already knew. The other kids, trying to play it cool, quieted down and listened to Nina, eyeing their own maps. The Oceanside Speech and Debate Pirates clearly did not perform much pillaging far from home. Nina took a step toward the postings, hoping she wasn't going to be responsible for all of them making it through the day.

"Wait!" Ms. Taylor called them back. Nina and the others turned to the pretty young coach, speeches scrunched in their hands, displaying their nerves by scowling or popping beads of sweat on their face. Nina didn't think she looked nervous, at least not like Erin with her green face, or Jamy with her bitten lips, or Travis with his rocking, but her gut was twisted and trying to get out her mouth.

"I'm so proud of you guys. Seriously." Ms. Taylor was about to cry, her voice quavering. Nina glanced down at the speech script in her hands, shutting down her reaction to her coach's emotional outburst. She could barely handle her own nerves.

"Don't freak me out, Ms. Taylor!" groaned Dylan, tucking in the volumes of excess shirt material. "See ya' later." He grabbed the map out of Nina's hand and ran away, laughing. Luckily, Nina remembered her code. She looked at Dylan's retreating back.

Kill, kill, murder, murder.

The group dispersed. Jamy held her map out again. "Nina, I'll share my map. You can help me find my room." She smiled nervously, but she was speaking at a rate Nina could understand this time. "Dylan might not admit it, but I will, this high school is crazy big. I've never been out of our county before. We sure don't have anything like this." They were weaving through the kids crowding around the postings, trying to get close enough to see the numbers. "I'm pretty sure our auction house couldn't hold this many people."

Packed in tight, the wet air smelled like an auction house. Pure nervous animal stench: salty sweat, dry-mouth breath, and methane. Nina stopped her lungs, and her brain, feeling an anxiety attack close at hand. Jamy looked on the verge of passing out. Nina got her to the posting for Poetry

Reading, finding her code and room number toward the bottom of the page. *Wow. I can't believe how many kids are doing poetry. There must be a hundred competitors listed here.* Jamy waited off to the side while Nina shouldered her way to her Dramatic Interpretation posting, which listed just as many competitors. Their rooms were at the same end of the high school; they moved quietly and quickly down the halls, two youthful, well-dressed girls, bearing down on the fear of the unknown.

Jamy left Nina at her room with a hug and a friendly wave, turning away with a determined shine in her eyes. Nina watched her go, wishing her well. She paused at her own door. The desire to slide to the floor was almost overwhelming. If she could stop for a moment, maybe rock herself back and forth briefly. Her right index finger slid under her bracelets and over a scar inside her left wrist, pressing a fingernail into the raised tissue, hard.

She stepped through the open door with faux confidence to find six professionally dressed students and a guy who appeared to be a college student. He stood out not only because of the stopwatch and official looking papers spread across his desk but also because of his scruffy chin, baggy jeans and layered tshirts. He didn't bother to look at her as she settled into one of the desks at the back of the room.

"M2?" He said to the desk.

"Pardon me?" Was he speaking to her? The other kids stared at her, no one saying a word.

"M2? Are you M2?"

"Oh, yes. Yes, I'm M2. My name is—"

"Doesn't matter. Okay, we're all here. C48, you're up."

A well-manicured boy in a crisp navy suit made his way forward, arrogantly stepping down the aisle to take his place at the front of the room. The handsome male in a nice suit created a twinge of homesickness, inspiring images of the crowded main streets of Beantown at lunch time.

C48? Does that mean his school brought at least 48 kids? That's one wicked huge team.

His performance was impeccable: his delivery was natural, smooth, the two character voices were believable. Nina was enthralled. He acted out a scene from *Of Mice and Men*, playing both the diminutive farm hand and the lumbering simpleton so realistically that Nina forgot she was sitting in a classroom at eight a.m. on a Saturday morning. She learned a lot in the next ten minutes, mentally noting the tricks she could pull into her own performance, like how to situate her body, how to use her eyes to keep the audience involved. She couldn't wait to tell Ms. Taylor about it. Suddenly, her nerves were steady, held in place by enthusiasm and the joy of being in the moment. This. This was why she had joined speech.

To become someone else.

CHAPTER 18
ADDY

Seething over the condescending comments of the black-suited, politicians-in-waiting, Addy shot laser beams into their backs. *No one gets to call my team hillbillies or junkies! Who do you think you are?* she shouted internally. The boys didn't care, they were barging down the hall to their predestined date with winning. Harumphing, she swung her gaze back to the tournament's posting wall. There were a few confused stragglers who didn't seem quite so sure of their destiny. She started toward them, thinking maybe she could help them get to their first round, if only to share her map. Kids were kids, whether or not she was their coach. Even the snooty ones.

"Ms. Taylor?" Tori had snaked back around the room and was now standing by Addy. The girl trembled, white faced, her usual bravado dissipated. Even her ponytail sagged.

"Honey, what is it?"

"My code isn't on the postings. Anywhere!" She wailed the last word.

"Hey, hey, it's okay. Maybe you wrote the number down incorrectly."

"No! I didn't!"

"Okay, okay. Sweetie. It's okay. We'll fix it." Addy put her arm around Tori's shoulders, steered her back to the registration desk.

"I'm going to be late. They won't let me compete." Tori dry sobbed. Addy projected calm, strength, imagery of steaming mugs of chamomile tea. *Here's to hoping my mental telepathy is working today.*

"No, no. The adults running this competition are here to help you. We'll get this resolved." They were almost to the table where she'd first encountered President Leila. A table that was now empty. *Crap.* Behind the table was a classroom door hung with a sign: Tab—Stay Out.

Tab must stand for Tabernacle? Tabloid? Tabulate . . . Yes, that made sense, Tabulation. *Here lies the monster's lair. Do I dare?*

Tori hiccupped, stressfully. *Yes, dare I must.* Addy stepped around the table, knocked on the warped steel, the threatening sign blocking the window. The door sprang open as if someone was waiting, crouched, on the other side.

Leila, the croucher, snarled, "Yes?"

Her taut, stunted body blocked the door, an evil gnome protecting her squatting rights.

"Leila, hi." Addy stood straight. *Didn't I see you in a Stephen King movie?* "Hey, I have a student here who was left off your postings downstairs. Her code is—"

"Go back, look at the postings. Kids always get that wrong."

"I'm pretty sure it's not there. If you could just check –"

"Go look at the postings." Rasping voice, no humanity.

She shut the door, squashing Addy's open-toed pump in the rapidly diminished door jam. There was a resounding metal clang when her foot painfully squirted free. *Damn.* Behind her, Addy heard a hitch and then a keening. Tori. Addy did not turn around. She sucked in all the air available in the hallway, turned the knob, and pushed the door back open.

"You can't be in here!" Leila screeched, waving her arms as if fending off a mugger.

"I'll stay right here, by the door. Listen, I'm a new coach? From Oceanside High School? I just need to find out what room my student's supposed to be in."

"Oh, for God's sake. What's this girl's name?" She'd dropped her arms but not her voice.

Addy gave her the name and code. Leila huffed around the room, a handful of helpers stepping out of the way when she came near. She stamped back to Addy, shaking a dog-eared piece of paper. "Her name is not on your registration."

The blood left Addy's brain, settled in her stomach. "Oh, I."

"She can't compete."

"We came all this way, I'll pay extra."

"There's no way I can fit her in now. This round of speeches has already begun." She turned her tiny back, her grey pin curls tightly clenching a No. 2 pencil.

"But what am supposed to do with her? We drove two and half hours to get here."

Leila didn't bother to face Addy. "You're going to have to work this out somewhere else. I've got a tournament to run."

Addy moved on wooden legs toward the door. *This sucks. Am I going to let this happen?* She stopped, not giving herself a chance to think before speaking. "I know this is a huge inconvenience but I'm not leaving until I find a way for her to compete. This is my error, not hers."

Leila did not answer, bent over a makeshift table created from rickety desks pushed together. She picked up a pencil, ignoring the one crammed in her hair, began listing numbers in a column. Addy peered over her shoulder, trying to decipher meaning from the numerical codes, holding her breath against the sting of cheap hairspray and fresh perm. Leila kept writing but growled, "Stand there as long as you like. My patience is wearing thin, though, I warn you."

"Leila, I understand you're crazy busy. I get that. But I can also see by the clock that this first round of speeches is just now starting." Addy spoke as fast as Jamy. "You can't tell me adding her in as last speaker somewhere is going to send this train off the tracks." Holy God, who just spoke? Addy became flustered, realizing an inner demon had escaped. She backpedaled immediately. "I know you're doing your best for all the kids, not just mine. I just think I could help find a place for her that wouldn't mess up the tournament for anyone . . ."

"Sweet mother of Mary!" Leila groaned. "Shut up, okay? What event is she in? What's her code?" The crinkly older woman physically hurt Addy with her glare. "I can respect standing up for your kid. But you have to get this right next time, princess. Your errors effect everyone."

Addy kept her gaze low, nodding submissively, hastily writing out Tori's information, handing it over wordlessly. Leila, in turn, scrawled a notation on another piece of paper, tore off a corner and handed it to Addy. "Tell your girl to give this to the judge. She'll go last."

"Thank you. Thank you so much."

"Fine. Go."

Addy escaped the room, sweat pooling in her bra and the small of her back. The waistband of her underwear would be damp for the rest of the day.

Tori was calm, giving her speech to the wall as Addy emerged, dazed. *Should I tell the girl she's mumbling? That her expression screams psycho killer? Maybe not now.* Tori beamed when she saw the paper in her coaches' hand. The relieved teenager said, "I knew you'd do it. Thank you so much, Ms. Taylor."

Addy wasn't sure what was more satisfying, that she *had* done it, or that Tori believed she would. They hurried down the passage, fluorescent lights humming, skirts swishing, steps synchronized.

CHAPTER 19
ADDY

Addy's mug rattled loosely in the car's cup holder as NPR's Monday morning newscaster lulled her into a passive driving state. Her eyes were swollen with lack of sleep, her brain swollen with apprehension of what was awaiting her at work. When she hit the speed bump in the OHS parking lot, coffee spurted through the drinking hole, burning her thigh. *Huh? What?* She startled. *How did I get here already?*

Ford's usual car, the Mercedes, lounged in the OHS front lot, giving Addy the eye as her Volvo squealed past. Addy drove around to the back of the school. She snuck in the back doors, slowly poking her head in and peering down the hallway. No one in sight. She slipped through the opening and practically tiptoed the one hundred yards to her classroom. She had purposefully exchanged her clickety-clackety high heels for soft-soled Danskos while dressing in black that morning, feeling like a spy. Or a goth prisoner on the run, reeking of coffee.

In her classroom, a huge gust of air escaped her lips as she lowered herself carefully into the bucking, duck-taped chair behind her desk. *I made it this far. I only have eight more hours of evasion ahead of me. I pray to all that is unholy that Ford becomes too busy to make his way down here.* A thought struck her. *Sorry kids, a lot of referrals are going to be written today. I've gotta' throw a few naughty goats into the vice-principal's fire or the volcano is going to explode.*

The Monday morning desk sprint kept her occupied, frantically writing notes on the board, finding examples, and making answer keys before the first period students swept in, bringing the thunder. She did not dare make any copies. Maybe not ever again.

The door surged open; Addy braced for the onslaught of students. Instead, it was an onslaught of righteous indignation and masculinity.

"Ms. Taylor!"

"Oh, Mr. Ford! Sorry, I didn't get—" She jumped up, knocking the chair over. *God. Damn. It.*

"You chose to avoid me this morning."

"No, I—"

"Save it." He glowered down at her. "Actions have consequences." He tilted his head, holding her gaze. "I suspect you already know that. Here, in my hand is your consequence."

"It was an accident! I didn't mean to set off the alarm." She gulped. *Again.*

"Calm down." He put the slip of paper on a teetering stack on her desk. "I know it was an accident." He paused. "Both times. But I did ask you to be in my office first thing." Addy squinted up at him, trying to decide if it was a facial tic or if he smiled. The dimple was alarming, charming, altogether unarming.

Ford brought her back to reality. "You're going to make it up to me by, first, holding fast to your promise to never again make overheads on a school copy machine. Second, you will learn how to disarm the building properly *and* apologize to the police chief for getting him out of bed before the crack of dawn. Even though, between you and me, I'm not sure he was in *his* bed, if you know what I mean."

"Ummm." She was confused. Did his voice just turn playful?

He cleared his throat, serious again. "Third, you're in charge of chaperoning the Homecoming Dance two weeks from now. The regular chaperone is in the hospital with liver failure. You're going to pick up his duty."

Addy's stomach sank. The dance fell on her only free weekend for that month. Rick was going to have a coronary.

"I can see by your face you're thrilled."

"Is there another staff member that can help me?"

"I don't know, you'll have to ask."

Addy quickly looked down, her eyes filled with tears. She'd worked an extra eighteen hours at the tournament on Saturday, and then wrote lesson plans on Sunday while simultaneously cooking lemon chicken for Rick and assuring him her every thought swirled around the awe-inspiring image of him. She walked into this day already exhausted. Now, further beaten down by Ford's heavy requirement thrown so unexpectedly on her back, she felt her will to continue breathing close to snapping. She bit the tip of her tongue until she tasted metal, berated her tear ducts harshly. Crying in front of her administrator would not make the load any lighter.

Ford, sensing female danger, smartly reeled in his testosterone, giving her the opportunity to re-group her emotions. He shoved his hands into his suit jacket pockets and said, "I know it's tough being the new guy, being in a place where you don't know anyone. Spending your time in this building." He looked down at her kindly, blue eyes empathetic. "It's my third year here. This small town school is hard to take sometimes."

She ventured a personal question. "You don't like it here?"

"Well, sometimes. I don't know. It can be pretty . . . " He straightened back up, seemed to remember he was her boss. "I'm going back to my old school in Portland next year. But I'm here for now. Like you. Hence coaching and chaperoning. Sorry."

Addy pursed her lips, unsure of how to respond to this personal connection. Part of her was disappointed to hear he wanted to leave, while the part of her that was anxious about being constantly chastised thought she could live with his absence, no matter how attracted she was becoming.

He leaned against a desk and asked, "By the way, how did the team do on Saturday?"

Addy peered into his face, believing his oceanic eyes were reflecting actual interest while her green eyes probably showed confusion and hesitation. Her girl parts were standing up, also taking a closer look. His gaze suddenly looked into her, not at her. *What is wrong with me? Seriously. He's been civil for less than one breath.*

She tugged her messenger bag out from under her desk, sorting through the hodge-podge of female detritus until she found the tournament document listing the results. Momentarily forgetting her disgruntlement over the Homecoming Dance, she told him about Erin and Nina breaking into the semi-finals, and how the rest of the team scored well in their three rounds but did not break into the final rounds. The kids came home excited, even the non-winners, claiming to be determined to use the feedback from their judges to improve before next weekend's tournament.

Ford looked at the clock, becoming distracted. "I'll get Candi to put Erin and Nina's placement in the announcements. Nice job, Coach."

He sauntered out, closing the door gently behind him.

Of course, she had not given Ford a detailed account of the tournament day, only the highlights. She "forgot" to mention Travis hissed "shit" in front of a judge when he forgot his lines, Billie disappeared only to be found some time later in an empty classroom with a boy from another school, Erin twisted her ankle and ended the day with ice packs and tears, Dylan returned from a bathroom break reeking of cigarettes, and Nina had some kind of melt down, not talking to anyone for two or three hours and refusing to get off the bus to eat dinner, staring ahead with pouting lips. By the time the slow line of cars drew into the pitchblack OHS parking lot it was 12:12 a.m.

To make matters worse, three of the students' parents did not show up, leaving Addy to re-pack her car with kids and gear and drive them to their scattered homes. The Volvo was empty and loud when she finally rolled up to her postage size front lawn, the early morning house dark and dreary, scary in the nighttime mist.

She'd hoped for a warm body and a loving heart awaiting her inside; instead, she had stealthily moved through the un-lit house, removing clothes before she got to the bedroom, where she found her boyfriend curled up on his side of the bed, in the position he'd been in when she left that morning. There was no sweet sticky note upon return. She'd slid silently between the sheets, not making a sound. Unfortunately, she wasn't quiet enough. He rolled over, and onto her, without a word, fumbling at her underwear.

She had frozen, debating her options. He tried thrusting himself into her, with her panties still on, grunting out bursts of Scotch-laden breath. She turned her head and struggled out from under him.

"Come on, Rick, I'm exhausted."

He lay on his back, too drunk to open his eyes. "Dammit Potato Face," he slurred, "Get out of my bed."

She gasped but refused to cry. *I should never have told him that nickname*, she thought, slinking out of the room, broken. In the living room, cold in only her torn panties, the street light strobed yellow across her face. Despite eyes scrunched tight, the tears escaped, hate-filled tears.

I don't have to take this. Do I? Do I have to take this?

That seemed a lifetime ago and Addy still didn't have an answer. But now, at least, she was snug in the safety of her classroom, away from Rick's heavy love, past Ford's reproachment. However, a thought stopped her mid-calm. The dance was going to be an issue for Rick. She had to figure out a plan of attack before broaching the subject. On the other hand, she was thrilled her interaction with Troy Ford ended on a positive note. She couldn't have born another day starting with conflict. She'd spent her whole life cowering in a corner; now the God of Argument and unrest seemed to have made Addy's corner his home.

CHAPTER 20
ADDY

Addy jabbed another bobby pin into the curls atop her head, dark blonde tendrils spilling out haphazardly. Turning the side of her mouth into a blowhole, she pushed a noisy rush of air into her face, moving curls out of her eyes. The mirror reflected a forlorn, freckled young woman with a wren's nest perched precariously on her head. She did not understand how she could have reached her mid twenties and still not mastered the physics of hair. She walked out of the bathroom, out of the house, into a sunny fall day, the sun twinkling off the placid ocean at the bottom of the hill.

If I was in Portland, there'd be two hairdressers and at least one girlfriend in a five block radius around my apartment. Here, I've got . . . mermaids.

One block down, she entered Rosie's Roost, praying Lizzie was on shift. Spying her through swinging kitchen doors, Addy sat at one of the six tables, all of which were empty. The dreadlocked waitress noticed her, her bright lips breaking into a smile, her uber-cool boots tapping out an uber-cool tune across the scarred wooden floor.

"Hey there! What's up? Alone again?"

"Yeah. Listen, I know this is weird but I have a girl question."

Through lips twisted in amusement, her smoky voice came out as a stage whisper, "Are you out of tampons?"

"No, no, nothing like that," she said quietly, beating down her shyness with the blunt end of her brain. "It's just that I don't know anyone in town, not really, and I was wondering-"

"Honey, you're adorable but I don't swing that way, not anymore."

Addy, thrown, proceeded with stuttery laughter. "It's my hair. I have to be at the Homecoming Dance in two hours, and I have no female in a two-hundred mile radius to tell me whether or not I look like a sad half-wit, a generic 80's girl, or a gloriously hot chaperone."

"Hmmm." Lizzie was not put off by the awkward, long-winded question. She pulled up a chair, backwards, and sat with her chin in her hands, pondering the tipping mess on Addy's head. "Not happy with the drunk Princess Leah look?" She cocked her head to the side, her shiny dreads dipping into her lap. "Take out your bobby pins. I'll fix it."

"Here? Now?" Addy's fingers were already digging out the metal sticks.

"Yeah. I don't think Sam's going to care, not as long as he gets to watch." She yelled back to the kitchen. "Right, Sam?" A pan clattered to the floor in response.

Twenty minutes later, Addy had discovered that Oceanside was a hotbed of freakish gossip and that her hair could be tucked neatly into a red-carpet chignon.

She stroked her smooth up-do, smiling up at the petite waitress. "Lizzie, you're truly amazing!"

"Bob doesn't think so." Lizzie, hands occupied with bobby pins, called across the restaurant to the only other patron, a logger reading a worn paperback, his mud-encased, cork-booted feet up on a chair. "Are you ready for more coffee, Bob?"

The bearded logger licked a thumb and turned a page, not looking up. "I was ready ten minutes ago, Lizzie."

Lizzie gave a low laugh, not hurrying to rectify the situation. She calmly smoothed the last few thick strands into place, fastening them securely with hidden pins. "There." She turned Addy to face her reflection in the plate glass window, the ocean a beautiful watermark, the weak October sun providing a golden sheen. Lizzie patted her cheek. "Thanks for giving me an art project for the day. Now, go on. Get your dance on."

Addy was pleased. The glass revealed a head of hair contained and tamed but, more importantly, there was a smooth image of two young women, grinning at each other. She had made a solid connection with another adult human being. She left happy, Lizzie following her out the door with nasty jokes about dark gym corners and teen pregnancy.

Rick's car pulled up to the house just as she reached the front door, his brown hair shining in the sun, a pleasant smile on his face. He let out a wolf whistle as he slammed the car door. "Wow, babe, you look beautiful. Nice." His athletic body hopped up on the stoop as she unlocked the door. "What time are we leaving?"

Addy had successfully circumvented any arguments about being gone another night; she invited Rick as her date, suggesting they pretend it was their prom. Rick knew poor, geeky teenage Addison had never been invited to any dances, but she'd been prepared for Rick to mock her, to squint his brown eyes and spew burning, sarcastic comments. Instead, he'd gone against type and agreed to go, even unearthing the old suit from *his* prom. Now, an hour to go, he had applied hair gel and body spray, and used a damp cloth to remove the layer of dust off the shoulders. He was ready.

She straightened his tie, tweaked his cheek. "I can't believe this still fits you! Come on, we better go. I have to get there before the kids."

Soon they were batting red, black and silver balloons away from their faces in the streamer-festooned gym; a disco ball lit up Addy's red satin sheath dress and Rick's matching tie. They were a beautiful couple in a shiny room, ready to celebrate despite the loss of the Pirate's last home football game. He looked around the nearly empty space, curious. "So. This is the gym. Damn. It's tiny."

Compared to their alma mater in a suburb of Portland, this gym was minuscule. Rick, a high school wrestler, was visibly disappointed but Addy felt nothing but satisfaction, smelling the faint, lingering odor of sweat, peering at the curling banners on the walls. There was even a speech and debate banner, albeit fifteen years old. Her new home. She liked it.

"Who's that guy?" Rick's muscular arm gestured toward Ed, hands on wide hips, arguing with the disc jockey trying to set up on the wooden stage embedded in the south wall of the gym.

"That's Ed, the social studies teacher I was telling you about. I asked him to help us chaperone." Addy was glad Ed was early. Kids were going to start showing up any minute, the thought making Addy antsy. Seeing the teens dressed up and nervous with their dates would be fun but she wasn't looking forward to confronting towering, drunk seniors. On the other hand, she figured that would be Ed's favorite part of the night. She did not feel bad, leaving the ejections to him.

Ed's tinny, grating voice floated over to them. "I don't care what you think. You're not playing this crap at a high school dance." He was stacking cds at the end of the music table, out of the dj's reach.

The dj tried to appease Ed, suggesting alternate albums, but Ed would only shake his head slowly, like he was trying to communicate with an idiot. Finally, to the relief of the dj, he sauntered across the gym toward Addy and Rick, a sour look on his face. Behind his back, the dj furtively retrieved at least half of the banned pile of cds.

"That guy must be a real hoot to work with." Rick's voice dripped with disdain, not trying to be quiet as Ed approached.

"Hi. Ed. Thanks for being here." She gestured to Rick, who had his hands in his pockets, rocking back on his heels, giving Ed the silent once over. "This is Rick, my boyfriend."

He nodded at Addy then swung his eyes over Rick's muscular body and spiky black hair, his mouth turning down at the corners. "Didn't know Addy was bringing a date tonight." He regarded Addy. "I always kinda' thought you were making up a boyfriend, throwin' the boys off the scent." The disco ball glinted off his balding head, turning the fringe of hair a sparkling pink, deepening the bags under his eyes. After an inappropriate amount of time, he reached out his hand. "Good to meet you." Their handshake was painful to watch, a silly, crushing affair.

Rick maintained a slight condescending smile on his face through the entire transaction, irritating Addy. She wanted him to be better than that, or at least better than Ed. Would it hurt to show kindness to the older man, ridiculous in a plaid shirt and paisley tie, his pants a finger-length too short? He was clearly a sad sack. She sighed, glad once again she was not encumbered with a penis and testosterone.

"Ed, did you bring the money box? Mr. Ford said he was going to leave it with you."

"Mi-ster Ford," he drawled, "told me he'd bring it."

"What? I thought he couldn't be here, that's why *I* had to be here."

"I think he changed his mind when he thought I might be handling money."

"Why would he care about that?"

"Let's just say he doesn't trust me."

There was an uncomfortable pause. Addy decided to stop asking questions.

While Ed waited for kids at the decorated table in the entrance, she sent a reluctant Rick and Michael Mason, the parent chaperone from the site council, to hang out in the parking lot and usher kids into the building as soon as they pulled in, giving them less time to hot box on campus. The other site council parent, Tisha Ives, came racing into the gym just ahead of the first crush of dancers. She was decked out in a black lace dress she likely wore to her own homecoming twenty years ago, perhaps slightly altered to show more of her bludgeoning bosoms and allow for her pot belly. Ed was thrilled to have her help taking tickets at the door. He was visibly not thrilled, however, to find the well-tailored Troy Ford also standing at the entrance to the dance. The vice-principal dropped a tan money box on the table with a clang, examined Ed knowingly, and then spotted Addy. She caught his gaze from just inside the gym doors.

Addy felt hypnotized under his penetrating intensity. She chose that moment to fade into the gym and circulate, make sure the music was playing, the corners were empty, the punch remained boring, and she maintained a distance from Troy Ford. Why was he looking at her so intently? There hadn't been time for her to screw up yet. And, she admitted to herself, his attention made her nervous, even more self-conscious than usual. Suddenly she felt overdressed, silly. *Why in the hell did I do this to my hair? I look like a fool.*

"Ms. Taylor! You're gorgeous!" Billie and Wyatt, followed by a handful of other students she recognized, pulsed and shimmered across the yellow gym floor, a kaleidoscope of color and shapes, youthful exuberance and joy turned to light and sound.

She laughed and talked with her students, bonding, free from academic expectations. When she spotted Rick and Michael coming in, she glided over to them, in the moment. Rick was also smiling, laughing, punching Michael in the arm hard enough to make his bright tie sling shot across his wrinkled denim shirt. They quieted when Addy approached, exchanging a quick look. *Yeah. That's not weird.*

"Hey babe. Wha's up?" Rick reached out to Addy, his long fingers grappling her satiny waist, leaning forward aggressively to give her a firm, wet kiss on the lips. She jerked away.

"What are you doing?! We're at school, remember?" Something caught her attention. She leaned back into him and sniffed his face. "What's that smell? Rick? Is that alco—"

Rick stiffened, looking past her.

"Good evening. Thank you for chaperoning," a deep voice rumbled over her head like a thunder boom.

Ah, hell. Of course Ford was behind her. She spun around, her skirt flaring like a Ginger Roger movie shot.

"No problem. Rick Hepner." Her boyfriend stuck his hand out with an air of belligerence. "And you?" Michael, the pudgy parent, edged away, fading into the shadows.

"I'm the vice principal, Troy Ford. Nice to meet you." Ford's blue eyes flicked to Rick briefly but remained on Addy. "Ms. Taylor is an excellent addition to our staff. We're happy to have her."

Behind her, Rick slid his hands back around her waist and pulled her against him. Addy froze for a second, trying to decide if it was more dignified to struggle or stay put, a mask of calm on her face. Inside, she was seething. *His testosterone is out of hand.*

There was a sudden, secondary silence hanging in the air as songs changed. From across the gym came a loud cry and a round of bellowing guffaws. Ford grimaced. "I better check that out. Have a nice night." With a nod, he strode away, tall and imposing even from the back.

Addy scrambled to break free. "What's your deal? I work here!"

Rick spread his hands wide, his brown eyes innocent. "What?"

Addy glanced away, breathing out her anger, not wanting conflict.

"That guy is a dick."

Breathing. Breathing. "Really? He said hi."

"What, now you like him?" Rick pushed off the wall he'd been leaning against, taking an angry step toward her.

"Like him? You mean, like a crush. Don't be dumb. I'm talking about being a professional." They glared at each other for a second, distracted finally by students waving her onto the dance floor. *Time to lighten this up.* "Hey, maybe we should go dance. Remember when we saw this band at Kell's two years ago?"

Rick's face un-pinched slightly as he eyeballed the chaos of dancers twenty feet from them. "Are there other teachers dancing?" He peered closer, dismantling the crowd, looking for adults. "Where *are* the other teachers? I thought I'd be meeting all the people you work with." He winked, trying to look blasé. "You know, my competition."

Addy blinked, seered to the bone by an epiphany. *Rick agreed to come tonight so he could pee on his territory.*

She stood for a moment, silently, facing away from her boyfriend. *Breathe. In. Out. Re-direct.* Turning back, she pasted a bright smile on her face and said, "Your biggest competition is right over there." She pointed out to the dance floor. "Fourteen year old Travis brought me a bunch of wilted wild daisies the other day. Keep an eye on that kid."

She got Rick out on the dance floor for a couple of songs, the tension dissipating as they joined one hundred teenagers bouncing around to Give Me All Your Luvin' and Sexy and I Know It, two songs probably filched from the censored pile. She relaxed, chuckled as Rick made himself the center of attention, delighting the teens with his sprinkler, lawn mower, and moon walking dance moves. Gavin, Ace and Travis, wearing their speech attire, came up beside him, emulating his moves, while the speech team girls egged on the spectacle with hoots and hollers. Travis seemed momentarily befuddled by an overly aggressive dance-off between himself and Rick but, like everyone else, thought it was a joke. Rick chilled out with a harsh glance from Addy, even joining the kids in laughter.

Addy was back to her happy place as she tripped out into the hall in front of the gym, Rick and Michael heading back out to the parking lot to check for errant children. Addy spent a couple minutes talking to Ed, who still manned the doors, a poorly-dressed, stoic sentry serious about his post. They talked school politics and horror stories from past school dances, Tisha bouncing in and out of the conversation. Addy eventually made her way back into the gym, wondering what was taking Rick so long.

"Ms. Taylor, you look lovely this evening." Ford loomed over her. Threatening, or a tower of safety, Addy couldn't decide.

She blushed, the tinge matching her dress. "Thank you."

"I appreciate you being here. I know it was last minute." He swept his gaze around the gym as he spoke, alert for foul play or inappropriate behavior, his thick auburn hair haloed in a silver light.

"Oh, sure, I don't mind." Addy wondered why she was lying but couldn't deny it felt good to have Ford look at her with an open, friendly face. She felt a slight tingle as his hand brushed her bare arm, the hairs raising on her sensitized flesh. Troy Ford confused her. Her body confused her. One minute she's glad this tyrant is moving back to Portland, the next she's rubbing against him like a cat.

Where is Rick?

Troy shifted his profile, turning to make full eye contact. He opened his mouth, about to say something, when a commotion at the gym entrance caught their attention. They couldn't hear the words over the music, only guttural tones and high pitched squeals accompanied by the vision of a red faced Tisha yelling at a shame faced Michael and a stone faced Rick, her breasts swinging with every jerk of her pointing finger. Ed hung back, out of the fray, appearing to enjoy the show.

As they hurried behind Tisha, Addy started to understand the gist of her tirade. Her shrill voice fought the pounding music for dominance and, in the hallway, won.

"I cannot believe you! You're disgusting, Michael."

The forty year old man bowed his salt and pepper head, shoved his hands in his dress pant pockets. "Tisha, I'm only here because you threatened me. Now you're makin' a mountain out of a mole hill. Keep this up and I'm goin' home."

Ford scrutinized the small group of adults, his eyes narrowed. "What's going on here? What's the problem?"

Rick snorted. "Nothin'. This lady needs to get a life."

Tisha exploded, the soccer mom unleashed. "You assholes were drinking! How responsible is that?! What if my daughter fell down and broke her leg? Who'd drive her to the hospital?!"

Suddenly everyone was talking at once, except Ed, who appeared relieved to be out of the spotlight. Luckily there were no kids within earshot.

Michael sputtered, loudly, "Rick brought a flask, it's no big deal, we're not drunk."

"Is this true, Mr. Hepner? You were drinking on campus?" Ford cut off Rick and Michael before they could answer, putting up an authoritative hand. "Never mind. This is ridiculous. Just go home. The dance is almost over and there's plenty of supervision without you."

Addy was dumbfounded, not sure whether to reach out to her boyfriend or not. *Is this true? Did he really bring a flask? I don't believe it.*

Rick's face was tight. "Fine. Get your coat, Addy."

There was no blood in her face, or in her brain. Her head was fuzzy, stuffed with cotton, laced with an acidic embarrassment. Unable to make eye contact with Rick, or anyone else, she mumbled a half-whisper, "I've gotta' stay. I'll see you at home."

He grabbed her arm, hard. "Don't be stupid. They don't need you."

She gasped, gritted her teeth, tried to pretend he wasn't hurting her. "I'll get a ride home." She tapped his hand, tried to draw his attention to the puckered, white skin around his grip.

Ford glowered, staring at Rick's hand on Addy's forearm. He slid forward, a vein pulsing in his forehead. Tisha pushed him aside, irreverent of his position of power, and stuck her face in Rick's. "Why don't you let her go, asshole? This isn't fucking 1950."

Rick threw up his hands, flinging Addy aside in the process. She would have toppled to the ground, unsteady on her stilettos, if Ed had not been there to grab her. She realized then Rick not only had been drinking, he was drunk. He'd never touched her before, not like this, and definitely not in public. His mode of operation was to be emotionally manipulative and sometimes verbally cruel, but immediately apologetic when he went too far. She smoothed the red satin over her hips, touched her hair, and steadied her hands, trying to figure out how to maneuver through the next few minutes. Rick marched away, an occasional stagger in his step, leaving her with a withering glare and a burn mark on her arm.

"Well, I—" she started.

"Don't you dare." Tisha's nostrils flared. "Don't you dare apologize for that asshole." She turned to Michael, the black lace enclosing her breasts taut with indignity. "Maybe you can catch a ride with him, you worthless piece of shit."

Troy Ford nodded. "I do believe it's best if you leave the premises, Mr. Mason."

Ford turned to Tisha. "And Mrs. Ives, as much as I appreciate all you've done here, you need to tone down the language." Tisha frowned, ready to go another round as Michael slipped away, the left over group in a loose horseshoe. Ford arched an eyebrow and, in a low voice, finished his thought. "Though you've said what I was thinking." He did not glance in Addy's direction.

"Amen, brother," said Ed, breaking his silence in order to agree with the athletic director for the first time in his career. He contemplated Addy out of the corner of his eye, guiltily. "Sorry."

Too stunned to respond, not sure what she would say even if she could speak, Addy spent the rest of the night hiding in corners, cleaning up spills or clinging to the gym wall for support. Tisha sought her out a couple of times but neither knew what to say; the ride home in Tisha's Taurus was equally as awkward, with a lot of conversation starters and little conversation. A thick, impenetrable bubble settled around Addy. The dome light revealed relief on Tisha's orange-tan face when they drove up to the curb in front of Addy's home. The house lights were off. The front door was buried in a black cave.

"Thanks, Tisha. And, again, I'm sorry about tonight."

"Please don't apologize anymore. Are you sure you want to spend the night here? Will you be okay?" Tisha's deeply grooved worry lines embarrassed Addy further.

"No, seriously, everything will be fine. Rick's not a bad guy."

"Well, you've got my number. You can stay with us, anytime."

Addy shut the car door, struggling not to grimace. Stay with Tisha? She hoped to God her relationship picked up, if that was the alternative. Tater tot casseroles, bunk bed in the basement, and overflowing ashtrays. Versus the erratic love of Rick? It was a tough choice.

The chill of the metallic doorknob halted her forward momentum. Did she want to keep going? Hell, they weren't married. Should she enter this door or find another? She didn't look around. The other doors were floating in an abyss, unapproachable for a wingless weakling.

CHAPTER 21
ADDY

The senior English class sluggishly took notes, doodled, or drooled quietly as Addy read a British war poem aloud. She looked up, noted the somnolence, closed the book and pried herself out of her tall chair. She was tired, too, but the teaching machine must march on.

"Siegfried Sassoon was writing about a soldier who died. He entitled the poem "The Hero." Yet, the soldier wasn't strong or brave. Do you think he was a hero?"

Some students opened up notebooks or began the search for a writing utensil.

"You don't have to write anything down. Let's just talk about it."

A field of nodding, blank faces.

She opened the book of war poems to page six and put it under the document projector. "Ok, do you consider the soldier, Jack, to be a coward?" She read the passage aloud again, with a bit more emphasis, hoping dramatic flair would at least irritate them awake.

> ... 'Jack', cold-footed, useless swine,
> Had panicked down the trench that night the mine
> Went up at Wicked Corner; how he'd tried
> To get sent home, and how, at last, he died,
> Blown to small bits. And no one seemed to care...

The discussion picked up a little, Dylan at one point falling out of his seat, tongue lolling, re-enacting the death of the soldier. Eventually, Addy got around to asking her real question.

"So, we've agreed he was afraid, tried to get out of the fight. But isn't that human nature, trying to protect ourselves? Look at it this way: he showed up. Right? He was there, in the trench, even when he didn't want to be. Isn't that in itself a type of courage?"

Nina, who rarely spoke in class, raised her hand. "Minimally. Sure, he was there, but real courage is not just showing up, you have to stand up and take action."

A pink-haired girl from the third row reacted. "Well, that's not fair! The soldier didn't ask to be there. They have to go wherever they're told to go." She rolled her eyes.

Dylan, of course, agreed with Nina. "Yeah, but a soldier can't just hunker down and call that good. Other soldiers will die because of his inaction. Whether he wants to help or not, it's his duty."

Jamy, clad in a pink cardigan, tentatively raised her hand and cleared her throat. "Same thing is true for regular people. If you see a fire start but stand there without doing anything, you're not a hero just because you didn't run away."

A lengthy boy next to Jamy nodded, making sure she saw him. "If you see a freak carjacking someone, you're evil if you *don't* try to stop it. Like Dylan said, inaction is just as bad as running away."

"Maybe if you're a cop. I don't think God expects me to give up my life. It's one thing to help, but a whole 'nother to put my life at risk," spouted the pink haired girl, defensive.

Nina bravely took a stand. "God doesn't have anything to do with this—you choose to live in a community, you also choose to take care of that community, no matter the risk. Otherwise, you might as well go live with the wolves." The teen was calm, graceful hands loose on her desk.

Addy was relieved, thrilled to witness a room full of kids analyzing strands of thought. She liked to see the hamster wheels whirring around in their brains. She kept the conversation going, saying, "Sure, but it's not always so easy to stand up and fight, is it? Many of us say we would—but would we really, in a moment of terror? Think about those girls on a Portland bus last week, the ones that beat up a fourteen year old girl. Not one person stepped in to help, to stop the fight. Not one. And there were at least fifteen passengers. The girl is in the hospital, in a coma."

Outbursts from around the room. "That's bullshit! Who does that? I would've stopped them. "

"Okay, calm down. Let's talk about this logically."

Pink hair was resolute, speaking up for the majority of humanity. "I'm not a cop—or a soldier! I don't want anyone to get hurt but I don't know how to save them, not if they're being attacked. I'm just a girl."

Nina, seemingly indifferent, asked a question to the air in front of her, her grey eyes unemotional. "If you came around the corner to find your best friend being picked on by a pack of kids, what would you do?" Her signature bracelets gave a low tinkle as she elegantly gestured to support her point.

Dylan, the littlest senior, possibly of all time, slapped Nina's desktop with a loud thwap and said, "I'd kick some ass."

Skeptical, the tall senior next to Jamy looked at Dylan. "It depends on how many of them there were. Are weapons involved? Are they comin' after me next?"

"So you're willing to face anything or anyone, but only if you know the person in trouble? And that you'll be safe?" Addy wanted to keep the ball rolling. She paced in front of their desks, enjoying the crackling energy tingling on her skin.

Dylan glared at Addy. "Jeez, okay! Not everyone's strong enough to be a hero! We get it."

"I think, more importantly, I want you to get that the world is not black and white." The young teacher was fired up, adamant, freckles alight. She continued to pace in front of the class, stopping in front multiple times to make eye contact. "Evil is not black and white. Heroic actions are not black and white. Everyday is full of surprises, many of which require action to restore balance. Will you be ready to step up? Because you can, you know. You can be the hero."

Briiing.

The bell rang. She couldn't have planned it better if she'd tried.

Addy, grateful for the break, sank carefully into the desk chair as the noisy crowd departed, propping her head in her hands. *What a crock. Who'm I to be lecturing on this? I hate discord more than I hate this goddamn rain. Hero? I didn't even stick up for my own boyfriend. I'm no hero.*

CHAPTER 22
NINA

Disheartened, Nina broke free from the small herd leaving the calculus classroom. Mr. Carter ended the period by standing, dejected, in front of a formula-laden blackboard, announcing calculus wasn't going to be offered next trimester, that the school administrators didn't believe it was fiscally responsible to run a class with fewer than ten students. All six of the current math students groaned, fully aware this was going to put them at a serious disadvantage on their college applications. Leaving the room, shoulders bowed, studiously eyeing the hall tiles, avoiding thoughts of her sinking future, someone grabbed Nina's calculus book out of her hands.

"Watcha' thinkin' about there, girly?" A towering, pimpled boy she didn't recognize was waving her textbook in the air above her head, straight out of a Bullies-R-Us manual.

"I know! Moonin' over our boy Jake, ain't 'cha?" Jake's slap-happy friend from the bus, the senior named Trent, was next to Acne Boy. Trent slithered into her space, standing so close she could feel his body heat. Nina hadn't talked to him, or Jake, since Jake introduced himself on the activity bus, only nodding an occasional hello in passing. But Jake wasn't here now, only Trent and Acne Boy.

"Can I have my book back? I doubt you have use for a math textbook." She tried to sound bored, keep her face passive. She wasn't sure if the dim-wit twins were engaging her in a light hearted moment ala first grade tactics, or if these boys had a mean streak they were raring to unleash.

Purposefully keeping herself from trying to grab her book out of the air, she leaned casually back against the wall, next to a cheery green paper Christmas tree.

"What? What was that, girly? I can't tell whatcher' sayin'." Trent's face turned cruel. "Talk normal."

Nina was pretty sure he was referring to her Bostonian accent but she didn't want to ask aloud for clarity. Mutely, she tried to push herself off the wall. Acne Boy swiftly moved forward, trapping her against the wall between his stiff arms, crumpling the paper Christmas tree under a clenched fist. Bad breath jettisoned from his thin lips into Nina's frozen face. Horrified, emotionally and physically, her mind couldn't process the moment, refusing to tell her what to do next.

"Another speech fag, come to join the fun." Trent sneered down the hall, jutting his chin at a burly boy lumbering toward them.

Wyatt. Gratitude washed over Nina, sagging her knees as Wyatt approached warily.

"Who're you callin' a fag, dickhead?" Wyatt moved slowly but steadily toward Trent.

"You, ya' pussy."

The pock-faced lackey holding Nina hostage backed away, eyes glittering as he watched Wyatt and Trent come toe to toe in the narrow high school hallway. Suddenly, she had room to maneuver. No adults around; kids were edging in closer, wanting a front row seat for the spectacle. Nina, on the other hand, craved nothing more than to be transported to another location, a quiet, solitary world. While she surreptitiously slid to the fringe of the crowd, Wyatt was busy transforming himself into the Hulk. Grabbing Trent by the armpits, Wyatt hefted the older boy into the air and shoved him against the wall. The paper Christmas tree ripped away beneath Trent's squirming, unable to withstand a secondary assault.

"Whad'ya call me?" Wyatt shook Trent, his feet swinging an inch above the tiles. "While you're hugging your little buddy here, the speech team is up against real schools. And we win. Stay away from my team."

Then he dropped the squirming senior like a sack of flour.

Trent, the varsity wrestler, couldn't stick his landing, falling to his knees, and then his hands. Before Trent could break out of his army crawl, Wyatt pushed past the kids in the hall, not even glancing at Nina. She watched him go, her shining knight in a letterman's jacket. Then she decided it would behoove her to wait in the OHS lady's room until the next bell. Better to irritate a teacher by being tardy than to draw the attention of Thing One or Thing Two again.

Her science class went by in a blur, interrupted by a trip to the office. The vice-principal caught wind of the incident, thanks to some chatty office t.a.'s, so she was called in to tell her side of the story. She kept it short and unemotional, making it clear Trent was the antagonist. Mr. Ford didn't make any comments, only taking notes. By the time school ended, Nina was calm. She made her way to the library for speech practice, glad Trent and Acne Boy were under wraps for a while. A smile quirked at the corners of her mouth as she rounded the book shelves and approached the library tables to find her hero telling his tale.

CHAPTER 23
ADDY

At the start of Tuesday's speech and debate practice, Addy schlepped in the last dusty box of playbooks from her car, pushing open the library door with her hip. Just inside, Tori grabbed the box from her coach, her straight blonde ponytail jittering in excitement.

"Ms. Taylor! Wyatt got in a fight!"

Addy whirled around. "What? Where is he?" She whipped her head back and forth, trying to spot the husky boy, praying he wasn't hurt. She didn't do well with blood. Tori pointed to the tables; there he was, sitting, calmly flipping through a dirt bike magazine.

"Wyatt. What's going' on? Tori said you were in a fight." She hovered, wringing her hands, whirring like a helicopter mamma.

Wyatt pushed back his chair, the heavy Carhart jacket scraping the table as he slowly stood and turned. Travis, his young cousin, came bounding up beside him, not letting him speak. "Man, you were awesome! Ms. Taylor, you'd be so proud of him, he was awesome!"

"So you said. Wyatt?"

"I'm sorry, Ms. Taylor." He spoke slowly, an ashamed look pulling his long face even longer.

"Sorry!" yelled Travis, the freshman hopping up and down. "You better not be sorry." Travis turned to the group. "He was protecting Nina. He was awesome."

Nina, spine ramrod straight, came into the library, arms across her chest, hands tucked into her sleeves. "It's true, he was trying to protect me." She was edging into the group.

154

"Protect you from what? Come on, guys, someone tell me what's goin' on." Addy paced her breathing, tried not to freak out.

Wyatt sat back down, sighing like an old man. "Look, it was no big deal." A flash of anger tightened his eyes for a moment though his delivery remained nonchalant, a boy describing eating a bowl of cereal or washing his face.

"Well, I mean, the fight part was no big deal. I was putting stuff in my locker when I heard a few of the guys giving someone shit. Sorry. Crap. I shut my locker and saw Nina down the hall, two senior wrestlers in her face. I went over to talk to 'em. Trent saw me comin' and called me a speech fag. Said we were a bunch a pu—. Well, you know."

He colored when he saw Addy recoil at the hateful expletives. The rest of the team had filtered in and were now silently encircling him, engrossed in his story. "I told 'im we compete against *real* teams, the big schools. Trent called me a fag again, so I grabbed him and pushed him against the wall."

"No!" Travis yelled. "He picked him up and *dangled* him—like Darth Vader dangling that Storm Trooper. He held up a senior, telling him off! It was awesome!"

There was a smattering of applause, hoots of admiration.

The young giant muttered darkly, agitated, "Look. I'm not awesome. I didn't do it to save Nina. I know what I *said*; I was just trying to look tough, dammit!" He took off his baseball cap and twisted it, hard. "The truth is, I lost my cool when he called me a fag. I wasn't trying to save anyone. I just let him get to me. Sorry, Nina. But that's the truth." His voice broke slightly. "I don't like to fight. I wasn't trying to save anyone, I just got sucked into it."

Everyone breathed, quiet. Wyatt cleared his voice, finally made eye contact with Addy. "And now I'm in trouble. I might get expelled."

"I'll talk to Mr. Ford, see what I can do." She doubted Troy Ford appreciated the nuances of this story. A strict no tolerance policy for violence was not up for debate by the administration.

"You know, Ms. Taylor, I can't play sports. I have a heart murmur. Did you know that? Well, I do. The school lawyer says I'm never allowed to touch a ball on school grounds. So here I am. A speech fag."

Stunned silence. Addy couldn't decide if it was more shocking to hear the big, sweet farm kid admit to a heart problem, describe hatred targeting her speech team kids, or for the overgrown child to toss off those horrific words so easily.

Wyatt explained himself further. "I just want to be part of something. I love sports, but I love being part of a team even more." His hand slapped the table. "This is kinda' my family now. It makes me feel good to have a place to go when I'm in trouble. It makes me mad those guys are tryin' to take that from me."

This was the most Addy had heard the boy speak, unless he was practicing lines from his speech. His passion infected the room, every teenager on the team mirroring his emotion.

"Speech fag. Let's not keep that as our motto," Gavin piped up. "I'm pretty sure the gay kids would be insulted if they saw that on the back of our team sweatshirts."

"I don't know," said Erin. "Maybe we'd get more kids on the team, appeal to the GLBT crowd. I know a few gay boys who freakin' love drama."

"We can talk about recruitment methods later." Addy put her hand briefly on Wyatt's head, tousled his hair. "You guys break up into partners, work on your stuff. You too, Wyatt. I'll go talk to Mr. Ford, see what he's planning."

As the kids wandered into corners to gossip while pretending to practice, Addy maneuvered Nina to a quiet spot.

"And you? Are you okay?"

"I'm fine." Her composed grey eyes shuttered beneath Addy's prying stare.

"Why were they harassing you? What did they do? Did they hurt you?"

"They didn't touch me. Trent and the other kid were just teasing me, that's all." Nina put her hand on Addy's shoulder, an adult gesture. "I'm fine, I promise. I'm going to go practice now, okay?"

Nina walked off, joining Tori and Ace at the new copy machine. Addy watched her leave, worried about her nonchalance but deciding Nina would rather talk to someone her age. Addy squared her shoulders. *Better go find Ford, get this thing sorted out.*

CHAPTER 24
ADDY

Treading down the hall to Ford's office, Addy's heart beat a little faster than was warranted by her pace. *Does this mean Wyatt's off the team? And more importantly, does my ass look fat in this skirt?* Pitter pat, pitter pat, Troy Ford, Troy Ford. The man who treated her like a child. The man who signed up a first year teacher as a coach and a dance chaperone. The man who publically ousted her boyfriend. She wanted to punch herself in the face for finding him attractive; her blood was heating up at the thought of the tanned crow's feet around his sea-blue eyes.

Her blood cooled when she heard her name float out of Ed's classroom. She had hoped she was passing by quick enough to evade interaction. *Hope in one hand, poop in another,* she thought.

She poked her head in his door. "Hey Ed. What's up?"

The chubby faced fifty year old had his feet up on his desk, streaming a basketball game on his computer. "Nuttin'. Just wanted to say hi." His nylon pants rustled as he awkwardly shuffled his legs off the desk, skewing piles of ungraded essays. "I'm dying of boredom since football ended."

She leaned against the doorframe. "I wish I could be bored, just for a week. I'm tired."

"I bet. How long does your debate thing go on?"

"Pretty much all year. We started in September but we don't stop going to competitions until the state tournament at the end of April."

Ed snorted, folded his meaty arms across his meaty stomach. "Jesus. That's crazy."

"I know, right? Some of the teams compete in the summer. Talk about dedication." Addy pushed off the wall. "Well, I better go. I have to talk to Ford."

She left Ed to his inappropriate use of school property, probably streaming sport's highlights and funny cat videos. She smiled, picturing Ed doing a search for Jedi Kittens. Then a boy no older than twelve, looking like an advertisement for Gap with his floppy hair and skinny pants, slid past her and silently disappeared into Ed's room. She heard Ed mutter something before his door clicked shut. *If that's his son, he may want to have a little talk with the mailman.*

Reaching the door of the school office, she was blinded by false cheer. Someone had gone crazy with the blinking holiday lights.

"Candi, is Mr. Ford available?"

Behind the high laminate desk, Candi's face registered Addy's appearance and then crumpled into a fake cringe. "Ew. No. Sorry Addy. He's got a parent in there right now."

The door to Ford's office burst open. A woman with black mascara running down her cheeks into multiple pockmarks uttered a threat as she hustled out. "You're done, Ford. You can't threaten my kid this way! You mother fu-"

"Mom!" Trent, Nina's bully, pushed the sputtering woman out of the office ahead of him, trying to keep her quiet. Clearly, she was a strong role model in his life.

Ford stood in the doorway, rubbing his hand over his eyes. "My God. This has been a long day. Candi, radio the custodian, tell him make sure that particular family leaves the building. If there's any problem, have him call me." He shifted his attention to Addy, frowning. "Are you looking for me, Ms. Taylor? I don't have a lot of time."

Responding to his curt tone, she started to step back and tell him to never mind. Then she remembered Wyatt's forlorn face. *I'm here for him.* "Mr. Ford, I-"

"Hang on. Candi, get Coach Pike up here. A couple of his wrestlers are in trouble." He strode back into his office, calling over his shoulder, "Come on in, Addy."

He called me Addy. She shivered, dread and pleasure coursing through her veins, causing her to blurt out words like projectiles. "Are you going to expel Wyatt?"

Troy Ford sat down behind a classic captain's desk. Picking up a pencil, he began tapping the eraser on the paper calendar in front of him. "Look, Addy. I've talked to Wyatt and enough other students to know Wyatt was not the instigator in this situation." He stopped tapping, leaned back. He shut his eyes, sighed, "I don't want that boy to get in trouble. But he did physically hurt Trent." He opened his eyes, looked at Addy. "Whether Trent deserved it or not doesn't matter. Wyatt has to go in front of the Expulsion Board, which will investigate and decide on the consequences. The rules are clear cut. There is a rigid, zero tolerance policy against violent contact."

"What about Trent? Did you hear the things he was saying to Wyatt? And he also had Nina cornered, but she won't tell me what he said to her. Trent started this thing."

"I know. I'm dealing with him. The problem is, he didn't touch anyone."

"Come on. Trent and another wrestler were totally bullying Nina and then Wyatt. I thought we had a strict no tolerance policy on that, too."

"Words are a lot harder to prove than the bruises Wyatt left on Trent's arms. Wyatt is not innocent." Ford's pencil beat a hard tune on the desk.

Addy tried to stand her ground. "We both know Wyatt didn't do anything. He didn't hit Trent, he just held him up. This isn't fair."

His words were clipped. "Ms. Taylor, I wish my job was about being fair. Instead, it's about upholding rules. Without rules, this building would not run. We'd have anarchy. But, like I said, I don't make the decision anyway. Alright, enough of this, I have a ton of work to do. Besides, isn't your team down in the library, unsupervised?"

"Yeah, they are. And about my team. Maybe they wouldn't be getting picked on if the school saw it as an actual team, not something to make fun of. I think the first step is for the administration to take the speech team seriously."

"I-" His eyebrows arched, showing surprise at her forceful tone.

"I'm not complaining, Mr. Ford, I'm offering a solution: how about giving Speech and Debate acknowledgement at the pep assemblies? And putting inspirational notes on their lockers? Just like they do with the other competitors here."

"Alright, I get it." Troy Ford looked at her with a tilted head. She couldn't tell if he was angry, frustrated, or simply uninterested. He continued, his face once again tired. "I don't disagree with you. But, seriously, I've got to finish these reports before five. We'll discuss this further another day."

She left his office without another word. Addy hoped the Expulsion Board would use common sense, consider the whole picture, not just the final action. *Again, hope in one hand . . .* She inadvertently wiped her hand on her skirt.

"Oh, Addy?" Candi's fake sweet voice screeched across an invisible chalkboard. Addy had almost made it to the outer door. "I'm glad I caught you. Remember, your quarterly grades are due tomorrow. I see you haven't input yours into the system yet." She tapped her gigantic computer screen with a pointy, day-glow green fingernail.

"Tomorrow? Crap."

Behind her, she heard snickering. Coach Pike, his beard freshly trimmed into a devil point, sat in the chairs against the wall, mocking her. His short, thin frame did not fill the chair, hardly any of the air above it. He crossed his arms and smirked at her as she made her way to the outer door. *What's with that guy?*

Addy didn't have time to worry about the weird football-cum-wrestling coach. Her grades needed to be entered in the next twelve hours? How? Pike was a health teacher and coach, how'd he get his done? She hurried out the door and down the hall, trying to make herself invisible until she reached the library.

She could hear Gavin and Ace, arguing over embargos. *At least they're talking about debate stuff. Or I'm assuming they are. Maybe they always sit around and talk about embargos.*

"The people of Cuba have no say over their stupid dictator; why should our embargo keep food and medicine from the island's poor people?"

Gavin poked at Ace's chest. "We're not keeping medicine from them—the dictator is."

"Boys," Addy interrupted. "Where's Wyatt?"

They broke off and looked at Addy. "His mom came to get him, the office called and said he had to leave campus."

"How 'bout Nina?"

"She didn't want to stay, she got a ride home with Wyatt. She said she'd talk to you tomorrow."

Addy mentally made a note to call her, make sure she really was okay. She briefly considered calling Nina's mother, but remembered Nina saying her mother was distracted and busy. She decided not to throw gasoline on a fire that seemed to have burned down. Besides, other fires were in immediate need of tending. For example, Jamy.

Billie was in a library corner with Jamy, cheering on the petite senior as if the poor girl was a cross country runner on the last stretch. Jamy did not look to be appreciating it.

"Jamy! Slow down." Quick mutters. " I mean it, slow down!" Dark, faster mutters. "SLOW DOWN . . . hey! I'm just trying to help!" Billie flashed a frown at Jamy's firm middle finger, and then placed her fists on her hips, about to break into cheer again.

Jamy had enough. She stood up and fired back, "It's not like you know what you're talking about, Billie."

Billie's apple cheeks blotched, water building behind her lashes. "Oh." She shoved her chair back, crossed her arms. "Thanks a lot, Jamy. Even my friends think I'm dumb." She let her long crimson locks fall across her face. A croak came from behind the shield. "I was only trying to help."

Jamy's face drooped, brown eyes wet with empathy, anger gone. "No, no! I'm sorry. I think you're super smart. Come on, who do I call every night for help with my AP government?" Her voice quailed. "I've been trying forever to get rid of this speech impediment. I sound so stupid!" Her straight bob swung around her cheeks with the force of her words.

Billie didn't stop crying, but she did wrap her arms around Jamy. Their red and brown hair mingled as they pressed their foreheads together.

Addy moved forward. "Girls?"

Both girls started talking at once. They assured Addy the argument was over, divulging the gist of the spat. Billie had urged Jamy to speak slower, more clearly, when presenting her poems. Obviously, yelling at the speed talker had not solved the problem.

Inspiration striking, the young coach picked up a pencil off the table and rubbed it down with the tail of her cardigan. She handed the yellow tool to Jamy. "Put this in your mouth."

"What?"

"Seriously. Clench it lengthwise between your teeth."

Jamy took it gingerly, placing it in her mouth with an inquisitive arched eyebrow.

"Wike wiss?" She asked.

Billie and Addy laughed. "Yes, like that," Addy said. She handed the teen her poetry manuscript. "Now, read the first two sentences aloud, slow, around the pencil."

"Ohhkwaay." Jamy read. The text sounded awkward but it forced Jamy to speak very slowly in order to pronounce every syllable. She looked at Addy and grinned, removing the pencil. "Hey, this might work." She gathered up her stuff and went off by herself to practice with the pencil, promising to get back to Addy in a few minutes.

Another fire bedded down. Look at me, coachin' it up.

After practice, Addy puttered around straightening chairs and throwing away scraps of paper. Finally, she gathered her books and papers, making her way back to her room in order to enter grades. Using her hips to push her way out the library door, she skittered forward when someone abruptly pulled the door open from the other side.

"Ed!" She caught her balance, dropping only a few papers.

"Jeez, Addy, sorry, thought I would help with the door . . ."

"Yeah, good job, Dad." The floppy haired boy she had seen earlier stood behind Ed, sneering in their direction then pointedly plugging back into his hand held device.

Ed flinched, gripping the door until his knuckles turned white. "This is my son, Matt. I'd introduce you but I hate to have you further witness his lack of manners."

The kid snorted, his eyes on the floor, music pouring from his headphones.

How did he hear that?

Ed ignored him, stepping back so Addy could fully emerge from the library. He locked the door while she gathered her papers. "Hey, Matt and I are gonna' grab some steaks at Rosie's if you want to tag along." He frowned. "Unless you're a vegetarian."

"Nope, I'm in no way a healthy eater." She glanced at her classroom door. "I totally appreciate the invite but, uh . . .

." She weighed her options, decided to be the responsible adult. "I have got to finish entering my grades." She frowned. "I'm going to be here for awhile."

Ed shuffled awkwardly, suddenly defensive. "Oh, yeah, of course. Oh, I just remembered, we need to get home anyway."

Did I say something wrong? Addy felt guilty but didn't know why. She left Ed and his son bickering in the hallway. *Wow, that kid has some pent up hostility. Poor Ed.* The prospective of a dinner with the two of them was unappetizing, but still better than her reality. She spent the next two hours in her classroom, entering grades from student assignments. The grading computer system was a nightmare to figure out. She wished Ed was still in the building so she could ask him how in the hell to submit the final reports. The training on the program consisted of, once again, being handed a business card with unintelligible directions and the voice of Darth Vader announcing, "If you can't figure it out, call the secretary. Don't lose your password."

Candi was long gone, probably bowling up a sweat, drinking Budweiser and laughing diabolically at the image of Addy trapped in the fluorescent glow of a computer screen.

Rick, on the other hand, probably imagined Addy dancing around the romantically lit staff room, drinking champagne in the company of three Chippendale strippers moonlighting as teachers. Her mind skittered away from the conversation he would want to have when she came in the front door, almost three hours after practice was over. She'd left a voice mail message for him, relieved he hadn't picked up. He was barely talking to her as it was, after the dance. Now her stuff was probably out on the lawn, waiting for her in a flaming pile.

Finally, she sweet talked the computer into accepting her work. The clock, very loudly, said ten minutes after eight. The chair creaked a listless response and then fell over when she stood up. She considered the carcass while denying her response, which was to lay down next to it and cry. Outside the window she could hear the ocean picking up energy. The winter wind blew off the sea and toward the school, the roar loud enough to be scary. *If we had a tsunami right now, I would die in this building, alone, smashed by a billion tons of white water and un-read Shakespeare textbooks.*

Thoroughly creeped out, she shut off her lights and stepped into the hall. The black, silent hall. The air left her body in a woosh. The back-up lights failed again, at least in her hall. Something or someone breathed on the back of her neck, the terror-induced hallucination prodding her nervous system into overdrive. Sliding around the corner, she could see the glowing exit sign at the end of the hallway, the only light in the building. The light was dim, but it was there.

Shaky hand slamming down the bar on the door, she gave herself permission to finally look over her shoulder.

There was a darker shadow within the dark shadow at the end of the hall. It appeared to be shifting, pulsing . . . wearing a porkpie hat.

Is that the principal? She squinted into the blackness, seeking a short Asian man in golf clothes. Nothing but dark.

Nah. Her body moved out into the night, her mind gladly followed. If the principal wanted to talk to her, he could seek her out in the glum light of day, like a living creature, not bearing a chainsaw or a hatchet. *Though I've never seen the principal in the light. Or at all. Maybe he's not real. No one can go to that many bureaucratic meetings and survive.*

CHAPTER 25
NINA

Nina stood in her kitchen, trying to block out the events of the day. Wyatt. That traitor. He wouldn't get out of her head, wouldn't stop laughing.

Wyatt saved Nina then crushed her completely within the span of a day; when he told the team he'd stepped into the fight not on behalf of Nina but on behalf of his homophobic penis, her heart literally shattered.

After the fight, and before practice, Nina spent the afternoon with an accelerated heartbeat, skipping to a happy beat. Actually happy. Someone stood up for her, took her side. At least, she thought Wyatt defended her. No. Then he admitted to not caring about her, only his stupid fragile ego, frightened into action by a gay slur. *Goddamn. I hate this school.* Rage straightened her spine, left her cold.

Once Ms. Taylor left the library, Nina became desperate to find a ride home, to at least physically transport herself away from the eighth circle of hell, the field of sewage. Her mother, of course, did not answer the page when she called her secretary at the hospital. When Wyatt's mother came to pick him up, she swallowed her pride, which, after such a beating, was fairly non-existent, and asked for a ride home. No one said goodbye as she followed Wyatt out the door; the team was too busy gossiping. No one seemed to notice as she crawled into the backseat of the Taurus, including Wyatt's mother, who backed out of the parking spot before Nina even had her door latched. No need to worry about an awkward silence; big momma had a lot to say about the fight, the suspension, and the high school administration.

The five minute ride to her house ended with the Taurus scraping the mailbox post, the yellow box left to cant, unhinged door flopping in the wind. Nina disembarked from the car with the quickness and agility of an acrobat, almost feeling sorry for the browbeaten Wyatt, under siege in the passenger seat. Almost.

The winter fog swirled wetly around her feet as the Wyatt family car slid around the corner, spewing gravel into the forest lining the road as it disappeared into the mist. Nina kicked at the partially frozen mud running over the sidewalk leading from the road to her yellow front door, deliberately trying to spatter the side of the cheery house with ugly brown earth. Despite the energetic hate focused through her toe, the clods fell short, landing soundlessly in the dead grass.

The chill followed her inside, a dark and unheated tomb. She cranked the thermostat, eschewing the fireplace. Cutting kindling and rounding up newspaper would require way too much effort. Stepping into the kitchen, flipping switches on the way, she found bare cupboards, an empty refrigerator, no note under flickering fluorescent lights. On the table were forms left for her mother to complete, the FAFSA information Nina needed to send out to colleges by next week. The forms were blank, the pen untouched, unmoved.

Wyatt's cackle continued to plague her, making her wince.

The voice mail light blinked on the landline phone. *That's odd, mom usually texts me. Maybe it's the school.* She punched the flashing red button.

"Honey, I'm not gonna' make it out there for Christmas." The message was from her dad. He sounded chipper and fake, like he was leaving a message for a client. She sat down on a kitchen stool, her legs too weak to hold her up. "I'm sorry, I really tried but I have to leave the country. China. I know it sucks but I'll bring you back something amazing. Call me back, tell me what you want. Think big. I owe ya'." Click.

Unrelenting, unceasing pain. An automaton, Nina's body carried her upstairs, into her bathroom. Not one thought crossed her mind as her body hung a towel over the mirror, pressed in the button lock on the door.

Sitting on the edge of the cold ceramic toilet, she discovered a shiny new razorblade in her hand. Still not thinking. Her body knew what to do with it, how to transform the pain. Not a sound crossed her lips as her thumb found the old white scars inside her elbow and started the flesh ladder anew, red droplets noiselessly spattering the white linoleum floor.

CHAPTER 26
ED

"Alright, I got what I need. Thanks for waiting. Do you wanna' get something to eat before I drop you off at your mom's?" Ed locked his classroom and glanced at his son.

Matt didn't answer his dad. He shuffled down the hallway, one step behind Ed, flicking through his playlist. *How in the hell does he not run into a wall?* Ed picked up his pace, considered ditching the kid. Just for a minute. His senses were redirected when he approached the library and heard fumbling on the other side of the heavy door.

He grasped the big brass handle and pulled. Addy shot through.

"Ed!" She caught her balance, scattering a few papers, before he could reach out to her.

"Jeez, Addy, sorry, thought I'd help with the door . . ."

"Yeah, good job, Dad." Matt chose this moment to step into Ed's world, give it a spin.

He glared at his boy, gut burning. *Not now. Please.* Matt, wielding a fine-tipped sword, knew just when to bury the tip. But the twelve year old seemed to stop paying attention, even when Ed asked Addy to dinner and the much younger woman started stuttering. He didn't seem to be paying attention when Ed lamely covered his embarrassment, blurting out some stupid shit about needing to get home. But, oh, the kid was listening, all right. His son dealt the death blow with perfect timing.

The tween pointed at Addy. "You think she bought that, Dad?" he yelled over his music.

Both Addy and Ed froze. Then the younger woman lurched, taking off down the hall, blonde curls bouncing with each step. With a wave behind her head, she called out, "Seriously, Ed, sorry. Some other time, kay?" She unlocked her classroom door with supernatural speed.

"Sure, sure, some other time. Take it easy," he called, clamping down on his son's wrist before the boy could open his mouth, yanking him down the corridor. Matt didn't struggle, just let himself be dragged along, a smirk tugging at the corners of his mouth.

A fine dampness engulfed them in the parking lot, a dank Pacific fog stinking of algae. Ed let go. *If I bruise him his mom will never let him come back.*

"What in the hell is wrong with you?" He leaned forward, each word bursting from his battered ego. And heart.

Matt scanned the air above his head. "Wrong with me? Classic."

"For Chrissakes! This ain't a goddamned debate!" Ed slammed an open palm onto a Honda Accord. Rust flakes sifted down to the ground. "If I'd talked to my pop like that, I'd be nursing a black eye!"

Matt shrugged, glancing casually around the parking lot, pursing his lips as if about to burst into a jaunty whistle. Ed could feel the thud of his heart in his ears, the vein in his forehead adding a secondary beat. *Why didn't I let her have that abortion?*

Sickened by his own thoughts, he fished linty Tums from his jacket pocket. Matt, drawing his hood up over his head, stood with his profile to Ed. He suddenly looked like the chatty five year old, fishing with his daddy, the sweet boy who poked Ed's belly and called him Pop-Pop. Ed could barely open his mouth to take the antacid medicine.

"Get in the car."

CHAPTER 27
ADDY

The boiler went out.

CLANK. CLANG. BANG. Hisssss. BANG.

The dying screams of the high school's ancient heating system scared students and staff alike, unsure if killer weightlifters were about to break through the walls, or if the walls were simply going to implode.

Addy sat braced half on, half off her stool in front of the fifth period English class. Many of the freshmen seemed to be equally unsure of how to react, some standing, some sitting, some under their desks. After the last ear-shattering bang, there was a moment of complete silence, the room a frozen tableau. Then one girl giggled, then another, then the rest of the class, letting out a collective burst of relief through laughter. Kids settled back into the hard plastic seats.

"Oh my God! I thought that was a gun!"

"I know! I think I need to change my underwear."

While the dark mirth was cathartic, Addy was saddened by the instinctive nature for kids to duck, that the possibility of a peer trying to shoot them was not outside of the realm of their possibilities, school shootings a scary reality. The lockdown drills were the opposite of reassuring; Addy had nightmares for days after each one.

The threat of violence passed but the steamy breath clouds and chilled fingers were real, the cold already creeping through the huge single pane windows facing the Pacific Ocean. Within minutes, kids were shivering, bombarding Addy with requests to go to their lockers for sweatshirts and jackets. She couldn't blame them, she'd already dug out an extra cardigan and put on her long rain coat, wishing she had pants rather than a knee length skirt with heels. By the end of the period, she wrapped another cardigan around her neck like a scarf and borrowed an extra pair of white athletic socks from one of the basketball players in her class, stretching the cotton as far up her leg as possible. She did not ask if they were clean. *I may not look pretty, or smell good, but I'm warm.*

Minutes before the bell was to ring, the intercom clicked on.

"This is Principal Nakamura." An irritated man's voice filled the classroom. "The boiler is broken. The parts won't be here until next week, during Christmas Break." The rarely heard, never seen principal of OHS cleared his throat. "Er, I mean Winter Break. It's not freezing so we're not cancelling school. Dress warm." Click. The Great Oz had spoken.

The room erupted in shouts. Addy let the frustration roll over her, unable and unwilling to quell their vocal outbursts. Why should she? She was cold, too, and equally as unhappy about having to sit in a meat locker for three more days. She watched from her stool without a word until the bell rang.

"Are we having speech practice today? I have to go to basketball practice first, if we are. I'll be late." Travis, the freshman, dribbled a basketball in the hallway outside her classroom, his orange hair an uncanny color match. He grabbed the door. "My partner's not here, anyway."

"We have to practice today. We have a tournament the weekend we get back. And we need to make sure everything is set for the Santa Pictures." Addy stopped Gavin before he could pass by on his way to the library. "Did you get the Santa suit from your grandpa?"

"Yeah, it's in the trunk of my car."

"Can you go get it? We need to make sure it's going to fit someone."

Gavin loped away, his black Converse slapping the tiles, high-fiving Ace as he passed the be-suited sophomore. Erin, Jamy, Nina and Tori were right behind Ace, chattering as they walked into the library. Noticeably missing was Travis's duo partner. Wyatt. Addy sighed, disheartened at the thought of the boy, sitting alone, in his bedroom, listening to death metal and playing Call of Duty.

She was pulled from her reverie by Ed erupting from his classroom, tugging a baseball hat on his head, jacket in hand. He glanced over at her while he sifted through his key ring, trying to fit the right key to his door, his hand shaking. "Hey, Addy."

"Wha's up, Ed? You taking off early?" She tamped down the awkwardness buzzing around her ears, hoping he didn't bring up his son. She hadn't talked to Ed since grade night.

"Pah. I have to get over to the bank, move some money around." He grunted. "Money I don't have." He stopped in front of her, bouncing on the balls of his feet. "How 'bout you? Got practice again?"

"Again. And again. For a few more months." She nodded toward the library. "But that's okay. The kids are pretty into it."

"Life of a coach. Make sure you're stayin' sane. Well, 'night." He trudged down the corridor, shoulders drooping, track pants swoosh-swoosh-swooshing. Addy wanted to run after him, give him a hug. *You reject his offer for dinner than hug him? No mixed signals, Addy.*

Addy moved into the library and gathered the students at the round tables, tethering herself to her charges, bolstering her spirits with their energy. *I'm an energy vampire.*

"Where's Billie?"

"She's coming after cheer practice."

"Okay. I'm not going to wait. We're going to hold a mini tournament." She did a head count. "There are seven of you. You're going to perform, one at a time. The team's going to be the audience, filling out a critique ballot for each speaker." She looked around the group carefully. "It's important you're honest. Being nice to your friends isn't helpful. Don't write things like 'I really like your speech' or 'that's a great topic.' You might as well stab your buddy in the back. It isn't going to help anyone win."

"Are you giving us permission to be mean?"

"No. You know what I'm saying, Erin. And I'm not only going to write suggestions on your ballots, I'm also going to score you. I'll give the best speaker first place."

"Whoopdee do. What do we get for first?"

"I'll buy the winner lunch at the next tournament."

"You already buy us lunch!"

"Jeez, tough crowd. Alright. The winner will get . . . to wear the Santa suit at the fundraiser next week."

Groans. "What?! That isn't a prize!"

"You guys are crazy!" Ace jumped up. "I totally would love to be Santa! Imagine freaking out those little kids!"

"Okay Ace. Reel it in. I don't know what you mean by that, but I don't think I'm going to let you be Santa." They laughed at his face.

"Ms. T?" Billie crouched next to her. "Can I try practicing an extemp speech with Ace?"

Addy turned to her. "You want to talk about current events?"

"Yeah, I watch CNN every morning. And my mom listens to talk radio all day." The teen blew a raspberry, pursing her highly glossed lips. "I can talk about family values and moral politics better than most of those guys."

Addy grinned. "I believe that, little missy. Give it a shot. Ace has a list of topics." *Good luck to you. I can't imagine anything more mind numbing. The judges will never see you coming, little miss thang.*

"Alright everyone, let's get going. Most of you have at least two speeches you've been working on, so pick one. I'll give you ten minutes to practice, then we're going to meet back here. Go."

While they raced into separate corners to perfect their delivery in front of a wall, Addy sat at the librarian's computer, trying to find an on-line schedule for the next competition. Suddenly, the phone next to her rang. She hesitated before picking it up, thinking she should let it go to voicemail since it was afterhours. Her hand hovered over the grimy library phone until she realized the caller might be a speech parent with a message for their child.

"Library." She was pleased with the official sound of her voice.

"Addy, hi."

"Rick? How'd you get me in here?"

"I tried calling your cell but you didn't answer. So I called the school and the secretary transferred me. She's not very pleasant, by the way. Her voice sounds like two cats, fucking."

"Classy, Rick. Must have been Candi. Surprised she's still here. What's up?"

"I just got a phone call from my mom. She says she needs to know when we're going to get there, how many days we're staying, if we'll be there for Christmas dinner, that kind of thing."

"Remember, I have that fundraiser next Tuesday. So we can leave Wednesday, or even late Tuesday night if you want."

He was quiet. "I forgot about that." His voice became irritated. "Wednesday is Christmas. I don't want to be driving on Christmas Eve or Christmas. This sucks."

"I know, I know, but it's only a couple of hours." She tried to lift his mood. "Look at it this way. The longer we're here, the shorter time we have to spend with our parents."

"Speak for yourself. *My* parents aren't a problem."

She agreed, in theory, her parents were generally unpleasant, bickering over who's turn it was to walk the dog, but that didn't mean she wanted to hear her boyfriend deride them. Defeated, she said, "You decide when we leave, it's fine, whatever."

Rick became petty, peevish. "Maybe I'll go without you, leave earlier."

"Why're you being like that all of a sudden? I never said I didn't want to go, I just can't leave until Tuesday night. Come on Rick."

"Whatever. I'll see you when you get home. I assume you'll be late." He hung up.

She held the phone to her ear, stared into space. Nina stepped in front of the librarian's desk. The tall, thin girl straightened the cardboard reindeer and sleigh on the counter, unsure if Addy had someone on the other end of the line. Addy didn't know if she was ready to talk yet, so just stared at Nina.

Addy sighed, hung up. "Must have been disconnected. Did you need something, Nina?"

Nina's pretty grey eyes were tired, puffy. "Ms. Taylor, I was wondering if I could go first. I need to catch up on some AP chemistry homework."

"Yeah, I don't see why not." Addy searched her face. "Anything wrong?"

Nina's shoulders moved back, her chin up. She grinned, showing perfect, white teeth. "No, I just have a ton of homework lately." Her long neck bent toward the wall clock. "Do you want me to call the gang back together?"

Addy put Rick's spiky voice out of her head, knowing she'd have plenty of chances to deal with their issues during vacation.

The kids gathered around her. Surprisingly, she relaxed over the next two hours, leaning back in her chair, wrapped in sweaters, socks and coats, entertained by her team. They put their hearts into their performances, delighting her with the polish and charisma they'd developed over the past few months. Travis wasn't so stiff anymore, Tori no longer smirked and paced, Nina didn't throw her hands in the air like an overwrought Hamlet every five seconds, Jamy taught herself to slow down by practicing enunciation around the pencil clenched between her teeth. Their dedication and hard work was paying off. She smiled and nodded at them, giving encouragement with her eyes and body language. She didn't have to say a word.

CHAPTER 28
ADDY

"**M**s. T, can you turn the heat up?" called Billie's voice from the damp, quiet darkness in the bowels of the bus.

"No!" growled Dylan, closer to the front. "I'm sweating. Turn it down!"

The OHS Speech and Debate Team members began to stir in the stiff mini-bus seats, awakened by the arguing and the uncomfortable temperatures. The crazy microclimates within the bus were driving Addy insane. She was sick of turning the heater up, turning the heater down, turning the radio up, turning the radio down, turning the heater up, while trying to maneuver the bus around blind corners on the snowy country highway leading into Portland. *Handles like a minivan, my ass.* In her wildest dreams, Addy had never have pictured herself captaining anything bigger than a four door sedan, maybe even a new Subaru Outback, but a bus? *I will not be mentioning this at my ten year high school reunion.*

"Dylan, move off the heater. Billie switch seats with him."

Mother Nature hit the rain button, cranked the dial to "deluge." Addy turned on the windshield wipers only to discover the seal was broken on the driver side, leaving a wide swath of water in the middle of her vision. She bent low over the ridiculously huge wheel, summoning her x-ray vision to find the road.

Thirty minutes out, Tori roused her sleeping teammates. Addy let the junior class president poke the slumbering bears, especially after witnessing their grumpy reactions. Addy was amazed by the blonde teen's whirl of pro-action;

she changed from pajamas into her power skirt suit under a blanket, used the heavy dew from the bus window to slick her pony tail into submission, handed out tournament schedules for the day, and made sure the boys retied the kindergarten-esque knots in their ties and exchanged their muddy tennis shoes for dress shoes.

That girl will be president of the world someday. Maybe she'll hire me to be her secretary. "Tori, can you help me figure out the directions?" Addy took the exit off Highway 26 to Pine Grove. "They're in my bag, under my seat." With Tori's help, they only got lost once, executed a twenty point turn on a dead end street, and made it to Pine Grove High School fifteen minutes before the tournament was to start.

"Okay, guys, as usual we're cutting it short. Make sure you have your speeches, I'll get your codes. Let's go."

The morning went by quickly. The small team bunkered down in a corner of the vast cafeteria, foraying out to their rounds, returning to eat junk food, practice their speeches, play video games, listen to their ipods, emit the stench of teen angst and scope out the opposite sex between performances. Addy checked in with them between judging rounds. She ended up being sent into a different speaking round every hour, six hours in a row, because the tournament director had not been able to procure enough judges, meaning the volunteers that did show up had to fill out ballots until their fingers arced into bent pieces of cement, permanently damaged by writing critiques for hours at a time.

Finally, she hid in a bathroom stall, reading a magazine in a crouch over the toilet until her thighs cramped. Praying there were no more ballots to be handed out, that every room had a judge, she snuck out, passing the judges' table nervously. No one stopped her. Not pausing or looking around, she bee-lined it to the Home Ec room, purported to have free food for the judges. She found a single dry slice of bread and wilted lettuce. She shrugged, adding mayo and mustard for flavor, and hopefully, calories. There was plenty of coffee in a gigantic urn, for which she was hugely grateful. Until she took a drink. Normally a black coffee kind of girl, she sought out creamer and sugar packets, craving the caffeine but barely able to cough down the burnt Folgers until she performed emergency surgery.

She sat in one of the chairs behind a row of ancient sewing machines, settling in with the latest edition of US Weekly. Engrossed in the life and times of Angelina Jolie, she jumped when the door opened. She tried not to look guilty when a handful of coaches entered.

"Ah, crap. I knew we were going to miss the sandwiches," said a man in his mid-thirties, sporting a Battle Star Galactica tshirt and long black hair tied in a ponytail.

"If it makes you feel better, I don't think there were ever any sandwiches. I stole someone's lunch out of the refrigerator. Shhh," a hulking older male coach responded. Addy couldn't see his face, only a wild, thick mane of white hair and a beat up leather jacket on the back of a gentleman who clearly had to shop at *Big and Tall.*

"Dude, you are not cool."

Laughter. They made their way to the coffee urn.

"I wouldn't do that if I were you, " Addy's voice cracked, wavered, forged ahead. "There isn't enough sugar in the world to change tar into coffee."

"Oh, I don't know," said the guy with the ponytail. "I'm adept at this particular form of alchemy." He poured the black brew into a used cup off the counter, no new ones in sight. "Though I appreciate the heads up. You're the new Oceanside coach, right?"

"Yes. Addy Taylor." She smiled shyly, getting up to shake his hand.

"I meant to introduce myself sooner. I'm Jeremy Catt. My school's in your district." His handshake was friendly, his demeanor calm and confident. "And this is Patrick.

Patrick Ogilvy. Be glad he's not in our district. His team is killing it this year."

Patrick turned away from the coffee urn, cup in hand, extending the other to Addy.

She tried very hard not to stare at the black eye patch covering his left eye. "Uh, hi." She hoped she didn't sound as stupid as she felt, looking everywhere but his eyes—*eye*—as she shook his hand.

"So, you have a thing for Pirates."

"What, no, I—" she spluttered.

His hearty guffaw resounded off the dingy walls. "Your sweatshirt, Ms. Taylor, I'm referring to your sweatshirt."

She looked down at the Oceanside Pirate biting a knife on her chest. Glancing back up, she lamely tried to save face, "Oh, yeah, my school's mascot." She trailed off, sat back down and fingered a magazine on the table in front of her, wondering if she should pretend to start reading, unsure of where else to look. *Why am I such a tool?*

Jeremy groaned. "Way to go, Patrick. Now we're going to have to wait another three months for her to speak again." He pulled out a chair next to her, sat down. "Seriously, Addy, ignore him. He only wears the patch to orchestrate awkward moments such as these."

Patrick snorted and also grabbed a chair with a huge, calloused hand, sitting down in a surprisingly graceful manner for such a bear of a man.

Fight or flee?

"You don't look much like a Pirate, even with the patch. You look more like a biker. Or Mad Eye Moody from *Harry Potter*." She held her breath.

"Well, now, I take that as a compliment," said the grizzled older man, pleasure on his face until he took a slurp of his coffee. "Jeremy, why don't you shut your word hole and make us some fresh coffee?"

Hanging out in the Home Ec room with Jeremy and Patrick, Addy found herself laughing numerous times, eventually comfortable enough to ask the questions she'd been squirreling away the last few months. The men seemed willing and able to answer her queries, as well as fill her in on the gossip in regards to Oregon's coaching circuit. By the time they were done, Addy wasn't nearly as intimidated by the debate coaches she'd moments before considered brilliant, omnipotent gods. Now she had dirt on most of them. She could stand tall in their presence, having only to remind herself of the torrid affairs in locker rooms, or drink fests on the empty busses, or the head banging to Bon Jovi at award ceremonies. *Brave of Jeremy to admit to that. I'll have to YouTube his long-haired head bang when I get home.*

"So, Addy I hate to break this to you, seein' how you finally pulled that stick outa' your backside, but you know your school is hosting the District tournament this year, right?" Patrick rubbed his eye patch as he spoke, as if he could polish it enough and finally see through it.

She went cold. "What do you mean?"

"Oh, you know, we've had a running bet whether you're a robot or just shy."

"Not about that! I'm talking about Districts. I have to put on a tournament? That's crazy. I have no idea how a tournament is run. Especially one that qualifies kids for the State tournament!" Horror dripped like tar in her veins.

"Patrick! She's not even in your District. This is my conversation to have, not yours." Jeremy twisted his lank, black ponytail, eyeing Addy sideways. "Don't worry, our district coaches will help you. You've met Juanita, right? She's in our district, too." He shrugged. "It's not a test or anything. It's just that it's Oceanside's turn in the rotation. Each school takes a turn hosting so there's a home field advantage once every five or six years."

"I'm pretty sure it's not going to be advantageous to my team to have me in charge," Addy grumbled.

Jeremy grinned, "Seriously, it's not as bad as you think. It's small, with less than ten schools." He patted her white-knuckled fist resting on the table. "We'll do it together."

Patrick swallowed hard, sputtering coffee. "Do it."

"Wha—I didn't mean it that way!" The younger coach dipped his head, embarrassed.

The conversation moved from fruitful to frustrating to fifth grade in the span of a minute. Addy extracted herself, leaving the men at the orange Home Ec table, claiming she needed to check on her kids. She found her way to the cafeteria, seeking out her team while avoiding the coaches running the judges' table.

The rest of the day sped by, the rush slingshotting her into the late evening.

Five of her ten students made it into the final rounds of their events; she was ecstatic. Jamy and Nina ran back from the posting wall, holding hands, jumping up and down excitedly. "We both made it to the Poetry final round!" One of them shrieked, Addy wasn't sure which one. Even the kids who were done for the day graciously let go of their gloom, for the moment, thrilled to be part of a succeeding team. Ace was in the Impromptu final round, Erin broke into the final for Oratory, and Tori was still competing in Radio. Gavin, Travis, Billie and Dylan did not break and so divvied themselves up, making sure each Oceanside competitor had a team member in the audience for support. The energy of the teens crackled, filling the air with delight.

Moving into the auditorium two hours later, waiting to hear the results, Addy and the team were jittery, giggling at the smallest provocation. Jamy, her pixie face glowing, hadn't stopped talking since she left her final round. No one could understand what she was saying, since she was telling story after story at the speed of light, but no one wanted to interrupt the stream of excited, happy chatter, instead choosing to flow with her. Other teams filtered in, filling up the theatre seats, bringing the noise level to astounding heights. Finally, the tournament director galloped in and waved them to quiet, his tie askew, his blue dress shirt adorned with wide, dark circles of sweat under the arms. Addy was glad she wasn't on stage with him, afraid his odor would bowl her backwards.

"We're almost ready with the results. I'll be back in a few moments. While you're waiting please send a couple people from each team back into the cafeteria to finish cleaning up your area. I say this with love: you guys are pigs." He slunk out of the spotlight, accompanied by groans and catcalls and a few beach balls.

The catcalls were rejuvenated within minutes when the tournament director, hair and tie flapping in synchronicity, hurried back across the stage, tapping the microphone. The noise died down almost instantly, a cold silence, not because the coach was on stage but because everyone in the auditorium simultaneously noticed something disconcerting; standing on the narrow steps leading up to the stage were two uniformed police officers.

The Pine Grove coach cleared his throat, leaned into the microphone.

"Will-" The feedback squealed loud enough to make Addy gasp.

Sheepish, he stepped back. "Sorry. Will the coach from Oceanside High School meet me at the stage steps?"

Silence. Addy felt the sound in the auditorium sucked into a void, the only noise a thrumming heartbeat in her ears. She turned to Nina beside her. "Did he just ask for me? Did I hear that correctly?" The senior's stunned grey eyes confirmed the odd request.

"Ms. Taylor? What's going on?" Her students were frantic as she pushed past their seats, grabbing at her skirt and jacket as she went by, their need to know turning physical. She had no answer for them, only a blank look, a whispered, "I don't know."

The officers and the tournament director ushered her outside the auditorium. Just outside the doors, she could stand it no longer, on the verge of tears. "What? What is this? What's going on?"

The woman officer, sensing the impending melt down, explained quickly. "No one's hurt. Your athletic director, a Mr. Ford, called us because he's not been able to reach you."

Addy pulled out her cell. She'd turned it off while listening to speeches and forgotten to turn it back on. Flicking the power button initiated a series of beeps, indicating a number of missed calls and texts. The officer continued.

"He called to tell you to start home right away." Addy sucked in her breath. The woman put a kind hand on her arm, squeezing. "You're fine if you leave now. Right now."

"I don't get it."

"Two of the three highways accessing the roads leading into Oceanside have major slides covering the roads. The road department says the debris won't be cleared for at least a day, especially while it's still pouring down rain. Unfortunately, the one highway left open is starting to flood. If you leave now, you'll be getting to the flood zone just as the ocean switches to an incoming tide. If you wait any longer, you'll have to spend the night on this side of the flood zone. Your athletic director wants you to try to get your team home before that happens."

Why did I move to the coast? What in the hell was I thinking?

The OHS team stealthily inched into Addy's vicinity, white faced teenagers listening to the adults make decisions regarding their lives. Addy recognized the feelings oozing off them from her own heart; it was lack of confidence in their leader.

"Are you sure we'll be safe?"

The other officer, an iron gray handle bar mustache twitching when he talked, joined the conversation. "You should be fine if you go slow. There don't appear to be any mudslide threats on Highway 53 right now. And if the water looks too high when you get to the flood zone, turn around. It's better to spend the night away from home than risk getting sucked down the river."

"Are you escorting me?" Addy was hopeful, wanting someone else to step in, be in charge. *I can't do this. Seriously. I can't. There's going to be another mudslide. I need someone else to drive. We're all going to die.*

The woman patted her arm again, her stiff dark uniform no longer comforting. "Honey, you'll be fine. We would if we could but this isn't an emergency. You just need to get going, and be careful."

Not an emergency?

Addy noticed Tori exchange looks with Billie as they scanned her face. She was bemused as the sixteen year olds pulled their peers into a huddle, Tori barking commands. "Dylan, you and Ace go back into the auditorium, grab any coats or backpacks left on our seats. Erin, can you run back to the cafeteria, make sure we have all of our stuff from there?" She looked at Addy, expectantly, offering the reigns with a twitch of her nose.

Addy awoke from her stupor, the synapses in her brain beginning to fire again. She spoke without forethought. "The rest of you, fill your water bottles, go the bathroom, meet back here in exactly five minutes. Tori, here's twenty bucks, run to the concessions stand, buy a bunch of granola bars and potato chips."

"Dinner on the bus, huh?"

"Yeah, looks like it."

Another coach, Juanita, her gentle face wrinkled with concern, bustled down the hall to the tense ball of people, carrying a large manila envelope and a handful of certificates. "Addy! I was in the tab room, heard you needed to leave early. Here."

She shoved the paperwork into Addy's stiff hands. "What else can I do?" she asked, rocking on the soft soles of her black walking shoes. Patrick and Jeremy came up behind her, also offering to help.

Sucking on a papercut, Addy grimaced. "Thanks, Juanita, guys. Unless you can abandon your own teams and drive us home, I think we're good." They exchanged phone numbers, knowing it wouldn't be much help once Addy was in the mountains, out of range.

The police officers edged away. Addy shook hands with them both, the woman giving her hand an extra squeeze. Addy smiled weakly. "Thanks for finding us. I didn't even know the police did this kind of thing."

The mustachioed cop said, "Good luck," and hurried his partner down the hall and out the door. Addy would have felt better if the female officer did not look so worried.

The kids completed their tasks in what seemed to be seconds and reported back to her, big eyes surrounding her, silently questioning.

I don't want to do this! I can't do this! Isn't there anyone willing to take over?

She drew a deep breath. "Ok, Pirates. Get your asses on the bus. Move. Move!"

CHAPTER 29
ADDY

"Ms. T, are we gonna' die?"

Yes.

"No. Dylan, sit down." She glared at them in the rearview mirror. "Come on, you guys! Put on your seat belts."

She heard scrabbling behind her, but no clicks.

"Ms. Taylor?"

"Put your seatbelt on!"

"Uh, I can't. There aren't any seat belts."

Safety first, unless it's money first. "Okay. Pack your bags in around you, keep the aisle clear, stay in your seats. If you go flying past me, grab onto my hair."

"Wow, that's love, Ms. T."

"I don't want your parents to sue me."

The mini bus was pushed around the highway by the wind gusts, pulled around by the rain funneling down the pavement. Addy wouldn't let the kids sleep, making them sing along with her to Jack Johnson and Adele, even Christmas songs, whatever it took to stay awake and focused, to keep the terror at bay. She was having an out of body experience, standing behind her own shoulder, watching this young woman she felt no connection with drive a bus through a dark and definitely stormy night into a flood.

By the time they traversed the mountain pass, fir trees waving frantically, rain made denser by dark fog, the bus floor was littered with Dorito bags, sunflower seeds and sticky puddles, not to mention errant dress socks, a pink high heel, soggy notebook paper and a deflated beach ball. Addy could hear the wind whistling through the unsealed metal trim on the windows as the mountain pass dipped down to the sodden coastal road.

She let the singers off the hook when Gavin started asthmatically wheezing. He was having a hard time breathing in the overly moist air and his inhaler was, of course, at home. This quieted everyone down, quick. Addy passed back a paper bag for Gavin to breath into, unable to think of anything else. Nina sat with Gavin, keeping him calm, holding the bag for him when his arms became weary. Despite his physical discomfort, Gavin seemed pleased to have the attention of the pretty girl, laying his head on her shoulder at one point, Nina caressing his hair like a mother with her child. Dylan sat facing the two, glaring.

They were approaching the flood zone. She re-focused her concentration, afraid she would run into unseen water and hydroplane. *Keep it pg back there, kids. I don't have time to worry about baby speechies right now.*

But before they encountered water, they encountered the police. Again. This time, the night sky a mile south of Oceanside was lit with strobing yellow lights, multiple cop cars blocking off Highway 101. One of the officers, hidden in the depths of a billowing, shiny yellow rain coat and wide brimmed hat, bent against the wind and made his way toward the bus as she slowed to a stop in the middle of the road.

She cranked open the accordion door, letting in swirling sheets of rain. The spray missed her but the bundled form in the front seat was not so lucky. Dylan shot upright, yelling, "What the—" His face shined with wet diamonds, more showering him as the door was held open.

"Sorry," shouted the state trooper, leaning into the bus's cavity, throwing an impish smile at the now sodden teen glaring down at him. Then the trooper turned to Addy, serious. "The road is flooded."

"Is there a detour?"

"Nope."

"Is there any way for me to get through here?"

"Big rigs like this have been crossing with no problem, but there is about six inches of water covering the road, more all the time. The flood is a couple of hundred yards wide. We're not letting cars or pickups through." He eyed the huddled teenagers in the back. "I don't know if you should try crossing with kids on board."

"Are you saying I can't, or that I shouldn't?"

"Like I said, you have enough clearance. But I wouldn't do it."

Addy's nerves were frayed. The thought of sleeping on this stinky, damp bus with the kids was not appealing; her credit card was maxed out, hotels were out of the question, she couldn't even buy these starving kids food. More importantly, Gavin was breathing like a log truck, blond spikes pasted to his sweaty head. He needed his inhaler, and there was no pharmacy open this late. *Go. Or don't go.* Both options carried danger. Which was the best for the kids?

The trooper blocking the door just looked at her, blankly. She eyed him speculatively, seeking an answer. He didn't have one. He didn't seem worried or upset, only irritated. That nonchalance spoke volumes to her, even if it was the calm, false voice of the devil. *Trucks are making it, we can make it.*

She wanted to ask "what's the worst case scenario?" but didn't want to hear "the bus rolling and filling with river water" so she put the question in lock-down.

"I'm gonna' try it."

She didn't know if her courage was inspired by desperation to help Gavin, or simply to have this over with. The trooper shrugged. "It's your call. The water starts on the other side of that cruiser. You should have plenty of room to get around the cars. I'll radio ahead, make sure no one is coming from the other side. Wait for me, I'll signal with my flashlight when you can go. Good luck. " He pushed the door shut, leaving a puddle running down the stairs.

I can't do this.

But Wonder Woman would. She'd do it. Addy became Wonder Woman. Looking down, the interior lights glinted off her metal bra and bracelets. *Okay, stop screwing around. Go.*

The trooper's flashlight arced across the highway, moving back and forth in short bursts. Addy turned on her blinker, started forward. Maneuvering through the police cars was stressful, with hardly enough room to keep her from scraping the black and white paint jobs. However, not as stressful as stepping on the gas, propelling a bus full of kids into a shallow river.

She drove into the water. *It's just a really big mud puddle.* She could feel the drag on the steering wheel immediately.

Dylan, his dark hair plastered against his white skin, was leaning over the rail in front of his seat. "Umm, Ms. Taylor?"

"I'm a little busy right now." Addy bent forward, her sternum pressed painfully into the wheel. Peering through the spattered, streaky windshield, her eyes kept trying to readjust, her brain unable to accept the living, moving surface that had replaced the asphalt. The swish, swish, squeal of the wiper amped her anxiety to the highest level sustainable for a human.

"Ms. Taylor."

Addy, irritated, ready to snap, opened her mouth to yell at Dylan.

Seeing her face, Dylan didn't speak again, instead pointed adamantly at the stairs beside her. Addy looked down. The floodwater seeped under the tri-fold door, slowly creeping up the metal stairs. Brown froth was already to the upper lip of the bottom step.

"Damn." She averted her eyes, face tingling as the blood departed her head. *That's not real. I'm watching tv. This is a scene from a movie.* The pull on the steering wheel was becoming unwieldy. The taut muscles in her forearms and triceps started to ache, book-lifting apparently not having prepared her for this adventure. *Steady on the gas. This too shall pass. Oh hell. I'm rhyming.*

She heard a hoarse whisper behind her. "It's almost to the top of the second stair."

She was glad Dylan had the sense to keep this information between the two of them, the rest of the team chattering excitedly amongst themselves, pointing out the windows like they were on the Pirates of the Caribbean ride at Disneyland. She tried not to look down but the temptation was too much. Glancing over, she was momentarily distracted not by the water on the stairs but by the heavy, musty steam. The white vapor floated above water filled with swirling dead leaves, multicolored plastic confetti, and indeterminable brown chunks. *If I spot a condom, I'm going to freak. 'Cause that's my breaking point. Garbage in the water.*

She tore her gaze away, fixed her stare on the job in front of her. She depressed the gas petal, gently, praying frantically, inarticulately. They continued to move forward. Addy's heart filled with icy sludge. Suddenly, she thought she felt them floating, perhaps moving sideways, not just forward. Before she could gather enough breath to screech in terror, the tires bumped and gripped. Slowly, oh so slowly, she pushed down further on the gas pedal, swallowing her scream.

Don't stall, don't stall, don't stall. The internal chant rang in her head for what seemed a lifetime, hypnotizing her. Her mind was on autopilot. She was afraid to flip the switch back to pilot. No need to disturb her catatonic state.

Dylan had his head hung over the rail. "The water's gone back down. I can see the bottom step again. At least part of it."

A minute later, "I can see the silver tread on the bottom of the staircase."

Then, the tension on her arms and chest muscles relented. The bus was on dry land. They were free.

Most of the kids cheered but she heard a few sobs intermingled in the noise. Or maybe that was her psyche, adding to the cacophony.

She drove past the northern police barrier, cops encased in shiny yellow plastic standing well out of the way. A hundred yards further, she jerked the bus onto a wide gravel shoulder. Addy threw off the lap harness, yanked open the door, leapt down the stairs, and burst into the wet night. Leaning against the bus, she vomited. And vomited some more. The tournament pizza and donuts provided generous amounts of adornment for the large black bus tires. The rain funneled down her face and over her long hair, darkening and weighing down her clothes, cooling the fire in her limp body.

Gentle fingers smoothed the hair from her forehead. Jamy, tiny Jamy, stood beside her. Addy shot up, moving her shaky sea legs squarely under her.

"I'm fine," she whispered. She cleared her throat, spit. "Thanks."

"No, thank *you*." Jamy touched her arm. "You were amazing, Ms. Taylor. You got us through a *flood*."

Addy tapped Jamy's cheek lightly, the rain glistening on the upturned teen's face. "Honey, I'm not amazing. Look at me." She chortled darkly, sweeping her hand over her spattered clothes. Then she realized she was appealing to her student to soothe her ego. *Jesus, get it together.*

The teen leaned her body into Addy's. The teacher stood strong, gave her a hug. Then she pointed at the white faces pressed against the steamy windows. "We think you should join the Coast Guard."

Addy laughed. It felt good. "I guarantee that is never going to happen. This mud puddle almost did me in." Despite her words, Addy was proud of herself. She'd made a tough decision and then pulled it off; no one else stepped in—she stepped up. She stood straighter.

Jamy started to talk again but Addy held up her hand. "Ok, ok, thank you. Let's get going; I have a feeling Gavin would be very grateful for a solid lungful of air." She steered Jamy ahead of her onto the bus. "Speaking of, I don't want to leave him and Nina without adult supervision."

Jamy gave her a quizzical look, one foot on the bus steps. She leaned back to Addy and whispered, "You know Gavin's gay, right?"

"Oh." *How did I miss that?* "Well, maybe someone should tell Dylan."

As everyone settled back down, and Addy's nerves reorganized themselves into human form, she eased back onto the asphalt, blackened by rain but blessfully visible. Even Gavin's breathing seemed calmer.

She smiled into the rearview mirror. Every face was turned toward her, waiting. Filling the uneasy silence with a new, softly confident voice, she said, "Ok kids. We've made it this far, we're going to be fine."

The road appeared to be clear.

CHAPTER 30
ADDY

Oceanside's weather-battered tower clock struck midnight as the small yellow bus rolled past, the face shadowed and blurred by the unrelenting torrent of water.

Weary, drained of life, Addy weakly spun the wheel, steering them into the high school parking lot.

"Why are so many lights on in the building?" Dylan palmed the steam off the window, trying to get a clear look at the high school, the front side of the building lit up like a Christmas tree.

Addy frowned, too tired to process. "I don't know. I don't think I turned on any lights when we left this morning." *This morning? Seems like last week.* "Maybe the basketball team just got back."

Ace moved forward to Dylan's seat. "My sister's in basketball. They got back this afternoon. They had a morning game." He blew out a frustrated breath. "They beat the road closures."

Addy didn't care about the lights, only her bed. She spoke loud enough for everyone to hear. "We're all tired but I need you guys to pick up the garbage off the floor, put it in this bag. The floor has to be cleaned up before I let you off this bus." She paused. "Except you Gavin. If you can get your mom here, you can go."

There were groans and muttered curse words. Travis kicked his backpack like a pouting toddler. Erin shoved trash into the plastic garbage bag and started bitching at him, her long black curls swinging with attitude. Addy ignored their behavior, understanding exactly where the feelings were coming from.

"Come on, hop to."

Jamy piped up from the back, "Ms. Taylor, is there any way you could tell us the results of our final rounds?"

"Oh my God. Kids. I'm so sorry." She rescued her messenger bag from below the seat she'd crammed it under, the papers Juanita handed her long forgotten. She groaned, slapped her forehead. "I'm a horrible coach."

Billie giggled. "We know. But we still love you."

Amid exhausted, manic laughter, Addy passed out the embossed finalist certificates. Addy, beaming, handed Jamy a Second Place certificate, then squealed like a poked pig when she saw Nina's certificate. Nina was the Poetry Champion. The team went crazy, whooping and high-fiving each other. Jamy, happy tears on her cheeks, hugged her new family. Nina merely seemed bemused, calmly sliding the certificate in her bag and cleaning up her seat area, quietly smiling at each congratulatory remark.

Everyone screamed when, suddenly, there was a pounding on the outside of the bus door. The tri-fold screeched open. Addy expected a grizzled, one-eyed killer with an axe. Not Troy Ford.

"What in the hell are you doing in here?!" The vice-principal's hair was askew, his thick sweatshirt crumpled, his cargo shorts sporting salsa stains. Or blood. He may not have been a killer but he looked crazed, his blue eyes wide and frantic. "You pulled in here ten minutes ago!"

"Mr. Ford!! What're you doing here?" Tori and Addy yelled the exact same words at the exact same time. They exchanged a look and burst out laughing, which only increased the bewildered look on Troy Ford's face.

Addy stood in the aisle between the front seats, acutely aware of her clinging, drenched clothes and stringy, wet hair.

He mounted the stairs, his eyes even with hers for the first time. His face was distraught, worry lines around his eyes.

Oh man. He found out how high the water was when we crossed.

He stepped further into the bus, ducking his head to avoid bumping his noggin. "Are you kids okay?"

There was a round of silent nods, no one sure what he wanted, visibly wondering if they were in trouble.

"Addy. Why are you wet? Are you okay?"

"I'm fine. We're all fine. Well, except Gavin. He needs his inhaler."

Gavin gave Ford a head dip, trying to be cool while wheezing and whistling with each breath.

Ford dragged his fingers through his auburn hair. "What can I do to help?"

She was surprised. "Umm, we need to get the bus clean, make sure all the kids get home. As a matter of fact, we can't get a hold of Gavin's mom. He needs to get home right away so he can get his inhaler."

"I can do that. Get your stuff, buddy. I'm parked right there." Gavin finished gathering his belonging, gave Jamy and Nina hugs, saying prolonged goodbyes, as if he wasn't going to see them in two days.

"Addy, can I talk to you for a minute?"

She followed Ford out of the bus the short distance to the cover over the front doors. She looked at him warily.

"I've been worried about you guys. I wish you would've called when you finally got on the road." He was clearly agitated. She could only hope he wasn't also angry. His eyes were seering into her own.

She looked away, crossing her arms over her damp chest. "You're the one who called the police to come find us?"

He responded quietly. "I didn't know what else to do. You weren't answering your phone."

She was abashed. "I forgot to turn it back on after judging rounds. I'm so sorry. I never meant to cause an uproar." She paused. "I would have called if I'd known you were worrying."

He breathed out loudly, rubbing the shadow on his chin with nervous energy. "It's not your fault. I'm just so glad you made it home safe. How was it driving through the floodwaters? I was afraid they wouldn't let you through."

"Uh. Yeah." Addy knew better than to admit how high the water had come into the bus. "It was nerve wracking but we made it."

His hand lightly came to rest on her upper arm. She shivered. He moved his hand in a caress, stopping at her elbow. He did not take his hand away, instead holding her in his gaze. She felt her eyes widen, then had to fight the instinct to close them and float into his arms. She could swear he felt the same, even stepping closer into her, but then he abruptly let go and swallowed, rubbing the stubble on his chin.

"Driving through a river." He shook his head. "Way beyond your contract, coach. Seriously, I'm glad you're okay." He cleared his throat, kicked a pebble from the toe of his Converse sneaker., bringing his foot into contact with her. "And the team. Glad the team's okay."

He peered back over his shoulder when someone called his name. Gavin was climbing into Troy's Toyota . "I better go. Poor kid." He stepped away from her but seemed hesitant. Was she imagining this exchange? She slapped herself internally. He'd made it clear numerous times he was not interested in a dunce like her. As their white breath mingled in the damp cold air she realized he must want to reprimand her but was afraid she'd crumble after her long day.

"Well. Tell your team to be careful getting home." His eyes landed on her briefly then away. "Why don't you stop in my office Monday, let me know the results of the tournament?" He paused. "Or you can call me tomorrow, I'll be around."

"Oh. Uh." She flushed. "I—"

He cut her off, his face shutting down. "All right then, we'll talk Monday." He swung away.

After a confused beat of time, she called after him, 'Thank you for driving Gavin home. And for making sure we came home!"

He waved without turning back.

An hour later, at one o'clock in the morning, Addy slunk through the front door of her house, trying to close the sticking wood without slamming it. Turning to face the living room, she saw she needn't worry about being too loud; a bottle of Scotch sat on the table next to the couch, two-thirds empty. The tv was on, static predominating the local airwaves at this hour. She switched off the big screen, as well as sporadically lit lamps. In the odorous master bedroom she found Rick, dressed, horn rimmed glasses askew on his nose, sprawled on his back, sideways across the queen size bed. His face was peaceful, a boy trapped in an adult's body. She silently backed out and shut the door.

In the guest room, she stripped naked, glad to finally be free of her wet clothes. And to be alone. She didn't bother making the futon into a bed, simply fell onto the couch, her skin bare to the rough denim cover, tucked under a makeshift blanket of coats pulled from the closet. She was asleep in one point four seconds. She dreamt of shifting waters and Troy Ford.

CHAPTER 31
ADDY

Addy hastily gathered papers and books off her desk, as well as the floor, preparing to meet the speech team in the library for practice. Ed poked his shiny head into her classroom.

"Whew." He crinkled his bulbous nose. "What's that smell?"

"Freshmen. Some of them have p.e. before this class."

"Ah. The anti-shower crowd. Hey, I see you're on the run but I was hoping I could talk you into helping at the track meet for awhile today. I'm supposed to be monitoring the high jump and the triple jump at the same time. Coach Pike believes I can divide myself in half."

"Oh, Ed, I can't, at least not until after speech practice. We're getting ready for district." She frowned. "As a matter of fact, I'm hosting the district tournament here. I'm kinda' overwhelmed."

He scratched his double chin, shifting his weight back and forth. "I'd love to talk to you about that but I gotta' go. Maybe I'll see ya' later?" He disappeared, leaving behind the sound of scritching nylon as he hurried down the hall.

I can't believe it's track season already. She looked out the window. The ocean was white capped and the Noble firs danced in the brisk spring breeze. It wasn't raining but it wasn't warm either. *Those poor kids. I can only imagine the goose bumps and white flesh on display right now.*

Stepping through her classroom door she heard whoops and laughter coming from the library. She sighed. The librarian sat at her desk, giving Addy the stink eye from under her iron gray beehive. Addy motioned for the kids to gather at the table, throwing a conciliatory grin and a shrug to the older woman. The librarian grumbled under her breath as she picked up her webbed Wal-Mart bag and lumbered out the doors.

Addy set up Erin and Nina to practice a debate round against Gavin and Ace. The girls spent most of their speaking time giggling, calling themselves "master debaters" over and over again. By the end of the debate, the boys were not talking to the girls, having stalked off to the bank of library computers in order to draft new arguments, and to avoid committing bodily harm to their teammates.

Addy realized she'd wasted the boys' time, and the girls', since they hadn't been practicing their pieces, either. She wasn't too worried about Nina, who appeared to have her poetry delivery in the bag. Besides, it'd been nice to see her acting like a silly teenager, joking around with her peers. Erin, on the other hand, needed help with her oratory speech. Her delivery was persuasive and entertaining, but many of the judges' complained about the lack of support from authoritative sources; that was going to be a challenge to repair, considering Erin was trying to persuade her audience lying was beneficial to society. Interesting topic, hard to sell. Even if the majority of people seated before the speaker lied up to thirty-two times a day. At least according to Erin—though she may have been lying.

Wyatt and Travis were side by side at the front of the room, practicing their Abbot and Costello duo script, staying loyal to the piece despite an avalanche of judges' comments declaring the comedy routine to be the least funny speech they'd seen since "The Exorcist." *Ah well. They won't win, but they're having fun.* It was good to have Wyatt back; Travis had moped around like a lost puppy while Wyatt was on suspension. The Expulsion Board thankfully allowed him to stay in school, only suspending him for a week and banning him from three weeks of practice and one tournament.

She paused to watch them, cocking her head as a thought struck her. *This script is annoying but the boys are making eye contact, projecting their voices, using their bodies dynamically . . . they're employing technical speaking skills. They're going to graduate and get a good job thanks to this gig. Hell's bells, I'm not wasting my time.*

Bemused, she made her way over to Tori, Billie and Dylan. They were working at the computers, updating the research on their speeches. "Can I help any of you? How's it going?"

Tori kept her face to the screen, a green glow cast on her pale face and hair. "I'm fine, thanks."

Dylan didn't answer, just waving his hand at Addy as if she was an annoying fly.

Billie looked up at Addy for a second, her apple red curls falling down her back, obscuring the Pirate on her tshirt. "I'm adding in some new sentences about child slavery. Will you listen to me in a couple minutes?"

"Sure. Do you need me to time you?"

"That'd be great, I'm afraid I'm overtime now."

"Better get that hammered down. We don't have too many days before District."

"Thanks for stressing me out!"

Jamy came up behind the group, twisting her necklace in nervous fingers. "I need to be timed, too. I don't know why, but I was really close to disqualifying with my time at the last tournament."

"I know why." Tori's straight blonde ponytail swung to the side as she turned to Jamy. The junior class president sat up straight, speaking thoughtfully. "At least I think I do. I've noticed I've slowed down. A lot. I think it's because I know my speech so well, and because I'm way more comfortable presenting to an audience than I was when I first wrote my speech. I've had to cut lines from my text a few times lately in order to stay in time." She smiled. "And God knows, Jamy, you could always use a little slowing."

Jamy scrunched up her face and stuck her tongue out at Tori. "For your information, I've mastered the pencil trick. I've slowed down a lot." Her voice dripped honey. "How 'bout you? Any luck finding a smile?"

"Hey!" Tori pretended to be mad, shaking an overdramatic fist in the air.

Dylan snorted loudly, his skinny fingers continuing to move across his keyboard. Jamy smacked him on the back of the head and skipped away.

Addy pondered Tori's theory. It made sense. "Listen up, guys," she yelled across the library, disrupting their activities and Jamy's escape. "Come here for a second."

"I want to re-time all of you," she said to the team grouping around her. "We'll start practicing with a stop watch and a friend giving you time signals. I don't want you to miss out on an opportunity to compete at State because you go over time at District." She had a thought. "Oh, I just had a good idea."

At the same time, Ace and Dylan moaned "Oh no!" The teenagers cracked up.

"Ha ha, hilarious," Addy fake frowned. "Do any of you have a video camera at home?" A couple of hands went up. "Ask your parents if you can bring them in. I'm going to record every one of you as you give your speech, then we'll watch it together and critique your delivery."

"Uh, Earth to Ms. Nineteenth Century. Most of us have cell phones. Not me of course, but everyone else. We can use those to record ourselves, it would be a lot easier. You can even email the video to yourself, watch it on a computer."

Addy smiled back at Erin, "Uh, Earth to Miss Smart Mouth. I want to watch it on a big screen tv, with surround sound and popcorn. Over and over again. Much easier if I can take home a big 'ol dvd and stick it in my machine. Yes, I said machine. We have a dvd player. Not even a computer at home."

The kids gaped at her, awestruck. Some of them probably didn't know what a vcr was, being born into the digital generation. None of them would know the joy of paying late fees at Blockbusters.

She laughed. "What? I'm a poor teacher. You've seen my car. What'd ya' expect?"

"Do you have an abacus at home? Grind your coffee with a pestle?" Erin cracked up the crew. Addy didn't mind that it was at her expense. She felt the warm glow over the group and basked in it. This time of the week was often her favorite, surrounded by energetic, hard working kids. Kids who wanted to be here, be with her. Sure, maybe it was a touch needy to find fulfillment here instead of at home, but could she help it if it was satisfying watching young people grow and feel like she had a hand in it? Teaching in the classroom was hard and rarely was the learning obvious. She was unsure kids were transferring her teaching into their thinking. Or doing. She knew her job was important, but she was never quite certain of her impact in Room Seven.

Coaching was different. There was immediate satisfaction. From the beginning of practice to the end, she was able to witness kids take her direction and get . . . better. In two hours. Jamy finding meaning in a new poem, Nina dampening her overacting, Gavin controlling his antsy feet and hands, Tori writing a succinct conclusion.

They were grateful. The team had come to trust her, be at their most vulnerable with her, willing to share their inner voices, accept that her suggestions were meant to help them improve, not to judge them. In this tiny school library at the edge of nowhere, she had found what she had always craved. She'd found trust and respect.

She wasn't entirely sure she'd earned it but by God she was going to bust her ass trying to keep it. The District tournament was coming up. She wouldn't let them down.

CHAPTER 32
ED

Ed wiped the beads of sweat off his ruddy brow, clipboard in hand, watching the home track meet at OHS.

The long jump and triple jump kids were in heaven, leaping with the wind at their backs. Their practice runs were spent goofing off, throwing their arms forward like Superman, heaved through the air by Mother Nature, creating some of the best distances Ed had seen in years. He was having as much fun as the kids, urging them on with shouts and laughter. The excitement created camaraderie between kids from competing schools, something he rarely saw on the athletic field, much less encouraged. But this moment in time and space was different, a peek into a world of acceptance he rarely believed in. Why not revel in the sun on his back, the sound of seagulls and pounding surf competing with kids hooping and hollering, the smell of fresh cut grass and sea brine carried on the strong gusts of wind?

"Nielson! Get over here!" Coach Pike yelled from the high jump pit. There was a group of tall eighteen year old's towering over him, jostling each other, trying to figure out who was going next. Pike looked terrified.

Ed's view of the world snapped instantly from Pollyanna to Gollum. "Yes, master," he muttered under his breath. The wind stinging his eyes became irritating, no longer fresh and fragrant. The smell of rotting clamshells was cloying, the whistles and bells and high-pitched teenage shouts made him want to plug his ears.

Dopy leprechaun, Ed thought, eyeing Pike's corduroy blazer, jeans and cowboy boots, his red beard annoyingly pointy. *He's not fit to run an event, much less an entire track meet. Forty-five minutes behind schedule! Why do the kids like this guy?* The popular upperclassmen spent their lunch periods in Pike's classroom, using his microwave and hot plate located below the charts on std's and proper hygiene. Ed never understood the draw of the dim-witted bastard. Ed was no romantic; he knew full well many of the high school teachers were burnt out or simply not capable. He probably fell into this category. He didn't give a shit, he needed the benefits. He just hated it that this particularly inept individual was loved by the students and, worse, given the head coaching position for every goddamn sport. *We might actually win a game if they let someone with a brain run the athletic programs.* Ed was tired of being the backseat driver.

"Yo, dude, Ford wants to talk to you. He's around here somewhere."

Dude? Is the guy twelve? "Did he say what he wanted?"

"I don't know, I wasn't listening. Can you find me a Diet Pepsi?"

Rather than giving in to his first impulse, which was to stab Pike with a rusty javelin, he squared away the high jumpers, got them arcing through the air again in an orderly fashion. He sent two freshmen hurdlers on a soda search, remaining on the lookout for Ford while huddling with the race conductors, creating a new schedule on the spot and making sure the starting pistol woman had her finger on the trigger. He couldn't decide if he was avoiding the vice principal or if he wanted to find him, end the suspense. Ford had been such a hard ass since football season, riding Ed for the stupidest shit, constantly making veiled threats, saying things like, "I've got my eye on you, Nielson." Ed's blood pressure, and waist size, had shot up since September thanks to the extra stress, constantly avoiding his dickhead boss just in case he had a pink slip in his metrosexual suit pocket.

I wish I knew what's been up his ass. I'm not schlepping a kid or padding state scores. What's he think I'm doing? Showing rated R movies? I learned my lesson with Reservoir Dogs.

The gun going off ten feet away made him jump. He glared at the starter, a math teacher who smiled back at him with a Cheshire grin. Looking past her shoulder, he saw Ford by the shotput ring. The gangling administrator came out to the track meet wearing an expensive grey suit. He stood out like a sore thumb; the competitors and coaches wore athletic clothes, while the dairy farmers, commercial fishermen, and loggers sported hickory shirts, hoodies or Columbia windbreakers. Even the town lawyer knew enough to change into a pair of jeans before coming to the school to stand in the brisk, briny wind, cheering her daughter in the 100-meter dash.

As he approached the shot putters, Ed grimaced. It bugged the shit out of him to see the girls talking to the athletic director, giggling and fawning like he was a rock star. There was Ford, eating it up, acting like he cared about the girls' performances. He asked them about the wind, their throws, the competition, and they were responding by tossing around their hair and inching up their shorts to show off long, lean, spray tanned legs. Ford caught his eye and maneuvered away from the teens.

"Mr. Nielson, I've been looking for you."

"So I hear."

"Candi tells me you agreed to take money at the baseball ticket booth at tomorrow's home game. While I appreciate your helpfulness, we won't be needing you. Not in that capacity."

"What? Did someone bump me? That's not fair. I signed up because I need the extra pay."

"I've given the job to someone else."

"Why? And what do you mean you don't need me in that capacity?"

"Mr. Nielson, you know and I know what is happening here. Soon, I'll be able to prove it. But, in the meantime, you are to go nowhere near school funds. Got it?"

"What in the fu—"

"Watch your language, Ed. This is a school function. Step carefully or I'm gonna' write you up for unprofessional behavior." Ford's eyes blazed. "God knows, you've deserved it for a long time."

Ed was not going to be bullied by this self-appointed dictator. He stepped closer, his scuffed tennis shoes toeing Ford's tasseled penny loafers. He had to crane his neck to look the son of a bitch in the eyes. "Be prepared Ford. My union is going to come down on you hard. And no way Principal Nakamura is on board with your crazy theory. I played golf with him last week; he knows I ain't no thief."

"Someone is, Nielson. And all evidence points to you." The tall man stood with his shoulders back, a righteous countenance on his face.

Fuming, Ed spun on his heel and marched off the track and into the building. He did not want to be fired for hitting that asshole. Ed had never stolen anything more than second helpings from the school cafeteria. He couldn't fathom why Ford continued to make these bullshit accusations and the stupid union couldn't be bothered to step in on his behalf. It was crazy. He had enough shit from his son and ex-wife, no way was he puttin' up with this at work. Tomorrow he was going to start looking for another job. He'd rather be a mortician than work in the public school system any longer.

CHAPTER 33
ADDY

Addy couldn't stop swiveling her head, searching for the source of the overwhelming sweet smell. Occasionally her sneezes smelled like honey, which the almighty internet claimed was perfectly normal, but that wasn't it. It was like being in a room with new diapers, a cloying deodorant odor . . . deodorant. That was it. She glanced at her classroom door, making sure it was shut, before she sniffed her armpit. Dammit. Her new, powder-fresh Suave stick had smelled pleasant this morning but, having spent the day in her under arm glands, the sickeningly sweet stink grew to unbearable proportions.

She wrapped her cardigan tightly around her, keeping her arms tucked to her side, awkwardly, as she slumped at her desk, green pen in hand, inking up reams of documents in preparation for this weekend's District Speech and Debate tournament. The unmarked pile far outweighed the marked stack. At eight p.m, it was demoralizing.

The wind creaked against the blackened windows. Looking up, she could see only her reflection. *I need some sleep. And a tan. I look like a ghost.* The sharp knock on the door caused her to jump and hover over her seat for a full second, furthering her ghostly appearance. Then her boyfriend walked in, his face twisted in anger.

Her stomach dropped.

"I take it you're not here to bring me dinner." She spoke quickly, tried to cut Rick off before he could talk. "Hey, sorry I'm so late, hosting a tournament is really kicking my-"

"Stop it!" His shout echoed off the walls, hung in the air, slowing down time.

She was suddenly scared. She wasn't sure why, gut instinct maybe. Rick was different somehow, a dangerous edge to his neediness. She straightened up slowly, the breath she drew in stinging her lungs. "Okay."

"What is wrong with you? Why can't you love me?" His volume dropped, the rasping quail piercing her ears, the quiet intensity even more frightening.

"What are you talking about?" She whispered, too, no air in her body.

"I love you so much. So much." His voice hitched then continued. "I've been waiting for the perfect time to ask you to be my wife." He paused, face hardening. "But you're always gone. You're only happy when you're away from me."

"I told you I was going to have to stay late." Her stomach dropped further at the mention of a proposal. *That can't be the right response.*

"Uh huh. And when you left this morning, did you kiss me goodbye? When was the last time you touched me?"

Have you been watching Lifetime TV again? Her mind quipped, unable to comprehend that this was real. His rage. His clenched fists. Rick's horn rimmed glasses seem to focus the hatred shooting from his eyes into targeted lasers. Addy could feel searing pain in her heart.

She stood up, walking toward him with hands outstretched, appeasing, placating. "Honey. Please. I love you. I've just been distracted."

He pushed her hands away, roughly, taking a step back. "How is it I can put you first but you can't do the same for me?"

"Rick, we both agreed to move here, knowing I was going to be working full time. I can't help it if they have me working sixty hours a week!" Now she was giving into her anger. "I'm tired! Goddamn it, I *want* to be home! I'm here because I have to be here!"

"You do *not* have to be here, this is your choice. Well, enjoy it. You can spend the night here, as far as I'm concerned." His face turned crafty. "Or you can go spend the night with your other boyfriend."

Her mouth fell agape. His jealousy had moved into fantasy.

"What in the hell are you talking about?" She threw up her hands. "You just found me here, at school!"

"Don't you yell at me." He knuckled the side of his head. He looked crazy. His eyes bore into her. "Your face is so guilty. You're here to cover your tracks." His voice rose again, almost a scream. He picked up a textbook from the desk, waving it in her face. "Well, you can't fool me, you fucking whore."

He threw the text. The heavy book smashed into her, slamming into an arm thrown in front of her, falling to the floor with a thud. She reeled in a half circle then froze, unable to move or speak, not sure if she was awake or dreaming, the pain in her arm too real.

"Nothing to say now, huh? Just keep standing there with that stupid look on your face. You're not leaving this room. Not until you tell me the truth!" This time, to punctuate his words, he threw his keys at her. Luckily, he missed, hitting the wall behind her. The key ring left a dent in the plaster. Her mind gibbered.

"No more, Rick! You're wrong, okay, and you can't treat me this way."

He laughed, the sound unhinged.

Beside Rick, the classroom door opened. Ed's pudgy body hesitated on the door jam. Addy had never been so relieved to see another face, especially one attached to a big body.

"Addy?" His voice was quiet, grey eyebrows raised in half moons of concern.

Rick rounded on him. "This is none of your business, old man."

"Huh. What's none of my business?" Ed looked tired, irritated.

"Get out, you fat fuck."

"I'm pretty sure that's not going to happen. Maybe you should go."

"Pshhhh. Asshole." Rick turned back to Addy, grabbing her by the shoulders, squeezing, hard. Then he shoved her. She stumbled back, releasing a woof as her back slammed into a protruding metal tray. "You can stay here. Don't bother coming home."

She couldn't keep her voice locked away any longer. Standing up straight, despite the pain, she opened her mouth, stopping both Rick and Ed, who was striding toward them.

"Who do you think you are?! Do not touch me. Ever. Again." Her rage, pent up over the year, boiled over. "You think you can keep me out of my house? Screw you! I'm calling the cops. You have tonight to pack up and get out."

"You think *I'm* just gonna' shrink up and whither away?" Rick stomped to the door, roughly shouldering past Ed, who had planted his feet, arms crossed in front of him like a blue collar genie. Rick yelled over his shoulder, "Watch your back, you ungrateful bitch."

"Get out. Get out! Get out! Get out!" she screamed, long after he was gone. Then she crumpled to the ground, howling in pain and distress but mostly anger. The howl filled the room, filled the building.

CHAPTER 34
NINA

The teens jostling Nina were hard-shelled shadows. Fighting her way to the front of the pack, she found the poetry section. Then the posting blurred in front of Nina. Her name was on the list. She was in the Final round at the District tournament.

What a bizarre day. Bizarre week, really. Nina's mother had been home for three nights in a row, making dinner as if she were a real care provider. She even asked to see Nina practice her speech. Nina was too nervous to perform for her, but they did discuss the poems she was using. Her mom enthusiastically asked questions, listened to the answers, and gave performance suggestions. Weird. Very weird. Then there was Ms. Taylor.

Nina couldn't be sure but she thought Ms. Taylor might have spent the last few nights at the school, or in her car. She sure looked it, her long curls a matted mess, her clothes suspiciously similar day to day. Normally, the woman was overly chipper, getting in their face about their lives and their speeches, but she'd been withdrawn the latter half of the week, speaking curtly and sometimes far too aggressively in inappropriate situations. She made Billie cry when she told her to stop bending over, that her cleavage was disconcerting to judges. Her actual wording was far more brusque, something about titties. Organizing and running a home tournament seemed to be too much for the young teacher to handle.

On the morning of the District tournament, Nina awoke with a flutter in her stomach. She dressed in a new outfit: a pencil skirt, fitted button down shirt, and stilettos. With her rich chestnut hair tucked into a modern twist, and a pair of accessory glasses, she felt the sexy librarian attire suited her. *First impression is everything*, she thought as she smoothed her shirttails into her pantyhose, eyeing her behind for lumps in the material. *I've got to be perfect today. I need to make it to State. Then on to Harvard.*

Her mother said she was going to give her a ride to the school but when Nina walked into their cheery yellow kitchen the room was empty save for the lingering smell of cigarettes, Chanel and a note in the middle of the slab table. Her mom wished her luck but she had an emergency at the hospital. Of course.

Gavin's mom didn't mind picking her up, but she took her sweet time, puttering up to Nina's house at the last possible minute. Hastily climbing into the back of their decrepit van, Nina caught her ankle on the door, snagging her nylons on the rusty metal. By the time they reached the school, Gavin chattering away happily with his hippy mom in the front seats, Nina had a run up the back of her calf from ankle to knee. Walking into the school, she stepped into a mud puddle, leaving the inside of her shoe sloshy. *Maybe I can use the mud to stop the run.*

Once inside, the day turned around. For whatever reason, her karma light switched on, her confident persona stepped forward and took over. Her countenance was serene, projecting dynamic charisma. She breezed through the multiple speaking rounds without incident, each performance giving her a rush of adrenaline. *My wet shoe is my lucky charm.* She moved to the front of the audience as if she was a queen, controlling the energy in the room. Every eye on her, captivated, unable to look away or even blink, as she embodied an island momma in the lilting accent of Jamaica Kincaid.

". . . This is how to bully a man; This is how a man bullies you; This is how to love a man, and if this doesn't work, there are other ways ..."

She did not remember most of the afternoon, but suddenly she was with the other hopefuls, jostling for space in front of the Poetry Final posting; her name was listed second out of seven finalists. Her eyes bleared with joy. Below her name was Jamy's. The familiar squeal at her ear made her smile, happy for her friend.

"We're both in Finals! We could both make it to State!" Jamy glowed, hands clasped to her cheeks. "I wonder if Ms. Taylor knows we're in." She looked around. "Who else made it to Finals?"

In the OHS cafeteria, the Pirate Speechies gave in to a minor scream fest when they realized how many of their mates made it into the final rounds; everybody but Travis and Wyatt had one more chance to compete for a slot at State. The boys took it with good-natured aplomb, offering their services as personal time-keepers to the highest bidders.

Just then Ms. Taylor staggered up to the group. She looked terrible. *Is her nose bleeding?* Nina leaned forward, trying to get a closer look without invading her space. Her space looked like it might smell. Bad.

Ms. Taylor held a tattered tissue to her nose. "I'm so proud of you!" Her eyes watered, her voices garbled. "You're amazing!"

Tori stopped celebrating long enough to dig a clean tissue out of her bag and hand it to her coach. "Thank you Ms. Taylor. Are you okay?"

"What, this? It's nothing. Sometimes I get a cold when I'm stressed out."

Billie giggled. "Hopefully, you're stressed out because we're all so good!"

"That's right. Don't worry about me, worry about getting to your rooms on time. Let's go!"

"Can you come watch any of us?"

"I wish I could. I shouldn't have left the tab room in the first place. I need to get back. But I also wanted to come down and let you know I'm proud and thinking of you. Break a leg, Pirates."

Nina joined the writhing mass of bodies exiting the cafeteria. *Is there something wrong with me? Why aren't I nervous?* But she didn't have time to ponder her spacey state of affairs. The best poetry speakers were gathered at the door of room fourteen, hustling each other as three judges made their way into the classroom, holding ballot packets before them like battering rams.

Nina eyed the adults calmly. Jamy, on the other hand, was a sweaty mess. Nina was more nervous for her than for herself, afraid her friend might pass out. She sat behind Jamy, rubbed her shoulders, reminding her to breath as the judges scribbled out preliminary information on the ballots.

"I don't know if I can," Jamy whispered, her head cranked around to look at Nina. "I'm so excited! I can not believe I made it to the Final round at District." She paused. "I don't think you understand, Nina. You came out of the gate a winner. I joined speech because I wanted to get over being shy, maybe do something about my speech impediment. Now look at me!" She bounced as she talked, trying to stay quiet, not draw the attention of the judges.

Nina was pleased Jamy saw her as talented. "Sweetie, you deserve to be here just as much as I do. You're going to be great. I know, I've seen it." She patted the nervous girl's shoulder one final time and settled back into her desk, taking the downtime to quickly flick through her manuscript, run through the words. Jamy was right about one thing. Nina was a winner.

CHAPTER 35
ADDY

The posting sheets blurred in front of Addy's tired eyes. Standing by the event tables in the OHS library-turned-tab room, she couldn't tell if she was looking at papers for the Dual event or the Impromptu event. She cranked closed fists into her eye sockets, twisting knuckles into her eyes like a sleepy three year old. The coaches were humming bees, swarming from table to table, moving the tournament forward, the unseen force behind the scenes, carrying kids from hour to hour, room to room, with the constant scritching of sharpened number two pencils. The force? Not her. No. The other district coaches bent over the event tables, filling scores into grids, making quick, intelligent decisions about how to proceed, a tight team of professionals. She'd spent the day three steps behind, no idea what she was doing, bewildered from the start.

The District Director, Jeremy, sent her a checklist two weeks ago to help her prepare. She'd completed every step, thoroughly, so she thought. She'd ended last night preparations with a self congratulatory pat on the back, proud of her ability to complete important tasks, of her ability to hold at bay her swirling terror about Rick and their future, about her ability to love well, her ability to ignore the two hundred and thirty six texts from her perpetually drunk boyfriend. *Boyfriend? Ex-boyfriend? No time to think about that now.*

Gloating soon became sorely inappropriate. The first coach showed up in the tab room, eyeballed her work, and paled. A frantic scramble ensued, correcting her errors before they could start the tournament. Juanita, the sweet older coach, gave her a motherly hug while Jeremy swung his long black ponytail in loops trying to crack her glum façade. The other coaches clucked appropriate words. *It's ok, we've all been new, it'll work out.* But Addy knew what they were thinking. Kind words did not mask their irritation with the village idiot. She tried to hide in the library stacks, melding with a bookcase, hoping Tolstoy or Bulgakov would stick out a hand and yank her into his pages, but Juanita gently led her to a table in reality, jammed a pencil in her hand and gave her a job.

Eight hours later, Addy was still there, tired, sick, the pencil in her hand doing the rubber dance thanks to intermittent shakes. Her current task was to go to each event table in the tab room, collect the lists of top speakers in each category, make copies of those lists, and give it to a runner who would take the copies downstairs. Thus, the Final Postings were born, the source of much angst and anxiety amongst the teen competitors in the cafeteria, waiting to see if they still had a shot at State. Realizing this, Addy read the papers in her hand.

Her knees went weak. Leaning against the over-heating copy machine, she noticed the other coaches watching her, exchanging grins. Jeremy folded his hands over his potbelly, resting them on a stretched tshirt Yoda. He rocked back and forth on his heels, chortling. "We wondered when you were going to notice."

"I have kids in District Finals!" She was shocked.

Juanita hugged her. "Congratulations! Why don't you take the Final Posting sheets down, share this moment with your kids? You deserve it. But hurry back, we still have a lot to do."

Addy floated.

In the cafeteria, she was almost trampled as she taped the posting sheets to the wall. Pushing her way free from the suits and skirts, she stood off to the side. It was hard to watch the children who turned away, faces falling, crushed after eight months of making themselves vulnerable, putting themselves in front of an audience to be critiqued and judged, practicing for endless hours, only to end with a fruitless search for their name on a list. A long, hard journey was over for these young speakers deemed not quite good enough to go on the next level. It hurt.

On the flip side were the winners. Not wanting to hurt the feelings of their friends who didn't make it to finals, many of the competitors, spying their name on the list, would temper their joy, trying to keep the glow contained, allowing only one short yelp or a quick round of hugs. But the Pirates were different. Addy's team was in the corner, freaking out, maniacally jumping around, no restraint in their voices. Wyatt and Travis were the only two not in a final round, but they didn't seem to care, giving tacit permission to celebrate by whooping and hollering right along with the rest.

Addy joined the happy fray and then herded them out, making sure competitors from other schools still in the cafeteria were okay. She gave hugs to broken children, then slowly made her way back to the tab room, trying to decide if she cared enough about her dignity to keep her blister-rubbing high heels on her feet. Passing an open classroom door, competitors filing in, she happened to catch the eye of one of the judges sitting in a student desk. It was Troy.

What's he doing here? The parents who organized the judging pool must have asked him to help out today. No one told me. It would have been nice to have a heads up. He was her boss, after all. A boss with full lips.

He made the "hey wait a minute" gesture at her and pried his lengthy body from the constricting desk. Joining Addy in the hall, he asked, "How'd our kids do? The people at the judges' table said we made it into Finals in a lot of events. Congratulations!"

"I know, I can't believe it. I'm so tired, I think I fell asleep and this is a dream." She swiped at her eyes, tried not to become distracted by the delicious odor of Old Spice trickling off the man in front of her. The scent reminded her of hot, steamy showers. It was disconcerting. She tried to stay in the conversation. "It helps that our District only has seven schools competing."

"Don't sell yourself short. The other schools are huge, 5A and 6A schools. Our tiny school is kicking some butt. You should be proud of yourself, Coach." His fingers brushed against hers then slowly withdrew, leaving his heady scent swinging in the air. "I'm glad I let the parent group talk me into this." His eyes crinkled, smiling, as he ran a strong hand through his thick, wavy auburn hair. "These kids blow me away. I can't imagine standing in front of an audience, talking about Iraq, or genetics . . . and making sense. I mean, really, these kids are amazing."

Addy had never heard Troy this energetic, upbeat. It was endearing to hear him praise her students, to know he gave up his Saturday to volunteer, actually enjoying himself. This was a different side of him, the teacher side. She liked it. Plus, he smelled so goddamned good.

She grinned, bemused. "I know. They continually surprise me," she said while thinking of his strong forearm almost touching her side, trying to use ESP to lift his hand and place it on her waist.

An adult voice called out to Ford, letting him know they were ready to start. He straightened up, out of Addy's space. "I'll check in with you before I go, see how they do. Are you in the library?"

She nodded as he went back into the room. He smiled at her, almost shyly, as he shut the door.

Today is a bizarre day. It's been a bizarre week.

She tried not to think of Rick, in a hotel room, stewing. Or, possibly, at their house, lighting her clothes on fire. She pushed those thoughts from her mind. No room for him today. Maybe not ever again.

Back in the tab room, the other coaches were taking the time to quickly jam limp sandwiches down their gullets before the final ballots started to return and they could begin compiling the data that would uncover the students who placed. And, most importantly at this tournament, the students who would be going on to State.

CHAPTER 36
ADDY

Addy went between two bookcases, bit down on the hem of her wool cardigan, and cried. Sobbed. Hunkered down and bawled.

Tears of happiness? Sadness? Fright? If she had to quantify, she'd say it was a blend, but mostly relief. Addy had tried to hold in the water works until the school building was empty, but it didn't quite work out that way. She'd walked into the day barely in control of her emotions, reeling from the incident with Rick, her empty bed, and the overwhelming stress of trying to put together the jig saw puzzle that was a speech tournament. By the time the award ceremony rolled around, the veil between woman and blubbering blob was thin and full of holes. Walking back to the library to give out the final paperwork to the coaches, the kids filing out the doors with trophies or tears, the veil crumpled under her grasping fingers. Hence, the fetal position on the library floor.

She couldn't believe it. Three of her students made it to the Oregon State Speech and Debate Competition. These same students started out the year having some vague notion that a speech team had something to do with lispers and stutterers. Now. Now they were going to State.

The award ceremony was a frozen moment in her mind. Nina, deservedly so, took first place in Poetry Reading. Billie, the perky, red-headed cheerleader, took second place in Extemporaneous Speaking, shocking everyone, including herself, with her ability to analyze politics and policy on the fly. Dylan was the biggest surprise, digging deep into himself to portray a realistic, heart rending character in his Dramatic Interpretation of an orphaned boy, receiving straight one's from his judges throughout the day, earning himself a first place trophy. Leaving the stage, tears dripped down his face. He ran to Addy and buried his face in her shoulder, shuddering. She knew he was thinking of his mother, wishing she were there. Instead, Addy was there. She poured all of her love into the embrace she gave the diminutive senior boy. The rest of the team did the same, curving around him as one, sensing the deep need in their friend. A friend who was part of their new family.

Some of the Oceanside kids were devastated when they didn't place high enough to go to State, especially Jamy and Ace. Ace came out of his final impromptu round with the assurance he'd dominated the room. The judges must have disagreed. Addy felt sorry for the boy, but he was only a sophomore, he had plenty of time to achieve the limelight. Same with Tori, Gavin, Erin, Wyatt, and the freshman Travis. Their pain was real but transitory and they knew it, at least on some level, behaving with dignity, allowing their winning teammates to savor their moment without guilt.

Jamy's pain was a bit more permanent, being a senior and having placed only third. She was now the alternate to State in Poetry; unless the first or second place winners dropped out for some unlikely reason, she was done. This was the end of the speech road for her. She graduated in a month. Knowing this, she was still Jamy, gracious, responding with a show of joy for Nina and her other teammates, putting aside her grief for the time being. She even laughed when Wyatt and Travis started cracking Tonya Harding jokes, offering to take out the winners with a crowbar to the knee in return for a year of homework.

The young coach was thrilled Billie, a junior, made the cut, but hugely grateful the two other seniors on the team made it to State. Nina and Dylan wouldn't get another opportunity like this, unless they decided to compete for a speech team in college. But what did Addy know? If someone had asked her at the beginning of the day if any of her kids would make it to State she would have hesitated. Not because she thought they weren't worthy. She knew in her heart they were bright, talented kids with as much brains and brawn as the next team over. No, really, the insecurity came from a deep fear she hadn't provided her kids with enough information or skills to win in this kind of competition, that she had held these kids back with her inept ability to give them what they needed. She felt bad when she remembered how she'd begrudged the coaching assignment in the fall, how she'd assumed the team was a joke that would quickly die away. Then, the kids took over. They wanted it to work. They wanted to learn, to perform, to excel, to prove their words had value.

"Are you okay?" Juanita crouched down next to her in the book stacks, holding out a tissue. "Ahh, the great melt down. Don't worry, Honey, it says a lot about your character that you waited until the show's over." She rubbed the young woman's back. "You probably won't believe this right now, but I see a great leader in you, Addy. Mark my words, you'll only get better. Soon, we'll be lamenting the day lil' ol' Oceanside got back on the circuit." The older woman's face was crinkly and kind, her dark eyes sparkly. "Okay. Wipe that snot off your face. The other coaches want to leave. Those cowards are afraid to come back here and say goodbye."

Time to get up.

Juanita helped her. Addy let her.

Two hours later, OHS was empty. The rooms were straightened, the garbages were empty, the tab room morphed back into a library. Wandering around in the dusky quiet, locking doors, Addy could find no evidence of a speech tournament. It was as if it had never happened.

Passing the office on the way to her room, she noticed a glow. Peeking through the window, she saw Troy Ford's door was open, his light on. She stepped into the office without thinking.

"Mr. Ford?" She called out quietly, moving past Candi's empty desk. A can of Aqua Net Super Hold sat next to the secretary's blackened computer screen.

The vice principal appeared in his door, filling the frame. Gone was his suit from earlier; he was wearing a blue, slightly crumpled t-shirt. He jammed his hands into the pockets of his baggy cargo shorts and leaned against the doorjamb. Her heart skipped and sang.

"Addy! What're you still doing here? I thought everyone was long gone."

"I sent everyone else home. I was just finishing up, making sure the classrooms were returned to normal so the teachers won't be mad on Monday."

"Yeah, good luck with that. Someone will complain, even if you leave a ten dollar bill and a chocolate bar on their desk." He grinned at her. "But don't worry about it. You guys did such a great job today, no one's going to be overly curmudgeon-ish."

She laughed. "Curmudgeon-ish? Is that a word?"

"Sure it is. You knew what I meant, so it must be a word." His grin was affable. Adorable, even. "I just made some coffee, want some?" He pulled two cups out of a cupboard by his desk. "And did you call me Mr. Ford when you came in? I thought we were long past that."

Addy didn't normally drink coffee this late. The digital wall clock read 8:30, which was earlier than she thought. Having no other plans and no big desire to traipse home to an empty house, she accepted a cup and settled into one of Ford's armchairs. *I mean, Troy's armchair. Troy. Now I can say it aloud.*

She eyed him curiously. "What are *you* still doing here? Don't you know it's Saturday night?"

"Ha. I don't have much of a life. Unless the surf's going off, I'm usually here." He leaned back in his chair, putting his long muscular legs up on his desk. He was wearing flip-flops. He gestured toward a few messy stacks on the side of his desk. "I've got plenty of stuff to keep me busy. And if I didn't, the principal or the school board always has more."

"I always forget we have a principal. I never see him." Addy was relaxing, winding down. Oddly enough, it was in her boss's office.

He rolled his eyes. "Tell me about it. That guy goes to more meetings than the President. I don't envy him. Just this week, he's had four meetings with the police chief."

Addy tried not to appear overly interested. *Police chief?*

Troy must have read her demeanor. "Oh, he's not in trouble. We've been investigating an embezzlement charge." Troy leaned forward, chin in his hands. "We've been keeping it quiet for obvious reasons, but we're pretty close to nailing the guy. Thank God. It's made for a stressful year, let me tell ya'." He tilted his head to the side. "But maybe I shouldn't say anything yet. Don't tell anyone, okay?"

"Don't worry, I don't talk to anyone. Except Ed. And he doesn't count." Addy held her breath at the expression that crossed Troy's handsome features. "Oh."

"Damn it, me and my big mouth. Addy—"

"I promise! I promise! Not a word." She gathered her courage, shyly. "But just for the record, and I'll never say another word about this . . . but I think you're wrong about Ed. He's annoying but he's a good guy."

Troy rubbed his hand over his eyes then sat up straight. "I wish I was wrong. I hate this crap. But I don't think I am. Anyway, it's almost over." He half-heartedly grimaced. "Sorry, I absolutely shouldn't have burdened you with this. But you cannot say anything to Ed."

"I know, I won't." She bit her fingernail. The feel of the room had shifted, sadly. "Well, I should be going. I'm going to bed and sleep for eighteen hours. It's been one heck of a week." She stood. "By the way, it meant a lot to the kids to have another one of their teachers here today. Thank you."

He walked her to the outer office door. "Seriously, don't thank me. This whole experience is making me re-think my view of small schools." He peered at her from under thick eyelashes. "This school."

"So why did you leave your last job? Wasn't it in the city?"

"Yeah. They were laying off administrators. Last hired first fired, you know. It was between me and a single mom. A lot easier for me to bum around. Besides, my karma needed the bump. And, now, they've asked me to come back so they can interview me for the head principal position." He paused, focus drifting out the window. But then he snapped back and went on. "Anyway, you're giving kids exactly what they need right here. Because of these kids, and you, Addy, I'm a little less worried about the future of the world."

Addy, wincing at the idea of the void Troy would leave in her current world, forced herself to laugh. "Okay, then, Mr. Hyperbole. I'll send the seniors your way when it's time to write letters of recommendations. Goodnight."

"Goodnight. And congratulations again, Addy." It was a full minute before she heard the office door's hard click behind her. Had he watched her walk away? She looked down at her pants. *Didn't I wear these yesterday?* A fog started to lift in her mind. She swiped a hand across her seat, praying she had not sat on a donut or ink in the past two days.

The automatic lights were coming on, the natural light almost gone. She was done here, at least for today. Time to go home.

CHAPTER 37
NINA

Water doused her constricted face, her hair, her back, as Nina leaned into the shower spray, eyes closed, reciting a new introduction she'd written for one of the poems in her speech. This version was much tighter, stronger. But for some reason she was having a hard time memorizing the new lines.

I can do this. I memorized The Merchant of Venice last year. For fun.

She pushed in the faucet and stepped onto the bath mat, mouthing the words, stumbling over them, her skin goose-fleshed from cooling water. Logically she knew she had her original performance down pat, that she had already won District with it the way it was. Emotionally, though, she could not let the flaw stand, no matter how small, even if the correction wasn't working. When she could momentarily suspend her chanting, she saw herself from a distance: she was obsessing.

I need to calm down. Channel this craziness.

The towel wrapped tightly around her, she sat on the toilet seat lid, resting her arm on her crossed legs. The scars and scabs on her inner arm were humming, calling softly to her. In a trance, she reached under the counter, pried the razor blade loose from its hiding spot, and wiped the blade clean on her towel. Once the silver blade pierced her skin, the words in her head dimmed.

CHAPTER 38
ADDY

"I hate starting new chapters," Addy said to Lizzie. "Life's too complicated. How do I know I'm starting the right chapter?" She sat at her favorite window seat in Rosie's Roost, hoping Rick wasn't going to sniff her out on this Saturday morning. She'd avoided him since their last blowout, but only through evasion, sprints and lies. Thankfully, the tourist crowds in Oceanside were thickening now that Spring had sprung, making it a easier for Addy to hide in public, or at least create a buffer of innocents. Rick spotted her a couple of times but, as long as she was surrounded by people, he didn't approach.

If only he would stay away from the house. She'd offered to be the one to move out, but he refused to move back in unless she stayed with him. Instead, he'd park outside and stare in the windows for hours. She'd pulled the drapes, changed the locks, and Lizzie occasionally spent the night, but she couldn't bar herself in forever. He'd proven he was no longer functioning rationally when it came to their relationship, especially when he was trying to solve problems with scotch. She couldn't control the way he thought of her, or treated her, but she could control her own actions. Right now she was choosing peace and quiet. A life of it.

"You can't control life, honey." Lizzie held back her dreads as she filled Addy's coffee cup. "You turn the page and wham. New chapter." She put down the carafe and put a hand on her hip. "Believe me, your new chapter was long overdue."

Addy felt, as always, she had to defend Rick. "He's not a bad guy. He's not evil. I just can't give him what he needs. And he's kind of overreacting."

"Yeah, kind of." Lizzie snorted. "You need to stop blaming yourself. And stop trying to protect him. He's not a child. If he's not happy with what you guys got goin' on, he can use his words, like a big boy. Not his fists."

"He hasn't hit me and you know it."

She pushed on Addy's tender shoulder, her dreads swinging into Addy. "Really? How's them bruises treatin' ya', girlfrien'?"

"C'mon."

"Baby Jesus didn't put that big bruise in the middle of your back."

Peeved, Addy looked out the window. Even in the sunlight, the ocean was faded bands of purple and grey, much like her bruises. "You don't need to be mean."

"Honey, I'm not trying to be mean. But you have to see that type of behavior is not normal. Way not normal." She patted Addy's shoulder, gently this time, picked up her carafe, and moved on to the next table, taking the scent of up-scale patchouli with her.

Rick had not wanted to hurt Addy. He'd tried to apologize yesterday, cornering her outside the local bank. His hurt, confused mind sought an un-findable clarity while Addy only wanted a safe distance between the two of them. He had seemed stable and calm for about one minute but then, abruptly, he tried to grab her wrist, quailing, "Why can't you love me?"

His red face, lips pressed into a thin line, mortified Addy. A woman emerging from the bank with two toddlers shooed her children to the opposite sidewalk rather than walk by the crazy man. Looking at Rick through the mother's eyes, she didn't blame her.

And looking at him through that stranger's eyes did something to Addy's vision, her perspective—her mind blossomed, opened in epiphany. *Who is that guy?* Rick was right. She didn't love him anymore.

She didn't know if the dissolution of her love was because of his growing skepticism, or if his skepticism was justified in the beginning. She couldn't untangle the timeline anymore. She only knew she wanted out of there, out of the relationship.

"No more of this, Rick. I'm done." She moved further down the sidewalk without turning her back, hands placating but out of reach. "I'm not putting myself into this position ever again."

"I'm trying to say I'm sorry!"

Not answering, she crossed to where the mother was handing out saltwater taffy to her children. She kept her eye on her fuming ex-boyfriend, edging past the family she used as a shield. With an audience, he didn't follow. No matter the depth and breadth of Rick's love and apologies, no matter if this truly was her fault, she was done feeling unsafe. Or unworthy. She might be the one that was evil, or at least an uncaring bitch, but she meant what she said. She was done.

She walked away, void of emotion, an automaton.

Lizzie's take on the situation was unpleasant to hear but the waitress did keep Addy grounded in reality. The past few weeks had been exhausting, her mind unable to escape the always spinning hamster wheel. She found herself nodding off whenever she sat down.

Paying Lizzie for the coffee and promising to see her that night, she moved into the stream of bodies on the late morning sidewalk, warm bodies bobbing along, talking, laughing, solving the world's problems. She moved with them, content for the moment to be part of an unthinking mass. When she did let herself think, it inevitably circled back to two things: feeling sorry for Rick or wondering why she couldn't cry. It was weird. At the best of times, she was a crier. She cried at cotton commercials, or when a puppy cuddled with a kitten. She cried when she listened to Dylan deliver his speech, every time, and she'd heard it ninety-seven times. But now that she had decided to leave Rick, she couldn't cry. She knew she was supposed to. Women in movies and books spent days sobbing, sitting around in their dirty bathrobes eating ice cream out of the carton. Sometimes, Addy tried to make herself cry, so she too could join the zeitgeist of today's unfulfilled woman. At best, she could squeeze out a few drips but by then she always felt so fake, like a paper cutout, that she made herself get up and do laundry or grade papers. At worst, she felt a nauseating guilt, picturing herself knifing Rick in the back, betraying the promise she had made to be with him. They weren't married, but they might as well have been, after so many years and experiences together. He'd moved out here for her.

The heaviest guilt, however, was over suddenly feeling so goddamn free and light, not having to worry about which Rick she was going to have to please when she came home, the manic or the depressive. Now she just had to please herself. Macaroni and cheese seemed to do the trick.

And her job. She was thrilled at how much satisfaction she could get from knowing she was making a difference in kids' lives every day and didn't have to go home and apologize for it every night. She was also grateful to have someplace to go. Teaching her classes and preparing her kids for the State tournament kept her occupied. The team was being extra nice to her, bringing her apples, donuts, and misshapen ceramic ashtrays from their art class. She hadn't told them about Rick, but they seemed to know. Either the small town gossip caught up with her or their years of experience with separated parents came into play. Either way, she loved the kids.

It was so much easier to think of the kids. Safer.

The State competition was in one week. Less than a week actually. They were going to leave on Thursday night so the kids would be well rested for their first round of speaking on Friday morning. They would be competing with the best of the best, the top kids from around the state, most of them coming from huge, well-funded schools with speech classes and three or four coaches. *But my kids are coming hungry. Watch out.*

Nina, Dylan and Billie's level of commitment stepped up to a level that would have been hard to match had Addy not suddenly been endowed with all the time in the world and a burning desire to fill the clock. She stayed late with them every night after school because they begged her. Even the kids who hadn't made it to State often stayed to give advice, videotape, research or run the stopwatch. Tori and Travis would stop by in their sweaty track clothes, stinking and full of commands. Gavin and Wyatt sometimes brought friends from the creative writing club by to provide fresh ears, and to show off their new-found acceptance in another world. Ace peppered Billie with political questions, irritating everyone with his righteously conservative approach to every issue but thankfully helping the cheerleader to keep abreast of political events. No one else wanted to talk about Syria, Afghanistan or the national deficit.

On the other hand, Erin and Jamy were willing to listen to Nina and Dylan multiple times in one sitting, working on the delivery of one word or phrase for hours. Jamy would sometimes disappear for a half hour or so, which bothered Addy, worried she was off on a crying jag, until she stumbled upon her one day tucked into a corner, practicing her own speech. Addy hadn't considered the possibility Jamy clung to the hope she might still compete, even though she was only an alternate. Addy let her be, even listened to her a few times, deciding it didn't hurt to let Jamy deal with this in her own way.

Addy's musing were put on hold as she contemplated four college aged kids standing in the middle of the sidewalk, eating ice cream, oblivious to the single dad with a toddler in melt down mode trying to get around them. She thought about turning back, going back home, but decided she was at the beach on a sunny day and should take advantage of it. Besides, Portland sidewalks were crowded like this everyday. *My life has changed so much. Is that a good thing or a bad thing? Maybe I should just go with the flow, not worry about definitions right now.*

But I should worry about Nina. While Jamy and the others seemed to be dealing with their stress in a normal fashion, Nina's focus was intense. Jamy and Erin were willing to listen to her for hours, but Nina continued long after everyone had glossy eyes and drool pooling on their chin. She deconstructed every poem, every introduction, every sentence, every word, adopting different interpretations and delivery methods until the team felt Nina should be re-named Sybil, the girl with a thousand voices. The pressure the teen was putting on herself was frightening. Yesterday she stumbled on a word, just one word, and made herself repeat it for a full ten minutes, into a tape recorder, before she would move on. The team thought she was dedicated, amazing . . . but Addy thought maybe she should talk to her mother, make sure she was letting go at home, giving herself time to relax. Dylan practiced every day, but he spent an equal amount of time screwing around, throwing pencils in the ceiling or hiding Erin's homework, which was irritating but healthily normal. Nina wasn't being normal.

Addy tilted her face to catch the damp, warm rays as she walked among the tourists bubbling around her on the sidewalk. *But who am I to judge normal? She's simply raising the bar and jumping for it. I should honor that. Help her.*

Lost in her musing and the warm weather, her reverie was interrupted by a honking.

Oh God, please, I'll do anything for that not to be Rick.

At the third honk, she couldn't ignore the noise any longer. Other people on the sidewalk were looking at her. She turned to see Ed, filling the interior of his mint green Prius. No matter how many times she saw him in his car, the choice surprised her—it was like coming across a banker wearing a tie-dyed tshirt and Birkenstocks. Luckily he waved and drove past, his elbow resting on his open window. She breathed a sigh of relief, waving after him, just one more man she'd been avoiding. Ever since Troy let it slip about the embezzlement inquiry, she'd avoided both Ed and Troy, unsure how to deal with the issue. *I am the worst friend ever.* Having only enough courage to internally deal with Rick, she put Ed, and Troy, out of her mind. Though Troy was a fairly consistent main character in her dreams . . .

They can figure out their own problems. Addy's long hair whipped her in the eye, the wind tossing it around. She tried to grab enough of it to pull into a pony tail but then stopped, coming to a decision. *There is one problem I can fix. Besides, it's time to grow up.*

She marched back up the main street and burst into Rosie's Roost with determination and excitement. Lizzie emerged from the kitchen with a fresh pot of coffee.

"What's got your knickers in a twist, girlfriend?" Lizzie smiled.

"When do you get off work? I want you to cut my hair. All of it. Off."

CHAPTER 39
ADDY

"**W**hy don't we take a break? Look, it's actually sunny outside. I'm gonna' run out to the track meet, see how Travis and Tori are doing." Addy stood up and stretched, her hands brushing through her new short hair. She couldn't get used to how light her head felt. Lizzie called it a French bob cut. The waitress had to be persuaded to cut it but once she saw Addy's mind was made up, Lizzie insisted she would only cut the 'lion's mane' if she got to choose the style. Luckily, Addy loved the look, sophisticated with a slight edge of punk.

Inside her head was a different story. Her brain was spinning; the kids were having the same problem as before District—they were no longer speaking fast out of nervousness and they knew every word and nuance so well that they had slowed way down from their earlier presentation times. Fog infused her brain, triggered by listening to the same section of Dylan's speech multiple times. He was overtime by thirty seconds; they needed to cut at least two sentences, if not three, before they left for State tomorrow. The decision was mind numbing. Every word was important at this point, since they'd already pared it down to the bare essentials. She was sure she was going to ruin his speech. Dylan simply looked at her with his sweet, trusting brown eyes, waiting to do whatever she suggested. She looked back at him, waving him up, out of his chair. "Come on, scoot. Move around. Let's get some blood pumping, walk around for fifteen minutes."

HOLLY L. LÖRINCZ

Billie peeled herself off the library computer, lifting her crimson hair up off the nape of her neck, blowing a raspberry through pursed lips. "Gahh. I can use a break. I'm gonna' stab myself in the eyes if I have to read anymore about starving African babies being raped. Good times, Ms. Taylor, good times."

Dylan jumped up, his small body doing jumping jacks, running in place, straight brown hair flopping in his eyes. "You're right, Ms. T, this feels good." He started breathing heavy. "Okay, I'm done now." Puffing, he dropped back into the orange plastic chair.

"Time to give up the cigarettes, Dylan," smirked Billie. She grabbed his hand and pulled him to his feet. "Let's go outside for a minute, get some vitamin D on your pasty face."

Ignoring the cigarette comment, Addy asked, "Do you guys know where Nina went? I haven't seen her in awhile."

"I thought she went to the bathroom," Billie said, as the three of them moved out of the library. "Maybe the siren song of the sun called her outside."

"Ooooh, poetic. Better not let Nina hear ya', she'll think you're tryin' ta' steal her place at State." Dylan laughed as he darted away from Billie's playful slap. The happiness ringing in the hallway was soothing to Addy, settled her nerves. Dylan would be fine . . . Rick would be fine. They'd all be fine.

Outside, the fragrant breeze was pleasant, lightly swirling her skirt around her knees, caressing her face. She turned her face to the warmth, closed her eyes briefly, the light breeze playing with her new short hair, a low blissful hum trilling from her chest. Billie and Dylan didn't say a word, understanding completely the sentiment. No one on the north coast mocked a moment in the sun.

The track swarmed with colors, flashing golds, reds, whites, blues, silvers. The wide scale bustle, mixed with the natural aesthetics, had Addy's heart beating a solid thump. Dylan and Billie sauntered off in search of their friends, with promises to return to the library soon. As he departed, Dylan held up a stopwatch he had pilfered off her desk, showing her a fifteen-minute rundown. Shaking her head, she turned away. After a few moments of cheering on the Pirates, moving from track to pits, she wandered over to the concessions stand. She was surprised to see Tori.

Addy raised her eyebrows. "I thought you were running. What're you doing in here?"

Tori grimaced, tossed her blond ponytail around, then smiled half-heartedly. "I ran my race already. A whopping fifth place, by the way. Then Coach Pike said he needed me in here." She shrugged. "Whatever. I don't really care." Then she started bossing the other three students around, barking orders. It was clear this was the race she really loved.

"Well, I'd like some popcorn, please. And seltzer water, if you have it."

"I don't know this seltzer water of which you speak, but here's a bottle of regular ol' water and some stale popcorn."

"Hmm. Thanks. I think my smart mouth is wearing off on you, Miss Tori."

"I hope so, Ms. T. By the way, I love the hair. Very cool."

Pike entered the snack shack. "Ya'all seem to be flappin' yer' lips, not getting' much done. You, make more popcorn. You, clean out that grease tray. You, run to the school, get some more coffee grounds from the kitchen." His beard proceeded him, next the pointy tips of his snake skin boots, then his short, stocky body. He noticed Addy leaning against the other side of the counter. She tipped her head, polite and he returned the favor. The stiffness between them had not eased, which no longer bothered Addy. She'd witnessed nothing but ignorant lesson plans, favoritism for popular athletes and quick to anger responses from him.

"Tori, I need that cash box. Here, use this one." He handed the girl an identical cash box, reaching for the one with Addy's freshly inserted coins. "And I need the balancing sheet, is it in here?"

Tori fluttered briefly. "Um, yeah, I think so, I didn't touch it. Did I do something wrong?" The overachieving girl wrung her hands with anxiety.

Pike was short, off-handed. "No, no. But the office needs this. Don't worry about it."

A whistle blew, another race started. Addy needed to get back to the library. "I'm heading into the building right now." She held her hand out, choosing to be nice, offering a verbal olive branch. "I can drop that off with Candi in the office."

Pike snapped the metal box to his chest, cradling it like an infant. "No," he said sharply. "I've got it." He wouldn't look at her. "I'm goin' in anyway." She watched as he turned abruptly, his two-inch wooden heels clicking as he marched out the door and across the parking lot, a Napoleon without the smarts or charisma.

She followed his path, entertaining herself with an internal stream of curse words and names, some wildly inventive. *I'll have to remember that one, my dad can use it on the guys in the factory.* She was glad when Pike turned off at the locker room, relieved to be free of his malignant presence.

Ed emerged from the office as she passed. "Addy. Have you seen Pike?"

She twisted her lips. "Unfortunately yes. He just went into the locker room." She started down the hall, throwing over her shoulder. "Oh, hey, he has the cash box, if that's what you're looking for."

As Addy's eyes swung forward, she cringed. *Ugh, why did I bring up money?* But then she turned around and walked back to Ed. *He deserves better.* "By the way, those high jump kids you've been helping are really taking off. I was just talking to Johnny Bergman; he said he got his personal best last week because of some move you taught him."

The older man's thick eyebrows shot up in surprise. "He said that?" Then his face settled back into its familiar jowly countenance. "At least one kid's doin' what I say. I need to get back out there but first I gotta' find Pike. Did you say he went downstairs?"

Scurrying toward the library, Addy un-hunched her shoulders, grateful to have escaped without explaining why she'd been avoiding him. *Maybe he doesn't realize it.* She was afraid to look behind her, ears tuned for following footsteps, releasing her breath only after she crossed the threshold. She shook her head. *Poor Ed.* Why did Troy say anything to her in the first place?

None of the kids were back in the library yet. She sighed. Sitting at the table closest to the computers, she pulled Dylan's script to her. *Back to it.* Billie came in, sat at her computer, muttering annoyance with Dylan, who had ditched her at the track meet to go find Nina.

The woman and the girl were startled to hear a high-pitched cry echo down the halls. They looked at each other, not moving until the next sound, a heart-rending scream, unleashed them from their paralysis.

Jumping up, racing through the doors, they were forced to pause for a second, not sure from which hall the terrifying noise was originating. "Down here!" cried Billie, pointing left with her chin. She and Addy broke into a sprint.

Skidding around a corner, they found a horrifying sight. Dylan screaming, kneeling over Nina's prone body. The girl's long hair was a lush splash of brown silk on the white tiles. She lay half in the restroom, legs propping the door open, her skirt hiked up to her thighs. Dylan, his shaking hands holding Nina's face, stopped screaming, started groaning.

"She's dead. She's dead. Oh, god, she's dead."

CHAPTER 40
ADDY

Wailing, wailing, wailing.

Addy craved desperately to cover her ears to block out the intense, high pitched sound. But as long as Dylan endured so would she. The ambulance siren was loud but the alternative was worse. At least there was a siren. That meant they were hurrying to save Nina's life. That she still had life.

The paramedics weren't thrilled to have Dylan and Addy in the back of the ambulance but also weren't willing to physically pry Dylan from Nina's side. And Addy couldn't let the two kids under eighteen ride away from her realm of responsibility, not with one frantic and the other unconscious. So, now, strapped onto a bench in the windowless back, boiling under the heated glare of the ambulance guy, her knuckles ached within the vice of Dylan's small but amazingly strong fingers. Nina's body swayed with the movement of the van, laying corpse-flat on a cot boasting a confusing amount of tubes and wires, some connected to her chest, some to her flaccid wrists.

Addy's focus bent again and again to those wrists, hands beseeching the roof for help, her shirt sleeves bunched up to reveal Nina's Achilles' heel. The poison line running up the inside of Nina's thin, pale arm was shocking, a cherry red streak bursting from the ladder of puckered, raw slashes above her elbow, up to her armpit. There was a murderous infection racing through her veins, making its way to her heart.

"I found my mom."

"What's that, honey?" Addy wasn't sure she heard Dylan correctly.

Dylan cleared his throat. "I found my mom. I was the first one in her room after she died." Holding Addy's hand, his knees pulled up to his chest, he looked like a sad kindergarten student, brown hair hanging in his haunted eyes. "She looked like that." He jerked his head toward Nina.

Addy squeezed his hand. "I know it looks bad. But you probably saved her life, Dylan."

"She doesn't look saved to me." He stretched his free hand across the narrow aisle. His fingertip almost touched the hollow of Nina's neck, then retracted and tucked back against his own neck, reaching for his pulse. The girl had no visible heartbeat, no pulsing skin, but the monitor blurted a steady assurance that the organ still functioned though a fever heat radiated off her skin. The paramedic in the back with them held onto a ceiling strap while adjusting monitors, visibly stunned by Dylan's quiet words. The man's attitude toward them eased, his body language and facial expressions becoming more sympathetic. They were annoying rule breakers, but human rule breakers.

Until he discovered the identity of Nina's mother.

"What? Her last name is DuBois? Oh my God, this is Margo's kid." He leaned forward, shouted at the driver. "Ed, you better step on it." Then he yelled at Addy, over the siren. "Does she know we're coming?"

Addy shook her head. "I don't think so. I've tried reaching her contact number but no one answers."

"Oh, I'm sure she's at the hospital. She always is. That is one woman you don't wanna' mess with." The guy looked young, too young to be in charge of a young, unconscious girl. "Zack, seriously, get the frickin' lead out."

They turned a sharp corner, a pole banged off Nina's ear, and she moaned, eyes fluttering.

"Dude! I said go faster, not kill us!"

Dylan glared at the paramedic as Nina resettled into silence.

Screeching up to Oceanside Hospital, the ambulance wheeled to the emergency doors, jerking to a halt.

"Alright, you two, out. Now. Get out of the way." The driver hurriedly dismantled his straps and hopped into the back, both paramedics grabbing monitors and wires, piling them carefully on the unconscious body of Nina, following Addy and Dylan out the doors. The hospital bay doors burst open.

A phalanx of scrub-encased hospital warriors marched forth, led by a stern Amazonian woman with Nina's regal bearing, porcelain skin and fine nose. Margo DuBois. The Administrator of Oceanside Hospital and Nina DuBois's momma.

"What're her vitals? How long's she been unconscious?" Margo did not run to her daughter's side. Nor did she appear distraught. Her questions were clipped, professional, directed to the paramedics, completely ignoring Addy and Dylan. Dylan held Nina's hand, Margo held her stethoscope.

Addy sadly acknowledged Nina's random comments about her distant, absorbed mother had not been overdramatic musings of a teenager. The woman was cold.

Nina was admitted and, after three hours, revived enough to be moved from the ICU to a private room. Addy wasn't allowed in to see her but she had a perfect view of the teen's door. Nurses and doctors went in and out but Margo had not appeared since Nina was first moved, staying only briefly, hurrying out with a beeping pager in hand.

Eventually, Addy sent Dylan home with Billie, who had stopped to check on Nina. Now that Nina was stable, Dylan and Billie needed to be at home, preparing to leave for State tomorrow, getting a good night's rest. Plus, someone needed to call Jamy, tell her she was no longer an alternate; Jamy would replace Nina, competing in two days. Billie's mother offered to drive Addy home, too, but Addy wasn't ready to leave yet. She'd call a taxi later.

She was drowsing when a nurse approached, informing her she could go in. Addy pushed open the door with trepidation, unsure of what she would see.

The girl appeared younger, unsure of herself, confused, but as striking as ever. When she saw Addy she burst into tears, too weak to lift her head.

"I'm so sorry, Ms. Taylor," she sobbed weakly, tears rolling down her cheeks, onto the crisp white pillow. "I've let you down."

"Nina, no! Please, don't ever think that!" Addy struggled to control her own tears, moving to stroke Nina's hair, comfort the shuddering girl.

"Yes, Ms. Taylor, she did let you down," said a gravelly voice from the doorway. Addy spun around to find Margo stepping into the room.

"There's no need to lie to the girl. She knows what she's done." She moved to the other side of Nina's bed, placing her hands on the edge. Her voice softened slightly as Nina's quiet sobs continued, only the mother's fingers revealing anxiety, creasing and recreasing the sheet. "You know and I know your cutting was a poor choice which could only lead to this. We've been here before, Nina."

"We?" Nina's voice was a whisper left unanswered.

Margo's face constricted, displaying pain and fear for the first time.

Addy smoothed the bandages on Nina's arms. *Should I be here?* "This has happened before, Nina? I wish I would have known. Maybe I could have helped."

Nina's eyes were blurring, giving in to the drugs dripping into her veins. She mutely looked away from Addy. Margo, on the other hand, snapped her head up, reacting as if Addy had slapped her. Curtly, Nina's mother asked, "You're the teacher? The one who got her involved in the debate club?"

"Yes," Addy stuttered, unsure of the emotion suddenly filling the room.

"Then you should have known to watch for this; it's in her file. You're around her everyday, how could you not notice?"

Stunned, Addy flooded with resentment. And guilt. *It's true, why didn't I notice? And what's in her file?* Catching sight of Margo's haughty face, Addy straightened, realized she'd been thrown under the bus. For Nina's sake, she swallowed her real response. "True. Absolutely. I'm so sorry, Nina, I failed to notice something was amiss." She touched her fingertips briefly to the girl's clammy cheek. "I'd give anything to not see you like this."

Nina shut her eyes for a long moment, her face struggling with a kaleidoscope of emotion. Slowly, her grey eyes opened, pierced Addy. "Ms. Taylor, this has nothing to do with you. I'm good at hiding my craziness. Mother taught me well." Nina's voice was weak but pointed.

Margo staggered this time, face white.

Addy tried to shrink up and vanish, not wanting to witness such ugly family dynamics. *Wow. These guys know how to carve on each other.* Her gaze dropped to Nina's bandaged arms. *Literally.*

"I'm not going to the State Tournament, am I?" The words twisted out of the teen. Addy shook her head. A blood red flush spread across Nina's face. After a beat of silence, the girl shuddered. Then she said, "I'm tired. Can we finish this later?" Her translucent eyelids fluttered closed, shutting down any further conversation.

Margo tentatively reached for Nina's face, but halted her hand in mid air, dropping it to tuck the blanket around her daughter instead. She followed Addy out of the room, shutting the door behind them. The hospital director began to stride away in the opposite direction but Addy called after her. "Ms. DuBois!"

Margo turned around, looking at her impatiently. "Yes?"

Addy wanted to make a quick getaway but her worry overrode her discomfort. "Will Nina be alright? Is there anything I can do?"

"Nina will be fine, I assure you." She sniffed. "And what could you possibly do? You somehow missed diagnosing a girl blazing with fever and infection. Do you think you can now provide her medical care? Or perhaps you think you can be her mommy?"

The harsh delivery was akin to poison on a dagger. Addy shook, taken aback, fighting the desire to run. But Nina was in that room, a girl in need of an advocate. "Look, Ms. DuBois, I know you're under a lot of pressure right now, but it's not like that. True, I should have checked in more carefully with Nina, realizing she pushed herself too hard. But you might want to consider your role in your daughter's care. You live with her. Clearly, I'm no doctor."

Margo paused, lips pursed, suppressing rage. "I run this hospital, Ms. Taylor. I'm responsible for every life in here, lives in real danger. I can't be at home to baby a seventeen year old who is perfectly capable to care for herself."

Addy's lungs expanded with anger, picturing Nina's unliving face on the floor of the high school. Quietly, very quietly, she said, "Yet, I think you know she isn't. Capable, that is."

"What?! Who are you to judge me? If I chose to put one person first, my daughter, hundreds would suffer. Go back to your classroom and shut the door. This is the real world." Margo gripped her hands in front of her. "Whether I like it or not."

Addy didn't back down. "I don't want to argue with you, or judge you. I want to help Nina. I love that little girl and I think you do, too."

Margo's dignified face pursed with anger, then wilted, collapsing. "Of course I love her! How dare you. I worry all the time. I should've been there, I should've seen this happening, but you—You!—don't have the right to call me out." The director stepped forward swiftly, palm raised. Addy backpedaled until she caught herself, held her ground. Margo seemed as stunned as Addy to find her hand in the air. She dropped it, her voice cracking.

"Her dad sent her out here so he wouldn't have to deal with her. And I did the same thing. Ignored dealing with her. I wanted her to be ok this time. I needed her to be ok." Margo slumped, aging by the minute.

Addy responded to the insecure, terrified mother finally free from the doctor façade, and softened her voice. "I'm sorry. You're right. I can't imagine how you feel." She wanted to touch the woman but didn't know if slapping was off the table yet.

"Good lord, who can? My child's been in our home, by herself, hurting so bad she can't function unless she digs into her flesh." Margo's voice hitched, her hands covered her face. "She almost died. Died! I'm here saving strangers while poison runs through my baby's veins."

The director swiped at her eyes, leaving black smears on the sleeves of her white lab coat. She patted her cheeks, surveyed the hall. Addy guessed she was trying to gauge how many of her employees had seen her transform into a human. Margo cleared her throat.

"Well. I think I'll go back in and sit with Nina." Her mouth twisted wryly. "Perhaps she'll be nicer to me if she's sleeping."

Addy smiled tentatively, relieved Margo was choosing her daughter. Margo did not smile back. She threw a stiff nod and strode into Nina's room, calling back over her shoulder. "We'll be speaking soon."

Addy paled. That didn't sound good.

I hope Nina wakes up. I hope she sees her mom there. I hope she's able to keep talking, really talking. Addy drug herself out into the misty night air. *And I hope I don't get fired.*

CHAPTER 41
ED

Ed stacked the last of the hurdles on the south side of the school, watching the track busses pull out of the parking lot. Yellow slugs following the slimy trail of Highway 101. Finally, the ambulances, the athletes, the staff . . . everyone was gone.

"Ed Nielson, please report to the office. Ed Nielson to the office." Ford's bleating voice trembled in the sea winds blowing across the outside speakers. Well, the humans had gone. Walking assholes apparently never left.

The social studies teacher zipped up his track jacket, collar brushing his scruffy chins, and shook his middle finger at the speaker.

As he crossed the parking lot to the front doors his butt cheek vibrated. Then again. He yanked the phone free from the small back pocket. Matt. His arthritic fingers bludgeoned the green button into compliance. "Hey, Buddy, wha's up?"

"Dad." His son's voice sounded small.

"What's the matter, Matt?"

A gulp. Then a cry. Ed's heart constricted. "Matt?!"

"Dad, you said you were gonna' be at my game today."

The air left Ed's lungs. *Dammit. Dad of the Year, once again.* Yet . . . there was a twinge of satisfaction. His smart-assed, eye-rolling, punk of a kid cared.

"Ah Jeez. I'm so sorry, Matt. I planned on it but we had an emergency here today. A girl got hurt, then they needed someone to stay with the track meet kids." *Only because Pike disappeared. Dickhead.*

There was a quiet pause, a sniff. "You didn't forget?"

"Well, kinda'." Ed spurted words like a car salesman, wanting to explain before Matt got the wrong impression. "I was leaving for your school when they found the girl. But, to be honest, then I did forget. I got wrapped up in getting everyone where they needed to be. I'm sorry, Matt." He entered the building, in no hurry.

"Is the girl okay?"

"She's been taken to the hospital. I don't know. She seemed pretty bad off."

There was a heavy quiet. "Wow. I'm sorry, Dad. I bet her mom was glad you were there."

Ed caught his breath. Matt thought he was the hero in the situation. *I'll tell him the truth. Later.*

"Listen, I'm gonna' be leavin' pretty soon; want me to stop by? Did your mom get any video? Any hits?"

"I have a lot of homework. But we have another home game Friday. Can you come to that one?"

Ed wound up the conversation, promising to see Matt in a few days. By the time he hung up, his bulky shadow drenched the office door. He pictured Ford crouched over his bowl of blood, communing with his boss from down under.

To be fired or not to be fired, that is the question.

"Ed, get in here."

He ground his teeth, then realized the command came from Al Nakamura, the principal of OHS, yelling from his throne at the back of the office. Al met Ed with his chubby hand extended, a grin on his affable face, while Ford lurked off to the side.

"Damn, man, I wasn't sure you worked here anymore." Ed plopped in a seat, crossed his legs in front of him, folded his hands over the basketball in his belly. He and Al had been around the block together a few times; Al was a known entity.

"Well, Ed, I've never been sure you work here. But little Lizzie assures me you're still around, and that you're sniffing around her mother. " He wagged his finger at Ed. "Stay away from my sister. Believe me, you go there, you're gonna' have to start eating pickled chicken feet. That woman refuses to eat anything unless it's pickled first." The principal shuddered then moved behind his desk, picked up a thick folder and waved it in the air. "Anyway, moving on, Troy here has something to say to you." He sat down, templed fingers under his jaw, giving the floor to the vice-principal.

Ed perked up. *What's this happy horseshit?*

Ford hovered, tossing his hair out of eyes like a girl, pulling nervously on his tie. "Look, Ed . . . " he stopped, cleared his throat. "I need to apologize to you." *Did his ridiculously square jaw tremble?* "I've been under the impression you were stealing from the school." He appealed to Ed with his hands, palm up. "In my defense, someone framed you." Ed wanted to sucker punch him as he tucked his hands into his suit pants pockets. Instead, Ed slouched.

Ford continued. "Stupid me, I bought it, hook, line and sinker. Now, I—"

"Enough of this," Nakamura bounded back up, spry in his khakis and golf shirt. "Blah, blah, blah, he's sorry. We have a thief on staff. Goddamn glad it's not you, by the way." He leaned forward. "But we know who it is." Slapping his massive cherry desk, the principal said, "You, Ed, can help us catch him."

Ed sat ramrod straight, a surge of energy humming through his body. It was an awakening.

CHAPTER 42
ADDY

Thursday morning, Addy zombie-walked into Oceanside High in time to hear Candi screech her name over the intercom. Entering the office she found Jamy sitting in a chair, swinging her legs, flipping through her poetry manuscript with a small smile on her face.

"Why're you here? You're not in trouble are you?" Addy sank, fatigued, into one of the office chairs. Jamy smelled innocent and sweet, like a toddler after a bath, with just the faint whiff of worry.

The girl's brown pixie cut jiggled with her delighted giggles, giggles a touch high pitched with hysteria. "No. At least I don't think so. I've never been in trouble. I think I'm here because I'm going to State!" The normally sedate teen yelled the last words, speed talking, deepening the frown on Candi's face.

Coach Pike walked out of the copy room carrying a stack of worksheet packets, his pointy red beard shining off the white paper. His voice crawled out of his throat. "You're not going to State. That's why you're here." His squinty eyes were black with evil. He turned to Candi, lightening the rasp, flirting. "Hey there, Sweet Cheeks, make sure the State funds they *won't* be using," he jerked a thumb at Addy, "gets put back into the budget. Football camps are expensive."

Candi smirked, decisively hitting keys on her keyboard as if she was actively moving money around at his command.

Addy sprang up, her short blonde hair standing on end like baby Medusa snakes. "What is this?" she yelped.

Exhaustion and frustration peeled back her professional tact, left it undone, her green eyes ablaze.

Troy's office door opened. Ford towered over Pike, making him suddenly inconsequential. "Pike, get out to the busses. There's a scuffle out there, go get the girls, bring 'em back here."

"Sure, boss." The skinny leprechaun snickered, wagging a finger under Addy's nose on his way out. She lurched back, glaring. She was about to open her mouth and let loose when Ford caught Addy's eye, shook his head and shrugged, his face sad.

"Come on in here." He motioned to both Addy and Jamy. As he held the door for them, he asked, "How's Nina this morning?"

Jamy spoke up before Addy, quickly but quietly. "I just came from there." The petite teen frowned but couldn't hold it. "She's doing okay. They're probably going to release her tomorrow. The poison lines are almost gone." Jamy stopped. "But I guess she's not really okay, is she?"

Hearing the term poison line said aloud discomfited Addy, who pulled Jamy to her, giving her a hug.

Addy asked, "How is she emotionally? By the time I left last night, she was distraught over missing State . . . and embarrassed."

Jamy ducked her head, "I think she pretended to be okay for my sake. She doesn't want us to worry. And she doesn't want me to feel bad about taking her place."

"About that. That's why you're both in here." Troy sat down behind his desk, sighing. "Jamy. This morning Coach Pike brought it to my attention that you're not enrolled in five classes. According to Oregon rules, you have to be a full time student in order to compete." He glanced at Addy then back to Jamy, who was getting smaller by the second. "You shouldn't have been competing at all this semester, but you definitely can't go to State. The school is already in danger of being fined."

The petite, shy teen twisted her head to look at the clueless young coach, reproach in her liquid brown eyes.

"I didn't know . . ." Addy trailed off.

"First things first. Jamy, why aren't you taking five classes?"

The senior blushed. "Well, I finished all my requirements, except English, and I'm taking that this semester. I'm also taking a bunch of electives. My fifth class was a t.a. period; the counselor put me with Coach Pike. I went to his health class everyday, but he never needed me." Both Addy and Troy were leaning forward, trying to follow Jamy's nervous, fast squirrel-speak. "After a week and a half, I just dropped it, and used that period as a study hall in the library. The librarian never said anything, so I figured I was okay."

Troy sat quietly for a minute, frowning off into the corner. A vein throbbed in Addy's temple, her heart beat lugging along to a weird tune. At twenty-three, she was going to die of a brain aneurism or a heart attack. *The human body isn't meant to be stressed like this. Chased by a lion, yes. Shitty boyfriends, dying girls and back-stabbing co-workers? No.*

Finally the vice principal spoke up. "Jamy, can the librarian validate you've been there everyday?"

"Yes, I promise."

"I think I have a solution. If the librarian is willing to sign off, I'm going to enroll you as her t.a. that period. Which means you'll have to finish out the year re-shelving books like crazy. Which you deserve for trying to manipulate the system." He grinned, lightening the mood in the room. "Okay. So. What time are you leaving today?"

Jamy and Addy both started talking at the same time, thanking Troy, asking questions. He raised both hands. "Jamy, class is going to start soon. I'll call the librarian, but why don't you go talk to her, warm her up to the suggestion."

Jamy gathered her stuff, hugged Addy again, and left, quickly, before anything more could happen. Addy turned back to Troy, holding onto the metal frame of her chair, preparing for the nuclear blast.

"Um, so a few things, Addy." Troy hung his head for a second, struggling to say something. After what seemed a lifetime, he looked back up, concern hanging on his features. "First, Margo DuBois is not your biggest fan. She's called and lodged a complaint against you." He sighed. "It sounds like you let a little too much off your chest at an inappropriate time."

Addy nodded, not sure how to defend herself.

His voice continued, soft. "This is serious. She has a lot of weight in this community. But I know you were trying to help the girl, to help Nina. There isn't anything you can do about it right now, but I want you to be prepared for fallout when you get back."

"I—"

"Hold on, Addy. I'm not done." His sigh sounded like a growl. "If the school does get fined for Jamy's thing, you're gonna' have to explain that to the School Board. Add this to Margo's complaint, Wyatt's fight, and the two building alarms you set off, well . . ." He cleared his throat. "Start prepping a persuasive speech to defend yourself."

Addy held her tongue but she wanted to punch something. Maybe Pike. Definitely herself. Ford's look of pity did nothing to stop the hydra monster eating her intestines.

He put both hands on his desk, leaned forward. "Goddamn Pike. That was a crappy stunt. He knew about the rule." Troy's eyes darkened. She kept her mouth shut a beat longer.

"Troy, I'm grateful. It's nice of you to go out of your way for Jamy." She swallowed. "And for your concern. I appreciate the words of advice."

He moved over to Addy's side. *Is he going to hug me or hit me?* Addy tried to maintain eye contact but her eyes skittered away. Her terror of the future battled with the immediate attraction to her boss. Which brought on more terror.

He spoke absently, peering down at her. "Jamy's a good kid, she's never been in trouble, she's always at the fundraisers, and she's a peer tutor in the remedial reading classes. If anyone deserves to go to State, she does. Besides, this was really more your error, wasn't it Addy?" He said it softly but it didn't dull the blow.

"I know, I know." *I thought we'd already covered this ground.*

"Do you like teaching? And coaching? Is it something you want to keep doing?"

He asked in a curious manner, not threatening. She pondered before answering, processing slightly slower than usual because he was standing right next to her, smelling of Old Spice and the sea. *Get it together, sister.* She did like teaching, and coaching, but was it worth it to do it again next year? Everything was so complicated, layered in expectation and responsibility at an impossible level.

Why does he care anyway? He doesn't really have the right to ask. He's leaving.

Troy's intercom buzzed. "Mr. Ford, Inspector Carlson is here, waiting." Candi said, irritatingly sweet.

Oh hell. That's not about me, is it? She fidgeted.

Troy sat back down. "Ok, Candi, one minute." He shrugged, "Sorry, Addy, I need to talk to this guy, and I know you need to get to your class. Don't worry, we'll work this out." He passed a card over his desk. "Will you call me from the tournament, let me know how it's going?"

He seemed expectant, nervous, as if she'd say no. Addy slid the card into her jacket pocket, thanking him, unable to look him in the eye as she hurried out. She'd failed so many times in the last few weeks. It was hard to see it reflected in his face.

What a mess. I thought adults had their shit together.

The English classes spent the day tiptoeing around their neurotic teacher, her green eyes glassy, her patience thin, energy sparking from her jittery fingertips. Students and teacher alike rejoiced at the last bell of the day.

I can do this. I can do this.

Addy gathered up Billie, Jamy and Dylan, crammed their excessive luggage into the recesses of the Volvo, and rumbled out of the Oceanside High parking lot, the ocean humming a sweet travelling tune. She cranked up the stereo, made them listen to "Eye of the Tiger" seventeen times. Then they sang it from the heart.

CHAPTER 43
ADDY

The kids were cowed as Addy's car turned onto the University of Oregon campus. Their trepidation twanged Addy's already frayed nerves. The three kids rarely travelled further than the country roads of Clatsop County, and none had ever been on a college campus. Addy had wanted to take the speech team to a university tournament earlier in the year but it was too expensive. Now she was wishing they'd scraped up the money somehow; Dylan, Billie and Jamy were going to be so intimidated by their surroundings they'd shrink into country mice as soon as city mice entered the room.

Peering out the back window with saucer eyes, Billie said, "This school is as big as our town."

"Dude, it's way bigger." Dylan, shorter than Billie, poked his head out the window to get a better look. "We don't have any buildings like that." He was pointing to the UO Library. "Hey there's a sign for Autzen Stadium! Can we find it, Ms. Taylor? I would love to see it!"

Billie jumped up and down in her seat. "Yah, yah, let's do it! I want to cheer there someday!" Addy raised her eyebrows, peering at Billie in the rearview mirror. Billie laughed, tossing her red hair out of her eyes. "What? I'm going to be on the debate team, too, don't worry, Ms. T!"

In the front seat, Jamy finally ceased her three-hour poetry chant and turned back to Billie. "What's Autzen Stadium?"

Dylan and Billie laughed. Dylan said, "Man, are you for real? Every Oregonian knows the home of the Ducks!"

"Ducks live in a stadium?" The girl seemed honestly confused.

"Come on! Seriously? I'm talking about the football team! You know, the Ducks!"

"You're telling me a football team has a duck for a mascot? Tooouugh."

"You're telling me this is the first time you've heard of the Ducks. Wow. I thought you were cool."

"I can't believe you want to cheer for a duck."

Addy picked up grainy, confusing maps from the information booth, drove the kids around the campus, pointed out buildings they would be competing in tomorrow and, if they made it to the upper rounds, Saturday. Winding her Volvo through narrow streets filled with half-dressed twenty-somethings toting backpacks and a lack of understanding regarding sidewalks versus the street, Addy ended the tour with an Autzen drive-by and a search for their hotel.

"Welcome to Motel Hell. Muwhaahaa." Dylan's comment was not far off. Hotel 99 was within walking distance of the State Tab room in UO's Erb Memorial Center—but it also boasted thin sheets, rusty water, orange carpets, and busy train tracks running behind the parking lot. Emerging from their rooms into the breezeway, Jamy tugged her door shut, locking it, and then rubbed her hands on her capri jeans. "Yuck. My mom would freak if she saw this place. She'd make us sleep in the car."

Billie nodded. "That's not a bad idea."

Dylan was unfazed. "Don't be wusses. You have a bed, electricity, and hot water." Sadly, this was probably nicer than the shed he lived in on the edge of town. Addy gulped down a lump in her throat as he hitched up his pants and started across the parking lot.

"We also have bed bugs and possibly the ghost of a murdered hooker," said Jamy with disgust.

Walking through Eugene's city streets, the teens amused themselves with various spins on the murdered prostitute's life and death. Some of them were entertaining, most were down right gross. Addy was relieved when they finally reached UO's Erb Center; horror stories had always given her an unpleasant stir and Dylan seemed to have an uncanny knack at creating disturbing imagery. She'd be sleeping with a light on tonight. Alone. In her creepy, creepy hotel room. Goddamn kids.

Appraising the historical, humongous, stone building, none of them could figure out where to enter. There were dozens of entrances, on multiple levels, none with signage for the High School State Speech Tournament. Signs for roommates, for rallies, for AA meetings, for banning pesticides, for banning Young Republicans from campus, for banning Log Cabin Republicans from campus, for banning pubs from campus, but not one sign about speech and debate. Billie did spot a sign about forensics, but upon closer inspection, they decided the clip art of an autopsy corpse and a bloody saw meant the sign referred to medical forensics, not analysis of meaning via the spoken word.

Eeny, meeny, miny, moe. Double doors to the left, encased in ornate wood carvings of salmon and Native Americans killing them. The tile inside flowed and ebbed, the spiral staircase climbed through air, suspended on cable reaching heights unseen from where the group stood, necks arched back.

"Hey, I recognize that kid," called Billie. "Let's follow him!"

Unsure of whether or not they were on their way to the men's restroom, a drug drop, or the State Tab room, Addy trailed her kids hot footing it up the stairs behind a lanky boy in a mis-matched suit carrying a naugahyde suitcase, clearly a speechie.

The tight band of tension across her chest relaxed a bit when she spied Jeremy, the long-haired coach from her district, across a room littered with small tables, chairs and lounging high school students. *How can these kids be so calm?* She almost broke into a run when he disappeared into a side room. She was preparing to hurdle a bunch of kids sitting on the floor playing a game of spoons but, luckily, Jeremy re-emerged. He broke into a grin when he spotted her. She reached him, walking nonchalantly, exuding cool.

"Addy! Good, you're here! Uh, what's that on your shoulder?" He grimaced, taking a step back.

She was afraid to look. Dripping down the sleeve of her cardigan was white goo flecked with black. She gagged. "That is either ice cream I didn't eat or it's a gift from a bird."

He grabbed a handful of napkins off the table beside him. "Let's call it a blessing. Like champagne on a maiden voyage."

"Yeah, it's just like that."

"I got your message. You've got a name change for the poetry event? Is everything okay?"

She gave his sympathetic ear a run down of events. Jeremy appropriately nodded at the right moments, easing her mind and her conscious, helping her relax. Then he trotted back into the side room, which turned out to be the State Tournament Tab Room, and reappeared with a packet of information, including competitor codes and speaking times. Like the coach he was, he turned to her kids, accepting the rush of questions with aplomb, answering questions calmly and succinctly. Within ten minutes, the Oceanside Pirates stepped off S.S.Frantic, able to move among the natives with ease. A better map and an understanding of the schedule helped.

They spent a minimal amount of time poking around buildings. The surge of hysteria had worn off, making them tired, so they headed back toward their hotel, fighting over restaurants along the way. Dylan ended the conflict by running inside a large building shaped like a Pagoda, cackling as the girls chased him. They settled in and ingested a ridiculous amount of Chinese food and virgin daiquiris. The waitress, dressed in a shiny kimono, brought them a dessert tray. Behind her was a large hulk of a man.

"Patrick!"

"Hey kid. Nice 'do. Very . . . adult."

She ran her fingers over her short hair, fluffed up the blond tips. "Thanks. Hey, where's your team?"

He slid into the booth across from Addy, his shock of white hair stark against the dull black patch. The older man shrugged and said, "I ditched them at the hotel with a chaperone, told them they needed to practice at least once more before I do a final run through with them. The lazy ingrates. I've told them they better step up or they have to write fifteen new debate cases when we get home, even though they're done debating."

She laughed. "Good! At least it isn't just us. If you gotta' lose, lose big, right?"

"Yep, that's right." He grimaced. "Frankly, some of my kids could stand to lose. They are getting way too cocky."

"You don't mean that! Not at State."

He tilted his head, inspected her. "Addy. Remember why we're here. It's not to get shiny trophies." He spread his hands wide, as if talking to an audience. "We're here to guide kids through the swamp, teach them how to jump, kick and find food." At her quizzical expression, he said, "I'm saying we're here to teach these kids how to survive in the real world, give them tools to help them maneuver through life. And I mean *all* the kids. I'm not just talking about my own team. Every kid here is brave enough to bare their brain to strangers. They all deserve our guidance." He wrinkled his brow, which shifted around his eye patch disconcertingly. "Remember that tomorrow, when you have to judge a few rounds. You're helping those kids, even when you give them last place." He jabbed the table, reinforcing his point. "Especially the kids in last place. They'll feel the sting and not want to feel it again, so hopefully they'll read your critique, try to improve next time. The kid that wins isn't actually learning much, is he?"

She nodded thoughtfully, hoping he was for real. He grinned, winked his good eye, and stage whispered, "But I do love them shiny trophies."

She laughed and spent the next five minutes soaking up his genius. The team waited impatiently, goofing off around the door. After the umpteenth evil eye and finger drawn across the throat, she gave up trying to get them to quiet down. It was time to refocus on her anxious charges.

She left the older coach at the table, her head full of tips and strategies. She gathered the kids and marched them back to the hotel, sequestering them in their Psycho-esque rooms, telling them to practice just to the point of scratchy throats. After calling to check in with Nina, who was doing homework with Erin in her hospital room, Addy made the rounds, timing the kids at least once, making sure they were under time. Ahhh, to get this far, to have jumped so many damned obstacles, only to be ousted because of a few seconds? Unbearable thought. But she also realized she was obsessing, she needed to back off, not scare these young souls any further. The kids didn't seem to notice, though; they were focused, on target. If, at this point, they didn't break into final rounds, they could leave knowing they had tried their hardest.

Bahhhh. Like that ever makes anyone feel better. To lose when you try your hardest is pretty fucking demoralizing. What happens next? Do you keep trying? Why?

She sighed, mentally slapped herself. Patrick was right. It was the journey that mattered here. She had to remember that, no matter how stressful the journey.

She made sure alarm clocks were set for pre-dawn, corralled promises for early bedtimes, prayed those promises weren't false, and dropped onto the dingy quilt in her room.

She left the bathroom light on, the tv on, and the curtain cracked a skosh. Despite the terrifying image of a bloody whore standing over her bed in the middle of the night, and the strobe of car lights piercing the open slash of curtains, her heavy eyelids overcame her racing heart fairly quickly.

CHAPTER 44
ADDY

After twelve hours of performing, they sweated and squeezed around a small round table in the banquet room, butt bones aching on hard plastic chairs similar to the Oceanside High School Library. Unlike OHS, however, was the crush of people sucking up the oxygen, pressing in on them from all sides. On the table were four plates of uneaten dessert, the sickeningly sweet stench spoiling the finite amount of breathing air.

Squealing feedback repeatedly assaulted their ears. President Leila, just as unpleasant on the stage as she was in a tab room, read the names from behind a podium while sending death rays at the sound-guy as she tried to adjust the microphone, read and adjust, read and adjust, read and adjust. Five hundred adolescents in the crowd held their breath, trying to decipher their names from the hellish garble. Despite this, Addy and her crew wouldn't depart the banquet room for a thousand dollars, not until the State Director finished announcing who would be moving onto semi-final rounds tomorrow.

Holding hands with the three Oceanside competitors, Addy was sure they looked like a coven, or at the very least a group engaged in a séance. When Billie was announced as a semi-finalist, the Pirates froze, unsure if they should believe their ears. Biting the hell out of the tip of her tongue, dew escaped the quivering lip of Addy's eye. This led to the entire table weeping silently, making the teams around them shift in discomfort. When Dylan and then Jamy were also announced as semi-finalists, they broke the rules: they screamed, long and loud. How could they not? In a million years, Addy never thought they'd get this far. She was shocked, swimming in bliss. Her three students, coming from a miniscule rural school, no speech class, no background, no trained coach—they'd surprised themselves by winning at District, and now her kids were here competing against kids from schools with over two thousand students, teams that had try-outs and a long history of wins. Now her kids were here, in the top fourteen of their events. All three of her kids. Her kids. Goddamn kids.

Back at the hotel, she removed Troy's card from her jean's pocket. She'd been keeping it close for two days now, waiting until it would seem like a business call. Not the breathy, hot exchange she wanted.

He answered before the first ring finished.

"Addy?"

"Troy—how'd you know it was me?"

"I got your number from the registry. I was going to call in case you forgot. Just wanted to see how you, I mean, the tournament is going."

She flushed with warmth and hope. He listened intently to her stories, her excited spewing over the kids and the competition. Then she heard herself and spasmed to a halt.

"Sorry, didn't mean to babble on."

"No, no, this has been great! I love hearing you so excited." Pause. "I mean, the kids are doing so well, the school will be thrilled."

"Well, the big test comes tomorrow. Do you want me to call again, let you know the final results?" she asked with bated breath.

"Uhh, maybe not tomorrow. I'm going to be in Portland. Meeting with some people from my old school."

"Oh, oh, sure. Well, I'll just catch up with you on Monday then. Oh, hey someone's knocking on my door." She rapped on the hotel wall next to her bed. "Coming! Gotta' go. Have a great weekend."

"Oh, okay. Goodnight, Addy," he said slowly.

"Night!" chirped and hung up.

Barking up a moving tree, Addy.

But late that night, Troy did not move away. He moved closer. He moved into her bed. He moved his hand up her trembling thigh, moved his fingers, gently and firmly, to exactly where they needed to be, moved his lips to her ear and whispered, "I've wanted you for a long time." She woke up wet and panting, the sheets twisted into a human shape.

The next morning, Billie's Extemporaneous Speaking round was scheduled first. Addy walked with the perky teen, Billie dressed in a tight skirt suit and a silky scarf, long red tendrils dripping from a loose knot at the back of her head, channeling a bookish Marilyn Monroe. The junior cheerleader had no apparent urge to contain her sex appeal. Addy fingered the hole in the elbow of her own cardigan, smoothed her shapeless wool skirt and sighed. Entering the Extemp prep room, Addy noticed only two other girls. The majority of the competitors appeared to be male, and seniors, meaning they had skill, and more importantly, experience. Billie, a junior, had smarts and looks. She also carried a fashionable tote full of dog-eared magazines and highlighted political essays; the other kids were wheeling in blue plastic tubs of alphabetized, cross-referenced current event files. *Use what you got girl. You're gonna' need it.*

Billie received three topics from which to choose and thirty minutes to prepare an organized, cohesive analysis. As the girl sauntered back to her table, a gaggle of kids waiting in the corner rolled their eyes, mocking Billie. Luckily, she didn't notice, but Addy's stomach tightened. As the coach, she wasn't allowed to stay in the room once Billie started to prep, but she did catch a glimpse of the choices: *Has China lived up to its fair trade obligations? Are planned cuts in U.S. military spending excessive? Should Iraq adopt a federal system?*

Hopefully Billie had a dictionary in her tote. Addy was stressed out just trying to understand the questions, she couldn't imagine coming up with a speech about China's trade obligations. Billie's face lit up, though, like a cheerleader handed pom poms made of moonbeams and fairy glitter. Addy slid out with a wave, feeling dumber just for having stood in the room with future Madeline Albrights and Henry Kissingers, Bushes, and Clintons. Well, maybe not Bush. Addy felt safe assuming Dubbya did not compete on a speech and debate team.

Back in the lobby at the posting wall, she found Jamy's Poetry Interpretation round had already started in a building half way to the next town. She'd never make it there in time. On the other hand, Dylan's Dramatic Interpretation round didn't start for a few more minutes and was in the Willamette building next door. A quick scan of the lobby did not reveal the swaggering, elf-like seventeen year old; if he was still here, he would have stood out. Dylan *was* wearing dress pants and a dress shirt with a tie. But his ensemble included ankle-high dress pants purchased on sale in the children's section of Fred Meyer's, a greyish-white dress shirt with the sleeves rolled up and the extra material safety-pinned in the middle of his back, and a bright orange knit tie. Knit. He didn't look serious. But by god, he was serious. Poor boy.

The door to his assigned room was closed with no window. Addy pressed her ear to the flaking green metal. She could hear nothing. Then, suddenly, someone inside was screaming. Addy almost ripped open the door. Luckily, the words sunk in before she could fumble her hands out of her pockets.

"The dingoes ate my baby!"

Ah. It was the girl from earlier this year, doing the Meryl Streep script about dingoes. She'd made it to State, too. *At least I know I'm in the right place.* Addy listened to the girl yell and cry for a few more minutes and then, when the room erupted into clapping, she went in. Dylan was in a chair in the back. He smiled when he noticed her threading her way back to him, muttering apologies for the winces and sore toes. As she sat down, she bent over to him and blasted him with her coffee breath, whispering, "Is it okay I'm here? Am I going to make you nervous?"

One of the judges swung around, frowning. Then he winked at Addy and turned back to his paperwork. Dylan raised an eyebrow and shook his head, sidetracked. He floated back to subvocalizing, practicing whispered chunks of his speech between speakers. She focused on the back of the judge's mohawked head, a college student even younger than Addy. How could he be qualified to judge at the State level? He must've competed when he was in high school, though judging by the size of the gauge in his ear she doubted he was a debater. Then she caught herself. Had she learned nothing from cheerleader Billie blasting the political crowd? Or shy Jamy slamming out poetry to an enchanted group? And here was Dylan, a skinny boy with a probation officer and a dead mom, getting right to the heart of an audience.

She gave an internal nod to mohawk guy's back. *Sorry dude.*

"O3?"

Dylan marched up to the front of the room, squared himself to the crowd. At the judges' nod, he bowed his head, took a small step forward and began.

"A twelve year old boy. Sitting at a dinner table, his momma kisses his hair as she hands him a glass of cold milk. His dad passes around the mashed potatoes. Sweet, right? Another twelve year old boy, sitting at a rickety card table, by himself, with dried bread and a withered apple, reading the back of a cereal box to keep his mind off the lice on his head. Not so sweet, but he's a survivor. In order to eat, to live, this boy has learned to follow . . . The Cider House Rules, by John Irving."

Dylan was a stern, polished performer, introducing his script, bowing his head, taking a half step back in order to move into the character's world. The next ten minutes belonged to him, entrancing the crowd, sucking them into the story.

Addy, moved as usual, cried along with the rest of the audience by the time he was done. In no way unbiased, she watched the rest of the performances and walked out believing Dylan had a realistic shot at the final round. He was just as good, if not better, than the majority of speakers in the room and, Addy believed, his choice of script was harder to perform and of higher quality. Again, though, she was biased.

Dylan was a helium balloon, shining, floating back to the lobby where they would be posting the names for the Final rounds. He had expended every drop of his energy. Addy couldn't be prouder.

Billie and Jamy were waiting for them, anxious to debrief. Billie had decided to speak on military spending, mostly because she had two articles referring to the budget and nothing on the other two topics.

"I don't think I nailed it, but I did okay. I forgot to give a roadmap in my introduction, so I think I confused the judges right off the bat. But once I got into it, I made solid points. Two of the judges would nod at whatever I was saying, and they all told me I did a good job when I was done." She pushed her hair up off her neck, massaging her own shoulder. "I'm just glad it's over."

Addy tried to read the girl's mind, her body language, decipher if she really was handling this as calmly as she seemed. After Nina, Addy never again would presume to take a kid at face value when they said they were okay, especially in high pressure situations like this. "You don't think you made it to the Final round?"

"No." She put a hand over her eyes for a second but then sat up. She squared her shoulders. "But that's okay. Don't get me wrong, I'd be stoked to be in Finals, I'm just not going to let it crush me." Billie's voice dropped to a whisper; she'd read Addy's mind. "I'm not Nina. I can roll with it." She grinned, broke the tension. "Besides, I've got next year."

Addy wanted to believe her. But she'd be there, just in case. She was learning.

Jamy nodded. "I wasn't supposed to be here in the first place. I'm grateful I got this far." These kids were being so mature and calm, Addy wondered when the shoe was going to drop.

Dylan half-frowned. "I don't know. I can't be that chill. I wanna' win." He kicked his feet up onto the chair next to him, put his hands behind his head. "I'm gonna' need some serious amounts of Skittles and gaming just to recover from the past few days. I can only imagine the load of candy necessary to save my soul if I lose."

Addy put an arm around his shoulder. "At least you're being honest. But, I'm tellin' ya', Dylan, you were amazing. I don't care if you make it to a Final round; you could skip all this and go directly to acting on a stage right now." She squeezed when he looked uncertain. "I mean it. Start memorizing Hamlet. Remember the little guys like me when you're famous."

He gave a shy smile, a child. He tucked into her. Billie and Jamy piled in. "Group hug! Group hug!" they yelled.

They had two hours to get some lunch. The kids chose a sushi restaurant next to the campus. They lived by a natural source of seaweed yet none of them had ever eaten it. While nervously awaiting new food and the final results, Dylan called Nina. Addy, sitting close, could hear Nina's tinny voice. She sounded strong. Dylan relayed what Nina was saying, telling them hi and that she was back home. Erin was staying with her when her mom was at work. She claimed to be better.

There was some individual, coded chatter and then Dylan was telling Nina not to make any decisions, they'd see her as soon as they got home. The four of them yelled out a chorus of goodbyes as Dylan hung up.

"She says her dad is coming to see her. She thinks he might try to take her back to Boston." He frowned. "She sounded tired. I'm glad Erin's there. I could hear her stupid stand up routine in the background."

Addy knew Nina was required to go to counseling sessions at least once a day; she almost thought Nina should be staying in some kind of facility, just until she was steady. But she wasn't the momma, she didn't have a say. Hopefully the dad could clean up the mess, give the world back to Nina. That girl had more potential in her stately pinky finger than any human Addy knew. The problem was keeping her alive, helping her realize she was strong enough to tap it, even on her own.

Addy rubbed her chest, bruised from life lessons, blow after blow in the past few months. Sometimes she was supposed to control everything, but sometimes, seemingly the most important times, she had no control whatsoever. Nina was out of her reach. Now. Back when she could have changed the stream of events, Addy had done nothing.

So, another life lesson. Not only was she supposed to occasionally control a situation, she was supposed to know, in the moment, that she was in the moment.

God. Damn. It. Being an adult sucked.

"Ms. T., I think we should head back, they'll be posting," Jamy straightened her pink cashmere sweater and cleaned up their area, dumping leftover wasabi and ginger. The kids had picked at the sushi for a moment or two, tentatively tasted the rolls, and then dove in like competitors at a food-eating contest.

Dylan tried to be nonchalant, leaning back to pat his bulging stomach. "Uh, could you pay for mine? I'll get ya' back. You know, when I'm famous."

And sometimes being an adult was okay. At least she had a Visa.

CHAPTER 45
ADDY

"**Y**ou spoke like, like, water moving over rocks," said a grizzled bus driver in a thread-bare flannel shirt. Jamy's hand disappeared in the friendly old man's paw, shaken enthusiastically. Then he picked up a judge's packet covered in scribbles off the desk he'd uncomfortably squeezed into for the past hour, listening to the Final round of Poetry. Jamy had been the last speaker, sweat sparkling on her upper lip.

There was a ringing born of hard clapping in the air. Well, actually, the applause was being drawn out, strenuously, by Billie and Dylan, who had not made it into the top seven final round of their own events and were now ferociously focusing their energy on Jamy.

Pride physically pressed on Addy, leaving her breathless. Jamy. Shy little Jamy, who spoke at the speed of light, afraid of interruptions before she could have her say. She'd strode to the front of the room when her name was called, a Jackie Kennedy crossed with Maya Angelou, lovely and strong. As the petite teen opened her mouth to begin, Addy clasped her hands together under her desk, squeezing until it hurt, fearful Jamy would start out too fast, as she was apt to do, shooting the audience with word bullets. Instead, the words tumbling from her mouth rang like a smoothly timed bell. The girl was sedate and charismatic, using her body and voice to share a full, rich interpretation of the poems. Addy's favorite poem was Jamy's concluding piece, *To Satch* by Samuel Washington Adams. Her blood zinged every time Jamy stretched her fintertips to the sky, sassily announcing to God "I'm gonna reach up and grab me a handfulla' stars!"

And that's what she did. She brought home the stars and a first place trophy. Jamy snatched the State Champion medal in Poetry right outta' the sky.

The girl's voice would never be caged again.

Knuckles in her mouth, rivulets of water streaming over her cheeks, Addy sat doubled over in her auditorium chair. *This is too much. Too much.* Minutes later, there was more.

"In the 1A/2A/3A/4A Sweepstakes division, the fifth place OSAA State Sweepstakes trophy goes to Oceanside High School!"

Confusion darkened Addy's high. *What? There must be some mistake.* Juanita, sitting in the row behind her, leaned forward, clapping Addy on the shoulder. "You did it! With the points from two kids in the top twelve, and one kid winning the whole enchilada, you earned that trophy!" The older woman pointed to Leila on the stage, expectantly waving around a two-foot statue.

Bewildered, Addy shoved Dylan and Jamy off their seats. "Kids! Go! She's talking about us!" The teens, fumbling, untangled themselves, picking their way past three or four seats before the wizened gnome on the mic boomed out, "Oceanside, this is a team win. Coach, come on up here and get your trophy."

"Sorry. Sorry," Addy mumbled, stepping over her kids doing jumping jacks of joy in the aisle. The other teams, including Juanita, Jeremy and Patrick, smiled at her from their seats. She surreptitiously took a few swipes at her damp face and checked her zipper as she stumbled through the jam-packed seats and down the aisle. *Shoulda' considered brushing my hair at some point today.* She realized she was slumping, submissive. *What the hell. Winners don't need to look good, we are good!* Her shoulders square, spine straight, chin up, she shook the President's hand, thanking her profusely.

Leila, tight grey curls framing a perpetually sullen face,

grasped Addy's hand for a beat longer than necessary. The old lady didn't smile but managed to growl, "You did good, kid."

The young coach, warmed by the floodlights and a sea of well wishes from the audience, raised the prize high, waving it at her team, applause boiling over her. The trophy, surprisingly light, felt good in her hands.

Addison Taylor knew she was no General. Addy was never going to marshal troops with a simple stern look, an authoritative point of the index finger. No, she was maybe Captain Taylor now, still gruffly asked for identification at every checkpoint. But. The shakes were settling down. Her identity was cementing into that of an adult, sometimes a competent adult, and a teacher. A real teacher. Even if she didn't have a real job when she got back home.

CHAPTER 46
ED

Ed tailed his target across the county, trying to stay behind dairy trucks or hay trailers. He'd even let his mustache grow in, hoping to project a chubby, graying Magnum PI. His mint green Prius didn't jibe with the image but what the hell? The burned out teacher was having more fun than he'd had in a long time.

But he was also getting frustrated. He'd been doing this for days now and he had to admit the trail had turned cold. Oceanside was not a hotbed of activity.

The suspect stopped at a tavern on the outskirts of town. *Thank God, thought I was gonna' have to piss in the Pepsi bottle again.* Ed waited five minutes, put on a bright red baseball cap for a disguise and nonchalantly planted himself in a corner of the bar, right next to a big screen tv. Three beers down, he realized he'd been a little too caught up in the baseball game. Mid-shout, Ed looked around. *Fuck. Where'd he go?*

Ed lumbered to his feet, checked the dark corners and made his way down the dank corridor to the men's room. Just past the bathrooms, he spied a heavy door cracked open. Sauntering past slowly, hat pulled low, he tried to look lost and confused. The beer helped.

Inside the dim room, cigar smoke swirled amid the loud voices of half-bagged poker players, including his target. Ed's eyes goggled as Coach Pike shoved a pile of cash toward a smirking man in a bad suit. *So that's what money looks like,* thought the teacher.

"You finally giving up there, big guy?" the man collecting the greenery said gruffly.

"Fuck you, Rosco." Pike nervously stroked his red goatee. "Just deal."

"You ain't got nothing left, Pike. I already got your fuckin' house."

Ed backed away, trying to keep the swish, swish noise of his rubbing thighs to a dull roar. He didn't need to hear anymore. His cell phone had recorded everything. Like the tough guy he was, Ed skipped to the bar. The cigarette-tanned barmaid snorted when he handed over his tie-dyed credit card. He gave her a jaunty wink. Back in the world of day, he played back the recording then erased the first twenty minutes of him slurping suds and cheering for the Red Sox. He hit save, raised the phone, and gave it a slobbery kiss. *I've just established motive. I da' man.*

Stroking his PI mustache, he drove toward the school, anxious to get there.

CHAPTER 47
ADDY

The golden orator, his hand raised in pontification, sparkled behind the glass in the trophy case. Addy's reflection, superimposed, responded in a whisper, practicing the speech she was about to give to the elusive Principal Nakamura.

"And I promise if given another chance—"

"Addy?"

She spun around. "Troy! I thought you had your final interview back at your old school today!" Light pierced the heavy darkness in her heart.

"I rescheduled. They'll let me come in next Tuesday."

She was afraid to ask if he was there for her. The disappointment would shake her confidence if he said no, but the responsibility of a yes answer might shake her even more. She turned back to the award cabinet, trying to compose her face.

Troy came up behind her, stood close. She breathed. "They're ready for you." His long fingers touched her hand, eyes sympathetic.

"They?"

"Margo DuBois is here."

She reeled then caught herself. "Oh."

"Nakamura wants to hear both sides of the story." His scent calmed her even while his words twisted her guts.

"He wants to see if I'm crazy, you mean."

Troy tried to lighten the mood. "You are a little crazy. That's what I like about you."

He likes me.

"Speaking of crazy, you didn't bring a union rep?" He shook his head. "You should have listened to me."

She paled further but squared her shoulders. "Huh. You might be right. But I'm crazy, remember? So far this year, I've started a fire, driven through a river, and chased away a boyfriend." She chewed the inside of her cheek. "Why clean up my track record now?"

"I'm gonna' suggest your lack of a boyfriend is not a bad thing." He shrugged his wide shoulders, put his hands in his pockets, grinned down at her.

"Uh. Okay." She looked at him sharply to see if he was kidding. "Is it okay for you to say that to me, being my boss and all?"

He spread his hands wide, "Maybe not for long."

It took her a second to catch his meaning. She punched him on the arm. "Hey, that's not funny!"

He took her punching hand, gently, and threaded his fingers through hers. Her heart skipped a beat, a thrill of happiness shooting up her spine despite the looming threat twenty feet away. He stared down at her, hard, and said, "Look. I'm here for you. But you don't need me, or even the union. You've spent the year teaching fourteen year olds, for God's sake! And you've driven through a river! Even if you get fired, you'll survive."

Addy absorbed the heat from his hand then pulled free. "Am I going to get fired, Troy?"

"I don't know." He paused, lips compressed. "Just explain yourself. You didn't mean to break the OSAA rule. And you didn't mean to offend Nina's mother. Right?"

She grimaced. "Right. And I didn't mean to ruin the copy machine, call in the police at four in the morning, let one of my students choke someone, or have another one almost die on my watch." She sucked in a lungful of air and heaved it back out again. "It's been a banner year."

He maneuvered her closer to the office. "Yeah, well, maybe not bring up all that stuff in the meeting." He turned away, seemingly with reluctance. "Come on."

She stopped him just outside the thick double doors of the big office at the end of the main office hall. "Hey. I appreciate your support. Seriously, I do. But I don't want you to say anything, okay? This is my fight, I can do this myself."

He nodded. "I know."

The doors sprang open.

Standing immediately in her path was Al Nakamura, the principal of OHS. Addy had seen the small, chubby Japanese man from a distance, heading meetings or sliding past her classroom door, occasionally waving from down the hall. His face, serious but kind, did not smile as he extended his hand, palm barely poking free from the sleeve of an orange argyle sweater. He was not an imposing figure, despite the power he held in his petite man-hands.

Margo, on the other hand, sat ramrod straight in one of the two chairs in front of Nakamura's oversized desk. *Talk about imposing.* Addy could barely look at her but she could smell her Chanel.

"Let's get this show on the road, shall we?" The principal motioned Addy into the armchair flanking Margo, leaving Troy to stand in the background. The chair felt like a trap.

As Nakamura made his way around the massive expanse of metal and plastic desktop, Margo turned to Addy and speared her with disdain. She said, "Let me be clear. I do not believe your teaching contract should be renewed for next year, considering your lack of common sense and decency while dealing with my daughter. You are not a good teacher."

Blood rushing to her face, Addy opened her mouth to speak, unsure of what would tumble out. Nakamura dropped into his chair and held up a hand, sighing. "Now,

Margo, we've talked about this. I'm not deciding anything until Ms. Taylor has a chance to explain her actions.

"Ms. Taylor. A few things." He leaned forward, intent on Addy. "One, how was Nina able to go missing from practice for so long before she was found? How are you conducting practices? Are you maintaining safe, responsible practices?" Margo interrupted with a snort. Nakamura shot her a dark glance, then refocused on Addy. "Also, Ms. DuBois has leveled charges against you concerning inappropriate remarks you made to her while her child lay in a hospital bed only a few feet away.

"What do you have to say in your defense, Ms. Taylor?"

Why did I say no to the Union rep? I'm an idiot. Pride goeth before the axe.

Addy took a deep breath and began. "Ms. DuBois," she said, peering at the hospital administrator through her eyelashes. "I'm devastated about Nina, and I'm so sorry for the role I played in Nina's illness. I'm relieved to hear she's doing okay."

"Hmph. Okay. Her father is taking her back to Boston. I don't know how okay that is. We'll see. I know it's what she wants right now. Who am I to stand in her way?"

There was no way Addy was going to answer that question, sensing the danger. Instead she said, "The kids will miss her. And I'm sorry for you."

"Don't you be sorry for me. Feel sorry for yourself."

"I understand your frustration and anger with the situation, but let's get back on track. Addy?" Nakamura tried to control the crackling emotions.

"It's true, the learning curve stomped me for awhile, but I think I'm starting to figure things out. Also, while I do believe I should have been more aware of Nina's depression, I'm not solely responsible for her actions." The young teacher angled her face at Nakamura. "When Nina left practice that day, she went to use the bathroom. When, after a few minutes, she didn't return, we assumed she'd gone out to the track meet. We looked for her outside and then returned to the building, keeping an eye out for her. While I'm responsible for my students, at some point I have to let them be responsible for themselves and then dole out the consequences when they falter. I had no way of knowing about Nina's personal demons, that I shouldn't let her go to the bathroom."

"Nina is special. I made the school aware of her time spent at Greenhaven's. It was in her file." Margo punctuated her words with a stabbing red fingernail.

Funny. How much time did she spend home, alone? Hypocrite.

Addy responded, flat-voiced. "Actually, I don't have access to student's personal files. The only flag I saw was the mark on her registration. When I asked the counselor, he said her parents were divorced, to watch for depression. Jeez, that's over half the kids here. Nina seemed a lot more stable than most of my students."

Both women faced the man across the desk.

Nonchalantly, Principal Nakamura picked up a pen and began making scratches on a notepad in front of him. "Alright. That's something we can fix. Communication regarding student histories and special needs. Check."

Check?! If it was always so easy, why wasn't it resolved earlier? Why did it have to come to this?

"Regardless, you crossed the line when you accosted me in the hospital hallway, Ms. Taylor."

Addy's jaw dropped. She couldn't control herself any longer. "Accosted you?! I asked how I could help! You attacked me, accusing me of ignoring signs of illness in your daughter."

Margo remained emotionless, stone-faced. "I'm referring to your comments accusing me of being a delinquent mother, inferring I'm unfit because I spend too much time at work."

"Ms. DuBois, I did no such thing. Not purposefully. My sole intention was to advocate for Nina. She told the team she was lonely; we saw her struggle to make friends and push herself to succeed academically. It's amazing that strangers can be aware of your daughter's struggles, even on a limited level, but you know nothing about her current unhappiness. Is that my fault?"

Margo spit out her words. "Do you see, Mr. Nakamura? This. This is what I'm talking about. This type of insubordination is unacceptable!"

Addy spoke before she could be restrained. "I'm not being insubordinate to anyone. First of all, you're not my boss. While I respect you and believe you do love your daughter, I don't need to kowtow to you. I wish to God I'd recognized how sick Nina was, but I will not accept the sole responsibility." Addy pushed her bangs out of her eyes, blew out her breath. Nakamura continued to listen, not interrupting. Addy dropped her voice, peeling the emotion out of her words as best as possible. "And you know it, Margo. You know it in your heart. I let her down, and so did you."

The hospital administrator shoved herself from the armchair, grabbing her satchel from the floor. Standing, tight as a spring, Margo directed her raised voice to Principal Nakamura. "Clearly you do not have control of your staff. I will be lodging a complaint with the School Board."

She stormed out, slamming the doors.

Addy burst out, "Mr. Nakamura! Please don't fire me!"

He stayed seated, calm. "Okay, bring it down a notch, Addy. No one's getting fired." The principal looked past her. "Come on, Troy, might as well sit down."

As Troy sat, the big man broke his silence. "So. What do you think, Al?"

Nakamura tugged at the collar of his cardigan, leaned back in his chair. "Seems to me we've got a volatile family situation, fraught with worry and tension, and Momma Bear is looking for a scape goat." Nakamura reacted to the relief washing over Addy's face. "Now, Ms. Taylor, I'm not saying you're totally innocent here. For one, you better tighten up your control over the students in your responsibility. I don't care what it takes, figure it out. We can't have freshman leaving English class to go to the bathroom only to end up as an Amber Alert."

She nodded. *I'm not sure how I'll make teenagers with free will do what they say they're going to do, but okay. GPS trackers it is.*

Nakamura sighed. "Don't worry about her complaint to the School Board. I'll explain the details to them. And you, Ford. You're going to the Board Meeting with me next Tuesday, to put your two cents in. They like you for some reason. I'm guessing you're on board." His faced creased into a grin as he eyeballed his vice principal.

Troy ignored Principal Nakamura's jibe, instead turning his head to stare at Addy. "Next Tuesday, you say?"

Understanding dawned on Addy. She started to shake her head and open her mouth to let him off the hook but he put his hand up and smiled. "It's fine. Really." Facing Nakamura, he asked, "What time is this shin-dig?"

Nakamura lifted his eyebrows but refrained from reacting to the weird exchange between Addy and Troy. He clearly did not know about Troy's interview. "It's at two, like usual," he said. Then he jabbed a finger at the air in front of the young teacher. "And Addy. Jesus. You cannot go spouting off to parents or community members, no matter how righteous your response. Seriously. Get it together, girl. You live in a small town now. You can have opinions —you just can't say them in public. Ever."

Troy watched her. His face held a look of warning. She agreed with a murmur, avoiding images of jailhouse stripes.

"Finally, this OSAA rule that Jamy Lock broke, not being registered in five classes this semester." he blew a raspberry. "What a load of crap that was. Pike. That guy." Nakamura shook his head. "He—"

"Al, we can't talk about that." Troy stood up, sat on the edge of Nakamura's desk. "Sorry Addy, nothing personal."

Nakamura stood up, too, clapping a hand on Troy's shoulder. "You're right, Kid. Me and my big mouth. Needless to say Addy, the OSAA isn't moving ahead with the charges, Troy cleared it up. The librarian's not thrilled to be doing you a favor, not after you tried to burn down her library, but she loves ol' blue eyes here." He slapped the v.p. on the shoulder again, jarring him. "Thank God, huh? Could you imagine stripping that girl of her trophy?"

Troy winced and stood up. "Okay, so we're good here?"

Addy was glad he asked though not sure she wanted the answer.

"Yes." Nakamura came over to their side of the desk. "I'll make sure your teaching contract is signed for next year —but I can't promise you the coaching contract. That still needs to be decided. The School Board needs to approve a permanent position. Good luck, Addy."

Troy rocked on his heels. "I guess this means you're staying in Oceanside."

Addy smiled at the two men. "We'll see. I haven't signed a contract yet."

"Psshh." Nakamura waved a hand in the air and then pushed them toward the doors. "Get out of here." He patted Addy gently on the back. "Next year won't be so bad, I promise."

She looked at Troy's receding back. *Maybe. Will you be here?*

CHAPTER 48
NINA

According to Dante, which form of evil is the worst? How is that particular evil punished?

Nina eyed the question on the make-up test in front of her, a bittersweet burn in her gut as she sat in the empty classroom. She knew the answer, of course; she'd studied *The Inferno* as a freshman in her old school. Thank God, since she'd been gone for a month while Ms. Taylor covered the epic with the senior class. She just couldn't help applying the question to herself.

Dante believed those who broke the bonds of family were among the worst. Had Nina dishonored her mother by not trusting in her, hating her instead of turning to her? She'd like to believe her mother, even her father, were at fault, believe they were the reason she hurt herself. They'd abandoned her, for goddsakes, hurt her first. She sighed. The truth was much more complicated. After days with an insipid psychoanalyst, an epiphany finally forced its way into existence: Nina was responsible for her reaction to the situation. She couldn't control her mother's life choices, but she could have sat her mom down, or called her dad, shared her feelings, even asked for help when she first started cutting. But she'd allowed pride and self-pity to dictate her actions. *Ah, geez, two more sins.*

Whatever. She'd come out on the other side. She had some new scars, and some new emotional baggage, but her dad was waiting for her outside, waiting to take her to a family counseling session. She bent her attention to the paper and scribbled out answers to the last two questions, forcibly removing herself from the equation.

Out in the hallway, she could hear Ms. Taylor approaching, talking to someone else, someone loud. Peeking out from under her bangs, she saw Mr. Nielson prop himself against the wall across the way, Ms. Taylor looking like a teenager standing next to him. Nina tried not to eavesdrop but it was tough, considering they were only ten feet away.

"Are you going to the board meeting on Friday? Big things afoot, should be interesting," said Mr. Nielson, gruff voice booming through the halls.

"Oh ? Well, I have to go. They're voting on whether or not OHS has a speech team next year." Nina perked up at that. *Why would they get rid of the team? We did better than the football team.*

"Well, bring a video camera, honey. Shit's goin' down, I tell ya'. And I have to miss it, my son has an award banquet's that night." Nina could hear the grin in his voice. "But I've got the inside track."

Ms. Taylor sounded confused, as usual. "What's goin' on? Why do you look so happy?"

"Addy, I can't say. I swore to keep my mouth shut. But know this: traitorous assholes get what they deserve." Nina smirked behind a hand. *I love it. Teacher drama.*

Nina wrote her name on the test, purposefully scraping her chair across the linoleum as she stood up. The noise brought in Ms. Taylor.

"You're done, I take it? Or do you have a question?" The teacher looked even younger than usual, wearing a speech team sweatshirt. Nina secretly adored the new team emblem, the hook-handed Pirate standing behind a podium. She planned on wearing her own team hoody back in Boston, bringing a bit of her west coast memories to Beantown. Maybe even bring it with her to Harvard, if they accepted her late application. The other item that would always travel with her was the team photo Tori brought her last week; the speechies had photoshopped her into the middle of the group. It was good to have smart friends. Good to have friends, period.

Nina handed over her test. "Thank you, Ms. Taylor. For everything."

She meant it.

CHAPTER 49
ADDY

"**A**ddy! Addy, wait!"

She hurried up the steps to the District Office, late for the School Board meeting; they were going to decide the fate of the OHS Speech Team for next year. Her first instinct was to keep going, to ignore Rick's plaintive cry, but she couldn't do it. Kicking herself in the non-existent balls, she went back down the stairs, walking across the freshly cut lawn to where Rick leaned against his car. *How did I not see him there? Ugh, my radar must be off.*

"Rick, I'm not trying to be rude but I've got to get inside. I'm already late."

"Yes, I'm sure you are. Nothing new there." His tone was light. He didn't look angry, or even crazy, just tired. "This'll just take a second. Here." He held out a manila envelope. "It's the rental agreement. I've taken my name off; the landlord is expecting the new papers."

She gently removed the yellow packet from his hand. His arm hung awkwardly in the air for a moment before reaching up to fidget with his horn-rimmed glasses. She feared he'd follow the draft of the papers, step into her space, but he did not move from the side of his car.

Instead he squinted at her. "I love you. I think you still love me. But I can't continue this way, beating my head on a wall. At least that's what my anger management guy says. So, let's finish this thing."

Addy thought she'd feel emptiness or a loss when this moment came. She had moved here with hope and wonder, never expecting to wander, hapless and lost, into single-land.

Having breeched the far side, she felt mainly relief. But maybe that was because she'd broken up with Rick a month ago and he was just now stepping into that reality. He always was a little slow.

Rick let her go, watching her walk away without an argument, without a word. For now, anyway.

Hurrying up to the door, she refused to look around, to betray the trace of guilt or worry she held for Rick. *He's on his own. Let him go. Let's hope he can do the same.*

Inside the meeting room, packed bodies overpowered diminutive folding chairs. A heavy odor of nighttime in late spring hung in the moist air. She kept her head down, threading to the back of the room, relieved the meeting hadn't started yet. Hiding in the back row, she picked grass blades off her ballet flats, surreptitiously scanning the room for Troy. A boyish grin met her search almost instantly. Troy stretched his lanky body back from the conference table in front of the room and mouthed something at her.

What? She mouthed back, purposefully not looking around to see who else was witness to this exchange.

Meet later? His lips over-exaggerated the two words, sending shivers down her spine and an electric current of hot gossip around the folding chairs, sparking yelps of muted laughter.

The soccer mom wedged in next to her turned to catch her response. Addy shrugged, blushing, playing it cool. They both knew she'd wait for him. No need to give the crowd anymore fodder for the fire.

No.

Screw it. Let's light this bitch.

"Eight o'clock, Rosie's," she yelled through cupped hands.

Troy's eyes widened and then he threw a thumbs-up signal over the buzz of the gossiping crowd.

The meeting proceeded through the reading of the minutes, old business, and, finally, new business. The first item of new business was from Troy, asking the School Board to approve his hiring of a new head football coach. The head of the board, a local lawyer from town, held out her hand for the paperwork. He handed around copies. The board members took a minute to peruse the contents, eying each other oddly, huddling for a consensus.

Whispers from the crowd wrapped around Addy. "What's going on? Why isn't Pike coaching next year? Well, I heard –"

Before she could hear what the soccer mom next to her had to say, the chairwoman declared, "Okay, Mr. Ford. We trust your judgment. But you better be sure about this." She sighed and then stated, clearly, into the tabletop microphone, "We approve the hiring of the new coach. Ed Nielson is now the head coach of the OHS Football Team."

There were shouts, laughter, arguing. Addy, flabbergasted flooded with relief. This meant they'd proved Ed hadn't stolen the money. Thank God. Addy knew he was innocent. Socially inept, maybe, but not a thief. And now he was Head Coach! *But what happened to Pike?* Dominoes clicked into place.

Pike had been the one stealing money. Her theory was confirmed by the whispered conversation between the soccer mom and the lumberyard owner next to her, describing the coach being dragged off in handcuffs from a late night poker game. Addy tilted her head, incredulous. She sucked in a huge gulp of air and let it out with a rush, suddenly aware of how worried she'd been. Maybe now Ed would have something worthwhile to occupy his time, give his teaching a little zing again.

She made up her mind to come to school board meetings more often. *You can find out so much about what's going on in your own building.*

"Seriously people? What is this, Portland? Let's settle down, show some decorum." The chairwoman pounded her gavel, obviously liking the heft and feel, hammering long into the silence.

"Just know, Mr. Ford, you're responsible for these coaches. You signed a contract, agreeing to stay on for at least another year, so I don't want to hear that you're letting things slide. Tight reigns, Mr. Ford. And a balanced budget." She peered at him solemnly over her reading glasses.

Troy seemed unfazed by the reprimand, nodding at the board with appropriate gravity and then turning to look at Addy. She exchanged a heavy glance with him, her heart dripping with relief. *He'll be here.*

"Mr. Ford, I believe you have another coaching issue you wanted to bring before us?"

Troy, still standing at the audience microphone, seemed unflustered by the stern row of administrators or the whispering crowd. *I wish I could be confident like that.* He looked like a gladiator, facing the lions with a half-smile. He handed out a fresh sheaf of paper to the board. They took another minute to peruse the details.

Is this about me? Am I sweating through my shirt? Why is it impossible to find good deodorant?

The chairwoman nodded at her comrades, moving back behind her microphone. "We have a few questions."

He waited quietly.

"First, you're asking us to add a permanent coaching position. That is a huge budgetary problem."

Troy nodded, serious. "I realize that, Madame Chair. But I'm hoping we can make this work, seeing as how the OHS Speech and Debate Team proved themselves a solid competitive group. They need a coach. Actually, they have a coach, if she's willing to continue in the position. I hope she is."

"Is this the same coach who set off the alarms twice this year, among other things?"

Addy sank in her chair, curious heads swinging toward her. *Nothing to see here, people.*

Troy didn't seem worried. "Yes." He grinned. "Did I mention she's a new teacher?"

The Board Members exchanged looks. The chairwoman crossed her arms in front of her. "Hmmmmmm." She leaned forward, staring at Troy.

The blood from Addy's face pooled in her feet. She slid further down the folding chair, hoping it wouldn't pop shut under her. The whispers from the crowd were confused. "Why'd the alarms go off? What in the hell is a speech team? We have one of those?"

Thunk. One swift drop of the gavel and the room was silent again.

"When you say they've proven themselves, what do you mean? I haven't heard of them winning any competitions."

"Beg pardon, ma'm. This is more of an individual competition, kind of like a track meet. We would celebrate if one of our athletes became the State Champion in the hurdles. Well, Oceanside now has the State Champion in Poetry Reading."

There were a lot of masked chuckles from the crowd. "Poetry? What the . . . we might as well have a champion basket weaver."

Addy grinned, twisting a strand of her short hair. She'd felt exactly the same way on her first day as a teacher in a new building, a new life, being handed a mandate to coach some weird team by an obnoxious man. She'd been wrong. So wrong.

Troy continued. "And the team took fifth place at State. Their first year!"

The board conversed a minute more, Troy pierced the crowd with his eyes. Finally, he caught her gaze, not bothering to hide his wink. The soccer mom guffawed, her belly quaking.

The chairwoman put an end to the chatter. "You say the coach may not be willing to return to this position next year? We will consider creating this as a permanent position only if the current coach is returning. We have no desire to waste time and money on a program that's going to die. But we'd like to move on; is she here?"

Troy maintained eye contact. "Addy?"

She stood slowly, surreptitiously unsticking her skirt from her clammy skin. *This is the point last year I would have fainted.*

"Ms. Taylor, please approach the Board."

Screw it. You know what to do. She stood up straight, threw back her shoulders, strode to the front of the room. Facing the rows of eyes, her voice projected crisply into every corner.

"Hello. I'm Addison Taylor." She stopped, out of habit. Then, surprisingly, found it was possible to think clearly—and to speak. "I started out this school year a new teacher. And, frankly, an unwilling coach. Now? Now. Well, now." She made direct eye contact with every board member and then Troy. "I wouldn't change my experience for the world. Yes, it was great to be handed a shiny trophy," she smiled as the audience chuckled. "And three of my kids are going to university next year with scholarships. Imagine! I helped kids go to college!

"But the best part . . ." She gulped down a sudden lump in her throat. "The best part is . . . these kids not only discovered their voices, they found the strength to use them. *I'm* just now figuring out how to do that.

"I'm so thankful to be part of this world, it, it . . . it's hard to put in words how fulfilling and awe-inspiring this experience has been." She glanced down at her hands and then back at the row of people in charge of her future. "Do as I say, not as I do, I guess." More encouraging laughter from the town of Oceanside. "Seriously, thank you. Thank you for giving me the chance to grow with these kids. I've learned as much from them as they've learned from me, that's for sure."

She breathed a beat.

"So, yes, I'll coach."

ACKNOWLEDGEMENTS

Thank you, Reader, for sticking it through to the end. I'm available for book group discussions if you're interested. Contact me through http://www.hollylorincz.wordpress.com.

Thank you Bryan Marvis for prompting, pushing, and pulling me through the creation of this novel—once you tricked me into writing it. You truly are a good friend. You helped me face my illness and stand back up, as a writer this time.

Thank you to my past students. Every one of you is a part of me. Thank you to my speech team kids from over the years. My God, I love you guys. I'm tearing up right now, running through the internal rolodex of names and faces. Your bravery changed me, made me step up.

Thank you to my peers, the teachers and coaches who have mentored me into becoming a successful educator and, hopefully, a decent human being. There are unfortunately too many of you to name, but I need to acknowledge my high school coach Dorthea Chevron, coach Patrick Leahy, teacher Beth Gienger, and student (long-graduated) Genna Hall as the most influential in those areas.

Thank you to the Burgess Writing Group and the Orange Writing Group for sending me to conferences and listening to chapter after chapter without complaint (as far as I know); thank you to my honest readers: Patrick Nelson, Jeff Kyriss, Robyn Clevenger Rose, Erika Recordon, Sandy Soderstrom, Miranda Sundell, Aina Tonjes and Heidi Gray; thank you to my Auggie for being so proud of his momma, the writer; thank you to SusieJo Lorincz for replacing my coffee-laced computer at a crucial time; finally, thank you to my agent, my dearest friend, Chip MacGregor, an actual industry guru who continues to believe in this project, and me.

I'm grateful to my community of family and friends for getting me here. Here is nice.

Made in the USA
Charleston, SC
12 October 2015